# TRUE I

MAX ALLAN COLLINS has earned an unprecedented seven Private Eye Writers of America "Shamus" nominations for his "Nathan Heller" historical thrillers, winning twice (*True Detective*, 1983, and *Stolen Away*, 1991). Termed "mystery's Renaissance Man" (by Ed Hoch in *The Best Mystery and Suspense Stories of 1993*), Collins has created three celebrated contemporary suspense series: Nolan, Quarry and Mallory (thief, hitman, and mystery writer respectively). He has also written four widely praised historical thrillers about real-life "Untouchable" Eliot Ness, and is an accomplished writer of short fiction: "Louise," his contribution to the popular anthology *Deadly Allies*, was a Mystery Writers of America "Edgar" nominee for best short story of 1992. He scripted the internationally syndicated comic strip *Dick Tracy* from 1977 to 1993, and wrote three *Tracy* novels. Working as an independent filmmaker in his native Iowa, he wrote, directed and executive-produced *Mommy*, a suspense film starring Patty McCormack, which aired on Lifetime cable in 1996; he performed the same duties for a sequel, *Mommy's Day*, released in 1997. The recipient of two Iowa Motion Picture Awards for screenwriting, he wrote *The Expert*, a 1995 HBO World Premiere film starring James Brolin. A longtime rock musician, he has in recent years recorded and performed with two bands: Seduction of the Innocent in California, and Crusin' in his native Muscatine, Iowa, where Collins lives with his wife, writer Barbara Collins, and their son, Nathan.

**MYSTERIES**
*Published by ibooks, inc.:*

# TRUE DETECTIVE

### THE FRANK NITTI TRILOGY, BOOK 1

# MAX
# ALLAN
# COLLINS

new york
www.ibooks.net

DISTRIBUTED THROUGH SIMON & SCHUSTER, INC.

*To Barb*
*with love*

A Publication of ibooks, inc.

An ibooks, inc. Book

ibooks, inc.
24 West 25th Street
New York, NY 10010

The ibooks World Wide Web Site Address is:
http://www.ibooks.net

ISBN 0-7434-5896-6
First ibooks, inc. printing February 2003
10 9 8 7 6 5 4 3 2 1

Printed in the U.S.A.

# A LIGHTBULB MOMENT
## An Introduction to *True Detective*

For the first few years of my writing career, I taught part-time at a community college. One of the ways I kept my sanity was by teaching a course on mystery fiction. It was in my capacity as a college instructor, then, that I re-read my favorite mystery novel, Dashiell Hammett's *The Maltese Falcon*, for the umpteenth time.

Perhaps it was that academic mode of thought that made me glance at the indicia page, note the copyright, and muse, "Nineteen twenty-nine . . . that's the St. Valentine's Day Massacre. That means Sam Spade and Al Capone were contemporaries."

In the comics field (where I also occasionally toil), this moment might be marked by a lightbulb going on in a balloon over my head. It was that kind of idea—the stray thought that lights up the world and changes everything, or at least a career.

For a long time I had been looking for a way to write private eye novels in the classic mode. I grew up on Hammett, Raymond Chandler, Mickey Spillane and dozens of their imitators, but my first published novels did not include the private detective narrator those writers made famous. Instead, at the University of Iowa's Writers Workshop, I wrote a trio of novels about three different protagonists: a thief, a hitman and a mystery writer; but in each case, the novels had roots in the P.I. form as much as the crime novel.

My lightbulb moment probably took place around 1974, not long before *Chinatown* came along, doing something of the same kind of P.I.-in-history thing I had in mind. And a couple of mystery writers, good ones (Andrew Bergman and Stuart Kaminsky), did their own period private-eye novels right around the same time.

Robert Towne's great screenplay for *Chinatown* loosely dealt with historical events, but his characters were fictional. Both Bergman and Kaminsky placed their P.I.s amid real people—chiefly, movie stars and various other Hollywood celebrities—but not in the context of actual events or specific crimes.

My concern, back at the end of the '60s and start of the '70s, was that the private eye character had become anachronistic—I did not (and still do not) care for the Marlowe type of noble-urban-knight detective carried over bodily into modern times (those times starting around 1963), a guy in a fedora and trenchcoat with a bottle of whiskey in his bottom desk drawer, who apparently stumbled into a time machine.

Such novels seemed to me forced, clichéd, ungainly pastiches of a form that was fixed in the amber of a bygone day. That was why my lightbulb epiphany was so crucial to me: I had come up with a way to write the private eye today . . . by setting the stories yesterday.

The first incarnation of the Nathan Heller character (the protagonist of the book you're about to read) was in a comic strip called "Heaven and Heller." An editor at Field Enterprises, around 1975, asked me to take a stab at creating a new story strip. That editor—Rick Marschall—was bucking the conventional wisdom, still held today, that story strips were no longer marketable.

The Heller samples (two batches were done—one by Ray Gotto, creator of the baseball strip "Ozark Ike"; another by Fernando DaSilva, the last assistant to Alex Raymond, creator of "Flash Gordon") had to do with a séance being held in Chicago by Harry Houdini's widow; the true-crime aspect of the Heller novels was there, in embryonic form.

"Heaven and Heller" was sold to Field Enterprises. But my visionary editor lost his job, and the contract was cancelled. "Heaven and Heller" went into the drawer. A few years later, Rick Marschall recommended me to the Tribune Company as the writer of "Dick Tracy," a job I held fifteen years (starting in 1977). . . . By the way—thanks, Rick!

In the meantime, *Chinatown* happened, and a good but short-lived period private eye TV series called *City of Angels* (co-created by Stephen Cannell and Roy Huggins) appeared, as did those aforementioned novels by Bergman and Kaminsky. The private eye in period setting was becoming a distinct if under-utilized sub-genre of mystery fiction.

But it still seemed to me that nobody had fully plumbed the potential of the P.I. in period. In fact, that was the problem: they were doing the private eye in period, but not in history. It occurred to me that Heller shouldn't just bump into real people, but that he should be involved in real events . . . that he should crack a real unsolved case. I was not thinking in terms of a series of novels, just one book, though I did contemplate the possibility of sequels (one of the reasons I made Heller a younger man in *True Detective* than most protagonists of private eye novels).

From the first inklings of Heller, I began gathering research materials, and the case that attracted me most—that seemed like a classic under-explored Chicago subject—was the attempted assassination of FDR that wound up taking the life of Mayor Anton Cermak. My fascination for that case had been sparked by a TV show I saw as a kid. . . .

One of the pop-culture touchstones that served to interest me in true crime and real detectives (or, should I say, real crime and true detectives) was the Robert Stack-starring television series, *The Untouchables*, based on a slightly fictionalized memoir by Eliot Ness (who was one of the real federal agents Chester Gould patterned his Dick Tracy upon).

*The Untouchables* had done a two-part episode about the attempt on Chicago Mayor Cermak's life, and it was typically inaccurate—the series, while wonderful, played fast and loose with the facts even as it pretended, courtesy of real newspaperman Walter Winchell's voiceover, to be a docudrama. Only the original two-part TV movie, "The Scarface Gang" (which aired on *Desilu Playhouse* and was a kind of accidental pilot film), hewed at all close to the facts of any of the cases the show explored.

Years later, digging into the research, I discovered a much better story in real life, having to do with Cermak's own attempt on the life of Frank Nitti. To say more would be to spoil the story you're about to read; but I will say that the facts of the Cermak case—and the mainstream historical accounts aren't much more accurate than the Robert Stack series—opened my eyes about the realities of Chicago crime and politics.

This book could not have been written without the research assistance of George Hagenauer. I don't use the word "assistant," anymore, because that doesn't do George justice—he has been my great friend and collaborator on these novels, not only helping with the research, but with the interpretation of that research. The plots have always been formed out of endless phone conversations in which George and I turn over all the facts like stones, looking for the wriggling, squirmy things underneath.

George now lives near Madison, Wisconsin, but he was born and raised in Chicago, and lived there throughout the writing of the first eight or nine Heller books. He—and another valued friend and Chicago historian, Mike Gold—helped me shape the character and the world of Nate Heller. Let me give an example.

When I first approached George, whom I knew through our mutual interest in collecting original comic art (we met at a comic book convention in Chicago), he was happy to help with the Chicago end of the research. Among other things, he said he could help with the sometimes complicated geography of the city and its many neighborhoods. He asked me about the story I had in mind.

"Well," I said, "Nate Heller is a young plainclothes cop who is forced to do something corrupt. He quits the force out of moral indignation, and opens his own detective agency."

When he stopped laughing, George said, "Max, you gotta leave all that Philip Marlowe nonsense behind, if you want to write about Chicago. This is the Depression we're talking about—a young guy would try to get on the Chicago cops for the graft. To take advantage of the corruption. And you couldn't get on the force at all without a Chinaman to pull the strings."

A Chinaman, he explained, was not an Asian gentleman, but someone rich enough, or anyway connected enough, to get a person a prized slot on the Chicago police force.

Later, George (and I think Mike Gold accompanied us on most of the trips) would walk me around the Loop, pointing out key buildings and the sites of various murders and other crimes. One time, we stopped for a Coke at a bar on Van Buren and George discreetly pointed out a transaction taking place: the bartender was paying off the beat cop.

"That's Chicago, Max," George said.

A very well-respected mystery writer wrote a negative review of one of the early Heller novels, criticizing my detective because he broke Philip Marlowe's "code." He could hardly have known that I set out with malice aforethought in *True Detective* to break every one of the rules that Chandler set for private eyes, in his famous "down these mean streets" speech. Heller takes bribes, he despoils virgins, he does any number of un-Marlowe-like things.

And yet I think he remains a hero, the best man in his shabby world— that much of Chandler I wanted to retain. The other thing was the easy-flowing poetry of Chandler's great first-person voice. (What came from Hammett was a certain way of looking at the world, and from Spillane came the level of violence and action, and Heller's thirst for getting even.)

Ironically, the use of Chandler-esque first-person in this novel was one of the most controversial aspects of *True Detective*, prior to its sale, anyway. Conventional publishing wisdom was, you didn't write a first-person novel as long as this one—readers didn't like being trapped inside one voice that long. Also, a mystery novel was supposed to be 50,000 or 60,000 words long—not over 100,000 words, like this one.

My agent at the time, a very prestigious one, didn't think *True Detective* should be about a private eye, and he thought the novel should be told in the third person, from multiple points of view. One of my favorite writers, a valued mentor of mine (very famous), agreed with my agent and told me either to re-work the novel as a non-P.I., third-person book, or just put it in a drawer.

I fired my agent, and ignored my mentor. (Fortunately, my other, even more famous mentor—Mickey Spillane—also read the manuscript, called me up and said it was the best private eye novel he'd ever read. Let me tell you—that felt good.)

Because this novel broke so many rules, I had to write it on "spec"—that is, I could not just send a proposal to one of my publishers and hope for a contract. The writing of it was an ordeal for my wife Barb and me. The historical nature of the novel meant that the research was ongoing and ever-shifting, and for the longest time, I could not get past the first chapter, which I rewrote and rewrote (and retyped and retyped on my trusty IBM Selectric). So I ended up selling one of our two cars to buy a newfangled gizmo called a word processor. It cost five grand and was an amazing machine, fast as the wind—16k!

Shortly after the manuscript was completed, I was informed by my wife that she was pregnant. After the ultrasound told us we had a boy on the way, Barb—caught up in the novel herself—asked if maybe "Nathan" wouldn't be a good name for our son.

"Okay," I said. "If we sell the book before you deliver the kid, he's Nathan. But if we haven't sold it, we'll go with something else—I'll be damned if I'll have a walking rejection slip running around this house."

Our son, Nathan Allan Collins, was born November 5, 1982.

*True Detective*—my original title, by the way, was *Tower Town* (how glad I am my editor asked to come up with something else!)—sold to the first publishing house my new agent, Dominick Abel, approached. The book won widespread and glowing reviews, as well as the 1983 Best Novel Shamus Award from the Private Eye Writers of America, in a very tough year—the other nominees included the likes of James Crumley, Robert B. Parker and Stanley Ellin.

In addition, the novel set me on a new path as a writer of historical crime fiction—eleven more Heller novels have followed, as well as four Eliot Ness novels and another half-dozen historical crime novels, including *The Titanic Murders*, a paperback bestseller a few years ago. Heller also led to my writing a graphic novel called *Road to Perdition*, which takes place in the same world of Frank Nitti, Al Capone and Eliot Ness that you are about to enter. But *Road to Perdition*, as successful as it's been (thanks to the Tom Hanks/Paul Newman/Sam Mendes film fashioned from it), is only a spin-off of the Heller series. Specifically, *Road to Perdition* grows out of the first three Heller novels, the "Frank Nitti Trilogy," of which *True Detective* is the first installment.

I hope you enjoy the novel. I think you'll find Nate Heller good company . . . even if he does take the occasional bribe. He sleeps around, too.

—Max Allan Collins
October 2002

He felt like somebody had taken the lid off his life
and let him look at the works.
—Dashiell Hammett

# 1
# THE BLIND PIG
## DECEMBER 19—DECEMBER 22, 1932

FRANK NITTI

I was off-duty at the time, sitting in a speak on South Clark Street drinking rum out of a coffee cup.

When two guys in topcoats and snap-brim hats came in and walked over without crawling out of 'em, I started to reach for the automatic under my jacket. But as they neared the table, I recognized them: Lang and Miller. The mayor's bagmen.

I didn't know them exactly, but everybody *knew* them: the two Harrys—Harry Lang and Harry Miller, the detectives handpicked by Mayor Cermak to handle the dirty linen. Lang I'd spoken to before; he was a guy about ten years my senior, thirty-seven or eight maybe, and a couple of inches under my six feet, a couple pounds over my 180. He had five-o'clock shadow and coal black hair and cold black eyes and the sort of shaggy eyebrows you don't trust; even the impression of hair was a lie: under the hat his forehead kept going. Miller was forty and fat and five eight, with a blank face and blanker eyes—the kind you can take for stupidity if you aren't careful. He was cleaning off the lenses of his wire-frames with a hanky, the glasses having got fogged up in the cold. His ears stuck out; when he put his glasses on, they stuck out more. The Coke-bottle lenses magnified the blank eyes, and it struck me he looked like an owl—an owl that could kick the crap out of an eagle, that is.

Before he was a cop, Miller was a bootlegger—one of the Miller Gang, who were West Side Boys. That made it Old Home Week: we were all West Side Boys. Maxwell Street, where my father's stall had been, was where I knew Lang from.

But I didn't know Lang well enough to merit the old-drinking-pals camaraderie he suggested in his words if not his tone: "Hiya, Red. Heard you hung out here."

Red wasn't my name. Heller was. Nathan Heller. Nate. Never Red, despite my mother's reddish-brown hair I was carrying around.

"The joint's halfway between Dearborn and LaSalle Street stations," I shrugged. "It's handy for me."

It was around three in the afternoon, and we had the place pretty much to ourselves: just me, the mayor's front-office dicks, the guy at the door, the guy behind the bar. But it was a cramped, boxlike joint with lots of dark wood and a mirror behind the bar and framed photos everywhere: celebrities and near-celebrities, signatures on their faces, were staring at me.

So were Lang and Miller.

"Buy you a cup of coffee?" I said, rising a little. I was a plainclothes officer, working the pickpocket detail, bucking for detective status. These guys were the best-paid detectives in town, sergeants yet, and they maybe didn't deserve respect, exactly, but I knew enough to give them some.

They made no move to sit down. Lang just stood there, hands in his topcoat pockets, snow brushing his shoulders like dandruff, and rocked on his heels, like a hobbyhorse; but whether it was from nerves, or from boredom, I couldn't say: I could just sense there was something I wasn't being let in on. Miller stood planted there like one of the lions in front of the Art Institute, only meaner-looking. Also, the lions were bronze and he was tarnished copper.

Then Miller spoke.

"We need a third," he said. He had a voice like somebody trying to sound tough in a talkie: monotone and slightly off-pitch. It should've been funny. It wasn't.

"A third what?" I said.

"A third man," Lang chimed in. "A third player."

"What's the game?"

"We'll tell you in the car."

They both turned toward the door. I was supposed to follow them, apparently. I grabbed my topcoat and hat.

The speak was on the corner of Clark and Polk. Out on the street the wind was whipping at package-clutching pedestrians heading for Dearborn Station, which was around the corner and a block down, where I should be getting back to, to protect these shoppers from losing whatever dough they had left after Marshall Field's got through with them. Skirts and overcoats flapped, and everybody walked with heads lowered, watching the pavement, ignoring the occasional panhandler; dry, wind-scattered snow was like confetti being tossed out of the windows during a particularly uninspiring parade. Across the way the R.E.A. Station was busy, trucks pulling in and out, others being loaded up. Four women, pretty, in their late twenties, early thirties, bundled with packages, went giggling into the speak we'd just exited. It was a week to Christmas, and business was picking up for everybody. Except for Saint Peter's Church, maybe, which was cattycorner from where we stood; business there looked slow.

There was no parking in and near the Loop (which was loosely defined as the area within the El tracks), but Lang and Miller had left their black Buick by the curb anyway, half a block down, across the street; it was the model people called the Pregnant Guppy, because the sides bulged out over the running boards. The running board next to the curb had a foot on it: a uniformed cop was writing a ticket. Miller walked up and reached over and tore it off the cop's pad and wadded it up and tossed it to the snow-flecked breeze. He didn't have to show the cop his detective's shield. Every copper in town knew the two Harrys.

But I liked the way the uniformed man handled it, a Paddy of about fifty who'd been pounding the beat longer than these two had been picking up the mayor's graft, that was for sure. And clean, as Chicago cops went, or he wouldn't still be pounding it. He put his book and pencil away slowly and gave Miller a look that was part condescension, part contempt, said, "My mistake, lad," and cleared his throat and shot phlegm toward Lang's feet. And turned on his heel and left, swinging his nightstick.

Lang, who'd had to hop back, and Miller, his face hanging like a loose rubber mask, stood watching him walk away, wondering what they should do about such unbridled arrogance, when I tapped Lang on the shoulder and said, "I'm freezing my nuts off, gentlemen. What exactly is the party?"

Miller smiled. It was wide but it didn't turn up at the corners and the teeth were big and yellow, like enormous kernels of corn. It was the worst goddamn smile I ever saw.

"Frank Nitti's tossing it," he said.

"Only he don't know it," Lang added, and opened the door on the Buick. "Get in back."

I climbed in. The Pregnant Guppy wasn't a popular model, but it was a nice car. Brown mohair seats, varnished wood trim around the windows. Comfortable, too, considering the situation.

Miller got behind the wheel. The Buick turned over right away, despite the cold, though it shuddered a bit as we pulled out into light traffic. Lang turned and leaned over the seat and smiled. "You got a gun with you?"

I nodded.

He passed a small .38, a snubnose, back to me.

"Now you got two," he said.

We were heading north on Dearborn. We drove through Printer's Row, its imposing ornate facades rising to either side of me, aloof to my situation. One of them, tall, gray, half-a-block long, was the Transportation Building, where my friend Eliot Ness was working even now; he seemed a more likely candidate to be calling on Al Capone's heir than yours truly.

"How'd you finally nail Nitti?" I asked after a while.

Lang turned and looked at me, surprised, like he'd forgotten I was there.

"What do you mean?"

"What's the charge? Who'd he kill?"

Lang and Miller exchanged glances, and Lang made a sound that was vaguely a laugh, though you could mistake it for a cough.

Miller, in his monotone, said, "That's a good one."

For a second, just a second, despite the gun I'd been handed, I had the feeling I was being taken for a ride. That somehow I'd stepped on somebody's toes and whoever it was was big enough and hurt bad enough to take it on up to the mayor, who Christ knows owed plenty of people favors, and now His Honor's prize flunkies were driving me God knows where—Lake Michigan maybe, where a lot of people went swimming, only some of them had been holding their breath underwater for years now.

But they didn't turn right, toward the lake; they turned left at the Federal Building—which meant the Chicago River was still a possibility  and the Union League Club ignored us as we passed. We turned again, right this time, at the Board of Trade. We were in the concrete canyons of the financial district now—and by concrete canyons, I mean just that: in the thick of Chicago's loop, you can see towering buildings at left and right and front and back. Chicago invented the skyscraper and never lets you forget it.

The dustlike snow wasn't coming down hard enough to collect, so the city remained gray, though touched with Christmas red and green: most office windows bore poinsettias, and every utility pole had sprigs of holly or balsam; and now and then an ex-broker in what used to be a nice suit sold bright red apples at a nickel per. Just a few blocks over, on State Street, it would've looked a little more like Christmas, albeit a drunken one: the big stores with their fancy window displays were high on drinking paraphernalia this year, cocktail shakers, hip flasks, hollow canes, home-brew apparatus. All of it legal, but a violation of the law's spirit, as if hookahs were being publicly sold and displayed, just because public opinion suddenly sanctioned smoking dope.

We passed the Bismarck Hotel, where the mayor often lunched; it hadn't been so long ago that the famous old hotel had changed its name to the Randolph, after its location on the southeast corner of Randolph and Wells, to assuage anti-German sentiments during the Great War, though nobody had *ever* called it the Randolph, and a couple years back the name went back to Bismarck, officially. We were on the Palace Theater side, where Ben Bernie and his Lads had top billing ("Free Gifts for the Kids!") and the picture was *Sports Parade* with William Gargan; across the street was City Hall, its Corinthian columns and classical airs making an ironic facade for the goings-on within. Then we crossed under the El, a train rumbling overhead, and I decided they were kidding about Frank Nitti, because the Detective Bureau was on our left and we'd obviously been heading there all along—only we went past.

In the 200 block of North LaSalle, City Hall just a block back, the Detective Bureau less than that, Miller pulled over to the curb again, NO PARKING be damned, and he and Lang got out slowly and I followed them. They drifted casually toward the Wacker-LaSalle Building, a whitestone skyscraper on the corner, the Chicago River across the street from it. A barge was making impatient noises at the nearby example of the massive drawbridges Big Bill Thompson gave the city, but its iron shoulders didn't even shrug.

Inside the Wacker-LaSalle, a gray-speckled marble floor stretched out across a large, mostly empty lobby, turning our footsteps into radio sound effects. On the ceiling high above, cupids flew halfheartedly. There was a newsstand over at the left; a row of phone booths at the right; a bank of elevators straight ahead.

Halfway to the elevators, more or less, in the midst of the big lobby, a couple of guys in derbies and brown baggy suits were sitting in cane-back chairs with a card table set up between them, playing gin. They were a Laurel and Hardy pair, only Italian, and Laurel had the mustache; both had cigars, as well as bulges under one arm. We were a stone's throw from the financial district, but these guys weren't brokers.

Hardy glanced up at the two Harrys, recognizing them, nodding;

Laurel looked at his cards. I looked ahead at the building registry, in the midst of the elevators with their polished brass cage doors: white letters on black, coming into focus as we neared. Import/export, other assorted small businesses, a few lawyers.

We paused at the elevators while Miller cleaned his thick wire-frames again. When they were back on his head, he nodded and Lang hit the elevator button.

"I'll take Campagna," Miller said. It sounded like he was ordering drinks.

"What?" I said.

They didn't say anything; they just looked at the elevators, waiting.

"'Little New York' Campagna?" I said. "The torpedo?"

An elevator came; a guy in another brown suit with matching underarm bulge was running it.

Lang put a finger on his lips to shush me. We got on the elevator and the guy told us to stand back. We did, and not just because he was armed: in those days when you were told to stand back on an elevator, you listened—there were no safety doors inside, and if you stood too near the front and took a shove, you could lose an arm.

He brought us up to the fifth floor: nobody was posted up here; no comedians with guns playing cards. Nobody at all with a bulge under his arm. Just gray walls and offices with pebbled glass in the doors with numbers and, sometimes, names. We were standing on a field of tiny black-and-white tiles—looking down the hallway at the receding mosaic of them made me dizzy momentarily. The air had an antiseptic smell, like a dentist's office, or a toilet.

Lang looked at Miller and pointed back to himself. "Nitti," he said.

"Hey," I said. "What the hell's going on?"

They looked at me like I was an intruder; like they didn't remember asking me along.

"Get a gun out, Red," Lang said to me impatiently.

"It's Heller, if you don't mind," I said, but did what he said, as he did likewise. As did Miller.

"We got a warrant?" I said.

"Shut up," Miller said, without looking at me.

"What the hell am I supposed to do?" I said.

"I just told you," Miller said, and this time he did look at me. "Shut up."

The blank eyes behind the Coke-bottle glasses were round black balls; funny how eyes so inexpressive could say so much.

Lang interceded. "Back us up, Heller. There may be some shooting."

They walked. Their footsteps—and mine, following—echoed down the hall like hollow words.

They stopped at a door that had no name on its pebbled glass—just a number, 554.

It wasn't locked.

Miller went in first, a .45 revolver in his fist; Lang followed, with a .38 with a four-inch barrel. I brought up the rear, thoroughly confused, but leaving the snubnose Lang gave me in my topcoat pocket: I carried a nine-millimeter automatic, a Browning—unusual for a cop, since automatics can jam on you, but I liked automatics. As much as I could like any gun, that is.

It was an outer office; a desk faced us as we entered, but there was no secretary or receptionist behind it. There were, however, two guys in two of half a dozen chairs lining the left wall · two more brown suits, topcoats in their laps, sitting there like some more furniture in the room.

Both were in their late twenties, dark hair, pale blank faces, average builds. One of them, with an oft-broken nose, was reading a pulp magazine, *Black Mask*; the other, with pockmarks you could hide dimes in, was sitting smoking, a deck of Phillip Morris and a much-used ashtray on the seat of the chair next to him.

Neither went for a gun or otherwise made any move. They just sat there surprised—not at seeing cops, but at seeing cops with guns in their hands.

In the corner to the left of the door we'd just come in was a coatrack with four topcoats and three hats; the right wall had another half dozen chairs, empty. Just behind and to the left of the desk was a water cooler and, in the midst of the pebbled-glass-and-wood wall, a closed door.

Then it opened.

Standing in the doorway, leaning against the jamb, was a man who was unmistakably Frank Nitti. I'd never met him, though he'd been pointed out to me a few times; but once having seen him, you couldn't miss him: handsome, in a battered way, fighter's nose, thin inverted-V mustache, faint scar on his lower lip; impeccably groomed, former barber that he was, slick black hair parted neatly at the left; impeccably dressed, in a gray pinstripe suit with vest, and wide black tie with a gray-and-white pattern. He was smaller than

Frank Nitti was supposed to be, but he was an imposing figure just the same.

He closed the door behind him.

There was a look on his face, upon seeing the two Harrys, that reminded me of the look on that uniformed cop's face. He seemed irritated and bored with them, and the fact that guns were in their hands didn't seem to concern him in the least.

A raid was an annoyance; it meant getting booked, making bail, then business as usual. But a few token raids now and then were necessary for public relations. Only for Nitti to be involved was an indignity. He'd only been out of Leavenworth a few months, since serving a tax rap; and now he was acting as his cousin Capone's proxy, the Big Fellow having left for the Atlanta big house in May.

"Where's Campagna?" Lang said. He was standing with Miller in front of him, partially blocked by him. Like Miller was a rock he was hiding behind.

"Is he in town?" Nitti said. Flatly.

"We heard you were siccing him on Tony," Miller said.

Tony was the mayor: Anton J. Cermak, alias "Ten Percent Tony."

Nitti shrugged. "I heard your bohunk boss is sleeping with Newberry," he said.

Ted Newberry was a Capone competitor on the North Side, running what was left of the old "Bugs" Moran operation.

Silence hung in the room like the smell of wet paint.

Then Lang said to me, "Frisk the help."

The two hoods stood; I patted them down with one hand. They were unarmed. If this was a handbook and wire-room setup, as I suspected, their being unarmed made sense; they were serving as runners, not guns. Lang and Miller taking their time about getting into the next room also made sense: most raids were conducted only for show, and this was giving the boys inside time to destroy the evidence.

"Let's see if Campagna's in there," Lang said finally, nodding toward the closed door.

"Who?" Nitti said, with a faint smile.

Then he opened the door and went in, followed by his runners, then by Miller, Lang, and me.

The inner room was larger, but nothing elaborate: just a room with a table running from left to right, taking up a lot of the space. At right, against the wall, was a cage, and a guy in shirt sleeves wearing a green accountant's shade was sitting in there with a bunch of money on the counter; he hadn't bothered putting it away. Perhaps it wouldn't all fit in the drawer. At left a young guy stood at a wire machine with a ticker tape in his hand, only this wasn't the Board of Trade by a long shot. Two more sat at the table: another one in shirt sleeves, his back to us, suitcoat slung over the chair behind him, four phones on the table in front of him; and across from him, a hook-nosed hood wearing a pearl hat with a black band at a Capone tilt. There were no pads or paper of any kind on the table, though there were a few scattered pens and pencils. This was a wireroom, all right. The smoking wastebasket next to the table agreed with me.

The guy in shirt sleeves at the table was the only one I recognized: Joe Palumbo. He was a heavyset man with bulging eyes and a vein-shot nose; at about forty-five, the oldest man in the room with the exception of Nitti, who was pushing fifty gracefully. The hood in the Capone hat was about thirty-five, small, swarthy, smoking—and probably Little New York Campagna. The accountant in the cage was in his thirties, too; and the kid at the ticker tape, with curly dark hair and a mustache, couldn't have been twenty-five. Lang ordered the accountant out of the cage; he was a little man with round shoulders and he took a seat at the table, across from Palumbo, next to the man I assumed (rightly) to be Campagna, who looked at the two Harrys and me with cold dark eyes that might have been glass. Miller told the runners to take seats at the table; they did. Then he had the others stand and take a frisk, Campagna first. Clean.

"What's this about?" Nitti asked. He was standing near the head of the table.

Lang and Miller exchanged glances; it seemed to mean something.

My hand was sweating around the automatic's grip. The men at the table weren't doing anything suspicious; their hands were on the table, near the phones. Everyone had been properly searched. Everyone except Nitti, that is, though the coat and vest hung on him in such a way that a shoulder holster seemed out of the question.

He was just standing there, staring at Lang and Miller, and I could feel it starting to work on them. Campagna's gaze was no picnic, either. The room seemed warm, suddenly; a radiator was hissing—or was that Nitti?

Finally Lang said, "Heller?"

"Yes?" I said. My voice broke, like a kid's.

"Frisk Nitti. Do it out in the other room."

I stepped forward and, gun in hand but not threateningly, asked Nitti to come with me.

He shrugged again and came along; he seemed to be having trouble deciding just how irritated to be.

In the outer office he held his coat open as if showing off the lining—it was jade-green silk—and I patted him down. No gun.

The cuffs were in my topcoat. Nitti turned his back to me and held his wrists behind him while I fished for the cuffs. He glanced back and said, "Do *you* know what this is about, kid?"

I said, "Not really," getting the cuffs out, and noticed he was chewing something.

"Hey," I said. "What the hell are you doing? Spit that out!"

He kept chewing and, Frank Nitti or not, I slapped him on the back and he spit it out: a piece of paper; a wad of paper, now. He must've had a bet written down and palmed it when we came in; hadn't had a chance to burn it like the boys inside did theirs.

"Nice try, Frank," I said, grasping his wrists, cuffs ready, feeling tough, and Lang came in from the bigger room, shut the door, came up beside me and shot Nitti in the back. The sound of it shook the pebbled glass around us; the bullet went through Nitti and snicked into some woodwork.

I pulled away, saying, "Jesus!"

Nitti turned as he fell, and Lang pumped two more slugs into him: one in his chest, one in the neck. The .38 blasts sounded like a cannon going off in the small room; a derby dropped off the coatrack. Worst of all was the sound the bullets made going in: a soft sound, like shooting into mud.

I grabbed Lang by the wrist before he could shoot again.

"What the hell are you    "

He jerked away from me. "Easy, Red. You got that snubnose?"

I could hear the men yelling in the adjacent room; Miller was keeping them back, presumably.

"Yes," I said.

Nitti was on the floor; so was a lot of his blood.

"Give it here," Lang said.

I handed it to him.

"Now go in and help Harry," he said.

I went back in the wire room. Miller had his gun on the men, all of whom were standing now, though still grouped around the table.

"Nitti's been shot," I said. I don't know who I was saying it to, exactly.

Campagna spat something in Sicilian.

Palumbo, eyes bulging even more than usual, furious, his face red, said, "Is he dead?"

"I don't know. I don't think he's going to be alive long, though." I looked at Miller; his face was impassive. "Call an ambulance."

He just looked at me.

I looked at Palumbo. "Call an ambulance."

He sat back down and reached for one of the many phones before him.

Then there was another shot.

I rushed back out there and Lang was holding his wrist; his right hand was bleeding—a fairly deep graze alongside the knuckle of his forefinger.

On the floor, by the open fingers of Nitti's right hand, the snub-nose .38 was smoking.

"Do you really think that's going to fool anybody?" I asked.

Lang said, "I'm shot. Call an ambulance."

"One's on the way," I said.

Miller came in, gun still in hand. He bent over Nitti.

"He's not dead," Miller said.

Lang shrugged. "He will be." He turned toward me, wrapping a handkerchief around his wound. "Get in there and watch the grease-balls."

I went back in the larger office. One of the men, the young, nervous one with the mustache, was opening the window, climbing out onto the ledge.

"What the hell do you think you're doing?" I asked.

The other men were seated at the table; the young guy who was half out the window froze.

Then somebody at the table tossed him a gun.

Where it came from, who tossed it, I didn't know. Maybe Campagna.

But the guy had a gun now, and he shot at me, and I got the automatic out and shot back.

And then he wasn't in the window anymore.

MAXWELL STREET

## 2

My father never wanted me to be a cop. Particularly not a Chicago cop, the definition of which (my father frequently said) was a guy with change for a five. He'd been a union man, my father, and had been jailed and beaten by police; and he'd always had disdain for Chicago politics, from the butcher down the block who was assistant precinct captain to "Big Bill" Thompson, the mayor who wanted to be known as the "Builder" when "Boozer" was more like it.

Pa would've liked nothing more than for me to quit the force. It had been a major stumbling block between us, those last few years of his life. It may have led to his death. I don't know for sure. He didn't leave a note that night he shot himself. With my gun.

The Hellers came from Halle, in eastern Germany, orginally, and so did their name: Jews in Germany in the early 1800s were forced to abandon their traditional lack of surname and take on the name of either their occupation or home area. If my name hadn't been Heller it probably would've been Taylor, because a tailor is what my great-grandfather, Jacob Heller, was, in Halle, in the late 1840s.

Which were hard times. The economy was doing handstands due to developing railroads and industry; technology was making jobs obsolete for everybody from the guy who weaved the cloth to the oxcart driver who shipped it. Unemployment flourished, while crops failed and food prices doubled. A lot of people headed for America. My great-grandfather hung on. His business was suffering, yes, but he had contacts with the richer Jews in Halle—moneylenders, bankers, businessmen—and when the region was rocked by political unrest in 1848, great-grandfather watched from the sidelines. He couldn't afford getting involved: his business depended on an upper-class patronage, after all.

Then the letter arrived. From Vienna, where great-grandfather's younger brother Albert had lived; *had* lived: he'd been killed in the March 13, 1848, revolt against Metternich. His brother left an inheritance, which had been placed in the hands of Rabbi Kohn, the rabbi of Vienna's Reform synagogue. Great-grandfather didn't trust the mails during such troubled times, and he went to Vienna to pick up the money. He stayed for a few days with Rabbi Kohn, and enjoyed the company of this kind, intelligent man and his gracious family. He was still there when the rabbi and his family were poisoned by Orthodox fanatics.

My great-grandfather was apparently hit hard by all this: political unrest had taken his brother from him; and in Vienna, he'd seen Jew kill Jew. He'd always been a very pragmatic businessman, preferring to be apolitical; and where religion was concerned, he practiced Reform Judaism rather than strict Orthodoxy. But now he renounced his faith altogether, and became apostate. Judaism hasn't been seen in my family since.

Leaving Halle couldn't have been easy, but staying would've been hard. The secret police that grew up in the wake of the revolution of 1848 were making things tough. So were the Orthodox Jews who attacked my great-grandfather verbally for his apostasy, and who spread the word to his wealthy clients that their tailor's late brother had been a radical. The latter didn't help business, certainly, nor did the general economic climate, and my great-grandfather decided, all in all, that America had to be a safer place to raise his family of four (the youngest, Hiram, having been born in 1850, just three years before the family immigrated to New York City).

As a youth, Hiram, my grandfather, worked in the family tailor shop, which was proving a moderately successful business, though Hiram never went into it. He went instead into the Union army at age seventeen. Like a lot of young Jews at that time, he wanted to prove his patriotism: Jewish war profiteers had been giving their fellows a bad name, and my grandfather helped make up for that by getting shot in both legs at Gettysburg.

He returned to New York, where his father had died in his absence, after a long hospitalization. His mother had died ten years before, and now his two brothers and his sister were squabbling over the business/inheritance, the upshot being that sister Anna left the city with a good chunk of the family savings, not to be heard of again for some years. His brothers, Jacob and Benjamin, stayed in New York but never spoke to each other again; they rarely saw Hiram, either, a nearly crippled, isolated man who was lucky to get his job in a sweatshop in the garment district.

In 1871 my grandfather married Naomi Levitz, a fellow sweatshop worker. My father, Mahlon, was born in 1875, my uncle Louis in

1877. In 1884 my grandfather collapsed while working and from then on was totally bedridden, left at home to look after the two boys as best he could, while grandmother continued working. In 1886 the crowded tenement building the family lived in caught fire. Many died in the blaze. My grandmother got my father and uncle out safely, then went back in after grandfather. Neither came out.

My father's aunt—who had left town with her estimated share of the inheritance—had got back in touch with the rest of the family, letting them know she was "successful." It was to her the two boys were sent. To Chicago. From the train to the streetcar, the wide-eyed boys were shuttled not to the Jewish section of the near West Side but to the section of the city known as the Levee. The First Ward—home of "Bathhouse" John and "Hinky Dink," the corrupt ward bosses; site of the most famous whorehouse in the country, the Everleigh Club, run by sisters Ada and Minna, and scores of lesser houses of ill repute. Their "successful" Aunt Anna was a madam in one of the latter.

Not that Aunt Anna was at the bottom rung; not when there were tenements housing row upon row of crib upon crib of streetwalkers taking a load off. Vile establishments, one of which was owned by the police superintendent at one time; several others by Carter Harrison, Sr., five-time mayor of Chicago. And then there were the panel houses, providing rooms furnished only with a bed and a chair, the former occupied by a girl and her client, the latter by the client's pants; and from a sliding panel in a wall or door, a third party would enter at an opportune moment and make a withdrawal, often at the very moment a deposit was being made.

At the other end of the spectrum were the Everleigh sisters and, before them, Carrie Watson, into whose parlor one could go at least five ways, as there were five parlors in her three-story brownstone mansion. There were also twenty bedrooms, a billiard room, and, in the basement, a bowling alley. Damask upholstery, silk gowns, linen sheets; wine served in silver buckets, sipped from gold goblets.

Then there was Anna Heller's house. Wine was served there, too; the dozen girls residing there had it for breakfast. This was around 1:00 P.M., and the third liquid meal of their (so far) short day: at noon a colored girl woke these "withered roses of society" for cocktails in bed; they dressed themselves with the assistance of absinthe, and headed down for breakfast. Soon the girls, in pairs, would sit at windows and attract the attention of male passersby. This would be done by rapping on the window and providing a glimpse of what a girl was wearing, if you could call it that: costumes ranging from Mother Hubbards made of mosquito netting to jockey uniforms to gowns without sleeves to gowns without bosoms (or rather, with bosoms out) to nothing. Business was brisk. And by four or five in the morning, the girls would find a novel use for a bed: sleep. Or drunken stupor.

It helped a girl to stay drunk at Anna Heller's. Anna was known to boast that no act was too disgusting or perverse for her girls—Circus Night was held three or four times a month—and heaven help the girl who made a liar out of Anna. It was said—though this one aspect of his aunt's business my father never witnessed—that Anna had in her employ six colored gentlemen who resided at a separate dwelling of hers; and that she would take business trips to other cities and return with girls from age thirteen to seventeen, having promised them jobs as actresses. The act Anna had in mind was a predictable one, though her variation wasn't. A girl would be locked in a room without clothing and raped by the colored gentlemen. In this way a girl became accustomed to "the life" and soon was having wine for breakfast. So it was said, at any rate.

My father didn't like his aunt; he didn't like her house or the way she slapped the drunken "chippies" (as she constantly called them) or the way she hoarded the money her girls made her. And *she* didn't like the way my father looked at her, a look of silent unveiled contempt (which my father was good at), and so my father got slapped a lot, too.

Anna and my uncle Louis got along fine. The parlor wasn't a fancy one, but it was upper-grade enough to occasionally attract a clientele that included ward politicans and successful businessmen, bankers and the like, and Louis must have liked the life these men led, or seemed to lead, and got a taste for capitalism. Of course Aunt Anna was a hell of a capitalist herself, so maybe that was where he picked it up. He probably learned to kiss ass watching Anna deal with the politicos and the posher types who occasionally showed up, and he put the skill to good effect by using it back on Anna, playing upon her pockmarked vanity. While Anna made my father stop school after the third grade, making him the bordello's janitor, Louis was attending a boarding school out east.

My father didn't like Louis much either, by this point. Louis didn't seem to notice, or care. When he was home from school out east, that is. If you called that house a home. Anna and my father did have one thing in common, though: a hatred of cops. Pa hated the sight of the patrolmen arriving for their weekly two dollars and fifty cents each, plus booze and food and girls anytime they were in the mood, which was every time. And Anna hated paying the two-fifty, and providing the booze, food, and girls. The beat cops weren't the only freeloaders: inspectors and captains from the Harrison Street police station held out a helping-themselves hand, as did the ward politicians, for whom my father also built a dislike. These were the same politicians, of course, who were among those my uncle Louis looked up to.

After eastern prep school, Louis returned to Chicago, and Aunt Anna sent him promptly off to Northwestern. And it was about then that she started taking her favorite nephew to the annual First Ward Ball, where Louis would not only see those admired politicians, but rub shoulders with them, and more important ones than just the First Ward ward heelers: Hinky Dink and Bathhouse John themselves, and most every other alderman in town, and bankers and lawyers and railroad executives and prominent businessmen, and police captains and inspectors and maybe even the commissioner; and pimps, madams, streetwalkers, pickpockets, burglars, and dope fiends. Everyone in costume, the men running to knights, gladiators, and circus strongmen, the ladies (most of whom were of the evening) to Indian maidens, Little Egypts, and geisha girls (costumes the newspapers understatedly described as "abbreviated"). The ball filled the Chicago Coliseum every year, a few days before Christmas, and added twenty-five to fifty thousand dollars to the Hinky Dink–Bathhouse John campaign fund.

"Bathhouse" John Coughlin, former rubber in a bathhouse, Democratic alderman from the First Ward, was the showman: he recited (his own) lousy poetry, wore outlandish clothes (lavender cravat and a red sash), and blew a fortune or two on the horses. "Hinky Dink" (Michael) Kenna was the brains, a little man who chewed on his cigars and accumulated a fortune or two while running the Workingmen's Exchange, a landmark Levee saloon; among his contributions to Chicago was establishing the standard rate for a vote: fifty cents. Their First Ward Balls were described by the Illinois Crime Survey as the "annual underworld orgy." Hinky Dink didn't care. "Chicago," he said, "ain't no sissy town."

But at the time Uncle Louis was being impressed by the balls of the First Ward, my father was long gone. In 1893, during the Columbian Exhibition—Chicago's first world's fair—business at Anna

Heller's had boomed, and extra girls were taken on, and Anna's iron hand had taken its toll: on the girls and on my father. The syphilis was probably starting to eat Anna's brain and possibly explained her erratic behavior. When my father exploded at her, his silent contempt finally erupting after his aunt slapped a young woman senseless, she came at him with a kitchen knife. The scar on his shoulder was five inches long. Pa stayed around long enough for the doctor Anna had on call to come sew up the wound, then hopped a freight south.

He got thrown off the train near 115th Street. The Pullman plant nearby was where he ended up working; a year later he found himself in the midst of a strike, and was one of the militant strikers who got laid off when the strike finally ended.

And so began Pa's union work: with the Hebrew Worker's Congress on the near West Side; with the Wobblies on the near North Side; as a union organizer; a worker at various plants, and involved with union actions and strikes. . . .

Uncle Louis took a different path. By now he was a trust officer with *the* major Chicago bank, Central Trust Company of Illinois, the famous "Dawes Bank," founded by General Charles Gates Dawes, who went on to be Calvin Coolidge's vice-president. Aunt Anna died in an insane asylum the year Louis graduated from Northwestern, so he was able to start out with a degree—and an inheritance, which is to say the money off the sale of the brothel and its hookers—and leave his sordid past behind him.

So the occasional meetings thereafter between my father and uncle were strained, to say the least—a polished young financier on his way up, and a radical worker into union organizing—and usually ended with my father shouting slogans and my uncle remaining quiet, expressing his contempt by not condescending to reply, which is funny because that was my *father's* favorite tactic. My father, despite his union activities, was not a man prone to losing his temper; his rage he swallowed, like an unchewable piece of meat that couldn't be spit out because times were too hard. But at my uncle, he would shout; at my uncle, he would vent his rage. So by century's turn, the two men weren't speaking; it made for no awkward moments: they didn't exactly travel in the same circles.

Also, by century's turn, my father was in love. Having been denied the education Louis got, he'd taken to reading, even before his union interests led him into books on history and economy. Perhaps that was where my father's capacity for smugness and contempt came from: he had the insecurity-based arrogance of all self-educated men. At any rate, it was at a cultural study program at Newberry Library that he met another (if less arrogant) self-educated soul: Jeanette Nolan, a beautiful redheaded young woman who was a bit on the frail, sickly side. In fact, it was repeated bouts of illness keeping her out of school that led her into reading and self-study (I never found out exactly what her health problems were, though I've come to think it may have been her heart). But this only made her all the more appealing to Pa. After all, his two favorite authors were Dumas and Dickens (although he once admitted to me his disappointment when he discovered that the same Dumas wasn't responsible for both *Camille* and *The Three Musketeers;* he had gone through many a year wondering at the versatility of the author Alexandre Dumas, till he found out that *pere* and *fils* were different people).

Not long after she and my father started to court, Pa landed in court, then in jail; his work with unions was repeatedly bringing him into conflict with cops, and his arrest came during a textile plant strike, landing him a month in Bridewell Prison.

Which was a hellhole, of course. A sandstone hellhole with no heat, no toilet facilities other than a five-gallon bucket in the corner of a rusty, paint-peeling cell with two wall-suspended bunks with straw mattresses and wafer-thin blankets, and a stench you could almost see. No water in the cells, though each morning at six, prisoners were given a few moments at a trough with cold running water before one of the two cell-mates got his turn at joining the parade of slop cans, which were carried from the cells and dumped outside in huge cesspools and then scrubbed clean with chemicals. And once a week, a gang shower. The shower came in handy after a week in a clay hole, which is where Pa was assigned: a stone quarry; a deep pit where big pieces of limestone got turned into little ones.

Pa was used to hardship; Aunt Anna had seen to that. And he was pretty healthy: he had the same framework as me, roughly six feet with one-eighty or one-seventy attached to it. But one month in Bridewell took its toll even on a healthy man, and he came out twenty pounds lighter—meals ran to a breakfast of bread and dry oatmeal, lunch of bread and thin soup, supper of bread and a concoction that was peas and fragments of corned beef swimming in something unidentifiable, all servings negligible, with the three pieces of bread the only thing that got him and the other prisoners through the day (one odd thing: Pa often said it was the best fresh-baked bread he ever ate), and he had a cough from breathing quarry dust, and was of course very proud of himself for the moral victory of going to jail over a union matter, and loved his martyr's role.

But Jeanette was not impressed, not with the glory aspects of it, anyway. She was horrified at the condition Pa was in after Bridewell, just as she'd been horrified the times she'd cleaned and bandaged him after strike-related beatings. Before he went to Bridewell, he'd proposed marriage; he'd asked her permission to ask her parents for her hand. She had said she'd think about it. And now she said she'd marry him on one condition . . .

So Pa left union work.

Pa was no stranger to Maxwell Street; he'd been there, from time to time, passing out political and union literature. He didn't want to work for a "capitalist" institution, like a bank (he'd leave *that* to his brother Louis); and he couldn't work in a factory   he'd been black-listed from most Chicago plants, and the ones where he wasn't black-listed would only present the temptation of future union work. So he opened a stall on Maxwell Street selling books, used and new, with an emphasis on dime novels, which, with school supplies—pencils, pens and ink, notebooks—attracted kids, who were his best custom-ers. Occasionally, a parent frowned upon the union and anarchist lit-erature that rubbed shoulders with Buffalo Bill and Nick Carter on Pa's stall; even the similarly politically conscious Jeanette was critical of this, but nothing could sway Pa. And Maxwell Street was a place where you could get away with selling just about anything.

About a mile southwest of the Loop, Maxwell Street was at the center of a Jewish ghetto a mile square, give or take, and on Maxwell Street it was mostly the latter. The Great Fire of 1871, thanks to Mrs. O'Leary's less-than-contented cow purportedly kicking a lantern over, left Maxwell Street, which was just south of the O'Leary barn, untouched. The Maxwell Street area had a big influx of new residents from the burned-out areas of Chicago, and the now densely popu-lated area attracted merchants—most of them Jewish peddlers with two-wheeled pushcarts. Soon the street was teeming with bearded patriarchs, their caftans brushing the dusty wooden sidewalks, their black derbies faded gray from days in the sun, selling. Selling shoes, fruit, garlic, pots, pans, spices . . .

By the time Pa opened a stall there, Maxwell Street was a Chicago institution, the marketplace where the rich and the poor would go for a bargain; where awnings hung from storefronts to the very edge of the wooden stalls crowding the curb, the walkway between so dark a tunnellike effect was created, and lamps were strung up so bargain hunters could see what they were getting· but not *too* many lamps, and not *overly* bright, because it wasn't to the seller's advantage to let the buyer get *too* close a look at the toeless socks, used toothbrushes, factory-second shirts, and other wonders that were the soul of the street. Whether the street had a heart or not, I couldn't say, but it did have a smell: the smell of onions frying; even the smell of garbage burning in open trash drums couldn't drown *that* out. Accompanying the oniony air were the clouds of steam rising from the hot dogs; and when the onions met the hot dogs in a fresh bun, that was as close to heaven as Maxwell Street got.

Pa and his bride moved into a one-room tenement flat at Twelfth and Jefferson, in a typical Maxwell Street-area building: a three-story clapboard with a pitched roof and exterior staircase. There were nine flats in the building and about eighty people; one three-room flat was home for an even dozen. The Hellers, alone in their one room, sharing an outhouse with twenty or thirty of their fellow residents (one outhouse per floor), had room to spare, and maybe that's what led to me.

I would imagine Pa was living your typical quiet life of desperation: his union work, which meant so much to him, was in the past; taking its place was his stall, in an atmosphere more openly capitalistic than the banks he loathed (and Pa was a well-read, intellectual type, remember; irony didn't get past him). So all he had in life was his beloved Jeanette, and the promise of a family.

But mother was still frail, and having me (in 1905) damn near killed her. A midwife/nurse from the Maxwell Street Dispensary, pulled her—and me—through; and, later, diplomatically suggested to them, separately and together, that Nathan Samuel Heller be an only child.

Big families were the rule then, however, and a few years later, my mother died during a miscarriage; the midwife didn't even make it to the house before my mother died in my father's bloody arms. I think I remember standing nearby and seeing this. Or maybe my father's quiet, understated but photographically vivid retelling (and he told me this only once) made me *think* I remembered, made me think it came back to me from over the years. I would've been about three, I guess. She died in 1908.

Pa didn't show his feelings; it wasn't his way. I don't remember ever seeing him weep. But losing mother hit him hard. Had there been relatives on either side of the family that Pa was close to, I might've ended up being raised by an aunt or something; there were overtures from Uncle Louis, I later learned, and from mother's sisters and a brother, but Pa resisted them all. I was all he had left, all that remained of her. That doesn't mean we were close, though, despite the fact that I was helping at the stall by age six; he and I didn't seem to have much in common, except perhaps an interest in reading, and mine was a casual one, hardly matching his. But I was reading Nick Carter by age ten and used hardbacks of Sherlock Holmes soon after. I wanted to be a detective when I grew up.

Conditions in the neighborhood got worse and worse; shopping in the Maxwell Street Market could be an adventure, but living there was a disaster. It was a slum: there were 130 people crowded in our building now, and the father and son who shared one room were looked upon with envy by their neighbors. There were sweatshops which of course got my union-in-his-blood father's ire up—and diseases (mother had had influenza when the miscarriage took her, and Pa used to blame the flu for her death, perhaps because in some way it absolved him); and there was the stink of garbage and outhouses and stables. I attended Walsh school, and while I managed not to get involved directly, there were gang wars aplenty, bloody fights in which kids would slash each other with knives and fire pistols at one another. And that was the six- and seven-year olds; the older kids were *really* tough. I managed to live through two years of Walsh before Pa announced we were moving out. *When?* I wanted to know. He said he didn't know, but we *would* move.

Even at age seven (which is what I was at the time) I knew Pa wasn't much of a businessman; school supplies and dime novels and such made for a steady, day-to-day sort of income, but nothing more. And while he was a hard worker, Pa had begun to have headaches what years later might have been called migraines—and there were days when his stall did not open for business. The headaches began, of course, after Mother died.

It couldn't have been easy for him, but Pa went to Uncle Louis. He went, one Sunday afternoon, to Uncle Louis' Lake Shore high-rise apartment in Lincoln Park. Uncle Louis was an assistant vice-president with the Dawes Bank now; a rich, successful businessman; in short, everything Pa was not. And when Pa asked for a loan, his brother asked, why not go to my *bank* for that? Why come to my home? And why, after all these years, should *I* help *you?*

And Pa answered him. As a courtesy to you, he said, I did not come to your bank; I would not want to embarrass my successful brother. And an embarrassment is what I would be, Pa said, a Maxwell Street merchant in ragged clothes, coming to beg from his banker brother; it would be unseemly. Of course, Pa said, if you *want* me to come around, I can do that; and I can do that again and again, until you finally give me my loan. Perhaps, Pa said, you do not embarrass easily; perhaps your business associates, your fancy clients, do not mind that your brother is a raggedy merchant—an anarchist—a union man; perhaps they do not mind that we both were raised by a whorehouse madam; perhaps they understand that your fortune was built upon misery and suffering, like their fortunes.

With the loan, my father was able to start a small bookstore in the part of North Lawndale we knew as Douglas Park, a storefront on South Homan with three rooms in the rear: kitchen, bedroom, sitting room, the latter doubling as my bedroom; best of all was indoor plumbing, and we had it all to ourselves. I went to Lawson school, which was practically across the street from Heller's Books. And the school supplies Pa sold, in addition to the dime novels he continued to stock, kept his store afloat. In twelve years he'd paid Uncle Louis back; that would've been about 1923.

I didn't know it then, because Pa never showed it, but I was the center of his life. I can see that now. I can see that he was proud of the good grades I got; and I can see that the move we made from Maxwell Street to Douglas Park had mostly to do with getting me in better, safer schools and very little to do with improving Pa's business—he still wasn't much of a businessman, stocking more political and economic literature than popular novels (Pa's idea of a popular novel was Upton Sinclair's *The Jungle*), refusing to add the penny candy and junk toys that would've been the perfect commercial adjunct to the school supplies he sold, that would've brought the Lawson kids in, because the school supplies and dime novels were the only concession he'd make to commerce, the only room he'd sacrifice to his precious books. And he didn't stock the religious books that would've sold well in this predominantly Jewish area, either; a taste for kosher food was about as Jewish as Pa got, and I guess the same has proved true for me. We're that much alike.

He wanted me to go to college; it was his overriding dream. The dream was no more specific than that: no goal of a son as a doctor, or a lawyer; I could be anything I wanted. A teacher would've pleased him, I think, but I'm just guessing. The only thing he made clear was his hope that business—either on Uncle Louis' high scale or his own low one—would be something I'd avoid; and I always assured him that he needn't worry about my following either of those courses of action. The only thing *I* had tried to make clear, since I was about ten years old, was my desire to be a detective when I grew up. Pa took that as seriously as most fathers would; but some kids *do* grow up to be firemen, you know. And when I kept talking about it on into my early twenties, he should've paid attention. But that's something parents rarely do. They demand attention; they don't give it. But then the same is true of children, isn't it?

To his credit, when he gave me the five hundred dollars he'd been saving for God knows how long, he said that it was a graduation gift, no strings, though he admitted to hoping I would use it for college. To my credit, I did; I went to Crane Junior College for two years, during which time Pa's business seemed to be less than prospering, with him alone in the shop, closing down occasionally because of headaches. When I went back to help him there, he assumed I was working to save up and go on for another two years of college. I assumed he realized I'd decided two years was enough. Typically, we didn't speak about this and went our merry private ways, assuming the hell out of things.

We had our first argument the day I told him I was applying for a job with the Chicago P.D. It was the first time Pa ever really shouted at me (and one of the last: he reverted to sarcasm and contempt thereafter, the arguments continuing but staying low-key if intense) and it shocked me; and I think I shocked him by standing up to him. He hadn't noticed I wasn't a kid, despite my being twenty-four at the time. When he finished shouting, he laughed at me. You'll never get a job with the cops, he said. You got no clout, you got no money, you got no prayer. And the argument was over.

I never told my father that my Uncle Louis had arranged my getting on the force; but it was obvious. Like Pa said, you needed patronage, or money to buy in, to get a city job. So I went to the only person I knew in Chicago who was really somebody, which was Uncle Louis (never Lou), who was by now a full VP with the Dawes Bank. I went to him for advice.

And he said, "You've never asked anything of me, Nate. And

you're not asking now. But I'm going to give you a present. Don't expect anything else from me, ever. But this present I will arrange." I asked him how. He said, "I'll speak to A.J." A.J. was Cermak, not yet mayor, but a powerful man in the city.

And I made the force. And it was never the same between Pa and me, though I continued to live at home. My role in "cracking" the Lingle case got me promoted to plainclothes after two years on traffic detail; and it was shortly after that that my father put my gun to his head.

The same gun I had used today, to kill some damn kid in Frank Nitti's office.

"So I quit," I told Barney.

Barney was Barney Ross, who as you may remember was one of the great professional boxers of his time, and that time was now; he was the top lightweight contender in the country, knocking on champion Tony Canzoneri's door. He was a West Side kid, too, another Maxwell Street expatriate. Actually, Barney still *was* a kid: twenty-three or twenty-four, a handsome bulldog with a smile that split his face whenever he chose to use it, which was often.

I knew Barney since he was baby Barney Rasofsky. His family was strictly Orthodox, and come Friday sundown could do no work till after Saturday. Barney's pa was so strict they even ripped toilet paper into strips so the family wouldn't be tearing paper on the *Shabbes*. For about a year, when I was seven or eight, right before we moved out of Maxwell Street, I turned on the gas and did other errands for the Rasofskys, as their *Shabbes goy*, since I was as un-Orthodox as my pa. Later, when I was a teenager in Douglas Park, I'd come back to Maxwell Street on Sundays, to work with Barney as a "puller" a puller being a barker working in front of the door of a store, shouting out bargains supposedly to be found within, often grabbing a passerby and forcing the potential customer into the store. We worked as a team, Barney and me, and Barney was a real *trombenik* by this time, a young roughneck; so I let him do the pulling, and I handled the sales pitch. Barney had turned into a dead-end kid after his pa was shot to death by thieves in the little hole-in-the-wall Rasofsky's Dairy. That's what turned him into a street fighter, and the need to provide for the family his pa had left behind eventually turned him into Barney Ross, the prizefighter.

Barney was smarter than a lot of fighters, but just as lousy with money as the worst of 'em. He'd been pulling in big purses for almost a year now; fortunately, his managers, Winch and Pian, were straight, and got him to make a couple of investments that weren't at the track. One of them was a jewelry store on Clark; another was a building at Van Buren and Plymouth with a downstairs corner deli next to a "blind pig"—that is, a bar that looked closed down from the street, but was really anything but (lots of things in Chicago looked like one thing outside and something else from inside). Barney planned to call the place the Barney Ross Cocktail Lounge someday, after Prohibition, and probably after he retired from the ring. His managers had a fit when he decided to keep the speak going, because Barney was a public figure in Chicago, with a wholesome image, despite a background that included being a runner for Capone and hustling crap games.

"So you quit," Barney said. He had a soft, quiet tenor voice, incongruous coming out of that flat, mildly battered puss of his, and puppy-dog brown eyes you could study for days and not see killer instinct—unless you swung at him.

"That's what I said," I said. "I quit."

"The cops, you mean."

"The opera company. Of course the cops."

He sipped the one beer he was allowing himself. We were in a corner booth. It was midevening, but slow; the night was just cold enough, the snow coming down just hard enough, to keep most sane folk inside. I only lived a few blocks from here, so was only moderately nuts. None of the other booths were taken and only a handful of stools at the bar were filled.

You went in through a door in the deli and found yourself facing the bar in a dark, smoky room three times as long as it was wide. The only tables were on the small dance floor at the far end, chairs stacked on the little open stage nearby—the nightclub aspect of the joint was on hold till Repeal. Boxing photos hung everywhere, shots of Barney and other fighters, in and out of the ring, with an emphasis on other West Side kids like King Levinsky, the heavyweight, and Jackie Fields, the welterweight Barney used to spar with; and, of course, the great lightweight Benny Leonard, who last year suffered a humiliating defeat attempting a comeback—Jimmy McLarnin put him down in six, giving him a bloody beating (the photos of Leonard on Barney's wall were from the 1917 championship victory over Freddie Welsh).

"Your pa woulda liked you quitting," he said.

"I know."

"But Janey ain't gonna."

"That I also know," I said.

Janey was Jane Dougherty; we were engaged. So far.

"You want another beer?"

"What do you think?"

"Buddy!" he said. He was talking to Buddy Gold, the retired heavyweight who ran the place for him and bartended. Then he looked at me with a wry little grin and said, "You're throwing money away, you know."

I nodded. "Being a cop in the Loop is good money in hard times."

Buddy brought the beer.

"It's good money in good times," Barney said.

"True."

"This Nitti thing."

"Yeah?"

"It happened yesterday afternoon?"

"Yeah. You saw the papers, I take it?"

"I saw the papers. I heard the city talking, too."

"No kidding. You serve lousy beer."

"No kidding. Manhattan Beer, what you expect?" Manhattan Beer was Capone's brand name; his Fort Dearborn brand liquors weren't so hot, either. "When did you decide to quit, exactly?"

"This morning."

"When did you turn your badge in?"

"This morning."

"It was that easy, then."

"No. It took me all day to quit."

Barney laughed. One short laugh. "I'm not surprised," he said.

The papers had made me out a hero. Me and Miller and Lang. But I came in for special commendation because I was already the youngest plainclothes officer in the city. That's what having an uncle who knows A. J. Cermak can do for you; that and if you help "crack" the Lingle case.

The mayor was big on publicity. He had a *daily* press conference; made weekly broadcasts he called "intimate chats," inviting listeners to write in and comment on his administration; and kept an "open door" at City Hall, where he could be seen sitting in shirt sleeves, possibly eating a sandwich and having a glass of milk, just like real people, any old time—or till recently, that is. Word had it open-door hours had been cut back, so he could better "transact the business of the mayor's office."

Today the papers had been full of the mayor declaring war on "the underworld." Frank "The Enforcer" Nitti was the first major victim in the current war on crime; the raid on Nitti's office was the opening volley in that war, Cermak said (in his daily news conference); and the three "brave detectives who made the bold attack" were "the mayor's special hoodlum squad." Well, that was news to me.

All I knew was when I went to the station after the shooting, I wrote out my report and gave it to the lieutenant, who read it over and said, "This won't be necessary," and wadded it up and tossed it in the wastebasket. And said, "Miller's doing the talking to the press. You just keep your mouth shut." I didn't say anything, but my expression amounted to a question, and the lieutenant said, "This comes from *way* upstairs. If I were you, I'd keep my trap shut till you find out what the story's going to be."

Well, I'd seen Miller's story by now—it was in the papers, too and it was a pretty good story, as stories went; it didn't have anything to do with what happened in Nitti's office, but it'd look swell in the true detective magazines, and if they made a movie out of it with Jack Holt as Miller and Chester Morris as Lang and Boris Karloff as Nitti, it'd be a corker. It had Nitti stuffing the piece of paper in his mouth, and Lang trying to stop him, and Nitti drawing a gun from a shoulder holster and firing; and I was supposed to have fired a shot into Nitti, too. And of course one of the gangsters made a break for it out the window, and I plugged him. Frank Hurt, the guy's name was—nice to know, if anybody ever wanted the names of people I killed. I was a regular six-gun kid; maybe Tom Mix should've played me.

It was a real publicity triumph, made to order for His Honor.

Only I was gumming it up. Today I told the lieutenant I was quitting; I tried to give him my badge, but he wouldn't take it. He had me talk to the chief of detectives, who wouldn't take my badge, either. He sent me over to City Hall where the chief himself talked to me; he, also, didn't want my badge. Neither did the deputy commissioner. He told me if I wanted to turn my badge in, I'd have to give it to the commissioner himself.

The commissioner's office was adjacent to Mayor Cermak's, whose door was not open this afternoon. It was about three-thirty; I'd been trying to give my badge away since nine.

The large reception room, where a male secretary sat behind a desk, was filled with ordinary citizens with legitimate gripes, and none of them had a prayer at getting in to see the commissioner. A ward heeler from the North Side went in right ahead of me and, without a glance at the poor peons seated and standing around him, went to the male secretary with a stack of traffic tickets that needed fixing, which the secretary took with a wordless, mild smile, stuffing them in a manila envelope that was already overflowing, which he then filed in a pigeonhole behind the desk.

The male secretary, seeing me, motioned toward a wall where all the chairs were already taken.

I said, "I'm Heller."

The secretary looked up from his paper work as if goosed, then pointed to a door to his right; I went in.

It was an anteroom, smaller than the previous one, but filled with aldermen, ward heelers, bail bondsmen, even a few ranking cops including my lieutenant, who when he saw me motioned and whispered, "Get in there."

I went in. There were four reporters in chairs in front of the commissioner's desk; the room was gray, trimmed in dark wood; the commissioner was gray. Hair, eyes, complexion, suit; his tie was blue, however.

He was referring to daily reports on his desk, and some Teletype tape, but what the subject was I couldn't say, because when he saw me, the commissioner stopped in midsentence.

"Gentlemen," he said to the reporters, their backs to me, none yet noticing my presence. "I'm going to have to cut this short. . . . My Board of Strategy is about to convene."

The Board of Strategy was a "kitchen cabinet" made up of police personnel who gathered in advisory session. I wasn't it, though I had a feeling the commissioner and I were about to convene.

Shrugging, the reporters got up. The first one who turned toward me was Davis, with the *News*, who'd talked to me more than once on the Lingle case.

"Well," he grinned, "it's the hero." He was a short guy with a head too big for his body. He wore a brown suit and a gray hat that didn't go together and he didn't give a shit. "When you going to brag to the press, Heller?"

"I'm waiting for Ben Hecht to come back to Chicago," I said. "It's been downhill for local journalism ever since he left."

Davis smirked; the others didn't know me by sight, but Davis saying my name had clued them in. But then when Davis wandered out without pursuing it, they followed. I had a feeling they'd be waiting for me when I left, though; Davis, anyway.

I stood in front of the commissioner's desk. He didn't rise. He did smile, though, and gestured toward one of the four vacated chairs; his smile was like plaster cracking.

"We're proud of you, Officer Heller," he said. "His Honor and I. The department. The city."

"Swell." I put my badge on his desk.

He ignored it. "You will receive an official commendation; there will be a ceremony at His Honor's office tomorrow morning. Can you attend?"

"I got nothing planned."

He smiled some more; it was a smile that had nothing to do with pleasure or happiness or even courtesy. He folded his hands on the desk and it was like he was praying and strangling something simultaneously.

"Now," he said slowly, carefully, looking at the badge on his desk out of the corner of an eye. "What's this nonsense about you . . . leaving us."

"I'm not leaving," I said. "I'm quitting."

"That is quite ridiculous. You're a hero, Officer Heller. The department is granting you and Sergeants Lang and Miller extra compensation for meritorious service. The city council, today, voted you three the city's *thanks* as heroes. The mayor has hailed you publicly for helping score a major victory in the war on crime."

"Yeah, it was a great show, all right. But two things fucked it up."

He squirmed visibly at having the word "fuck" said in his office, and by a subordinate; this was 1932 and school children weren't using the word at the dinner table yet, so it still had mild shock value.

"Which are?" he said, struggling for dignity.

"First, I killed somebody, and I wasn't planning to kill anybody yesterday afternoon. Let alone a kid. Nobody seems too concerned about him, though. Nitti's boys say he has no relatives in the city. Claim he's from the old country, an orphan. But that's *all* they claim; they aren't claiming the body. That goes into potter's field. Just another punk. Only *I* put him there. And I don't like it."

The smile was gone now; a straight line took its place, a pursed straight line. "I understand," the commissioner said, "you weren't so self-righteous one other time."

"That's right. I helped cover something up, and it got me some money and a promotion. I'm from Chicago, all right. But awhile back I decided there's a line I don't go over anymore. And Miller and Lang forced me over that line yesterday."

"You said two things."

"What?"

"You said two things got . . . gummed up. What's the second?"

"Oh." I smiled. "Nitti. We went up there to kill him yesterday. I didn't know that, but that's what we were up there for. And he fooled all of us. He didn't die. He's in the hospital right now, and it's beginning to look like he's going to pull through."

Nitti had been taken to the hospital at Bridewell Prison, but his father-in-law, Dr. Gaetano Ronga, had him transferred to Jefferson Park Hospital, where Ronga was a staff physician. Ronga had already issued statements to the effect that Nitti would live, barring unforeseen complications.

The commissioner stood; he wasn't very tall. "Your allegations are unfounded. The address at the Wacker-LaSalle Building was believed to be the headquarters for the old Capone gang, now under Frank Nitti's leadership."

"It was a handbook and wire room."

"An illegal gambling den, yes, and in the course of your raid, Frank Nitti pulled a gun."

I shrugged. Got myself up. "That's the story," I said.

"Keep that in mind," the commissioner said. There was a tremor in his voice; anger? Fear.

"I will," I said.

I turned and headed out.

"You've forgotten something."

I glanced back; the commissioner was pointing to my badge, where I'd laid it on his desk.

"No I didn't," I said, and left.

"So what's bothering you?" Barney said. "Killing some innocent kid?"

I sipped at my third beer. "Who's to say he was innocent? That isn't the point. Look. I held on to this goddamn thing"—I patted under my arm, where the automatic was—"because my father blew his brains out with it. Anytime I take it out of its harness, somewhere in my brain I keep the thought of that. So that I won't take using it lightly. Only I *did* use it, didn't I?"

"Yeah." He patted my drinking arm. "But you ain't takin' it lightly."

I found a smile. "I guess not."

"So where do you go from here?"

"To all one rooms of my apartment. Where else?"

"No, I mean, what kind of trade you gonna take up?"

"I only got one trade. Cop. For what it's worth."

We'd talked about it plenty of times, Barney and me. That one day I'd quit the department and open my own agency. I'd talked about it with my friend Eliot, too; he'd encouraged me to do it, said he'd help line some business up. But it had always been a pipe dream.

Barney stood up and got a funny little smile going, a little kid smile, and motioned with a curling forefinger. "Come with me," he said.

I just sat there with half a beer in my hand, giving him a "what the ———" look.

He grabbed me by the coat sleeve and tugged till I got up and followed him, back through the deli and out onto the street, where the snow had stopped and the city had got quiet, for a change. There was a door between the blind pig and the pawnshop next door. Barney searched for keys, found some, and unlocked the door. I followed him up a flight of narrow stairs to a landing, and then did that two more times, and we were on the fourth floor of his building, which ran mostly to small businesses, import/export, a few low-rent doctors and lawyers and one dentist. Nothing fancy, certainly. Wood floors, glass-and-wood office walls, pebbled glass doors.

At the end of the hall the floor dead-ended in an office that bore no name. Barney fished for keys again and opened the door.

I followed him in.

It was a good-size office, cream-color plaster walls with some wood trim, sparsely furnished: a scarred oak desk with its back to the wall that had windows, a brown leather couch with some tears repaired by brown tape, a few straight-back chairs, one in front of the desk, a slightly more comfortable, partially padded one behind it. The El was right outside the windows. It was a Chicago view, all right.

I ran a finger idly across the desk top. Dusty.

"You can find a dustcloth, can't you?"

"What do you mean?"

"Well, it's your office. Leave it filthy if you want."

"My office?"

"Yeah."

"Don't go *meshugge* on me, Barney."

"Don't go Yiddish on me, Nate. You can't pass."

"Then don't go Jewish on me when you tell me the rent."

"For you, nothing."

"Nothing."

"Almost nothing. You gotta live here. I can use a night watchman. If you ain't gonna be here some night, just phone in and I'll cover for you somehow."

"Live here."

"I'll put a Murphy bed in."

He opened a door that I thought was a closet. It wasn't. The office had its own washroom: a sink, a stool.

"Not all the offices have their own can," he said, "but this was a lawyer's office, and lawyers got a lot to wash their hands over."

I walked around the room, looking at it; it was kind of dingy-looking. Beautiful-looking, is what it was.

"I don't know what to say, Barney."

"Say you'll do it. Now, in the morning, you want a shower, you walk over to the Morrison." The Morrison Hotel was where Barney lived. They had a traveler's lounge for regular patrons who were in town for the day and needed a place to freshen up or relax—sitting rooms, shower stalls, exercise rooms—one of which had been converted into a sort of mini-gym by Barney, with the hotel's blessing. "I'll be working out there most mornings," Barney continued, "and at the Trafton gym most afternoons. You're welcome both places. I'm training, you know."

"Yeah, *somebody's* got to pay for all this."

Barney was known for being a soft touch: a lot of the guys from the old neighborhood had taken advantage of him, hitting him for loans of fifty and a hundred like asking for a nickel for coffee. I didn't want to be a leech; I told him so.

"You're makin' me mad, Nate," he said expressionlessly. "You really think it's smart to make the next champ mad?" He struck a half-assed boxing pose and got a laugh out of me. "So what do you say? When do you move in?"

I shrugged. "Soon as I break it to Janey, I guess. Soon as I see if I can get an op's license. Jesus. You're Santa Claus."

"I don't believe in Santa Claus. Unlike some people I know, I'm a *real* Jew."

"Yeah, well drop your drawers and prove it."

Barney was looking for a fast answer when the El rumbled by like a herd of elephants on roller skates and provided him with one.

"No cover charge for the local color," he said, speaking up.

"Don't you know music when you hear it?" I said. "I wouldn't take this dump without it."

Barney rocked on his heels, smiling like a kid getting away with something.

"Let's get out of here," I said, trying not to smile back at him, "before I start dusting."

"Nightcap?" Barney asked.

"Nightcap," I agreed.

I was having one last beer, and Barney, staying in training, was just watching, when a figure moved up to the booth like a truck parking.

It was Miller; the eyes behind the Coke-bottle glasses looked bored, half-asleep.

"How's the fight racket, Ross?" Miller asked, in his off-pitch monotone, hands in his topcoat pockets.

"Ask your brother," Barney said, noncommitally. Miller's brother Dave, also an ex-bootlegger, was a prizefight referee.

Miller stood there for a while, his capacity for making small talk exhausted.

Then moved his head in a kind of sideways nod, toward me, and said, "Come on."

"What?"

"You're coming with me, Heller."

"What is it? Visiting time at Nitti's hospital room? Go to hell, Miller."

He leaned over and put a hand on my arm. "Come on, Heller."

"Hey, pal, this is where I came in."

Barney said, "I'm going to land you on your fat ass, Miller, if you don't take your hand off my friend."

Miller thought about that, took the hand off, but out of something closer to boredom than fear from Barney's threat.

"Cermak wants to see you," he said to me. "Now. Are you coming, or what?"

MAYOR CERMAK

## 4

I'd never spoken to Mayor Cermak, but I'd seen him before; almost every cop in Chicago had. His Honor liked to pull surprise personal inspections on the boys in blue and then carry his criticisms to the press. He claimed he wanted to weed the deadweight out of the department, to cut down on the paperwork, to have a maximum number of men out on the streets at all times, battling crime. All this from a mayor with the behind-his-back nickname Ten Percent Tony, whose political life seemed a study in patronage; who as Cook County commissioner (a position also known as "mayor of Cook County") had given Capone free reign (well, not exactly "free") to turn the little city of Cicero into gang headquarters, with it and nearby Stickney becoming the wettest of the wet in this dry land, as they were simultaneously overrun with slot machines, whores, and gangsters. Cook County, where two hundred roadhouses had been personally licensed by Tony; where Capone dog tracks flourished thanks to an injunction by a Cermak judge; where Sheriff Hoffman permitted bootleggers Terry Druggan and Frankie Lake to leave his jail most anytime they pleased, and they consequently spent more time in their luxurious apartments than behind bars, though Hoffman eventually landed behind bars himself—for thirty days—after which Cermak gave him a post with the forest preserves at ten grand per annum; and, well, all this "reform" talk coming from Cermak sounded like a crock of shit to most Chicago cops.

But we cops didn't underestimate our mayor. We may have referred to him as "that bohunk bastard," among other things, and, like most other civil service employees, hated or feared him or both, and at the very least resented the "for sale" nature of positions and promotions; but we didn't underestimate him. We knew him to be unfailingly familiar with every operation in his administration—from beat cop to building inspector, from clerk to cabinet officer; and he brought a level of competence, even administrative brilliance, to the office of mayor, equaled only by the level of his paranoia, which he manifested in his incessant wiretapping, mail interception, use of surveillance, planting of undercover men, and seeking out of stool pigeons—all within his own administration.

Cermak was a roughneck made good. He was foreign-born (a first for a Chicago mayor), brought to this country as an infant, from Czechoslovakia, and went no farther than third grade. By age thirteen he was working with his father in the coal mines of Braidwood, Illinois; by sixteen he was a railroad brakeman in Chicago. A brawler and two-fisted drinker, he was soon leader of a youth gang that based itself in a saloon; this rising star attracted the local Democratic organization, and young Tony was suddenly a ward heeler. He purchased a horse and wagon, started hauling wood, and built a business, using his political contacts to good advantage. He became secretary to an organization called the United Societies, a lobby of saloonkeepers, brewers, and distillers; he maintained this position when, in 1902, he entered the state legislature—showing his versalitity by simultaneously serving as state representative and lobbyist for the saloon interests.

From the state legislature Cermak went to the city council (a step up: an alderman got a bigger salary and had more patronage at his disposal), then on to baliff of municipal court, commissioner of Cook County Board and, by '29, head of the Democratic organization of Cook County. His mayoral victory in '31 was by the widest margin in Chicago history; he had crossed ethnic lines to build coalitions within his party, and put together a machine. It was a lot like what Capone had done.

Cermak probably had no idea, till tonight, that I lived across the alley from him. He lived in the Congress Hotel, and had a view of the park, I'd bet; I lived across the alley in the Adams Hotel, a residential hotel that was not a flophouse, but it sure didn't have a view of the park. It had a view of the back of the Congress, is what it had.

I wasn't home when Miller came calling on me, of course, but evidently somebody—Cermak's fabled espionage system, I supposed—had known enough about me to gather I'd be at Barney Ross' speak. After all, somebody had known enough about me to know where I'd be yesterday afternoon. I was starting to feel like an open book. A well-thumbed one.

It wasn't much of a walk from Barney's building to the Congress; just follow the El up Van Buren a few blocks—the wind off the lake seemed more cool now than cold, the powderlike snow blowing around a little—then down State Street, past Congress and up Harrison, past my hotel, all three less-than-luxurious stories of it, and on to Cermak's.

As we walked, I was thinking about how my hotel didn't have a lobby, just a narrow stairway that hesitated at a check-in window at the right as you came in. But the Congress, now that was a hotel; the lobby was high-ceilinged, ornate, lots of red and gold with plush furniture to sink down into while you waited for some society girl. Or while you waited for somebody to pick somebody else's pocket, because that was the only reason I'd ever had for being in the Congress lobby before. Of course I'd also done some pickpocket duty in the corridor of fancy shops in the Congress, Peacock Alley. But this time I was going in to go up to a penthouse. Even though I hadn't been given much choice, it wouldn't be so bad, going first class for a change.

We went in the alley way.

And I don't mean Peacock. Just the alley; in the service entrance.

In a narrow vestibule, rubbing shoulders with some mops and buckets, hobnobbing with a couple of refuse cartons, I reached a hand out to push the button on the service elevator and Miller batted it away casually.

"We'll walk," Miller said.

"Are you kidding? What floor is he on?"

"Three."

"Oh."

We walked the two flights; evidently it wasn't enough for the rich folks in the lobby not to see me · I was even persona non grata to the hired help who might ride the service elevator.

The exchange at the elevator, incidentally, was the extent of conversation between Miller and myself since leaving the blind pig. Miller seemed distant behind his Coke-bottle glasses; about as personable as a potted plant. He wasn't somebody I particularly wanted to know any better, so I didn't press it.

Miller knocked twice and the pale gold door opened and a detective I'd seen around but whose name I did not know answered with a gun in hand. He was a skinny guy with a pencil-line mustache and a dark brown suit that hung on him like it had been a good buy but they didn't have his size. His hat was off and his mouth hung open; he wasn't the brightest-looking sort I ever saw, and my guess was he was temporary · Lang would be back as soon as the finger healed.

We went in, Miller first, and he pointed me to a sofa that looked, and was, about as plush and comfortable as the furniture in the Congress lobby. This was a sitting room or living room or whatever, with chairs and a couple of sofas, a fireplace and a glass chandelier, and various furniture that was probably named for some French king with numbers after his name. The only light on in the room was a standing lamp over in one corner, and it was consequently a little dark in there, like a cloudy day.

Across the room from me were windows looking out on Grant Park and Michigan Avenue; the south corner suite, this was. In front of me was a coffee table, a low marble-topped one, with a silver champagne bucket full of ice and brown bottles. Beer. The only thing between me and the view of the park was an empty chair, not a soft-looking, plush chair, but a wooden one with a curved shape to its back, like a captain's chair, or a throne. It was not a chair that had come with the room.

Miller parked himself over by the window, leaned against the sill, and looked out; he was miles away. The other guy, who introduced himself as Mulaney, sat as far away from me as he could and still be in the room, over on a sofa at left. He had put the gun away shortly after we entered. There was the faint sound of a radio playing Paul Whiteman from next door, off to the left, beyond Mulaney.

To my right, on either side of the fireplace, were doorways standing open; from the room beyond the door nearest me came the muffled sound of a flushing toilet.

His Honor, hitching up his trousers a bit, rolled into the room like a pushcart.

"Heller!" he said, beaming, like we were the oldest, bosomest of buddies, thrusting a hand forward; I stood and took it—it was a bit damp.

He gestured for me to sit and I did. He went to his chair across from me but did not sit, as yet; he just stood there studying me, with the friendliest of smiles and the coldest, hardest of eyes. Like Miller, he wore glasses with round lenses—but the frames were dark and thick and clumsy and rode his face uneasily, like the foreign object they were.

He was in his shirt sleeves and suspenders, but his tie wasn't loosened 'round his neck; he looked a bit like a participant in the Scopes trial, if cooler. It was, in truth, a bit warm in the room, and he bent down and pulled a bottle of beer from the champagne bucket and took an opener from somewhere and popped the cap and handed me the bottle. All the time smiling, almost apple-cheeked, a big man, barrel-chested, thick-bodied, broad-shouldered, larger than life, getting himself a beer now.

We sat there silently, each of us having a couple of swigs at his beer.

Finally I said, "This is good beer."

The smile turned into a grin, and the grin seemed more real. "It beats that piss Capone bottles and calls beer, by a hundert miles," he said.

"There's no label."

"It's Roger Touhy's beer. The beer he bottles isn't for sale. It's for friendship. The beer he sells, he sells by the barrel, to the road-houses, saloons, and such. All outside of Chicago."

Roger Touhy was a bootlegger in the northwest suburbs; the sort of safe, minor-league gangster Cermak could control.

"Well, it's the best beer in or out of town," I said.

Cermak nodded, his smile gone, his expression thoughtful. "It's the water, you know."

"Pardon?"

"They got an artesian well near Roselle. The finest, purest water. That's Touhy's secret."

We sat and drank for a while. Periodically, Cermak would seem to wince or something; put a hand on his stomach.

"And how is your uncle Louis?" Cermak said, putting the half-empty bottle of Touhy beer on the marble-top. "I understand he had kidney stones."

"Why, uh, yes," I said, startled that Cermak had remembered me and my connection to my uncle, "that's right. But he's, uh, he's over it, I think."

Cermak shook his head gravely. "You never get over that. I had 'em, you know. Goddamn stones, if you pass 'em, it's like pissing glass."

I suddenly realized that Cermak didn't remember me, or that particular piece of patronage; he just had done his homework.

He offered me another beer and I turned it down: I'd already had three or four at Barney's, and I was feeling the effect. This guy was too cute, too cunning to deal with tipsy.

"I suppose I should get to the point," he said. "You're a busy man. I don't want to waste your time."

He said this quite ingenuously, as if he didn't sense the irony of the mayor of Chicago not wanting to waste one of his cop's time. One of his *ex*-cops, at that.

"I want you to take this back," he said, and he reached a hand out behind him and Miller came over and reached in an inside jacket pocket and withdrew something and filled Cermak's hand with it. Cermak showed me what it was. My badge.

"I can't do that," I said.

Cermak didn't hear that, apparently.

"What I have in mind," he said, putting the badge on the marble-top, "is you joining one of my hoodlum squads. We've got the world's fair coming up, you know, and I've got some promises to keep. And I keep my promises, Nate. Can I call you Nate?"

"Sure," I shrugged.

Cermak took a swig of the beer and said, "I'll have no truck with lawlessness, Nate. I promised Chicago I'd run these gangsters out of town, and by damn I'm going to do it. I won't have 'em working their shady games at the fair."

I nodded.

"Yesterday is an example of what we need to do, where these hoodlums are concerned. You—like Sergeants Miller and Lang, and some of my other top people—will be sworn in as a deputy coroner so you can go all over Cook County picking up these gangsters."

"Your Honor," I said, "I killed somebody yesterday. That isn't my idea of how to do *anything*."

He rose; his face got very red. And then he exploded.

"It's a *war!* It's a goddamn *war!* Don't you know that? I'm giving you an opportunity that any cop in town, *every* cop in town, would give his left *ball* for, and you—you "

He touched his stomach with the flat of one hand; he squinted.

"Excuse me," he said, and left the room.

I could hear Paul Whiteman again, faintly. Over by the window, Miller, looking out at Grant Park, said, "You better listen to the mayor."

I didn't say anything.

There was another flush, and Cermak came back in; he didn't roll in this time. He seemed old. He was only in his late fifties, but he seemed old.

He sat. "I made some campaign promises. I said I'd salvage Chicago's reputation. I said I'd drive the gangsters out. I told important people in this town that the town would be safe for a world's fair. A fair that could restore Chicago's dignity. Her reputation."

"Do you really think Chicago's reputation was enhanced by what happened yesterday?" I said.

He seemed to think about that. "We were shown to be courageous."

"Some people say it was *real* police behind the guns at the Saint Valentine's Day Massacre, too, you know."

He glared at me; it was like an oven door opening and the heat hitting you in the face. "What the hell is *that* supposed to mean?"

"It simply means," I said, trying to drain all the smart-ass out of me, "that headline-making violence adds to the city's bloody reputation no matter *who* is pulling the triggers."

He touched his hands together lightly, prayerlike. "Suppose yesterday had gone differently. Suppose that young man had not been in the window. Suppose the only person to die in that room had been Frank Nitti. A message would've been sent. To the gangsters. To the public. That this administration is not fooling around."

"Somebody did die, and it wasn't Frank Nitti. That's the bad part, isn't it, Your Honor. The public sees a shoot-out involving police, and several people are shot, but the big fish gets away. Oh, Nitti took a fall, all right—only he's going to get up again. Nitti's going to live."

Cermak nodded, suddenly lost in thought. "Yes," he said. "I believe you're right . . ." There was a pause the word "unfortunately" might have filled. ". . . and while the world would be a better place without Mr. Nitti, we're not murderers, after all. He did shoot Sergeant Lang, and Sergeant Lang returned fire, and that's the end of it."

I glanced over at Miller. He didn't seem to be listening; he was still looking out at the park.

"Could we speak in private, Your Honor?" I asked.

Without turning, Cermak said, "Sergeant Miller . . . you and Mulaney go and have a smoke in the hall."

Miller shambled by, without looking at me; Mulaney followed him out, or anyway the oversize suit he was wearing did, taking him along.

When the door had closed behind them, I said, "Are you really aware of what happened at the Wacker-LaSalle Building yesterday?"

"Suppose you tell me, Nate."

I did.

He listened with a rather glassy, frozen smile, and when I finished, he said, "It's a funny thing, Nate. You can have a dozen witnesses to an event, to an accident, a crime, and you can end up with a dozen damn versions of it. It's human nature. Take the Lingle case." And here he paused and broadened his smile momentarily, as if to say, *You remember the Lingle case, don't you, Nate?* Then he picked my badge up from the marble-top, looked at it, tossed it on the sofa next to me. "You'll be a sergeant for a while, and a lieutenant by next year this time. Sergeant's pay is twenty-nine hundred dollars, but you'll get deputy coroner's pay, which is three thousand sixty. Lieutenant's is thirty-two hundred. That's a thousand-dollar raise for you, isn't it, Nate?"

Cermak talked about that extra grand like he wasn't a millionaire, like it meant something to him; or maybe that's why he *was* a millionaire: because a grand did mean something to him. Like it did to me.

"And the salary isn't everything," he continued, with an offhand gesture, a little smile, a shrug. "There are extras. I don't have to be specific, do I, Nate?"

"You don't have to be specific," I said.

He sat and stared at me and smiled at me and it was like having a shotgun smile at you and I finally had to look away.

When I did, he said, "I think the boys have had time enough for their smoke now, don't you?"

"Sure."

He got up and went to the door and called Miller and Mulaney back in; then, his upper lip pulled back over his teeth, a hand clutching his stomach, he excused himself and left the room again.

"Does he do that often?" I said.

Miller, who had resumed his post by the window, said, "He has to take a shit now and then. Don't you, Heller?"

"Not every five minutes."

Cermak came back in, sat down, seemed embarrassed, smiling, gesturing awkwardly. "Sorry about the interruptions. I got the trots to beat the band today. It's my goddamn stomach. Ulcer or something. Colitis, gastritis, the docs call it. About as bad as goddamn kidney stones."

"Your Honor . . ."

"Yes, Nate?"

I held the badge out toward him. "I can't take this back."

He didn't understand for a second; it was as if he thought I were fooling. Then his smile fell like a cake, and his eyes could've turned Medusa to stone.

When I could see he wasn't going to take the badge, I put it on the table, next to the bucket of ice and beer.

And now Cermak softened his gaze, like somebody fine-tuning a radio.

"Mr. Heller," he began (not "Nate"), "what is it you want?"

"Out. That's all. I don't like killing people. I don't like being used. By you, by your people. By anybody. Just because I helped you people cover up that fucking Lingle case, that doesn't mean that every time there's a dirty goddamn job to do, you go pull Heller in off the street."

Cermak folded his hands across his troubled stomach. His expression was neutral. "I don't know what you're referring to," he said. "The Lingle case was prior to my administration, and it's *my* understanding that the murderer was convicted and is serving his sentence right· now."

"Yeah. Right. Look. All I want to do is quit the force. That's all I'm after."

"Nate." So it was "Nate" again. "We need to present a unified front on this matter. You killed a man. You have an inquest to attend, when? Day after tomorrow?"

"Tomorrow. Morning."

"If my people tell conflicting stories, it will reflect badly on *me*. On *all* of us. It will get very complicated. *You* are the only officer who killed anyone in that office, Nate. Surely you don't want this to linger on, to fester in the public's eye."

The beers from Barney's, and the one Touhy, were knocking at my bladder door. I asked if *I* could leave the room this time, and Cermak, looking weary (or pretending to—who knew with this guy?), assented, pointing, as if he hadn't already made the direction of the bathroom perfectly clear.

I walked through a big fancy bedroom, where against one wall a rolltop desk was stuck, looking about as out of place here as me. But what really struck me as wrong were the three suitcases, the four boxes of personal papers and other work-type stuff, and the steamer trunk, all standing at the foot of the bed, like a crowd at a political rally. Cermak was going someplace.

I let the beer out, then came back and sat down.

"Taking a trip, Your Honor?"

Absently, he said, "Florida. Taking Horner down there."

Horner was the recently elected governor of Illinois—one of Cermak's more recent miracles: a Jew elected to the state's highest office. It was a cinch Cermak wasn't going along to help Horner write his inaugural address; they were probably going there to divy up patronage jobs.

"You don't exactly travel light, do you?" I said.

Cermak looked at me, pulled away from whatever strategy he was forming to use on me, and said, "Oh, that. I'm moving out of here. I'll be living in the Morrison Hotel after I get back."

That's where Barney lived; small world.

"Why? This is a terrific view."

"There's a penthouse bungalow on top of the Morrison, with a private elevator. The security'll be better. I'm taking on a few extra bodyguards, too. You can't wage war on the goddamn underworld without getting 'em irritated at you, you know," and he gave out a forced chuckle.

"I'd imagine Nitti's pissed off," I admitted. Nitti was, after all, about the extent of this "war" Cermak kept talking about. The rest of the "war" seemed to be restricted to busting beer flats on the North Side, where private citizens were brewing suds in their apartments to make a few extra depression dollars.

"Yeah," Cermak was saying, rather grandly, "they're fitting me for a bulletproof vest. I think that's going too far, but I suppose there is *some* small danger. . . ."

What was he trying for now? My sympathy? Maybe I was supposed to admire him; or maybe this was a role he liked to play just for himself.

"I better be going, Your Honor," I said, getting up.

He stood, too; put a hand on my arm. I could smell his breath; it smelled like Touhy's beer, not surprisingly. But his expression was sober, somber. "What will you be saying at the inquest tomorrow?"

"The truth, I suppose."

"Truth is relative. Even off the force, I can be of a little help to you, you know. Have you decided what line you'll be going in?"

I shrugged. "I only have one trade."

Cermak looked surprised; he took his hand off my arm. "What do you mean?"

"I'm a cop, a detective. I'm going private, that's all."

"Who with? Pinkerton's? You got something lined up?"

"My own little agency."

"I see." He was smiling again; I didn't like that. "When were you planning to get started?"

"Right away."

He shook his head sadly, continuing to smile. "That's a shame, really it is."

"What do you mean?"

"Oh, the paperwork on these matters. A goddamn shame. The red tape. Sometimes an application for a license can be turned down for, oh, the most trivial of reasons. For no reason at all, actually."

"So that's how it is."

He pointed a finger at me like a gun. "I'll tell you how it is. You go out of the department under a cloud—you tie yourself up in a police scandal, where month upon month goes by, trial upon trial drags on, and you're not going to get a private detective's license, not till it's over, maybe not till never. I won't have to pull any strings to make that happen. *You'll* have made it happen."

I thought it over.

"You know I'm right," he said.

I nodded. "Suppose I agree to corroborate Lang and Miller's story."

"You'll have a license tomorrow."

I thought some more. "When the trial comes up, suppose I double-cross you. Suppose I tell a different story. Like maybe the real one."

Cermak beamed. "You wouldn't do that. You're not a stupid man. Licenses can get revoked for no good reason, too, you know. The Lord giveth and He taketh the hell away, too, Heller."

For the first time, I realized, Miller was looking at me; his body was still turned toward the window, but his head was turned my way, casually.

"I'll do it," I said. "Goddamnit."

"Good." He took his gaze off me. I felt he'd forgotten all about me already. He didn't look at me as he said, "I think you know the way out," and, with a faint grimace and with a hand on his stomach, went in the other room.

## 5

Miller took me back down the way we'd come in; you know—the scenic route between my hotel and Cermak's: the alley. It was okay if you liked fire escapes, bricks and cement, and garbage. And Miller.

Who delivered me to the front door of the Adams and, hands in his topcoat pockets, eyes unfathomable behind the glasses, said, "So you ain't as dumb as you look."

I was getting fed up, and was beer-brave. I said, "Neither are you, and that's no compliment. Why don't you flap your ears and take a flying fuck, lardass?"

His head tilted back; it was just the slightest movement, really, but it seemed sinister, somehow, coming from him. He said, "You ought to be on the radio, Heller. Cross us, and maybe you will be."

"What's that supposed to mean?"

"Cross us and see, wise guy."

I hit him in the stomach. With every fucking thing I had.

And he went down. It was like seeing a building fall under a demolition ball. It was beautiful.

When he was on the pavement, I reached inside his jacket, and tugged his .45 revolver, the same one he carried into Nitti's office, out of his shoulder holster, and stuffed the barrel in his fat gut. I stayed in close to him, right on top of him, not letting the gun show, just in case somebody going by on foot or in a car or something might take notice and stop. Not that that would happen: Harrison wasn't particularly busy this time of night (it was about eleven); it was also Chicago, and not a great place to go wading into something that looked dangerous.

"What the hell are you doing, Heller?" he said. His monotone voice was breathy; there was fear in it. I liked that.

"Telling you to get your butt off the pavement and walk around the corner, back in the alley."

He had nothing smart to say; the remark about radio had about used up his wit inventory for the night. He gave me that mean owl look and got up, slowly, as I kept right with him, my free hand in the crook of his arm, the revolver buried in his side now, and I noticed for the first time that he smelled of lilac water. It didn't do much for him. I walked him around the corner into the alley, and we stepped back into a small, courtlike area back of the Adams.

It was dark, but light from the street let us see each other, not that either of us were wild about it. The El rumbled in the background, like an earthquake happening a country over. I didn't make him back up against a wall; I'd already taken this too far, thanks to the beer, and the crap I'd had to take these last couple days. But I had something to say, and I said it.

"I made a deal with Cermak," I said, "and I'll stick to it. When Nitti's trial comes up, I'll be playing parrot to you and Lang. Don't worry about it."

"Then what's this about?" Miller asked.

"Cermak wanted to know why I turned my badge in. Everybody wants to know why I'm so upset over Frank Nitti getting shot. I couldn't care less about Nitti. I don't like being put in a position where I have to kill some damn kid, but never mind. You and Lang are the ones who fucked me over. You pulled me in on something and didn't tell me what the score was. People get killed in this town for any old reason—no reason sometimes. So I don't appreciate you pulling me in unawares on a raid that turned out to be a hit—on Frank Nitti, no less. Thanks to you, my life isn't worth a plug nickel. Nitti'll probably have all three of us hit. Haven't you figured that out yet?"

Miller just looked at me.

"Sure you have," I said. "I saw in the papers where there's a police guard on Lang's house. Watching the wife and kid. Seems there were threatening phone calls."

Then he said, "They wouldn't kill cops."

That rated a laugh. "Right. Like noboby would dare kill a state prosecutor. Only Capone killed McSwiggin. And nobody would dare kill a reporter. But Jake Lingle is real dead. We can be real dead, too, and in the wake, you should pardon the expression, the papers'll be full of us, full of how dirty we were, full of how we were on the take, and most of it'll be true. And then it won't be cops dead. It'll be crooked cops dead, and who'll give a damn?"

We stood and looked at each other in the darkness.

And when I got tired of looking at him, which didn't take long at all, I dumped the slugs out of the revolver's cylinder and they rained on the pavement. Then I kicked 'em away. Handed him the gun.

"Fly home, Miller. Sleep. Dream."

He glared at me. As much as that owl mask could glare. He said, "You haven't heard the end of this, Heller."

"Touch me, and I'll tell the world the real story. Kill me, and a lawyer will open the envelope I left him, in case something happened to me. The envelope with my statement in it." That last part was a bluff, of course, but by tomorrow afternoon it wouldn't be.

Miller cleared his throat, spat a clot of something to the right of me.

"Get out of here, Miller."

He did.

Pretty soon I was in my one-room apartment in the Hotel Adams, on my back in my underwear on top of the blankets; the radiator in the little room was overambitious tonight, so there was no need to climb under the sheets. The lights were out, but some neon pulsed in from out on the street, three floors below. I was on the third floor, just like Cermak. And, like the mayor, I was getting ready to move out—only *I* couldn't afford the secluded suite atop the Morrison, though Christ knows I could've used the protection.

What I'd told Miller was right: there was good reason to expect a reprisal from the Nitti forces. I hadn't told it to anyone—not the commissioner or the hundred other people I tried to turn my badge into, not the mayor, not even Barney or my girl Janey when I had called her last night, briefly, to assure her everything was all right—but one of the main reasons I turned my badge in was to send a message to Nitti: To let him know I was unhappy about being sucked into something I had nothing to do with. If he and his boys had been paying attention yesterday at the Wacker-LaSalle, they might have picked up on that. And my quitting the department over the incident would confirm it, I hoped, and might indicate my intention to tell the truth at Nitti's trial.

Except my intention to tell the truth at the trial had changed. I'd done a deal with the mayor, to tell the story his way. Otherwise, no op's license. I could lie now, to the mayor, and tell the truth later on the witness stand. But, as Cermak had pointed out, my license could then be revoked, if for no other reason than I'd waited all that time to change my story. If I had to corroborate Miller and Lang's story at the inquest tomorrow, under oath, and then went back on it later,

that'd be perjury. Testifying against Nitti could get me killed, however, in which case not having an op's license would be something I'd
get over.

I was tired. It had been a long, draining day, but my brain kept
buzzing; it buzzed about half an hour, anyway, at which time (approximately   these things are hard to pinpoint) I went away. I dreamed
about Nitti and Cermak and Miller and Lang and Little New York
Campagna and all sorts of people, and I won't go into it, but it wasn't
a nice dream, and it climaxed with somebody grabbing me upright in
bed, by the front of my T-shirt, only that part wasn't a dream, I
finally began to realize.

My first thought was Miller: He'd come back to beat the crap out of
me, despite my threats of envelopes and attorneys. Then somebody
turned on the lamp on the dresser next to my bed, and I saw two
guys in gray topcoats with black Capone hats with pearl bands; they
would've looked like twins, only they were a Mutt and Jeff pair. Jeff
was particularly unimpressive, one of those guys who when he needs
a shave looks like his face is dirty. Mutt, unfortunately, a big swarthy
guy with a wart on his cheek the size of a knuckle, was the one
hoisting me up by my T-shirt.

"You're coming with us, Heller," he said, and goddamnit, that was
enough. How many fucking times were people going to grab me and
take me someplace I didn't want to go, and since the place these guys
were going to take me was probably for a ride, I got my hand on my
spare pillow and slapped the guy with it.

It surprised him, anyway, and knocked his hat off. It didn't hurt
him much, but it did give me time to take the automatic out from
under my other pillow and show him, and Jeff.

They were tough guys; probably as tough as Miller and Lang,
maybe tougher.

But they had woken up a guy in his sleep who had been pushed
once too often in too short a time, and I must've had a look on my
face that said they might die, because they put their hands up and
Mutt said, "Heller! Please. This ain't that way. We ain't even
armed."

That didn't sound right.

"It's true," Jeff said. "Can I take my coat off?"

I was off the bed now, standing on the floor; the wood was cold
against my bare feet.

"Slip out of it"—I nodded—"but nice and easy. I haven't killed anybody all day. Help me keep it that way."

Jeff slipped out of the coat, no tricks at all, and held his dark gray suitcoat open and there was no shoulder holster.

"You do what he did," I told Mutt.

Mutt slipped out of his topcoat; his suit was a blue pinstripe, but there seemed to be no gun under there, either. I had them both put their hands against the wall, or actually one of them put his hands against the door, because there wasn't wall space enough in that room for two people to be frisked against any one wall; and, standing there in my underwear, I frisked them, and they were clean.

"Sit on the bed," I told them.

They sat on the bed.

"Tell me what this is about," I said, and got my pants on, taking my time, keeping the gun on them, buttoning my fly one-handed.

"Mr. Nitti wants to see you," Mutt said.

"Oh, really? Isn't he a little under the weather to be having visitors?"

Jeff said, "He's gonna be okay. No thanks to you coppers."

I motioned with both hands, including the one with the gun in it. "Hey. I'm not a copper anymore. And I wasn't in on it."

"You was there," Jeff said accusingly.

"And that was the extent of it," I said.

"Maybe so," Mutt said, "but Mr. Nitti wants to see you."

"So you come break in my apartment and put the muscle on me."

Mutt pursed his lips and moved his head from side to side slowly. "We got the key from the guy at the desk. It only cost a buck. You got great security here, pal."

"It's okay, I'm moving tomorrow. You boys can go now. Tell Mr. Nitti I'll talk to him when he's feeling better."

Mutt said, "This is a friendly gesture. He just wants to talk. That's why we didn't come heeled."

I thought about that.

"I still don't like it," I said.

"Look," Mutt continued, "you know if Mr. Nitti wants to see you, Mr. Nitti's gonna see you. Why not do it now, when you got a gun on *us*, and when he's on his back in a hospital bed?"

I nodded. "Good point. Car downstairs?"

Jeff smiled a little. "You bet."

"Okay," I said. "Let me get my shoes and socks and shirt on."

They watched me dress; it wasn't that easy to do while keeping a gun on 'em, but I did it and Mutt sat in back of the big black Lincoln with me, as we took Monroe Street over to the near West Side, to Jefferson Park Hospital.

There were four more guys in topcoats and hats in the corridor on the third floor where Nitti had his private room. The lighting in the corridor was subdued—it was roughly three in the morning now—and I saw no doctors and only one nurse, a woman about thirty-five, stocky, dark-haired, scared shitless. Nitti's room was halfway down the corridor, and I stood outside with Jeff while Mutt went in.

Mutt didn't come out: a doctor did. A rather distinguished-looking man in his late fifties or early sixties, short, medium build with a paunch, gray-haired with a gray mustache. He had a near-frown on his face when our eyes met; he didn't approve of my being here, I could tell already. In fact I could tell he didn't approve of me, period.

"I consider this ill-advised," he said, as if my being here was my idea. I told him it wasn't.

"Frank being here *is* your idea, though, isn't it?" he snapped, in a whisper.

"Actually, no," I said. "I got pulled into this by the short hair."

"You're the one who killed the boy."

I nodded.

He sighed. "My son-in-law insists on seeing you."

"You're Dr. Ronga?"

"That's right." He didn't offer a hand to shake; I thought it best not to offer mine. "I wouldn't have agreed to this at all if I couldn't see that Frank might get agitated if we refused him, and he does not need to get agitated right now."

"He is going to live?"

"No thanks to you people, I would say he is. I would say he's got as much chance to live as you do to drive back across town safely."

I glanced sideways at Jeff. "That could depend on who's driving, Doc."

Ronga said, "Frank needs rest and quiet. Absence of worry and shock." He pointed a finger at me. "Which might open the wounds and cause a hemorrhage—if that happens it *could* prove fatal."

"Doctor, I have no intention of agitating Mr. Nitti. I promise. Whether or not Mr. Nitti has any intention of agitating me is another story."

Ronga gave out a terse, humorless laugh and held out an open, yet somehow contemptuous, hand in a gesture that said, Go on in.

I went in.

Nitti was sitting up in bed; his reading lamp was on, otherwise the room was dark. He wasn't hooked up to tubes or anything, but he didn't look well; he was even paler than usual and seemed to have lost about fifteen pounds since I saw him last—yesterday. He gave me a little smile; it was so little his mouth curved but his mustache didn't.

"'Cusa me if I don't get up," he said. His voice was soft, but there was no tremor in it.

"It's okay, Mr. Nitti."

"Make it 'Frank.' We're going to be friends, Heller."

I shrugged. "Then make it 'Nate.'"

"Nate."

Mutt was standing on the other side of Nitti's bed; he came around to me before I could approach Nitti's bedside, and said, in an almost gentle way, "You're going to have to let me have your gun."

"This isn't a great place for a scene, pal."

"There's six of us here, Heller, me and five guys out in the hall, plus I think Dr. Ronga would be willin' to take your appendix out with a pocketknife."

I gave him the gun.

Nitti made a little gesture that meant I was to sit down in the chair that had been provided for me next to his bed.

I sat. Seeing him up close, he didn't look any worse. He was bandaged around the throat, from the slug he took in the neck, and he didn't seem to be able to move his head, so my chair was seated at an angle where he didn't have to.

"You didn't know, did you?" Nitti said.

"I didn't know," I said, and I told him how Miller and Lang had picked me up at that speak and brought me along for the ride, without telling me the score.

"Bastards," he said. His mouth was a line. He looked at me; his eyes were calm. "I'm told you quit the department."

"That's right," I said. "I've had it with those sons of bitches."

"You were the one that got an ambulance called. Those bastards woulda let me bleed awhile."

"I suppose."

"Since you quit, that means what? What are you gonna say at my trial? They'll try me for shooting that prick bastard Lang, you know."

"I know."

"You read that load of baloney in the papers that Miller's giving out? Is that the story they're going with?"

"More or less, I guess."

"You going along with it?"

"I'm going to have to, Frank."

Nitti didn't say anything; he looked straight ahead, at the wall, not at me.

"Cermak had me in for a talk," I said.

Nitti turned his head to look right at me; it had to be painful—he moved like the Man in the Iron Mask. His teeth were together when he said, "Cermak."

"I'm opening up a little private agency. Cop is the only trade I got. Cermak'll block my license if I don't play ball."

Nitti turned his head back and looked toward the wall again. "Cermak," he said again.

"And I killed a guy up there, Frank."

Nitti's mouth twitched in a one-sided smirk. "Nobody important."

"Not to you, maybe. I didn't like doing it. And since I'm the only copper up there who managed to *kill* somebody, I'm the one to take the fall if the stories don't jibe."

Nitti didn't say anything.

"If you have any other ideas, I'm open," I said.

Nitti said, "I don't suppose you'd want something with my outfit."

I shook my head no. "It'd be no different than the cops. It's something I want out of altogether. Thank you, though, Frank."

Nitti's eyes looked at me. They were amused. "You're a pal of Ness', aren't you?"

"Yeah," I said, smiling a little, suddenly feeling embarrassed. "But I ain't no Boy Scout."

"I know," Nitti said. "I remember the Lingle case."

A voice behind me said, "Frank. Please." It was Dr. Ronga.

"*Un momento, Papa,*" Nitti said.

Ronga shook his head, shut the door, and Nitti and I—and Mutt, who was seated over in the corner—were alone again.

"I want you to know," Nitti said, "that I hold you no grudge. I understand your position. No reprisals will be taken against you. At this time, I don't even think reprisals will be taken against Lang and Miller. The bastards. They are not worth the trouble. As Al used to say, 'Don't stir up the heat.'"

I smiled a little. "Did he say that before or after Saint Valentine's Day?"

Nitti smiled a little, too. "After kid. After."

"I better be going. You get some rest. If you want to see me again, just call. You don't need to send anybody for me."

"Good. But stay a few moments. There are some things you need to know."

"Oh?"

"You know Cermak was ours, don't you? Al helped get him in, you know."

I nodded. Cermak's association with the Capone gang went back at least as far as when Tony was "mayor of Cook County," and let Cicero happen.

"But now this fair is coming in. This world's fair. And there's gonna be a lot of money to be made. People coming from all over. Hicks and high-hats and everybody between. And they're gonna want things. They're gonna need things. And somebody's gonna provide things. Whores. Gambling. Beer—on the fairgrounds if it's legal by then, in the speaks if not. Either way, it'll be our beer they're drinkin'. Lot of money to be made. I ain't telling you nothing you don't already know.

"But the bankers and the other swells, they know Chicago's got a bad rep. In fact, this fair they're throwing is supposed to bring people back here, to see what a great place this is, safe, wonderful, and all. So how can somebody like Ten Percent Tony clean the city up and still give the people what they want—like whores and gambling and booze—and keep his pockets nice and full, too? By putting the screws to us, the old Capone mob. The feds got a lot of mileage out of sending Al up. Your pal Ness got lots of press, 'Eliot Press' we call him, the fed who announces his next raid in the papers." He laughed, and flinched just a bit.

I said, "So Cermak's connecting with the smaller mobs, then. Roger Touhy. Ted Newberry. Small fry he can control, manipulate."

Nitti looked at me so hard it about knocked me over. "And throw us to the goddamn wolves. The people who made the son of a bitch."

"You're probably right, Frank. But what does it have to do with me?"

Nitti smiled. "I just thought you'd like to know that Ted Newberry put up fifteen thousand dollars for anybody who'd bump me off."

I leaned forward. "You're sure of this?"

"Dead sure. And added to all the other ways those sons of bitches Miller and Lang screwed you is they weren't gonna cut you in."

I just sat there.

"Just thought you'd like to know," Nitti said.

I stood. "Thanks, Frank. I hope you get well."

"You know," Nitti said, "I believe you do."

ELIOT NESS

## 6

The fix was in at the inquest. It was held in a meeting room at the morgue, presided over by the coroner. Since all the cops on Cermak's hoodlum squad were officially deputy coroners, the phrase "conflict of interest" might come to mind. But not in Chicago.

Cermak had covered himself, where I was concerned: I was never asked to give my version—or any version—of Frank Nitti being shot. A signed statement by the still-hospitalized Lang was entered, which covered the Nitti shooting, and Miller testified to his part in the proceedings and backed up Lang's story (though he had not been in the room with us). The questions the coroner asked me were limited to the second, fatal shooting, with the foregone conclusion that the truth on the Nitti matter had already been entered into the record.

The rest of the (you should excuse the expression) gang from the office at the Wacker-Lasalle all testified as well: Palumbo, Campagna, the accountant, the two runners. None of them were asked anything about the Nitti shooting—and, in fairness, none of them had been in the room when it happened, so why should they  and all of them confirmed my version of the death of one Frank Hurt (which sounded like something Nitti might've muttered deliriously on his way to the hospital). Hurt panicked, Palumbo said; the kid had commented on having an out-of-state warrant against him and not wanting to go in for a showup, and Campagna had suggested he take the ledge over to the fire escape while he had the chance. And I'd come in and somebody had thrown him a gun and I'd shot him. Everybody told it the same; nobody (including me) seemed to know where the gun had come from.

I think Nitti had put the fix in, too; I was starting to be glad he and I'd had that little talk. Both he and Cermak had made the inquest easy for me.

So it was cut-and-dried. But it didn't start till ten-thirty, and with all those witnesses, it dragged on, and I missed a lunch date with Janey. I caught her in the office at the county treasurer's at City Hall by phone, about two, and apologized for standing her up.

"Did it come out okay?" she said. There was just the slightest edge of irritation in her voice. "The inquest?"

"Yeah. I came out smelling like a rose. So why do I feel like I need a shower?"

"There's a shower at my place," she said, sounding friendlier.

"Yeah, I remember."

Janey, incidentally, was a lovely girl of twenty-five years and 125 well-placed pounds; with darkish blond hair worn short and wavy, and dark brown eyes highlighted by long, standing-at-attention lashes. She was smart as she was beautiful, and she let me sleep with her once a week or so, as soon as I started talking marriage. We'd been talking marriage for almost three years now, and I'd given her a little diamond last year. I only had one problem with Janey: I wasn't sure if what I felt for her was love, exactly. I also wasn't sure if it mattered.

"I'll make lunch up to you," I said.

"I know you will," she said, like a threat.

"How about tonight? I'll take you someplace expensive."

"I'm working late tonight. You can come out to my place if you want. About nine-thirty. I'll fix sandwiches."

"Okay. And tomorrow night, we'll take in the Bismarck dining room."

"I'd settle for the Berghoff—that's expensive enough."

"We'll do the Bismarck. It's a special night. I have something special to tell you."

Real special: I hadn't broken it to her yet that I'd quit the department.

"I already know, Nate," she said.

"What?"

"It was in the papers today. Just a little footnote to one of the follow-up articles on the shooting. That officer Nathan Heller had resigned to pursue a career in private business."

"I, uh—I wanted to tell you about it myself."

"You can, tonight. I'm not crazy about you quitting the department, but if your uncle Louis has offered you a position, I think that's fine."

Janey was like that: jumping to conclusions based upon her own desires.

"Yeah, well, let's talk about it tonight," I said.

"Good. I love you, Nate."

She didn't whisper it, which meant she was in the office alone.

"Love you, Janey."

That afternoon I moved out of the Adams and into the office in Barney's building. Barney had moved fast: a big brown box was against the right wall as you came in, next to the closet door. The box was a Murphy bed; he'd even got sheets and blankets for me, which were in a drawer at the bottom of the box, under where the bed fell down out of it when you pulled the latch, which I did. It was a double bed, no less; Barney was being optimistic for me. I stretched out on the bare mattress. It wasn't as comfy as Janey's bed, but it beat the hell out of what I had at the Adams. I studied where some paint was starting to peel on the ceiling, for a while, then got up; put the bed back up and in.

The closet was hardly spacious, but it was roomy enough for my three suits. And I had a box of books and other personal junk, which I slid onto the shelf at the top of the closet; it just fit. My suitcase went on the floor in there; I figured to live out of the suitcase, till I got some kind of dresser or something.

Which presented a problem: How could I make this place look like an office and not a place I lived in? I didn't think *that* would impress prospective clients much: an office with a dresser and a Murphy bed in it, an office that was obviously where this poverty-stricken private dick was forced to live. It wouldn't inspire confidence.

Well, the Murphy bed I couldn't do anything about; but I could get around the dresser. I'd get ahold of a couple filing cabinets, or maybe one big multi-drawer one, and file my clothes and such in the bottom drawers. And speaking of bottom drawers, I could then file my underwear under *U*, I supposed. I smiled to myself, shook my head; this was ridiculous. What was I thinking of, giving up the cops and a life of crime for this? I was sitting on the edge of the desk, laughing silently at myself, when I noticed the phone.

A black, candlestick phone with a brand-new Chicago phone book next to it. My flat-nosed Jewish mother, Barney Ross, *did* work fast. Bless him.

So I sat behind the desk and I tried it out. I called my uncle Louis at the Dawes Bank. He and I weren't particularly close, but we kept in touch, and I hadn't talked to him since this mess began, and I thought I should. I also thought he might be able to get me a couple file cabinets wholesale.

I had to go through three secretaries to get him, but I got him.

"Are you all right, Nate?" he said. He sounded genuinely worried. But this was Wednesday, and the shooting was Monday, and I didn't exactly remember Uncle Louis calling on me at the Adams to express his concern.

"I'm fine. They had an inquest today, and I'm completely in the clear."

"As well you should be. You deserve a medal for shooting those hoodlums."

"The city council's giving me three hundred bucks. Me and Miller and Lang, each of us get that. And commendations. That's like getting a medal, I suppose."

"You should be honored. You don't sound it."

"I'm not. I quit the department, you know."

"I know, I know."

"You saw it in the papers, too, huh?"

"I heard."

Where would Uncle Louis have heard?

"Nate," he said. "Nathan."

Something was coming; otherwise it would've just been Nate.

"Yes, Uncle Louis?"

"I wondered could I have lunch with you tomorrow."

"Certainly. Who's buying?"

"Your rich uncle, of course. You'll come?"

"Sure. Where?"

"Saint Hubert's."

"That's pretty fancy. My rich uncle's going to *have* to pick up the tab if we go there. I never been there before."

"Well, be there tomorrow, promptly at noon."

"Promptly, huh? Okay. You're the boss; you're the only rich relative I got."

"Dress nice, Nate."

"I'll wear the clean suit."

"I'd appreciate that. We won't be dining alone."

"Oh?"

"There's someone who wants to meet you."

"Who would that be?"

"Mr. Dawes."

"Yeah, sure. Rufus or the General?"

"The General."

"Say, you aren't kidding, are you?"

"Not in the least."

"The biggest banker in Chicago wants to see me? Former vice-president of these United States meets former member of the downtown division's pickpocket detail?"

"That's correct."

"Why, for Christ's sake?"

"Can I count on you for noon, Nathan?"

Nathan again!

"Of course you can. Hell. Maybe we can stick Dawes for the check."

"Noon, Nathan," Uncle Louis said humorlessly.

I sat looking at the phone, after hanging up, for maybe ten minutes, trying to figure this. And it just didn't figure. Cermak and Nitti wanting to see me was one thing; Dawes was something else again. I couldn't work it out.

And I had forgot to ask about the file cabinets.

At about six, I went down onto the street and found another cool evening waiting for me—the day had been cloudy, no snow, a little rain, and the sidewalk was shiny, wet. Van Buren Street itself, though, sheltered by the El tracks, looked dry. A streetcar slid by, obscuring the store across the way—Bailey's Uniforms—for just a moment. I walked to the restaurant around the corner from Barney's building; it was a white building with a vertical sign that spelled out

B
I
N
Y
O
N
,

S in neon-outlined white letters against black, with the word "Restaurant" horizontally below in black cursive neon against white. Not a cheap place, but they didn't rob you either, and the food was good, and since I'd missed lunch I decided I could afford something better than a one-arm joint.

I couldn't afford it, really: I'd get one more paycheck from the department and then would have to dig into the couple thousand I had salted away—a combination of the remainder of the small estate my pa left and money I'd been putting aside for a house for after Janey and I got married.

I had about an hour to kill before hopping the El to go out to
Janey's flat on the near North Side, so I hit Barney's blind pig again,
and Barney was in there, sitting in a booth with a hardly touched
beer; he lit up like July 4 when he saw me.

I was embarrassed. What can you say when somebody goes that far
out of his way for you?

"Might've made up the bed, you thoughtless bastard," I said, with
a sour smile.

"Go to hell," he said pleasantly.

"I tried to call you at the gym this afternoon, but couldn't get you."

"I was doing roadwork around Grant Park. I usually do that in the
morning, but I had some business to do, and Pian and Winch insist
on that roadwork, 'cause my wind ain't my strong point."

"You had business to do, all right. Going out and getting that Murphy bed, and getting a phone put in. You forgot to get me a file
cabinet, you know."

He shrugged. "They couldn't deliver till tomorrow."

"You're kidding."

He wasn't.

I said, "I hope you know I'm paying you for all this."

Barney nodded. "Okay."

"You might have argued a little."

"That gracious I'm not."

Buddy Gold came over from behind the bar and leaned in to our
booth, raising his furry eyebrows sarcastically. "You got a phone call,
Heller—that fed friend of yours."

I took it behind the bar.

"Eliot," I said, "what's up?"

"Nate, can you get free?"

I looked at my watch; I needed to hop the El in half an hour to
keep my date with Janey.

"Is it important, Eliot?"

"I think it's something you'd find interesting."

Eliot tended to understate, so that meant it was probably crucial I
come.

"Okay. You going to pick me up?"

"Yes. I'm at the Transportation Building, so it won't be more than
ten minutes. I'll try for five."

"Okay. You know where I am, obviously. Want to stop in for a
beer?"

"No thanks, Nate." There was a smile in his voice; he liked to pretend he didn't have a sense of humor, but he did.

"Why don't you pick me up in that truck of yours, the one with the prow on the front end? You can just butt your way in, pick me up, and get a little work done on the side."

Eliot allowed himself a short laugh. "Why don't I just honk instead?"

"And I thought you had style," I said, hanging up.

I tried to call Janey to tell her I'd be late, but she wasn't home yet. So I went back to the booth.

"What does Ness have going?" Barney asked.

"He didn't say. Sounded like he was in a hurry to get there, wherever it is we're going. I haven't talked to him since this brouhaha started brewing. I do know he's involved peripherally. I saw in the papers that he and another prohibition agent questioned Campagna and Palumbo and the others when they were still in custody, that same day of the shooting. I meant to give him a call, but I didn't get 'round to it."

That wasn't quite true: in a way, I'd been ducking Eliot; not consciously, exactly, but I hadn't gone out of my way to see or talk with him, because he really was one of the few straight-arrow law enforcement officers in Chicago, and I liked him, and had earned a certain amount of his respect, and I didn't know if I wanted to talk to him about the shooting until I found out exactly how I was going to be able to play it. And now that I knew—knew that I'd be playing Cermak's crooked game, out of necessity   I didn't know if I wanted to tell Eliot the truth, even off the record.

Eliot was, after all, one of the primary forces behind Al Capone's fall. The original Prohibition Unit had proved as corrupt as it was underpaid and poorly trained. That had been a Justice Department operation, but was transferred after an inauspicious seven-year run to Treasury in '28. In '29 Eliot, then only twenty-six and only a few years out of the University of Chicago, was chosen to command a select detail. He scoured personnel files for honest men, found almost no prospects among Chicago's three hundred-some prohibition agents, and finally came up with nine (and even of these "untouchables," one did prove crooked, a sore point with Eliot). The members of Eliot's detail were young—thirty or under—and expert marksmen, and included specialists in wiretapping, truck-driving, shadowing suspects on foot or by car, you name it. They shut down breweries and distilleries, made speakeasy raids, hitting Capone hard in his pocket-book; and they put together enough evidence to indict Capone and some of his cronies on "conspiracy to violate the Volstead Act."

But Nitti was right about Eliot's weakness for publicity. The effectiveness of his efforts was somewhat hampered by a tendency to inform the press of his battle plans, so that cameras would be on hand when the ten-ton truck smashed open the doors of a Capone brewery. And Eliot and his squad by no means single-handedly "destroyed" the Capone empire. For one thing, it was Elmer Irey, of the IRS Enforcement Branch, and Treasury Agent Frank Wilson, among others, who nailed Capone on tax evasion. And for another thing, the Capone gang was still around and doing quite nicely, thank you.

About five minutes had gone by since Eliot's call, and I was getting up to try Janey one last time, when I heard his honk. I reminded Barney to keep trying Janey till he got her, and went out and climbed in the front of Eliot's black Ford sedan.

I was barely in when Eliot pulled away.

"Where's the fire, chief?" I asked him.

He gave me a sideways glance and tight smile. "Your old stomping grounds."

Eliot had a certain grace; even sitting behind the wheel of the car, he seemed somehow intense and relaxed at the same time. He was of Norwegian stock, with a ruddy-cheeked, well-scrubbed appearance, a trail of freckles across the bridge of his nose; a six-footer with square, broad shoulders, he looked like somebody who could be Eliot Ness, if you were told that. But left to your own devices, you might take him for a young business exec (he was only twenty-nine, not that much older than me—but then Capone, at the time of his fall, had only been thirty-two, not the fortyish mobster of *Scarface*). He was wearing a tan camel's hair topcoat, a gray suit and maroon tie peeking out. His hat was on the seat between us.

"Ever hear of a guy named Nydick?" Eliot said.

"Nope."

"He's wanted for a couple of robberies: a shoe store, which is pretty much for sure, and a bank robbery, just for questioning."

"So?"

"The mayor's hoodlum squad is going to pick him up; they'll beat us there by ten minutes, probably."

"The mayor's hoodlum squad. As in Harry Miller?"

Eliot looked at me with a nasty little smile. "You got it."

We were on Clark Street now, going past Dearborn Station, then soon up an incline onto Twelfth Street, which rose over the train yards. It was a dark night, with little slashes and splashes of light coming from the yards: trains pulling in; barrels with fire in them; lit-up cabooses.

"Where are we headed, exactly?"

"The Park Row Hotel. It's at forty-one-forty. That's       "

"I know where it is."

That was only five or six blocks from my old neighborhood, where my father's bookstore had been; alderman Jake Arvey's territory, adjacent to Cermak's district. A middle-class, working-class Jewish community; not seedy, but not the Gold Coast either.

It was where both Lang and Miller lived.

"About a year ago," Eliot was saying, "when they were investigating the shoe store robbery, Lang and Miller cornered Nydick. And Nydick got the drop on them, somehow, and disarmed them, kept 'em captive for over an hour."

"I'm starting to remember this," I said, nodding.

"Pretty humiliating for a couple of tough guys like those two," Eliot said.

We were riding through the north end of the Maxwell Street district, Maxwell Street on our right, Little Italy on our left—not that you could tell the difference: tenements were tenements.

"There's also a rumor," he said, "just a rumor, mind you, that Miller and Nydick's wife are . . . acquainted. That it was her that led Lang and Miller to Nydick the time he disarmed and humiliated 'em."

"So where does the woman stand? With her husband or Miller?"

Eliot shrugged. "I don't know. My guess would be she doesn't stand at all. More like reclines."

"For both of 'em?"

He shrugged again. "This is just rumor. But I've been monitoring the hoodlum squad on the police radio in my office, and after what happened with you the other day, I thought you'd find Miller's further adventures . . . interesting."

"What's your connection?"

"You. My excuse is the bank robbery, which involves interstate transportation of a stolen vehicle. And Nydick is wanted for questioning in some Volstead-related matters."

"You mean he drinks?"

Eliot grinned this time. "That's what I hear."

I shook my head and smiled. I knew it was more than just our friendship that had sparked Eliot's interest: the mayor's hoodlum squad was indulging itself on his turf. The cops weren't supposed to raid Frank Nitti; *Eliot Ness* was supposed to raid Frank Nitti. Miller and Lang (and even yours truly) had got the kind of press thunder Eliot loved. Look how he showed up after the Nitti shooting, to ride the story's coattails and make it into the papers.

"So you came out all right on the inquest," Eliot said, as he weaved around streetcars and other vehicles. He wasn't going quite fast enough to need a siren, which was a good thing, because he didn't have one. He did have credentials in his billfold with the name Eliot Ness on them, which was one of the few ways in Chicago to get out of a speeding ticket without handing over a couple of bucks to the traffic cop.

"Yeah," I said. "All clear."

"Listen," he said. Quietly. "You don't have to tell me what went on in there. At the Wacker-LaSalle, I mean. You don't have to explain."

I didn't say anything.

"Your turning your badge in is enough explanation," he added.

But it was clear he wanted one, and since even speeding through traffic we were still a good twenty minutes away from the Park Row Hotel, I told him what had really happened. And I told him about my arrangement with Cermak, and my meeting with Nitti, too. I left out Nitti's condescending remarks about him.

"This is all off the record, Eliot."

He nodded, sighed heavily, passing a truck that might have been hauling beer.

"It took guts to turn down the hoodlum squad post," he said. "It paid good *over* the table, let alone under. But I'm glad you quit . . . even though you were one of the few contacts I had on the department I could trust."

"For a Chicago cop," I said, "I was honest. Which means anywhere else, I'd be in for twenty years."

"Thirty. Did you see what the Crime Lab made out of the note Nitti tried to eat?"

It had been in the papers.

"Yeah," I said. "It sounded like a grocery list . . . 'call Billy for dinner' . . . 'potatoes' . . . I think it was just notes he'd made for himself on any sort of mundane matters, which he scribbled a bet on and had to eat."

"The chief of detectives says it's an underworld code," Eliot said with a straight face.

I looked at him with a straight face, and we both started laughing.

"You know," I said, "Cermak and company can't be sleeping too good, with Nitti alive and well."

"I think you're right. Did you see the *News* tonight?"

"No."

"Cermak gave a speech about driving the gangsters out of the city"—he paused for the punch line—"then he left for Florida."

We were only a couple blocks away now, driving through a shopping district.

Eliot, suddenly serious, said, "About that guy you shot . . . I know it's bothering you. I've shot men myself, and I think I know how you feel. I know I hope never to kill anybody or anything again. But you were in a position where it couldn't be helped. Just let go of it, Nate, and be glad you're a private citizen again."

There was silence, as the Park Row loomed up on the right, its blue-and-red neon sign glowing. It was a big brick building squeezed into the middle of a block like a fat lady in a movie-house seat.

"I'll be glad to help you get set up as a private cop," Eliot said as he pulled over to the curb, half a block from the hotel. "I used to work as an investigator for a retail credit company, you know. I can get you some work."

We got out of the Ford and headed for the front door. I stopped him and looked into gray eyes that were kind, even a little innocent. I said, "They say a guy's rich when he's got one good friend. With you and Barney on my side, I'm rolling in it."

He smiled, looked away self-consciously toward the hotel entrance, and said, "Let's go see what the mayor's top men are up to."

Across the modest lobby of this primarily residential hotel was the check-in desk, behind which was a switchboard, where a sandy-haired woman of about forty-five wore a purple-and-white floral dress and a harried expression.

"Are you *more* police?" the woman wanted to know.

Eliot nodded, flashed her his credentials, which she looked at but didn't read.

"That fat creep held me down here at *gunpoint*," she said, voice trembling, holding a fist up, "like I was a *criminal*."

Her indignation seemed righteous: she looked like somebody's mother. She probably was.

"What do you mean?" Eliot said.

"They asked to see Mr. Long. Five officers. I told them room three-sixty-one. The fat one with the thick glasses sent the others upstairs and said he'd stay down and watch me so that I couldn't *warn* Mr. Long. And then he held a gun on me!"

Eliot shot me a quick, disgusted look.

"They're still up there?" he asked.

"Yes," the woman said. "One of the other officers came down, and said, 'We got him.' And then he went up, too."

"When was this?"

"A couple minutes before you came in, detective."

We took the elevator up to the third floor. A man in a brown rumpled suit and brown hat stood in the hallway, gun in hand, guarding a dowdily attractive woman in her thirties in a blue-and-white-pattern dress, and a boy in a blue-and-red-striped sweater who was maybe twelve. The boy was quite understandably confused, looking all about him, looking at the cop, looking at his mother, the mother staring off into space, a somber, somehow resigned look on her face.

We had just reached them when we heard the shots.

Three of them, each on the other's heels.

The woman's composure broke; she screamed "No!" and the cop restrained her, and the kid hung onto her, afraid.

"What do you think you're doing?" the cop said as we moved by, pointing the gun toward Eliot, who flashed his credentials at the guy.

"I'm Eliot Ness. And I'm going in that room." He pointed to the room with the number 361 on it, across from where we stood. He didn't have to say, *Care to try to stop me?* I doubt the cop would have, even if he didn't already have his hands full with the woman and boy.

Eliot put his credentials away and took his gun out and opened the door.

A man was sprawled on his stomach over by a far window; nearby there was a chair, a calendar on the wall, a dresser with an open drawer. On the dresser, a scrawny two-foot-tall Christmas tree roped with tinsel sat in a little green wooden stand that looked to be home-made. The man was bleeding; there were three entry wounds in his back, three bloody scorched bulletholes against the pale yellow of his shirt. If this guy wasn't dead or about to be, I was the Marx Brothers.

Speaking of comedy, Miller was standing over the apparent corpse with a gun in his hand; smoke trailed out the barrel like a ghost.

Two other plainclothes cops, neither of whom I recognized, were closer to us as we came into the hotel room: a stocky guy with a mustache, and a stocky guy without a mustache. The one with a mustache was near the door; the one without was over at the left, by the double bed, which had a cream-color bedspread and a nightstand with phone. Everybody looked at us—except the guy on the floor.

"Ness," Miller said, something like surprise registering on the blank putty face, eyes wide behind the Coke-bottle lenses. "Heller? What the hell. . . ?"

Eliot bent over the body. Eased him over, barely; put him back.

"Nydick," he said to me. I was still over by the door. "I think he may be breathing, but it's a habit he's going to break real soon." He looked at the cop near the phone. "Call an ambulance. Now!"

The cop did as he was told; in sotto voce, he could be heard asking the switchboard for Mount Sinai, the closest hospital.

Eliot rose, staying by the body. "How did it happen, Miller?"

"What jurisdiction you got here, Ness?"

"I have jurisdiction anywhere I damn well want it. This man was wanted for questioning in several federal matters, if it matters. How'd it happen, Miller?"

Miller put his gun on the dresser, under the Christmas tree, like a gift; it was the only one. He pointed at the open drawer, where a little .32 lay; the drawer was otherwise empty.

"He went for the gun," he said, like the bad actor he was. "I had to shoot."

"Three bullets in the back," Eliot said. "That'll slow a man down."

Miller continued. "The boys came up and broke in and secured the suspect. I came up and sent the wife and kid out, and I read him the warrant. He grabbed it and tore it up." He pointed. The warrant lay on the floor, not far from Nydick, torn in two.

I said, "Are you sure he didn't try to eat it?"

Miller got a little red. "*You* got no jurisdiction *anywhere*, Heller, so shut the hell up."

Eliot said, "Then what happened?"

"He was sitting a few feet from that dresser. Then he turned and tried to reach in a dresser drawer for that pistol. I couldn't take any chances. I fired and he fell."

Eliot turned to the cop near me. "Why didn't you just *grab* Nydick?"

The cop made a helpless, shrugging gesture. "I wasn't close enough." The other cop, having finished with his phone call, was staying in the background.

"How about you?" Eliot asked him. "Why didn't you grab Nydick when he went for the gun?"

"I started to jump over the bed, but—Miller, he—already fired."

Eliot glared at Miller. "Let's step out in the hall." He pointed a finger at first one, then the other cop. "You two stay put. Make sure your suspect doesn't make a break for it."

When we got out in the hall, the wife, being held by one arm by the cop in the brown suit, said, "What in God's name happened in there?"

Eliot said, "Are you Mrs. Nydick?"

The woman lowered her head. "I'm Mrs. Long."

Miller said, "That's the name Nydick was registered under."

Eliot said it again: "Are you Mrs. Nydick?"

She nodded, looking at the floor. "He's . . . dead, isn't he?"

"He's been shot," Eliot said. "It doesn't look good for him."

She kept nodding, kept looking at the floor. She didn't ask to go in and be with her husband; she just nodded and looked at the floor. The boy started to cry. Nobody comforted him.

A few other guests were cracking their doors and peeking out. In a loud, firm voice, Eliot said, "This is a police matter—go about your business." The doors closed.

Then he took Miller by the arm and led him down the hall and around a corner, glancing back at me to follow, which I did.

With a smile that was in no way friendly, he backed Miller up against the wall, gently.

"Didn't you kill somebody else this year?" he asked.

Miller nodded. "A thief. I don't like thieves. Nydick was a thief."

"Ever meet Nydick before?"

"No."

"He didn't hold a gun on you and your partner Lang once?"

"No. That . . . story got around, but it was just a story. Nobody can . . ."

"What?"

Miller swallowed. "Nobody can prove it happened."

"I see. Boy, the hoodlum squad's going all out. First you and Lang nail Nitti. Now the notorious Nydick. What next?"

"We're just doing our job, Ness."

Eliot took him by one arm and squeezed and said, "Listen to me, you trigger-happy son of a bitch. I got my eye on you. You keep turning your job into a shooting gallery and I'm going to fall on you like a wall. Got me?"

Miller didn't say anything, but he was shaking—it was barely perceptible, but he was shaking.

Eliot turned his back on him and started to walk away. Then he glanced back and said, "How long do you think your buddy Cermak is going to back you up on these pleasure cruises? The word's out about Newberry offering fifteen grand for Nitti dead, you know. And if that wife of Nydick's isn't your girl friend, I'll invite you over for Christmas dinner."

Miller started to blink behind the glasses.

"Oh, by the way," Eliot added. "Heller wasn't here tonight. Neither one of you needs the stink that might raise, and Heller's along innocently, just 'cause he happened to be with me. I'll tell your boys, and you tell 'em, too. The civilians won't remember how many cops they saw. Got it?" He turned to me. "Anything you care to add?"

I said, "Give me a minute with him alone, Eliot."

He nodded and walked back around the corner and down the corridor.

Miller looked at me and tried to get a sneer going; he didn't quite manage. "I don't like the company you keep," he said.

"Maybe you picked the wrong person to pull in out of a speakeasy to do your shit work for you."

"What's the idea of bringing Ness into this?"

"Ness has been in since the first day, but never mind. You and Lang should've told me about Newberry, Miller."

"I don't know what you're talking about."

"Let's just say if Nitti has a relapse and kicks the bucket, I'll expect my five thousand. Give my love to Lang. Tell him when his finger heals to stick it."

"You're dead, Heller."

"Sure, why not, what's another body to a big-game hunter like you? Some free advice: I don't know what you and Nydick's little lady had going, but I don't think she expected you to kill him. I hope you

can get her to get her story together. You just got to start letting
those close to you in on your plans, Miller. See you in court."

I left him there to think about that and joined Eliot, who was waiting by the door that said EXIT over it.

"Take the stairs down," he said. "Find your way home. The ambulance and reporters'll be here anytime. You don't need that kind of
publicity."

I grinned at him. "Don't tell me Eliot Ness is helping cover something up?"

He laughed a little, but his heart wasn't in it. He'd been sickened
by what he saw here tonight.

He said, "That guy really puts the 'hoodlum' into hoodlum squad,
doesn't he?"

And opened the door for me to leave.

GENERAL DAWES

## 7

Chicago is a city where rich and poor stand side by side, ignoring each other. Take the block where my office was. Starting at the deli on the corner and looking down toward Wabash, you'd see Barney's blind pig, a pawnshop, a jewelry store, a flophouse, a sign advertising a palm reader one floor up—buildings wearing fire escapes on their faces like protective masks, looking out stoically on the iron beams of the El; not the classiest landscape in the world. But just around the corner from the deli, right before Binyon's, was the Harvard-Yale-Princeton Club, and across the street from Binyon's was the Standard Club, the Jewish equivalent of the Union League. Some of the richest men in Chicago walked under the SC canopy into the gray, dignified Standard Club, while around the corner and down the block, winos slept it off in a "hotel for men only."

Saint Hubert's, the restaurant General Charles Gates Dawes had selected for our luncheon meeting, was on Federal Street at the foot of the Union League Club, where he'd be able to stop in after his conference with the two Jews (even though neither Uncle Louis nor myself had been raised in that faith, we were, technically, so "tainted"). Maybe the General would have a smoke on his trademark pipe with its low-slung bowl while chatting with another top "bankster" (as big-shot bankers were often referred to by lesser Chicagoans, like yours truly) in the room at the Union League that had been papered with a million dollars in failed stocks and bonds. The Million-Dollar Room, like so much else in Chicago, had been made possible by the depression; and it was sure heartening to know that the banksters were taking the hard times with a sense of humor. My uncle Louis, of course, was a member of the Standard Club, but we couldn't go there for lunch with General Dawes because Dawes wasn't a Jew—it worked both ways, you know. It just worked the other way more often.

It was a walk of only a few blocks. The temperature was in the forties and it looked like rain. Perfect weather to go to Saint Hubert's English Grill—Federal Street was like some narrow, gloomy London bystreet, anyway. All that was missing was the fog, and my state of mind provided that.

I hadn't woken up till about eleven, because I had come back to Barney's speak last night, after taking a streetcar back to the Loop, too late to go out to Janey's, and had tied one on. So I awoke fuzzy-mouthed and like-minded, and didn't have time to take up Barney's standing offer of using the traveler's lounge at the Morrison to freshen up, and made do with the sink in my office bathroom. I felt it was a major accomplishment getting up, dressed, relatively clean, and to Saint Hubert's by three minutes after noon. But from the look on my uncle Louis' face as a pink-coated waiter showed me to the table he and the General were sharing, you'd think I was three days late. Christ, I'd put on the clean suit as promised; wasn't that enough?

Apparently not. My uncle stood and gave me a smile and a glare; the smile was forced—the glare wasn't. He gestured toward a seat; the General rose, as well.

First, my uncle. He was a thinner, taller version of my father, wearing a navy suit with vest and bow tie. His hair and mustache were salt-and-pepper, heavier on the salt, and he had the paunch that a thin man can get in his middle age, if he's eating well.

And the General. He was in his mid-to-late sixties, one of those men who manage to look lanky and beefy at the same time, with a long face, its most prominent feature a long, low-slung nose that seemed designed to go with the long, low-slung pipe clutched tight in his lips. He, too, had salt-and-pepper hair, but heavier on the pepper, and the faintly amused smile and bemused eyes of a man so self-assured that it never occurred to him he was superior to you: that, after all, was a given. He wore a dark gray suit with a lighter gray pinstripe and a gray-striped tie. He offered a hand for me to shake, and I did. It was a firm grasp.

I sat. I knew about the General. He was Chicago's number-one Good Citizen. Not just a banker, but a public servant. The "General" title came from his serving under Pershing as the U.S. Army's purchasing agent in the Great War, after which he authored the Dawes Plan for postwar European reconstruction. He was comptroller of the currency under McKinley and, of course, vice-president under Coolidge. He'd even done work for Hoover: recently, he'd headed up the Reconstruction Finance Corporation, to provide emergency support for banks hit by the depression, but he had had to resign to save his own bank and, by a remarkable coincidence, the RFC had loaned his bank $90 million just three weeks after he resigned as RFC president.

But even a cynical soul like me had at least one good thing to say about Dawes. In memory of a son who had died at twenty-two, he established a hotel for down-and-outers at six cents a bed and three cents a meal; the Dawes Hotel for Men was the Ritz of flophouses and a genuinely charitable endeavor.

Dawes sat and so did my uncle, who made the introductions, as if we didn't all know who we were. They were drinking tea and soon I was, too. The atmosphere of Saint Hubert's was that of an old Dickensian inn. The pink-coated waiters had English accents, presumably real. Prints of fox hunts and other pip-pip-old boy sporting events hung on the rough stone walls, and a fireplace across the room was providing warmth and a homey feeling. The ceiling was low; long clay pipes hung from its beams, and a few of the all-male guests were smoking them—the pipes, not the beams.

No clay pipe for the General, though: he took too much relish in the monster he was already smoking, with its special fire bowl designed to trap in its false bottom the tobacco tar distilled in smoking. This was not the first thing the General told me about over our lunch, but when I did express interest in his unusual pipe, he perked up, as if he had suddenly realized we were both of the same species, and promised to send me one, which he did. He kept his promises. But I never used the pipe.

He sat leaning against one elbow, pulling on the pipe, and, looking about the place, said, "I'm reminded of England."

No kidding!

"When I was ambassador," he said, "I grew to love London. What do you think of Leon Errol?"

"Pardon?" I said.

"Leon Errol," Dawes said, with enthusiasm. "The renowned comedian, man!"

"Oh. Sure. Leon Errol. Yes. Funny. Funny man."

What the hell did Leon Errol have to do with London? He wasn't even English.

"Allow me to tell you a story," Dawes said, and smiling to himself, he leaned forward and told us a story, not looking at either Uncle Louis or me during the telling.

When he gave his first formal dinner as ambassador to England, in attendance were Her Royal Highness Princess Beatrice, the prime minister, the Japanese ambassador, the Spanish ambassador, Lord and Lady Astor, among many others, including several famous authors and artistes, among them Leon Errol, who was strangely absent when the prim and proper dinner began. But suddenly things began to go awry. One of the waiters, who had a rather large mustache, began filling water glasses with lemonade; he removed plates before guests had finished the course at hand; he began to pass a tray of crackers then spilled it onto the plate of one of the guests; he stumbled while carrying a tray and nearly upended it in a lady's lap; and, finally, he dropped a spoon, kicking it under the table clumsily, and took a candle from the table and got down on hands and knees and searched.

"And then Lady Astor, bless her," Dawes smiled, "saw through our ruse. For you see—"

"Leon Errol was the waiter," I said.

Dawes looked surprised. "You've heard the story?"

My uncle was giving me a look-to-kill.

I tried to cover. "My uncle told it to me. It's one of his favorites of your stories."

Dawes seemed faintly embarrassed. "You should have stopped me—"

"No," I said, "I wanted to hear it again, from the source's mouth. You tell it much better than my uncle."

Dawes beamed, and looked across the table at Uncle Louis. "I don't remember telling you that one before, Louis. Is that really one of your favorites?"

"Oh, yes," Louis said, beaming back.

"Mine, too," Dawes nodded. He turned his distant gaze on me. "I took the liberty of ordering for you, Mr. Heller, since you were a bit tardy."

Tardy? What was this, fucking school?

"Not at all," I said. "What are we having?"

Dawes relit his pipe. "Mutton chops, of course. The specialty of the house."

Mutton? Jesus Christ!

"My favorite," I said.

"Mine, too," Uncle Louis nodded.

I was starting to understand why my father had hated Uncle Louis. But I was wrong about the mutton chops—they were thick and juicy and good. And when the General ordered plum pudding for us, I didn't argue; I trusted his judgment about such things by now, and that too proved, as the General said, a culinary delight. The General had a way with words: he left no cliché unturned.

"Of course they lack the brandy so necessary in the making of proper plum pudding," the General said after we'd finished it. "But the law is the law. Even in England, I refused to serve liquor at embassy functions, out of regard to the prohibition laws in force at home."

"But liquor wasn't illegal there," I said.

"I was a representative of the United States government," he said, matter-of-factly. As if that explained it.

"General," I said, "it was a wonderful lunch. I'm honored you asked me . . . though I'm still confused as to why."

When Dawes smiled, he smiled with his mouth closed; that's the way he was smiling now, at any rate.

"Is it such a surprise to you," he said, "that one public servant should want to meet, and honor, another?"

"I hope it won't be rude of me to say this," I said, "but neither one of us is a public servant, at the moment. We're both, you might say, in private business."

Uncle Louis shifted in his seat.

Dawes nodded. "That's fair. But you were recently honored by the city council for meritorious, *hazardous* service, in the line of duty, as an officer of the law."

"Yes."

"And now you've chosen to leave the department."

Not again!

"Sir," I said, "my decision to leave the department is final."

He sat back, looked down his pipe at me. "Fine," he said. "I respect that." Then he leaned forward, just the slightest bit conspiratorial. "That, in fact, is why you are here."

"I don't understand."

Uncle Louis said, "Let him explain, Nate."

"Sure," I shrugged.

We had been there an hour and a half, and the room was emptying out: with no liquor served on the premises, the long lunch hour for executives was less common. It had been this near-privacy in a public place that the General had been waiting for.

"You're familiar with President Hoover," he said, with no apparent humor.

"We've never met," I said, "but I have heard of him."

"Are you aware that he is the man who put Al Capone away?"

I grinned. "I always thought my friend Eliot Ness had something to do with that."

"Indeed he did," the General said, nodding sagely. "A good man. He is part of what I am talking about. You see, there were some of us here in Chicago . . . in positions of responsibility . . . who began to feel, a few years ago, that Mr. Capone and company were giving our city more than just a 'colorful' reputation. Chicago had come to be viewed as a happy hunting ground for gunmen and other criminals, and, while I undertook a European campaign to defend her good name, Chicago to a degree did deserve this stigma. This colony of unnaturalized persons, which Mr. Capone came to symbolize, had undertaken a reign of lawlessness and terror in open defiance of the law. My friends on Wall Street were beginning to ponder upon whether or not their money was safely invested here. The time had come to act."

The time had also come for me to ask a question, because the General paused dramatically, here, to light his pipe again.

So I said, "How does this make Herbert Hoover the guy who got Capone?"

He shrugged facially. "That is just a way of putting it. The efforts actually began before Mr. Hoover reached office, but it is well known that for many months, every morning, when he and Andrew Mellon would toss the medicine ball around on the White House lawn, the president would ask Andrew, who is a personal friend of mine and the secretary of treasury, if that man Capone was in jail yet. So it has been the interest and support of Mr. Hoover that made the end of Mr. Capone possible. You see, prior to Mr. Hoover reaching office, several of us here in Chicago had devised a two-part plan. First, a world's fair. What better way to restore Chicago's image in the eyes of the nation, of the world. What better way than to attract millions of people from around the globe to our fair city on the lake, to prove to them that the average person in Chicago never so much as *sees* a gangster."

I would've liked to have met that average person, but never mind.

"We felt we needed a good ten years to do the exposition up right.

We would call it 'A Century of Progress,' and it would take place in 1937, the hundredth anniversary of the incorporation of the city   "

I interrupted. "But you're planning it now for *this* summer. And it's still called 'A Century of Progress,' isn't it?"

"Yes," Dawes admitted, "but, after the Crash, the city needed the exposition more than it needed correct mathematics."

Uncle Louis said, "Fort Dearborn was a village in 1833. That's a century, isn't it?"

"Hey, it's okay with me," I said. "Hold it any year you like. I think it's a good idea. Good for the city; it'll bring some money in."

The General smiled and nodded, as if he hadn't thought of that before but it was a good idea.

Then he continued. "When we were first discussing the possibility of an exposition, we knew that for it to truly be a success, for the point we were seeking to make to be made, Mr. Capone would have to be excised. And then we would need to restore the law and order that preceded him."

"Excuse me, General," I said, "but Big Jim Colosimo and Johnny Torrio preceded Al Capone, not law and order."

My uncle gave me another sharp look; like a knife.

But the General only smiled enigmatically. "Shall we say the *relative* law and order that preceded Mr. Capone."

"All right," I conceded.

"This was when some of us here in Chicago, who were concerned, and who had certain influence—and since I was, at that time, still vice-president of these United States, I did have influence—thought something should be done. I arranged for a special prosecutor, a Dwight Green, to begin dealing with Mr. Capone and company. A two-part attack was devised. Mr. Ness and his 'untouchables' would damage Mr. Capone financially, while Mr. Irey of the IRS attempted to put our income tax laws to a *good* use, for a change. The first of the gangsters to go to prison for tax evasion, you may remember, was one Frank Nitti, with whom I believe you are acquainted."

"Him I've met."

"Of course these things go in cycles, and Mr. Nitti is no longer in prison, though Mr. Capone is, and will be for some time. As you so rightly pointed out, Mr. Heller, the gangster element was with us long before Al Capone, and will go on being with us for time immemorial, human nature being what it is. But it should remain in its back-alley place, inconspicuous, within bounds. It should keep out of City Hall, for one thing."

I sipped my tea. "You've got a Republican to thank for *that*, sir."

Uncle Louis closed his eyes.

"True," Dawes said, "but I will not take credit nor blame for William Hale Thompson. The man was a public drunkard, his campaign tactics an embarrassment, his connection with the Capone crowd, the obvious graft, the embezzlement"—he glanced about Saint Hubert's sadly  "all crowned by the absurdity of his anti-British stance, demanding 'pro-British' textbooks be burned, threatening to 'whack King George on the snoot.' As ambassador to Great Britain I was personally ashamed by such remarks coming from the mayor of my own great city. 'Big Bill,' as he is so quaintly referred to, bankrupted this city, humiliated and disgraced it, to a degree that, well . . . how should I put it?"

"Like Capone," I said, "he had to go."

"Precisely."

"And now in his place you have Cermak," I said.

Dawes sighed heavily, nodded. "Still, there are things to be said in Cermak's favor. When city employees under Mayor Thompson were having payless paydays, Commissioner Cermak's county employees were paid regularly. His fiscal skills were an encouraging sign. But I have always had misgivings about Mr. Cermak."

"I thought you bankers were all behind him," I said. "He's one of your own, after all."

Dawes smiled again, but barely concealed his contempt for the subject at hand. "A. J. Cermak sitting on the boards of a few minor banks does not make him 'one of our own.' But you are correct, Mr. Heller. There was Cermak support among financial and commercial leaders of Democratic leaning, certainly. And we Republicans could hardly be expected to rally around William Hale Thompson's bid for a fourth term."

"I seem to recall," I said, somewhat coyly, "Cermak nominating a friend of yours as favorite-son candidate for president at the national convention last month."

That was Melvin Traylor, president of the First National Bank and perhaps the only banker in Chicago of nearly equal stature to the General.

"Yes," Dawes nodded, "Melvin was a major Cermak supporter. And Frank Loesch, of the Chicago Crime Commission. There were any number of Cermak-for-mayor businessmen's committees. Many of us came to support Mr. Cermak, as the 'lesser evil.'"

"Well," I said, "he *has* been helping you bankers out on the tax front, hasn't he?"

Uncle Louis said, a bit testily, "Which is only fair, since he must come to the banks to obtain loans for the city."

The General dismissed all that with a wave of the hand. "That would be the case under any mayor, under current conditions. The major reason Mr. Cermak gained the support of business was his promise to 'redeem Chicago,' to restore her good name. To put an end to all gangster operations during the fair."

"Did you really believe that?"

"Yes, within reason. As we've both said, gangsters will always be with us. The people who come to our fair will occasionally seek that which is not offered there. So I would not expect, for example, a gentleman from Des Moines having a great deal of difficulty finding a glass of beer to drink while in Chicago this summer."

"Cermak's declared war on crime. Isn't that what you want?"

"Bloody headlines are not what any of us want. The fair is designed to paint a whole new picture of Chicago. And blood is not the sort of paint we have in mind."

"I can see that," I admitted.

"Now. You may be wondering where you fit into all this."

"Yes."

"I'm merely hoping you'll be civic-minded when Mr. Nitti's trial comes up, before too long."

"Civic-minded?"

"Yes. I would hope you would take the stand and tell the truth."

"Which truth is that?"

Dawes looked at me hard. "*The* truth, man! The truth. Whatever it is. Wherever the chips may fall."

"Okay," I said, unsurely.

"Like the city council," he said, with humor, "I believe a sense of civic duty should be rewarded."

"That's nice. How?"

"I understand you've opened a private agency."

"That's correct."

"I understand further that you were a member of the pickpocket detail."

"Yes."

"We'll have our own security force, at the fair. I would like them instructed in the ways and means of the pickpocket. I would like you to do that. And I would like you to spend a day or two at the fair, each week, yourself, when your schedule allows, to supervise them, doing spot checks, perhaps nabbing an occasional pickpocket personally."

"Fine," I said.

"Would a retainer of three thousand dollars be sufficient?"

"Oh, yes."

"Good. Now this is all tentative, mind you. Contingent upon your performance at the trial."

"Oh."

"Come and see me afterward. And we'll draw up a contract." He stood. So did my uncle Louis. So did I.

He offered his hand for another shake, and I shook it, and said, "Well, thanks for the offer. It's very kind of you."

"Most of my troubles have come from attempted acts of kindness," he said. "But most of my happiness has come from the same endeavor. It will be illuminating to see into which category you fall."

"Right," I said.

Out on the street I said to Uncle Louis, "What was that all about?"

"Isn't it self-evident? He wants you to tell the truth at the trial."

"We're talking about *the* truth, here? As in, what *really* happened?"

"Of course."

We walked with hands in topcoat pockets; the wind off the lake was finally kicking in. It was down in the mid-thirties now.

"He wants to expose Cermak?" I said. "I don't get it. That's just more bad Chicago publicity."

"Exposing Cermak would be the best thing in the world for the General and his high-hat friends, Nate. The bad publicity could force Cermak to resign, on account of 'health problems.' He has 'em, you know."

I had a sudden image of Cermak getting up and heading for the toilet.

"Yeah, I know," I said.

"And if he doesn't resign, it'll scare him into cleaning up his act. He won't send his hooligan squads around assassinating gangsters anymore. And he may keep his own associations with gangsters a bit closer to his vest."

"Maybe you're right," I said.

"Besides," Uncle Louis went on, "Cermak is a Democrat. This'll provide a nice cloud to hang over him when reelection comes around, and we'll get a *real* Republican back in. It's going to be a cold day in hell when a Democratic machine runs Chicago again, after Cermak gets dumped."

"Well, it's already getting colder, you know, Uncle Louis."

"What do you mean?"

"I can't sell Cermak out. At least I don't see how I can. He can yank my license. I won't be able to work. I won't be able to carry a gun, either. And maybe Ted Newberry or Roger Touhy'll send some guys over to take me for a ride."

"Well," Uncle Louis said, "think it over. Cermak is powerful, but the General is *power*. When he said Hoover was the guy who got Capone, he was just being nice, you know. It's Dawes who did it. Well. Here's the Standard Club. Let's talk soon, Nate."

And my uncle patted me on the back and entered the gray old club. I walked around the corner, turned down a panhandler's request for a dime, and went up to my office, and called Eliot.

## 8

"That looks like a Murphy bed," Eliot said, coming in the door and pointing at the Murphy bed.

"There's a reason for that," I said, sitting behind my desk, feet up, like a big shot.

He took his topcoat off, walked to the straight-backed chair in front of my desk, and turned it around, and draped the coat over it, and sat backward in it and faced me; his face was deadpan, but he was smiling around the cool gray eyes. "You didn't say anything about living here, too."

I shrugged. "I'm not nuts about it getting around."

He pointed again, this time at the varnished-pine four-drawer file in the corner behind me, to my left. "I suppose you got your shorts filed under *S*."

I reached over and pulled the bottom file drawer out and pulled out a pair of shorts. "Under *U*," I said.

Eliot started laughing till his eyes teared; so did I. A couple of tough guys.

My own laughter under control, the shorts on the desk in front of me like something I was working on, I said, "Well, this used to be a lawyer's office. I suppose he had briefs to file, too."

"Enough," Eliot said, wiping his eyes with a handkerchief. "Brother. You've really hit the big time, haven't you, Nate?"

"The biggest," I said, filing my shorts away. "Everybody in town is trying to hire me or bribe me, shut me up or make me talk. I'm popular."

"Seriously?"

"Yeah. Did you know General Dawes and me were thick?"

"Yeah?"

I held up crossed fingers. "Like this. Guess which one I am. He wants me to tell the truth on the stand, when Nitti's trial comes up."

Eliot thought about that. "He wants you to sell Cermak out, you mean?"

"Yowsah."

Eliot took his hat off and tossed it on the desk. "Well, Cermak is making the wrong kind of headlines."

I nodded. "Don't want to scare potential fairgoers off, you know."

"The fair *is* Dawes' baby, remember. Him and his brother Rufus, who's the president of the thing. You mean to say, he came right out and asked you . . ."

"Not really. My uncle Louis had to explain it to me. Dawes is a walking garden of platitudes; I needed a translator."

Eliot smiled. "I've met him a couple of times. Didn't make much of an impression on me."

"Don't you know he's the guy who got Capone?"

"What? What am I, chopped liver?"

"You were Dawes' tool, my boy."

"Sure," he said, his smile turning to a smirk.

I decided not to pursue the issue; why burst his bubble?

I had asked him to come over here—it wasn't much of a walk from the Transportation Building—to show him my office and to allow him to speak freely, without the other prohibition agents at his office overhearing. I wanted to find out about the Nydick inquest, at which he'd been a witness this morning.

"It was a circus," Eliot said, disgustedly. "The second inquest this week where the coroner sat in judgment of the actions of police officers who, officially, are deputy coroners. Sometimes I think the reason justice is blind is 'cause it's looking the other way."

They had started out at the morgue and moved to the Park Row Hotel where the crime was reenacted—theoretically for the sake of the jurors, but really for the press photogs. (Eliot said this with an uncharacteristic disdain for publicity; on the other hand, this publicity wasn't his.) Mrs. Nydick's attorney had charged that the shooting was unjustified, and that no revolver had been in the dresser drawer before the hoodlum squad entered to arrest her (now-deceased) husband. Miller had to fend off the attorney's questions about possible animosity toward Nydick, but the coroner put an early end to that, saying that if the attorney was going to be belligerent, he wouldn't be allowed to cross-examine witnesses at all. Miller was exonerated.

"What do you make of it?" I asked.

Eliot shrugged elaborately. "I think the wife set her husband up for her boyfriend Miller to collar, but Miller, on his own initiative, decided to take the opportunity to bump the husband off. And I think the wife took that less than kindly, and sicced her attorney on Miller."

"She might've done that just to make herself look good," I said. "It makes the cover-up look more legit to have some of these questions raised and quashed, you know."

He nodded. "You may be right. And she may not be his girl friend at all. We're just guessing. At any rate, Miller planted the gun."

"If all the guns Lang and Miller planted bore fruit," I said, "we'd be picking bullets off trees."

"Ain't it the truth. The other detectives seemed embarrassed, testifying. I think they felt taken, like you did."

"You don't think they were in on it?"

"Naw. I think Miller planted the thirty-two in the drawer with his back to them. That's my guess, anyway."

"It's as good as any," I admitted.

Eliot looked around. "It's a nice office. Bigger than mine."

"Well, you don't live in yours."

"True. Why'd you give up your room at the Adams?"

"It was getting old, living in the lap of luxury." I explained my night-watchman arrangement with Barney.

"Sounds like a good deal for both of you," Eliot nodded. He reached into an inside pocket. "Say, I've already talked to this guy, and he may have something for you." He handed me a slip of paper across the desk.

I read it aloud. "Retail Credit Company." There was a name and a number, too, and an address in the Jackson Park area.

"Real glamorous work," he said. "All the pavement-pounding a man could hope for. Checking credit ratings, investigating insurance claims. You know—exciting stuff."

"I appreciate this, Eliot."

He shrugged. "What about Sunday?"

"What about it?"

"Christmas, Nate. How about having Christmas dinner with Betty and me."

"Yeah, well that's awful nice of you, but I don't celebrate Christmas, particularly. I'm sort of a Jew, remember?"

"You don't, so why should I? Come on over. We got a huge turkey and only a handful of relatives. Plenty of room for an honest private detective."

"And for me?"

"And for you. And why not bring Janey?"

"Can I call you later? If Janey's already got something planned, then . . ."

"I understand." He stood; pointed a finger at me. "But if she doesn't, you better both be there."

"Okay. You rushing off, already?"

"I got a press conference this afternoon. We're announcing raids for New Year's Eve. Assuring the public that we're arresting only owners, not patrons."

"It'll probably be legal *next* New Year's, you know."

"I know, and it's fine with me. But till then, I got to at least go through the motions." He had his hat and coat on now. "Let me know if you change your mind about Christmas."

"I will."

"Good. I got a real nice lump of coal for you, tied with a big red ribbon."

The office was a little cold; the radiator behind my desk seemed largely ornamental. "I think that may come in handy."

"It might," he smiled, waved, went out.

I called the Retail Credit Company in Jackson Park and arranged with the manager, a Mr. Anderson, for a meeting next Monday afternoon. He was friendly, glad to hear from me, expected my call Eliot had really laid some groundwork for me, and that was a nice Christmas present; even better than the coal he'd promised. Then I called the phone company to see if my agency could still get into the '33 phone book, and made it just under the wire. A-1 Detective Agency, Nathan Heller, President. The A-1 should get me listed first in the Yellow Pages, and that alone could bring in some clients.

And I called the other agencies in town to let them know I was in business, and that I could handle their overflow at a reasonable rate: ten dollars a day and expenses. That appealed to a couple of the medium-size agencies, where there were three or four operatives, and occasionally the work load did get too big for them to handle. My rate for the general public would be twenty dollars a day plus expenses, though I didn't plan to post it; better to size a client up and slide the rate up or down, as traffic would allow—in times like these, down was where most of the sliding would be, I supposed.

This took the better part of the afternoon, and at four I got a small suitcase with some toiletries, a change of underwear, a clean shirt, and my relatively clean navy pinstripe, and went over to the Morrison Hotel, to the traveler's lounge, where I showered and shaved, leaving the suitcase and dirty clothes in a locker, before heading over to City Hall to meet Janey.

By that time it was five and already getting dark; the neons gave off a funny, halfhearted glow in the dusk, an effect amplified by the mist, which was what the cloudy day had decided to give us instead of rain or snow. Christmas was looking to be gloomy and wet, not cheery and white. The streets were filled with rush-hour traffic as I walked the concrete canyons to City Hall; once there, I stood within the high marble lobby waiting for Janey, watching city employees get out of there as fast as possible—all of 'em except Janey, of course.

Janey was, like a lot of City Hall employees, a patronage worker. She worked in the county treasurer's office as a clerk, though she did a great deal of secretarial work for the man who ran the office, Dick Daley. The county treasurer was an obese drunken gambler named McDonough; his secretary, the de facto county treasurer, was Daley. Because a lot of the patronage workers in the county treasurer's office were, like Janey, from the Back of the Yards (which is to say the area that included the Union Stockyards), there was a problem for some of the clerks: they couldn't read or write. Janey's father, a drugstore owner and political precinct captain, had seen to it that she got a high school education in a neighborhood where that was an exception, and she had managed to pick up some secretarial skills, which led to her doing a lot of secretarial work in the county treasurer's office, some of it for Daley, whom she seemed to greatly admire.

A mutual friend at City Hall had introduced us almost three years ago, about the same time Janey went to work there. It was a bit unusual for anybody to move out of a neighborhood in Chicago, but I could well see why she might want to get the hell out of the Back of the Yards. The stockyards gave the nation its meat and the South Side its jobs, but it also gave the air a stench; and her neighborhood, Bridgeport, despite her father's relative affluence and influence, was a shabby little collection of frame houses and rented two-flats, though a lot of people found it a pleasant enough place to live. But Janey didn't, and at age twenty-one she had married a man named Dougherty, who was ten years older than her, lived on the North Side (and was a political associate of the powerful alderman Paddy Bauler), and ran a saloon, which became a speakeasy, and one drunken evening was hit by a streetcar and killed deader than he was drunk.

Janey had been a widow for about a year when we met; she rarely spoke of her late husband, and what I mentioned above is the extent of what I knew about him. What I knew about her was that she did not return to the Back of the Yards after the death of her husband, but instead took a flat in the rooming-house district of the near North Side, an area of drearily similar, soot-stained stone houses, dirty alleys, and window after window with the familiar black-and-white card reading ROOMS TO RENT. Nearby were the fancy apartments and homes of Lake Shore Drive, and the shade-tree-lined streets of the Gold Coast back of them. For someone like Janey, who had an eye on the finer things, this must have provided inspiration and irritation, depending on her varying moods. And they did vary.

The security guards were starting to talk quietly to one another, glancing over at me with obvious suspicion, when at ten after six, Janey finally emerged from an elevator. She looked stunning: her eyes, with their startled lashes, leaped out of her face, and her lips were appropriately red and bee-stung. She walked over like a model, her hands in knit cream-color gloves riding the pockets of her brown alpaca coat, thumbs out; the coat had a big double-breasted collar that rose around her neck, around which was a pale brown scarf, and there were two big buttons above the coat's belt, and two below, and she wore a fur felt hat with a brim that dipped just above one brown eye. A small cream-color purse was tucked under one arm.

I was leaning against a pillar. She approached me and looked up at me with a cute, arrogant smile. "I had to work a little late. For Mr. Daley."

"Fuck Dick Daley," I said.

I hadn't said it loud, but my voice carried a bit in the echoey corridor, and a security guard turned and looked at me with wide eyes.

But Janey didn't shock easy. She just said, "Maybe I would, if he weren't engaged," and her smile got even more arrogant, and even cuter, and she turned her back on me and walked toward the doors. I followed her.

Out on the street, I looped my arm in hers and said, "You just kept me waiting because I've had to stand you up a couple times these last few days."

The smile showed teeth now, and they were cute, too, and the arrogance was pretty much gone. "You're right. But I did have some work to do. And I had to freshen up. It isn't every day we go to the Bismarck dining room."

"No, it isn't. In fact, I've never been there before."

"I've been there with Mr. Daley for lunch lots of times."

"You're a damn liar, Janey."

"I know."

At the intersection of LaSalle and Randolph, the big Bismarck Hotel, rebuilt in '27 on the site of the original hotel, lorded it over German Square, where German clubs, shops, and steamship offices converged at the west end of the Rialto Theatre district. The elaborately uniformed Bismarck doorman let us in and we went up the wide, red-carpeted steps to the huge lobby and into the main dining room.

We checked our coats, and Janey was even lovelier under the alpaca: she wore a rust-color soft wool dress with a gentle V neck, trimmed in white, and a creped, belted skirt. She left the fringed scarf on, and her hat, as we entered the dining room.

"You went to work like this?" I whispered to her, as the maître d' showed us to our table.

"Of course," she said, not whispering. Then in an affectionate if mocking whisper: "But the scarf and the hat are for you alone, dearest."

"You're too good to me."

"I know."

We had a table for two over to one side, and we sat and took the place in for a while, while a boy in a white coat filled our water glasses with water and ice. The walls were hand-carved walnut, the south one hung with tapestries on either side of a mantel, and brass chandeliers fell from the ceiling. But the room was not what I had expected: it was all very modern, on the art-deco order. The Berghoff, the German restaurant where Janey and I occasionally dined, was a bustling, no-nonsense affair, famous for pigs knuckles and sauerkraut, not atmosphere; but here I had expected an old-world peasant aura, and instead got German modernism. Germany's idea of itself was changing, and the Bismarck dining room reflected that.

Well, I'd already been at one quaint old-world restaurant today, and since it wasn't every day (it wasn't every week), (make that month), that I ate at two top restaurants, I decided to enjoy myself.

We made small talk throughout the meal (we both had Wiener schnitzel and potato pancakes) and Janey, though generally a good poker player, was not hiding her anxiety. She wanted to hear all about my new job, but she didn't want to act like she did, so she was waiting for me to tell her of my own accord. And it was killing her.

Finally, while she ate cheesecake with strawberries and I drank coffee, I said, "I don't think you're going to like my new job."

She kissed her bite of cheesecake and strawberries off her fork and shrugged a little and smiled. "You can't expect your uncle Louis to start you out at the top. These things take time."

"Janey, I didn't say anything about Uncle Louis getting me a job."

That caught her with a forkful of desert in midair. She returned fork to plate and with folded hands looked across the table at me with wide brown eyes that I could've dived into, and said, "I don't understand. You left the department. What else. . . ?"

"You know what I've always talked about."

"I do?"

"Well, *think* about it, dammit. We're supposed to be engaged. You're supposed to know me better than anyone."

She thought, and played with the diamond ring, turning it slowly from side to side, just a bit. "I know what you've always dreamed about doing. But it's so impractical."

"Well, that's what I'm doing."

"You mean you're going to be a private eye. Like Ricardo Cortez in that movie we saw."

"Yes, but I don't think I'm going to get a smoking jacket or a pretty secretary right away, like Cortez."

"Neither do I."

"And I'm not *going* to be a private eye. I *am* a private eye. Detective. Operative. Whatever."

She nibbled at her cheesecake.

"I thought you'd be unhappy," I said.

"Did I say I was unhappy?"

"No. I'm psychic."

"Did you think about asking your uncle Louis for a job?"

"No."

"Well, why did you quit the department, anyway?"

"Why do you think?"

"Because you were involved in that Nitti shooting? So what?"

I hadn't really told her that whole story yet; maybe it was time. Maybe I should tell her what really happened. If she was going to be my wife one of these days, I ought to trust her. She should've been told days ago.

I told her.

She shook her head, angrily, as I finished up. "They just came in and grabbed you, didn't even tell you what they were up to? Louses. Bums." She shook her head again. "But why quit over it?"

"Don't you understand? Don't you understand why they picked on *me*?"

She shrugged. "The Lingle case, I suppose."

"That's right."

"And they'll expect you to testify for them at the Nitti trial."

"Well, I will testify for them."

"If you stayed with the department and testified, you could get something out of it. Why quit, and help them cover up, and get nothing out of it?"

"Because I am getting something. I'm getting my private op's license in return."

"Oh."

I told her about the Cermak meeting; that impressed her. She loved that part. And I told her about Nitti, which impressed her in a different way: it seemed to scare her a little. And then I told her about Dawes, and she *really* liked that.

"What's *wrong* with you, Nate? Why don't you take advantage of Dawes' offer?"

"Three grand for supervising some pickpocket operations at the fair *would* be easy money; it'd make my first year in business a rousing success even if not a single other client walked in my door."

"That's small potatoes. You can get something better out of Dawes and your uncle. You could get a *real* job, with a bank or a business or something."

"No. You don't seem to get it, Janey. I *am* in business. I'm the president of A-1 Detective Agency. How 'bout some support here? How about you back me a little?"

She looked blankly at the center of the table, where a candle in a silver deco centerpiece glowed. "Where do I fit in? What about us? Our house?"

"I still have that money in the bank. I haven't had to dip into it yet. But I do think we should wait a year and see how I'm doing. If the money's coming in okay, and I haven't had to dip into the nest egg, we can start looking for that house. Does that make you happy?"

She looked up, found a little smile for me. "Sure it does. I only want what's best for you, Nate."

"Then believe in me."

"I do."

"Would you like to see my office?"

"Of course I would."

"It's a short walk; pretty short. Over on Van Buren and Plymouth."

"Near the Standard Club?"

"Yeah. 'Round the corner from there. Hey, I'll treat you to a cab, if you're not up to a walk."

"I'm up to a walk, Nate. Let's get our coats."

So we walked back, in the mist, arm in arm; she snuggled up next to me, but seemed distant, for being so close. She smelled like flowers; I couldn't tell you what flowers, exactly. But I can smell 'em right now . . .

And at the building, I unlocked the street entrance and had her go on up, and followed her up the stairs, and then led her to the office and let her in. Turned on the light.

"A Murphy bed?" she said.

"I live here, too," I said.

"Well, it's no worse than the Adams."

"It's better. Here I can have female guests, if I like."

"Let's make that singular, okay? Female guest?"

"Okay," I grinned. "What do you think?"

"It's pretty roomy. For one room."

"Take a look at this." I opened the door to the washroom.

"Deluxe," she said, ambivalently.

I put my hands on her arms. "Look. I know this isn't anything special. But it's all I got. And it means a lot to me."

"I'd rather hear you say that about me."

"Honey. You know I love you."

"I love you, Nate," she said, flatly.

I took her in my arms and held her close; she responded, but her heart didn't seem to be in it.

So I kissed her. Long and hard, and put everything I had into it, including my tongue in her mouth, and she came around; she came on fire, and clutched at me with something like desperation.

She took the alpaca coat off and laid it gently on the desk. She stood with hands on the hips of her smart rust-color dress and said, "I've never used a Murphy bed in a box; only ones in the wall, like at my flat."

I shrugged. "Why, you want to see how this one works?"

"Yeah. I'm interested."

I took the bed down out of its box; it was made: that was probably why I'd been three minutes late for lunch at Saint Hubert's earlier.

"No big deal," I said.

"Oh I don't know," she said. "Get the lights, would you?"

I got the lights.

Neon pulsed in from the street as she undressed. She did it slowly; there was no tease to it, she was just methodical: loosening the belt, unsnapping some snaps under one arm, slipping the dress up and over her head, laying it on the desk. And then she was in a camisole and lacy, flared panties. The points of the perfect handfuls under the camisole poked at the cloth; the lacy panties rode her thighs, a garter belt riding the panties, dark sheer brown hose rising up her thighs to where the bare stretch extended to where the flared panties came down, and then the flared panties came down, and her heart-shaped pubic tuft called to me. She lifted the camisole over her head and the pink points of her breasts scolded me. She stood there with hands on bare hips and basked in the neon and, head back a bit, smiled her impudent, cocky smile, knowing how beautiful she was, knowing the power she had, and walked slowly over and began undressing me.

She had a Sheik in her hand, in her palm. She'd carried some with her, apparently—we kept a supply at her flat—and had got it from her purse at some point, unbeknown to me, and was now slipping the condom down over me, tenderly, lovingly.

She was the first girl I ever knew who preferred being on top; I didn't mind. She rode me well, and I could watch her, see how lovely she was, as she reared her head back, lost in herself, as was I, and I put my hands on those breasts, filled my hands with those soft firm breasts, filled my mouth with as much of them as I could, and thrust into her, controlling her from below as best I could, and she rode me, slowly, and she rode me, not slowly, and she clutched her breasts and moaned and moaned till the moan was too loud to be called a moan, and too pleasure-filled to be a scream, and I emptied my seed up into her.

Into the condom, actually.

"I wish I was really in you," I said.

She was still on me; she smiled down, sadly. "You'd like a son, wouldn't you?"

"I suppose. I'd like a family. With you."

She got off me, gently, disappeared into the washroom, the cheeks of her rear jiggling engagingly as she went. She was in there awhile, and there was a flushing, and water ran, then she came back and had some tissue and removed the condom from me and went and disposed of it.

She walked to the desk and got into the panties and camisole and came back to bed; we crawled under the covers. She cuddled to me, nuzzled my neck.

We were quiet for a long time—maybe half an hour. I thought she was asleep, but suddenly she said, "Do you think you could still take Cermak up on his offer?"

"What?"

"You know. Get back with the department. Be a sergeant, a deputy coroner; be on one of his special squads."

"On one of the hoodlum squads? You want to hear something about the mayor's hoodlum squads?"

I told her about the Nydick shooting.

"I don't see how that has anything to do with you," she said afterward.

"The hoodlum squads are vile even for Chicago, Janey. I don't mind a little honest graft, but this has got out of hand. Janey. You know how my father died."

"He killed himself with your gun. It was a long time ago, Nate. It's time to let go of that."

"It wasn't that long ago. It was a year and a half ago. He did it because I gave him money."

"I know, I know. You wanted him to be able to renew the lease on his store, and you gave him the thousand dollars you got, along with your promotion, for testifying in the Lingle case. It's an old story, Nate. You got to let go of it."

"I gave him the money and told him I saved it, but he found out from somebody where it came from and he killed himself with my gun."

"I *know*, Nate."

"And now I've killed somebody with that gun. Somebody I didn't even know, all because my reputation as somebody you can buy in a murder case preceded me. Everybody in town thinks I'm for sale."

"Everybody in this town *is* for sale."

"I know that. I'm no virgin."

"You aren't?"

"Cut it out. I just got to live with myself."

"I thought you wanted to live with me."

"I do. I want to live with you, marry you, have babies with you, live happily ever after with you."

"That's a nice dream. It's a dream that could come true real easy, if you just took one of those offers."

"What offers?"

"Cermak's offer. Or Dawes'. Dammit, Nate, even Frank Nitti offered you a job. That would've been money, too."

"Are you saying you'd approve of that?"

"It's not my business how you make your living. If I'm going to be your wife, it's my business to give you moral support."

Say good night, Gracie.

"Look," I said, "I've always wanted to be a detective. The cops turned out not to be the place to do that. Now I've got a chance to try it on my own, for real. It may not pan out. But can't you let me *try*? Can't you give me, say, a year? Just put that moral support you're talking about behind Nathan Heller, President, A-1 Detective Agency, for a year, and if I'm not at least matching my income as a member of the Chicago P.D., I'll hang it up and go to Uncle Louis and beg for a job. Fair enough?"

She thought about that, then nodded. Smiled. "Sure."

She cuddled to me awhile.

Then she said, "You know, working at the county treasurer's office is really interesting. You see a lot of important people; you see a lot of important things happening. Take my boss, Mr. Daley. He's about your age, Nate. Just a couple years older. He's so dynamic. He's involved with the tax end of things, sure, but mostly he's involved in the political end. I pick up on more of that than most people, you know, because my father's a precinct captain, you know. And Mr. Daley, he's just a little older than you, and there he is, in there distributing the jobs, handling the ward committeemen from all over the city, dealing with powerful men, in a powerful way. And then at night he takes night school, can you imagine? He'll be a lawyer before you know it. He lets me help him more than most of the others, because he knows my father so well, and he knows I'll cover for him, if he needs it, when his night school cuts into his duties."

"It's too bad you're already engaged," I said. "Then you could marry the little Mick."

"Oh, he's engaged, too, you know that," she said distantly. Then, catching the slight, wrinkled her chin and said, "Nate, I'm just trying to make a point."

"Which is?"

"Daley's going places."

"He can go to hell, as far as I care."

"You're jealous."

"Pissed off is more like it."

"Oh, Nate. I'm sorry. . . . I just want *more* for you. I just want you to live up to your potential."

I didn't say anything.

She studied me in the near dark.

She kissed me on the mouth; I didn't kiss back.

"What's wrong?" she grinned, impishly. "Did I take it all out of you?"

I couldn't help grinning back. "Let me do it without using anything."

She kept smiling, then said, "All right," and started climbing on top of me.

"No," I said. "I want to be on top, Janey."

"Okay, Nate. I want you on top, too."

I got on top; I got in her. I'd never been in her without a Sheik before; it was wonderful. It was sweet. It was warm and sweet and wonderful and I pulled out. Rolled over on my back.

"Nate!" She put her hand on my chest. "What is it? What's wrong?"

"Janey, would you mind getting your clothes on?"

"What?"

"Please."

"What did I . . . ?"

"Nothing. Please. Just do it."

She got out of the bed slowly. There were tears in her eyes; she dressed quickly. Put on her alpaca coat. I was dressed by now myself; I got my topcoat on and walked her out of the building and to the El.

We stood and waited for the next train in silence.

Just as it was pulling in, I said, "Janey, I'm sorry. It's just that . . . well, I've had people trying to control me, to manipulate me all week. I've been bribed just once too many times this week."

She looked at me; the brown eyes were wet, the bee-stung lips were tight, trembling. She took her gloves off, removed the engagement ring, pressed it into my hand.

"Merry Christmas, Nate," she said, and turned toward the waiting train.

Then she turned back, quickly, and kissed my cheek, and got on the train and was gone.

I went back to my office and sat behind the desk, looking at the rumpled bed, smelling her in the room, the flowery perfume scent, the musky scent, too. I could've opened a window and got rid of it. But I didn't. I figured I'd be rid of it soon enough as it was.

It was only nine-thirty. I called Eliot and said I'd be over for Christmas.

HOOVERVILLE

# 2
# THE LONG BELLYACHE
## JANUARY 7—APRIL 8, 1933

GEORGE RAFT ▪■

## 9

The body was in a ditch near a telephone pole. No snow. Tall brown weeds leaned in the wind, and the ground was mostly sand with pebbles mixed in, so that our feet made a crunching sound as we approached. The nearby road was gravel, and there were ridges of sandy mud near the ditch, creased with tire tracks, pocked with footprints. A small middle-aged man in a cap and a heavy brown jacket stood near the body, as if claiming it for his own. Next to him was a heavyset man in a western-style hat and a hunting jacket with a badge pinned on it—the sheriff, apparently. Otherwise there was no one around: just the body in the ditch.

Back of the two men and the body, sand dunes rose. The dunes were spotted with khaki-color brush, like gigantic scalps with the hair mostly fallen out, leaving only occasional sick patches behind. Bare trees, skinny, black against a sky such a faded blue it might have been wearing out, stood close together, watching from atop the dunes, some of which ran to a hundred feet; skeletal branches touched to form a black-lace pattern against the horizon. The bitter cold air and the desert-like dunes mocked each other, and the wind blew like a bored fat man with a sense of irony.

We were on a back road near Chesterton, Indiana, about fifteen miles east of Gary, five miles west of nowhere. It was Saturday morning, about seven, and I would rather have been sleeping. But Eliot called and said he was picking me up; there was something he wanted me to see.

The something was the body in the ditch.

Eliot bent over the body, which was sprawled on its side, wearing an overcoat, a hat partially covering the face; he lifted the hat off, set it easily to one side.

"It's Ted Newberry, all right," he said to me.

The man who seemed to be the sheriff thought that was meant for him. "Thought as much," he said. He was about fifty-five with a vein-shot nose that indicated he didn't keep all the laws he was theoretically hired to enforce.

"I'm Ness," Eliot told the apparent sheriff. "A couple more people from Chicago will be showing up soon. A representative of the police department, and the deceased's lawyer."

"What do we do with the body?"

"What do you usually do?"

"We don't have a morgue; we use a local mortuary."

"Use it, then."

"It's okay if I call 'em now?"

"I think that'd be wise. It's a cold enough day, but this boy isn't going to keep forever."

"I got to walk to that farmhouse," the sheriff said, pointing with a hand distorted by a heavy cotton glove. Then he put the hand down and waited for something, and what he got was silence. When Eliot failed to fill the silence, the sheriff grinned, shrugged, said, "Don't have a police radio in my car yet. Like to have one."

Eliot just looked at him, and the sheriff kind of nodded and walked off, his breath preceding him like smoke from a steam engine.

Eliot stood and looked at Newberry. I did the same, but from more of a distance. In life Newberry had been a jaunty sort; hail-fellow-well-met, though I'd never met him. But he had a reputation as such. A big, dark-haired roughly handsome gangster, about forty. Now he was a body sprawled in a ditch, with his pockets turned inside out.

The guy in the cap and brown jacket said to Eliot, "I found him. 'Bout daybreak."

Eliot nodded, waited for more information to come. It didn't.

"Was there anyone else around when you found him?" Eliot asked.

"No. I was by myself."

Eliot pointed to Newberry. "What about him. Was he by himself?"

"I should say."

"Is there anything else you can tell me about this?"

"Looks to me like this boy was took for a ride."

"Stand over by your car, would you?"

"Are the reporters coming soon?"

"Sooner or later."

Reluctantly, the guy went over and stood by his flivver.

Eliot came over to me and shook his head. "Publicity seekers," he said.

I resisted any ironic comment.

"Come over and take a look at Ted."

"I've seen dead bodies before."

"I know you have. Come on."

We walked to the body and Eliot knelt over it again and pointed to Newberry's belt. The buckle was large and jewel-encrusted: diamonds and emeralds.

"Ever see one like that?" Eliot asked.

"Yeah. Jake Lingle had one on, the day he was shot."

Eliot nodded. "Capone gave more than one of his pals fancy belts like that."

"And more than one of 'em ended up like Ted, here."

"Lingle included," he said guardedly.

"Lingle included," I said.

Jake Lingle was a subject Eliot had never broached with me directly, though I knew he wanted to, knew his curiosity was killing him and had killed him repeatedly since he'd known me, but out of a sense of courtesy toward me, he'd resisted the urge. My involvement with the Lingle case predated my friendship with Eliot, which had come about when I got into plainclothes, which had come about after my testifying at the Lingle trial. Which meant that Eliot and I would not have become friends if the Jake Lingle case hadn't elevated me to the status of a detective, a peer of the great Eliot Ness.

He said, "You could look at this as an appointment with Capone that finally got kept."

"How do you mean, Eliot?"

He stood, shrugged, still glancing down at the body. "I'm just thinking of a certain morning when Ted and his boss Bugs Moran were delayed a few minutes on the way to meet with the rest of the boys, and when they finally got there, Ted spotted a squad car parked in front of the garage, and he and Bugs and Willie Marks ducked in a café to avoid what they figured was the cops running a petty shakedown. Know what morning I'm talking about, Nate?"

Eliot was giving me his best melodramatic deadpan, now.

"Yeah, yeah," I said.

February 14, 1929. Saint Valentine's Day.

I bent over Newberry's body and had a close look; it wasn't hard to reconstruct what had happened. He got the bullethole through the hand, with accompanying powder burns, when, in an effort to keep from getting shot, he'd grabbed a gun pointed at him; that same bullet, or another one from the same gun, had shot off his left earlobe as he struggled. That point, probably, was when he got his skull bashed in, and only then came the final bullet, the one that killed him (unless the bashing had already done the trick): a single execution-style slug, fired from behind, at the base of the skull. There wasn't much blood, here. He'd been killed elsewhere and dumped in the dunes, pockets pulled inside out, in a nod toward faking a robbery.

Eliot was looking at the tire tracks. He studied them for a few minutes, then turned to me. "The car came from the west, dumped Ted, turned around, and went back the way it came."

I moved away from the body, pointing at it as I did. "He had a place near here, didn't he? A summer home?"

Eliot nodded. "At Bass Lake. They probably killed him there."

Last night, at about two, Newberry's lawyer, at the prompting of a worried crony of Ted's who said Ted was two hours late for an appointment, had called the detective bureau and asked if his gangster client had been arrested, and got no answer. Then the lawyer had called Eliot at home and asked if the *feds* had his boy, and Eliot had told the lawyer to go jump and went back to sleep. A writ of habeas corpus was filed, and by early this morning the chief of detectives and Eliot were in the former's City Hall office, both officially responding to the lawyer that Newberry was not in custody. And at that point the word came in that a body answering Newberry's description had been found in Indiana.

Shortly after the sheriff had returned from his phone call at a nearby farmhouse, a dark blue Cadillac sedan pulled up and a short squat man in a blue pinstripe with a diamond stickpin hopped out; he was Newberry's lawyer.

"Hello, Abe," Eliot said, as the little man trundled toward the body in the ditch.

Without acknowledging Eliot's greeting, the lawyer looked at Newberry and, as if speaking to Ted, said, "Where's the county official?"

The sheriff, standing in the road, called out, "Me, mister!"

The lawyer walked up to the sheriff and said, "That man is Edward Newberry. Where will his body be taken?"

The sheriff gave him the name of the mortuary.

The lawyer nodded, said, "We'll be in touch," and got in his Cadillac and drove off.

The man in the cap and brown jacket was still over by his flivver, standing first on one foot, then the other. He said, to no one in particular, "Where's the reporters, anyway?"

"Stick around," Eliot said, and advised the sheriff the same thing, then nodded to me and we walked back to his Ford.

"Aren't you going to wait for the press, Eliot?" I asked him.

He shook his head no. "This is nothing I want to be part of. You, either."

On the way back to Chicago, Eliot said, "That's Nitti's work, of course. So much for Ted Newberry as the mayor's handpicked candidate for running gambling on the North Side."

"That still leaves Touhy in Cermak's pocket."

"Touhy's nothing. Nitti's made an important point here. Newberry offered fifteen thousand for Nitti dead. Well, Nitti's alive and Ted isn't."

"I wonder how Cermak's favorite bodyguards will take the news of Newberry taking a ride."

Eliot smiled a little. "I wonder how Cermak will take it."

"Why'd you want me to see that, anyway?"

Eliot, watching the road, said, "It concerns you."

"Sure. But you could've phoned and told me about it. Why'd you want me along? Outside of me being charming company."

"Newberry was Cermak's man."

"So?"

"He's nobody's man, now."

"Point being?"

He glanced at me, then back at the road. The dunes were still around us: it was like the Midwest was doing a bad but impressive imitation of Egypt.

Eliot said, "Maybe this opens the door for you telling a different story at the Nitti trial."

"Like the true story, you mean."

He shrugged. "You might want to consider it. Newberry's an example of how Nitti operates. And Newberry's also an example of Cermak's current lack of strength in mob circles."

"So, what? You're saying if I stick with Cermak's team, I'm ditchbound? That's bullshit, Eliot. Nitti knows I'm an innocent bystander in this. You notice that was *Newberry* dead back there, not Lang or Miller. Frank Nitti doesn't kill the messenger; he kills the guy who *sent* the message."

Eliot just drove.

I kept talking. "Just because Cermak isn't aligned with a gang of any power, at the moment, doesn't mean he isn't going to be again, soon. He's been playing this game a long time, you know. And if I cross Cermak, I'll get my op ticket, and my gun permit, pulled. Get serious, Eliot."

Eliot didn't say another word to me till he pulled up in front of my building on Van Buren; not until I was getting out, feeling just a little irritated with him.

"Sorry, Nate," he said. "I just thought you should see that back there."

I could feel my face was red, and it wasn't the cold. "Christ, Eliot, what is it you want out of me? Are you such a goddamn Boy Scout you expect me to tell the truth because it's the truth? You been in Chicago too long to be *that* naïve."

Which was a lousy thing for me to say, because Eliot might have been a lot of things, but naïve about the Chicago facts of life he wasn't.

He gave me a sad little smile.

And said, "I just don't like the idea of you getting on a witness stand and perjuring yourself."

He didn't add "again," but the word hung in his eyes, and it was that fucking Lingle case again, wasn't it? Coming back to haunt me.

I nodded at him to let him know I understood he meant well, and shut the door on the Ford, and he drove off.

It was a little after eleven, and I hadn't had any breakfast, so I went into the deli on the corner for an early lunch. I ate my usual pastrami sandwich but, despite my hunger, barely got it down. Eliot had bothered me, whether I wanted to admit it to myself or not. I sat nibbling dill pickles absently for maybe half an hour, sipping at a ginger ale, when Barney came in through the door that connected the deli with his speak, noticed me, and got this silly grin, like it just occurred to him that he was top contender.

"There's somebody you got to meet," he said, leaning against the table, not sitting down, pointing with a thumb back at the door he'd just come through.

"Does she have nice pins?" I asked.

"It ain't a woman, Nate."

"Then I ain't interested."

"Nate, it's a famous guy."

"Barney, *you're* a famous guy, and I'm not interested."

"Some mood you're in."

"You're right. I'm sorry. I better start being nice to you or you'll start charging me rent. Who do you want me to meet? Some other goddamn fighter?"

His grin got silly again. "You'll see. Come on."

I finished off the last dill pickle and got up and followed him into the speak. The place was about half-full, and the patrons, all of them men, were craning their necks back to see the far corner booth by the boarded-up street windows, talking among themselves as they did. We headed to the booth that was causing the commotion.

For a second, just a second, I thought it was Frank Nitti. The same slicked-back blue-black hair, the same swarthily handsome, hooded-eyed look, though this guy lacked Nitti's vaguely battered quality, sported no pencil-line mustache, and was younger, thirty-five or forty. Like Nitti, he was immaculately groomed, in fact was a snappy dresser, sporting a dark gray pinstripe with lavishly wide lapels, and a black shirt with white tie. And, like Nitti, he wasn't a big man; he was sitting down, but you could tell standing up he wouldn't be more than five six or so. This was a more conventionally handsome Frank Nitti, with a little Valentino tossed in.

Barney and I stood next to the booth and the man smiled at us, rather remotely, while Barney introduced us.

"Georgie," he said, "this is a childhood pal of mine, Nate Heller. Nate, this is George Raft."

We sat in the booth across from Raft, and I smiled at the actor and said, "I'm embarrassed. I should've recognized you."

Raft shrugged, barely perceptibly, smiled the same way. "Maybe if I been flipping a coin."

I nodded. "I saw that picture. Pretty wild."

We were talking about *Scarface*, the big hit of the year before, which had made Raft a star; it had caused a lot of controversy in Chicago, opening months later than anywhere else in the country, the local censorship board having fits over its depiction of their city (even though it was Chicago's own Ben Hecht who wrote the picture).

"I hear good things about it," Raft said. "I didn't see it myself."

Barney explained. "George never looks at the pictures he's in."

"Why's that?" I asked Raft.

"Who needs it?" he said. "I probably look terrible. My face'd scare babies."

He didn't seem to be kidding. I suddenly realized his remoteness wasn't a tough-guy pose, but a sort of shyness.

"Georgie's in town doing some personal appearances," Barney said. "What's the name of the new picture?"

"*Undercover Man*," Raft said noncommittally.

"Oh?" I said. "Where you appearing?"

"At the Oriental Theater," Raft said. "I come out and talk to the folks, the orchestra plays, and I do some dancing. Did you see *Night After Night*?"

"Sorry, no," I said.

"That was a pretty good one. Not so much gangster shit. Got to do some dancing."

"Mae West was in that," Barney said, eating this up.

"Yeah," Raft said, smiling faintly, "and she stole everything but the camera."

"How do you two happen to know each other?" I asked Barney, nodding at Raft.

"Oh, Georgie's a big fight fan," Barney said. "He was a fighter himself, weren't you, Georgie?"

Raft laughed a little. "Seventeen bouts and ten knockouts."

"That's a good record," I allowed.

"Not when it's you getting KO'd," Raft said.

"You won a few," Barney said.

"Three," Raft said, holding up three fingers.

Buddy Gold came over for my order. I asked for a beer. Neither Barney nor Raft was drinking anything. I knew why Barney wasn't drinking: he had a fight coming up later this month in Pittsburgh, with Johnny Dato.

"Don't you want anything, George?" I asked him.

"I don't drink," Raft said. "Bring me a coffee, would you, Buddy?"

"Sure thing, Mr. Raft."

Raft looked my way and said, "I been following Barney's career real close. He's won me some money. I admit to knowing more about boxing out of the ring than I did in it. I was a fight manager for a while. Discovered Maxie Rosenbloom."

Something was ringing a distant bell in my mind; like the round-ending bell in the ears of a canvas-prone fighter who's just been saved by it.

"Weren't you involved with Primo Carnera?" I asked.

Raft seemed to flinch at that, again, barely perceptibly. Out of the corner of my eye, I could see Barney's grin disappear. I'd opened a door better left closed   I'd been rude to Barney's guest. But I let it ride.

"Not really," Raft said. "A friend of mine owned a piece of him."

"Owney Madden, you mean," I said.

"Yes," Raft said.

I could tell this was making Barney uneasy, so I didn't pursue it. It was natural that an honest fighter like Barney would be embarrassed by one of his friends being connected to Primo Carnera and Owney Madden. Primo Carnera was the big, lumbering heavyweight brought over from Italy who, through a succession of fixed fights and sportswriters on the take, was elevated to the Championship of the World. Carnera was a slow, awkward giant with a glass jaw, but he made good show business, until a real fighter, Max Baer, took the championship away from him, and damn near killed the poor clown in the doing. New York gangster Owney Madden owned Carnera, and Madden and George Raft were lifelong friends. The story I'd heard had Raft, just prior to his Hollywood days, slipping a mickey to "Big Boy" Eddie Petersen, a fighter who had refused to take a dive; Raft's mickey had paved the way for Carnera's first major victory—at Madison Square Garden, no less.

I knew Barney knew this story: it was him who told it to me, with some disgust, when he was noting the climb of this guy Raft in the talkies, this guy who used to be Owney Madden's boy. But that had been a year ago, before Barney was into the heavy purses—and the papers—and before he met Georgie at Arlington Park, where they shared a mutuel love.

"I kinda hate to admit how I got a lot of my boxing savvy," Raft said.

"Why's that?" I asked.

"Well, the boxing arenas were my stomping grounds, back in my pickpocket days. And I understand you're an ex-pickpocket detail dick. Maybe you don't want to be seen in public with an ex-dip."

I smiled at him, a bit charmed in spite of myself. "Some of my best friends are pickpockets. And as long as they sit *across* the booth from me, we stay friends."

"I understand you're a private dick now."

"That's right."

"Barney says you got an office upstairs."

"That's right."

"How 'bout giving me a tour? Who knows, I might have to play a private dick in a movie someday."

"Sure. You never know. Barney? You coming?"

Raft got out of the booth. "I'm expecting a phone call, Barney. Would you mind sticking around, in case it comes in? I'm on suspension from Paramount, at the moment, and my agent's trying to work something out for me."

Barney shrugged, smiled. "Sure. See you guys in a few minutes."

Raft climbed into a black formfitting coat with a velvet collar, pulled a pearl-gray hat down over one eye. With his high trousers, spats, and pointy shoes as shiny as his hair, he seemed a movie star's idea of a gangster—or was it the other way around?

He followed me through the deli out onto the street and up the stairs to my office. He hung his coat and hat on the tree by the door, and took a seat across from my desk before I'd even got behind it. It was clear this was more than a movie star wanting to meet a real private detective for research purposes; besides, I had a feeling George Raft was one Hollywood actor who didn't need help researching underworld-related matters.

I got behind the desk; Raft was eyeing the box against the wall. "That looks like a Murphy bed," he said.

"I'm supposed to be the detective," I said.

He smiled; wider, more at ease. "I spent years sleeping in worse places than my own office . . . lofts, pool halls, subways. Times are tough. You're lucky to be in business."

"You're kind of lucky yourself."

He got a silver cigarette case out from his inside coat pocket. "You said it. You mind?" I nodded I didn't, and he lit up a long cigarette with a bullet-shaped silver lighter.

"What's this really about, Raft?"

"Let's keep it friendly. Let's keep it 'George' and 'Nate,' all right?"

"Sure, George."

"I get the feeling, from that remark about Carnera and Madden, that you know a little about me."

"I know you used to be a bootlegger for Madden, and that he helped pull some strings to get you started in Hollywood."

Raft shrugged. "That's no secret. The columnists have had hold of that, and it hasn't hurt me. Nobody thinks a bootlegger's a bad guy; nobody who drinks, that is."

"You don't drink."

"I grew up in Hell's Kitchen. It was no fuckin' picnic. I was in a street gang with Owney. You woulda been too, if you grew up where I did. He went his way, I went mine. I was never a hood, really. I used to see them, though, when I was sitting 'round the dance halls. Sharp young hoods in candy-stripe silk shirts, flashing their roll. Was I green with envy. They had money to spend and their pick of the skirts, and I wanted a candy-stripe silk shirt so bad I was ready to pull one off the first guy I could catch alone in a dark alley."

"But instead you became a movie star."

Raft's hooded eyes blinked a few times, his face impassive. "I'm no saint. I was a pickpocket, a shoplifter. Then I found a trade—dancing. I got into taxi-dancing, I worked up a Charleston act, eventually. Did some vaudeville. Owney was in Sing Sing through all this, but when he got out, after Prohibition came in, he helped me climb. I worked the El Fey with Texas Guinan, and I was doing a little bootlegging on the side, for Owney. And Owney helped me make it to Broadway, and Hollywood. And I ain't ashamed of that. What are friends for?"

"This is all real fascinating," I said, "but what the hell does it have to do with me?"

Raft inhaled on the cigarette. Blew smoke out, like a movie tough guy. "This office. Barney set you up, right? Did a friend a favor?"

"Yeah. Right. So?"

"Friends do favors for friends. Sometimes you even do favors for friends of friends."

"You ought to sew that on a sampler, George."

"Don't be testy. I didn't come 'round here to look up Barney Ross; that was just for appearance sake, though Barney don't know that. It's you I come to see."

"Why, for Christ's sake?"

"I used to work at a place called the Club Durant. Jimmy Durante's place. There was a small garage below street level, connected with the club, that was the largest floating crap game in New York. That's where I got to know Al Brown."

"Al Brown."

"I saw him later, at El Fey's. And he was a good friend of Owney's, too. They were business associates."

"Oh. That 'Al Brown.'"

"Yeah. That one. I was in New York last week, and a friend asked me to do a favor for Al Brown."

"Why you?"

"It had to be somebody neutral. Somebody who could come around and see you without anybody getting any ideas. But somebody important enough for you to take it seriously."

"What does he want?"

"He wants you to come see him." Raft reached in his other inside pocket, withdrew a flat sealed envelope. Handed it to me.

Inside was a thousand dollars in hundreds, a round-trip ticket to Atlanta on the Dixie Express, and credentials identifying me as an attorney with the Louis Piquett firm.

"These tickets are for Monday," I said.

"That's right. I'm told if there's a conflict, they can be switched to any other day next week. No pressure, Nate."

"Do you know what this is about?"

Raft got up. "I don't want to know what this is about. But I can guess. If it doesn't have something to do with another friend of mine, Frank Nitti, getting shot up by your mayor's favorite cops, I'll go back to taxi-dancing."

I got up. I extended my hand to Raft, who smiled tightly and shook it. "Sorry I was a wiseass," I said.

"I take it you'll do it."

"Why not? A grand is a nice retainer for a guy that sleeps in his office. And it isn't every day that George Raft stops by to play middleman."

"It isn't every day you take on Al Capone for a client," Raft said, and we went down and spent some time with Barney.

AL CAPONE

I took a sleeper to Atlanta, catching the Dixie Express at Dearborn Station early Monday afternoon; the next morning I was having breakfast in the dining car, finishing my last piece of toast as the train steamed into Atlanta's Union Station at half past eight. I caught a taxi, my topcoat slung over my arm (it was sunny, about sixty degrees not a Chicagoan's idea of a winter morning), and waited till I was in the back of the cab before I said, "McDonough Road and South Boulevard."

The cabbie turned and looked at me, a skinny guy with a Harry Langdon deadpan and a drawl you could hang a hammock on. He said, "Mister, that's the pen."

"Right," I said, and gave him a sawbuck. "This should take about an hour round trip, and you get another one when it's over."

He smiled, shrugged, left the flag on the meter up, drove the four miles to the address I'd given him.

He pulled over by the side of the road, shut the motor off, and waited, as I got out and approached the small barrack from which a blue-uniformed, armed guard came out and asked me my business here. I told him, and he passed me on, and I moved down a walk to a second barrack in front of the barred gates stuck in the midst of a thirty-foot gray granite wall. A second uniformed guard, carrying a Winchester rifle, asked me the same thing as the previous one, and asked if I had a camera or a weapon. I said I had neither.

At the gate in the massive wall, its stones haphazardly cut and set, no doubt reflecting the attitude of the labor that had done the job, a guard looked at me, through the bars, and asked me my business here, for the third time. And one side of the gate groaned open.

Inside the massive granite main building, I was led by a guard to a little desk in the big main corridor; at the end of the corridor was a steel gate, and guards with clubs were watching as blue-denim-garbed inmates shuffled hurriedly along. I was given a small blank sheet of paper on which I was to put the name of the prisoner I wished to see, which I did—ALPHONSE CAPONE—and was told to give my own name and address, and reason for calling upon said inmate. I listed my real name, but gave the address of the Piquett law firm, and stated my business as legal representative. This wasn't a lie, as I was representing that firm, but it did tend to give the impression that I was an attorney.

The guard passed my slip of paper to a second guard, who relayed it to a convict runner stationed in the corridor beyond the second gate, who was sent to fetch the prisoner. The guard and I talked about the differences between Chicago and Atlanta weather, the guard coming to the conclusion that he was glad he lived in Atlanta, and me coming to the silently held conclusion that I was glad I wasn't a prison guard. When five minutes had passed, the guard led me to a nearby reception room about the size of my office, and had me sit on the near side of a long, bare wooden table. I could see a partition that ran underneath the table to the floor—to prevent the passing of items, I presumed—but there was no wire mesh separating the two sides of the table. The walls were gray stone with the windows high and barred. Other than the table, the room was completely bare.

Five minutes later a guard with a club escorted a prisoner into the room; the prisoner was about five ten, weighed perhaps two hundred pounds, and had a nice tan. His thinning dark brown hair was prison-short, his eyebrows bushy and his gray eyes piercing, surrounded by dark circles that showed even against the tan; they were the kind of dark circles that come from genes, not lack of sleep. The head was shaped like a squeezed pumpkin, and along the left cheek were two scars, a long and a short, the latter deep and pronounced; under the jaw, riding a nearly nonexistent neck, was a third scar. Without the guard, he came around the table and sat across from me; with a thick-lipped smile that showed no teeth, he nodded at me, fishing in the pocket of his faded denim jacket for something. It was a cigar; a thick, six-inch one. He fished some more for some matches and lit it. Without saying anything to me, by gesturing with the cigar, he asked if I cared for one, and I shook my head no. He looked over at the guard with a benevolent smile and nodded, and the guard left the room. And Al Capone and I were alone.

He extended his hand to me, and the smile increased, showing some teeth. I shook the hand; Capone had slimmed down, but his hand was still pudgy, soft. His grip wasn't.

"So you're Heller," he said.

"I'm Heller."

"We never met, but you did me a favor once."

I wasn't sure I knew what he meant. I said so.

"No matter, no matter. Sure you don't want one of these?" He waved the cigar; it smelled pretty good. "Two bucks. Havana."

"No thanks."

He leaned on one hand, cigar in his lips, cocked upward. "It ain't so bad in here, you know. This is the first rest I had since Philly."

He was referring to the year stretch he'd done after he was picked up a few years ago in Philadelphia on a gun-carrying charge. Speculation was he'd sought the rap for a cooling-off period, his old mentor Torrio, who was putting the national crime combine together, having advised him to lay low in the wake of the bad publicity of the Saint Valentine's Day Massacre, among other excesses.

"Still, they screwed me," he said philosophically. "Eleven years the fuckers gave me, when they promised me a couple years tops, if I gave 'em their guilty plea. Those bastards, their word means nothin' to 'em."

"It looks like Atlanta's agreeing with you."

He shrugged, smiled some more. "It's the tennis. Exercise and sun. It's okay. Be nice if there was some women in here, but what the hell, you can't have it all. You know Rusty Rudensky?"

"No."

"Good little safecracker. Did some work for me years 'n' years ago. Turned out to be one of my cell-mates. I'm in with seven other guys, in case you think this is the fuckin' Ritz. But Rusty's okay. He knew the ropes, fixed it up so a trusty pal of his who drives a supply truck can smuggle cash into me. That buys privileges with guards you don't think we're alone just 'cause you're supposed to be my mouthpiece, do you?—and it helps keep me protected. You know, there's a lot of little shots want to take a shot at a big shot. So I got cons playin' bodyguard for me in here, just like Frankie Rio in the old days."

A wave of something went over his face; the smile went. Referring to life on the outside as "the old days" was what did it.

"I'm doin' all right, Heller," he said, as if trying to convince himself. "They got me workin' in a shoe factory, cobblin' shoes, can you buy it? Eight hours a day for seven bucks a month. Hell of a deal, me with a million bucks in half a dozen banks. Sittin' in a hole like this."

I didn't say anything; I still didn't know what I was doing here, but it was his nickel. His grand, actually.

"I could be in Florida right now," he mused, looking up, like Florida was heaven. "I got a wife and a boy at Palm Island, ya know. I idolize that boy; he's gonna be goddamn president. If I could be with him and his momma in Florida, I'd be the happiest man in the world. God, I'd love to lay under those palm trees. God, I'd love to be at Hialeah followin' the ponies."

I'll be damned if I didn't feel a little sorry for him, but then he pointed a finger and the cigar in his mouth right at me, like two gun barrels, and his beady gray eyes in their dark sockets bored into me, like I'd done something to him.

"And your pal Ness and those other dumb bastard feds go and nail me on a *bookkeeping* rap! A damn tax rap, and now I'm in here, and the rest of 'em are out there splitting up what I built!"

The beady eyes glowed with something that was scary; the fat head seemed like a skull somehow—a skull with eyes.

"They're going to fuck it up, Heller. They're gonna piss away what I made, what I . . . created. If I don't stop 'em." This was said with religious certainty.

I ventured a question. "Who, Mr. Capone?"

"Let's make it 'Al,' okay? What's your first name? Nate? Nate. Nate, Frank's a good boy, he really is. He's family. But he just don't got what it takes to fill my chair."

Nitti. He meant Nitti.

"Now, I know all about what you've been through. I know you got sucked into hitting Frank with Cermak's goons. I can tell you without a doubt that Frank don't hold nothin' against you. You were honorable, quittin' that scumbag police force. Bunch of fuckin' crooks. I hate 'em damn near as much as the politicians, two-faced fuckin' crooks. I thought Cermak was different, but he's like the rest. Just another politician spending half his time covering up so the public don't see he's a thief."

"Mr. Capone "

"Al."

"Al. What am I doing here?"

"You're here 'cause I need somebody I can trust. You showed yourself to be honorable, and I ain't forgetting the time you helped me out in the past, though maybe you didn't know it was me you was helping. I can't call on any of my boys, 'cause I gotta handle this . . . from the outside. And I don't want to mix my brothers in, if I can help it. 'Cause I don't want to go up against Frank, toe to toe, 'cause, what the hell, he's out there, and I'm in here, and how the hell we gonna go toe to toe with bars in between."

"I don't understand."

"Understand this: I'm gonna be out of this cage before the year's over. *I'm* gonna be sitting in my chair, not Frank. But it's gonna take time. I shelled out two hundred grand and then some to a big shot in Washington who's gonna open these gates up wide, right from D.C. And I got five of the biggest attorneys in the land getting me ready for being sprung. But it'll take time, and in the meantime, I don't want Frank and the rest of them bums flushing my empire down the shithole."

"What makes you think they're doing that?"

He shook his head, sadly; puffed the pool-cue cigar. "I thought Frank was smarter than this. No kiddin', I did. I thought he learned from my mistakes; I thought he learned my lessons. You can't stir up the heat. That's the one mistake I made, and I learned to correct it, but too late, I guess, or otherwise I wouldn't be sitting in here. I stirred up the heat. I put too many bodies on the front page. People want candy on Valentine's Day, not headlines."

I said nothing.

"I tried to play peacemaker, you know. All along, I done that. Just last year, 'bout this time, when I was waiting in the Cook County Jail, they brought that crazy bastard Dutch Schultz and Charlie Luciano in to see me. They been feuding. It was Schultz's fault, horning in on Charlie's territory. The dumb bastard Schultz wouldn't listen, and I didn't end up gettin' nowhere, but the point is I *tried*, my natural bent's to be a peacemaker. Only how do you make peace with Dutch Schultz? If I'd had him outside, I'd've shoved a gun in his guts."

Capone's cigar, in one pudgy hand now, had gone out; he lit it again, and I sat patiently waiting to see where I fit in.

"When I heard what Frank's planning, I sent word to him: don't do this, Frank. You'll stir up the heat, Frank. You can find a better way,

Frank. And you know what he says, what the lawyer says he says? He says, you're inside, Al, and I'm out, and, all due respect, I gotta trust my judgment. I'm outside, he says, and I'm handling things. That's what he says."

There was a great sadness, greater frustration, in his face.

Then he smiled, a small, private smile.

"You know what Frank's planning?" he asked innocently.

"No."

"Guess."

"I—I can't."

"Go on. Guess."

"Gang war? He hit Newberry the other day."

Capone grinned, said, "And about time! That bum jumped from side to side whenever the wind blew his way. He shoulda got his February fourteenth '29. No, you can kill somebody, from time to time, if you don't do it on no big scale, and you don't make a habit of it. But there's some people you just can't hit."

"Like who?"

"Like the mayor of a big city."

"What?"

"Cermak. Frank's gonna hit Cermak."

He leaned back and puffed his cigar and smiled at me, quietly, amused by the look on my face no doubt.

"You're kidding," I said.

"Yeah, I'm kidding. I paid you a grand and brought you down on the Express to tell you my life story."

I thought about it. "I saw Nitti in the hospital," I said. "He hates Cermak, all right. I guess it's possible he'd do something like that . . . but it seems—"

"Crazy? It's suicide, Heller. Times are hard; the booze business is comin' to a close. And I got to take my business into quieter areas. I made plenty of progress with the unions, for instance. That's the future, Heller. But there ain't gonna be a future, not for my business, if the guy I give it for safekeeping to goes around shooting the mayor of Chicago."

"He's not going to shoot him himself, for Christ's sake—"

"No! He's crazy but he ain't insane. Don't be dumb."

"How's it going to happen?"

"I don't know exactly. That's where you come in."

"Me?"

"I got certain lines of communication; I picked up on some of it, but not all of it. I know where, and sort of when. I even know who the triggerman is."

"So tell."

"Cermak's going to Florida. I wish it was me, not him. Going to Florida, that is, not gettin' hit. He's going to Miami for patronage. Cermak fucked up royal, you know, when he backed Al Smith clear till the last minute, and didn't deliver the important votes to FDR at the convention. He hopped on the bandwagon at the last minute, but he's still shit with the White House, so he's gotta go down there while the president-to-be holds court, and beg for scraps. Kind of a laugh, the king of patronage havin' to be a beggar. Well, Cermak'll be down there a week or so. And sometime during that week, the hit'll go down. Doing the hit outa town, that's Frank's idea of keeping from stirring up the heat. Jesus. Anyway. That's all I know."

"You said you knew the triggerman."

"I know who they plan to use as of today; it could change. We're talkin' next month, and things change. But it's part of why I sent for you, Heller. First, you're a cop; you can handle this. You can tail Cermak, and even if you get seen, so what? You're no hood, just an honest citizen takin' a vacation. And bein' a cop, you can use a gun if you have to. And you'll have a gun permit, don't worry. You'll be down there as a licensed private cop with a gun permit. I got connections in Miami that'll see to that."

"There are plenty of people just as capable as me, Al. So why me?"

"The triggerman's name don't matter. But let me put it this way he's a blond boy. About twenty-eight, thirty. And you seen him before." He grinned at me. "Get it?"

I got it.

Because suddenly I understood what favor it was I'd done for him once; what work I'd done that I didn't know was for him.

In the summer of 1930, Alfred "Jake" Lingle walked down the steps into the tunnel running under Michigan Avenue to Illinois Central Station, to catch the one-thirty racetrack special to Washington Park. As he walked along within the tunnel, reading a racing form, smoking a cigar, wearing a jauntily cocked straw hat, a jauntily cocked .38 was placed just over the back of his collar and a bullet went up through his brain, and he fell dead, on his racing form, cigar still burning.

His slayer, who also wore a straw hat as well as a medium-gray

suit, was blond, about five ten, weighed perhaps 160 pounds, and
seemed to be in his late twenties. He had held the gun in his left,
gloved hand, and dropped the snubnose to the cement, just as Lingle
was dropping. And the blond gunman ran. He ran through the startled crowd, pushing his way back to the stairs Lingle had come down,
ran back up to Michigan Avenue, crossing it, running west onto Randolph Street, where a traffic cop stationed at Randolph and Michigan,
in response to someone's cry of "Get that man," took pursuit. The
cop got within arm's reach of him, getting a good look at the blond,
but stumbling, and then the gunman angled down an alley and, presumably, followed the maze of alleys back into the Wabash crowds,
where he was lost.

And so Jake Lingle, reporter, was dead. And Chicago, particularly
his employer Col. Robert R. McCormick (who had never met this
particular employee—he had four thousand), was outraged. It was
obvious that this sixty-five-dollar-a-week police reporter had "got the
goods" on gangland, that he "knew too much" and so had been struck
down, martyrlike. The Colonel in Tribune Tower offered a a twenty-
five thousand dollar reward for information leading to the murderer's
conviction; other papers and civic groups kicked in, bringing the tally
to over fifty thousand dollars. The fallen hero, this "first-line solider"
in the war on crime, would be avenged.

Then, to Chicago's embarrassment (and Colonel McCormick's),
Lingle turned out to be, well . . . he turned out to be Jake Lingle;
sixty-five-dollar-a-week legman with the *Trib* whose yearly income
was easily over sixty thousand dollars; who was known in gangland
circles as the "unofficial chief of police" because of the clout he could
wield, for a price, if you wanted a speak or a brothel or what-have-
you sanctioned by the powers-that-be; whose Lincoln car was chauffeured; who owned a summer home on the Michigan lakeshore, and
another in Florida; who lived in a suite at the Stevens Hotel, when in
Chicago; who played the stock market and the races with equal abandon; whose closest friend was the commissioner of police, next to Al
Capone, of course, who gave him the diamond-studded belt buckle
he wore at the time of his murder.

The gun that killed Lingle was traced to Peter von Frantzius, who
had also supplied the machine guns used on Saint Valentine's Day.
He admitted having sold this gun and several others to one Ted Newberry.

Newberry was, at that point, in Capone's camp, leading some to believe that the Big Fellow had turned on his old friend Lingle. After all, story was that after Capone got out of jail in Philly, he had snubbed his old pal Jake, rather than give him the usual exclusive coverage. Al, in Florida at the time of Jake's murder, pooh-poohed that to the press.

And a rival tied to the old Bugs Moran faction, Jack Zuta, seemed to be the likely suspect for engineering the Lingle hit; after being grilled by the cops, Zuta was killed, apparently by Capone people avenging the death of Al's old pal Jake.

This did not satisfy Colonel McCormick, who financed his own investigation, and a combined effort between the state attorney's office and *Trib*-financed investigators led to a fellow named Leo Brothers. The investigators, it was rumored, had got a tip on Brothers from Capone himself, eager to help get the heat off in Chicago, thanks to the bad publicity Lingle's murder had generated, the worst since February 14, 1929.

Brothers, a labor-union terrorist on the run from St. Louis authorities, was thirty-one, with wavy light brown hair. He was mute throughout the proceedings, and even during the course of the trial; rumor had it he was taking the fall for the mob, for pay. One of his lawyers was a former *Trib* staffer, a friend of Lingle's; the other lawyer was Louis Piquett, also a friend of Lingle's, who had seen Lingle shortly before the murder and was a witness in these very proceedings.

There were fifteen witnesses. Fourteen of them had been in the tunnel with Lingle and had seen the blond killer flee. Seven of them identified brown-haired Brothers as the blond; the other seven didn't. Still, Brothers was convicted, and sentenced to a strangely lenient fourteen years for the cold-blooded assassination, a sentence that finally got a public comment from Brothers: "I can do that standing on my head."

It was widely held that the prosecution's case was won by the fifteenth witness; a witness who could identify Brothers as the blond, though this witness (bringing the total to eight who could identify the killer) had not been in the tunnel; but up on the street: the traffic cop who had pursued the killer, who had nearly caught him, who had seen him clearly. Me.

"Jake Lingle," Capone said, almost wistfully, "was a pal. Paid him one hundred thousand dollars for protection on my dog tracks, and got nothing for my money. Then he cut me out of the wire-service action, servicing the handbooks; twenty-five hundred of 'em in the city, it adds up. Then he starts doing business with Moran, on the side. And all the while he's going to my tailor charging four and five suits at a time to my account. Well, something had to give."

I didn't say anything.

"You did us a favor," Capone said, "helping us put the wrong man away."

Meaning Brothers.

"And now it's gonna come in handy," he said, "because you're the only guy who ain't a hood who can recognize this blond guy Nitti's sending to hit Cermak. Ain't that lucky?"

I smiled. "Lucky," I said.

That day I chased that blond kid and lost him had led me to plainclothes, which led me to Nitti's office, which led me here, sitting in front of Al Capone. Who I was about to work for again.

"There's nine grand more in it," he said. "That's ten grand total. And all you got to do is stop it."

"How?"

"That's up to you. But I suggest you do it quiet. If you spot the guy, take him someplace and handle it."

"I'm no killer."

"Did I say kill him? I said stop him. How you do that's between you and him." He smiled broadly, with those fat, faintly purple lips. "Then when that traitor Cermak comes back to Chicago in one piece, I let Frank know who saw to it."

"Nitti won't be happy with me," I said.

"You won't matter. You won't have had nothin' to do with it. It'll be me. Me, sitting here in fuckin' prison, still on top of things. And Frank and the boys'll know better next time."

Behind me, a voice said, "Time."

It was the guard, sticking his head in, almost embarrassed to be interrupting.

Capone nodded to him, and the guard retreated back outside.

I stood. "Aren't you going to ask me if I'm going to do it?"

"Oh, you'll do it," Capone said, standing. And he went out, leaving me alone in the room with the bars on the windows.

He was right, of course: I'd do it. Not just because it was Al Capone asking, and it would be unwise to say no; not just because there was ten grand in it, though that was no small part of it.

It had to do with something Capone couldn't even guess.

I wanted to catch that blond killer, this time.

The Morrison was the tallest hotel in the city and, if its advertising was to be believed, the world. The main building was twenty-one stories, with a tower going up another nineteen, with a flagpole atop that, the gold ball atop the flagpole the highest point in the city. Cermak was living in the bungalow atop the tower; if he wanted to ride higher up, he'd have to climb the pole and sit on the ball.

It was Wednesday morning, but I was still tired from the Atlanta trip; I'd got in at Dearborn Station at two yesterday afternoon, giving an unintentional scare to a couple of pickpockets who apparently didn't know I was off the force. I'd spent the rest of the day in my office doing Retail Credit checks over the phone and, after a bite at Binyon's and a solitary nightcap at Barney's, I'd gone up and pulled down the Murphy bed, the plan being to sleep till noon; any noon. But a phone call from Eliot had woken me at seven-thirty this morning—he wanted to meet me for coffee at eight; we settled on nine, in the Morrison Sandwich Shop.

I went in the hotel's main lobby, which was pretty plush: gray marble floors, walls inlaid with marble and wood, overstuffed furniture, bronze lamps, potted ferns, high vaulted ceiling. To the right was the marble-and-bronze check-in desk, to the left a bank of five elevators, one of which I took up to the fifth floor. Most of the hotels in the city were in trouble; one, the Blackstone, was about to go under. But the Morrison Hotel was doing fine, having cut its rates in half; even a relatively posh joint like this had to make concessions for the depression.

I showered and shaved in the traveler's lounge, went to my locker to get dressed; I was buttoning my pants when I felt a finger tap on my shoulder. I turned.

It was Lang.

It was the first I'd seen him since Nitti's office. His five o'clock shadow seemed even darker this time; maybe he was down here to shave. He was in a rumpled suit that looked slept in, and his bald head caught the overhead light and reflected it. His black eyes were shiny, too, and he had something like a smile going, though there was more than a little sneer in it.

He kept tapping the finger against my chest. "You doin' anything special here, Heller?"

"That finger's healed nicely," I said.

He prodded me with it, kind of hard. "It's healed fine."

I grabbed it, twisted it; he grimaced but said nothing.

I said: "Didn't your friend Miller give you my message? You're to keep your distance from me. I don't like either one of you bastards."

I let go of him. He backed away, holding the finger, his reddened face screwed up, and glanced behind him, wishing Miller were around to back him up. He wasn't.

"I just wanted to know what you're doing here, Heller," he said lamely.

"I'm using the traveler's lounge, Lang, just like you are. I presume you're using this 'cause Cermak won't let you use the facilities in his fancy bungalow. Or maybe His Honor just keeps 'em tied up."

"You think you're pretty funny."

"No, I think you're pretty funny. Now excuse me." I put my suit-coat on, and my hat, slung my topcoat over my arm, ready to leave; he held a palm out, in a stop gesture—but he didn't touch me.

"Look," he said. "Maybe we should get off each other's backs. We're in this together, right?"

I said, "Three peas in a pod, that's us. At the trial. But till then, keep your fucking distance, okay?"

He shrugged, almost embarrassed. "Okay," he said.

Eliot was in a booth in the sandwich shop, sipping coffee; he gave me a weary little smile as I joined him.

"Just saw a friend of mine," I said.

"Who's that?"

"Lang."

"No kidding. You boys keep it friendly?"

"Sure. We're pals."

"He must be looking after Cermak." Eliot pointed upward with a thumb. "That bungalow's something, I hear. Steinway in the living room. Three master bedrooms. Library. Kitchen, dining room, the works."

"Must pay to be a servant of the public."

Eliot laughed humorlessly. "So they tell me."

"What's the word from the streets, on the Nitti hit?"

Eliot shrugged. "People seem to think Nitti was going to use Little New York Campagna as a triggerman, to bump Cermak, and Cermak got wind. Newberry, either at Cermak's suggestion or to be a good team player, offered fifteen thousand dollars to have Nitti hit first. Box score: Nitti's alive, Newberry's dead, Cermak's hiding upstairs."

"Think he's in danger?"

"I hear he bought a bulletproof vest. But, no, I don't think so. Too much publicity. Frank Nitti isn't stupid enough to shoot down the mayor of Chicago."

"He was planning to."

"He could've got away with it, before the shit hit the fan. The Cermak hit could've been pinned on any number of gangs, not just the Capone faction. But after all that's happened, no . . . I'd say Cermak's safe. Nitti's too smart for that."

I nodded. A pretty waitress with blond hair in a pink-aproned outfit came over. She gave me a nice smile and I asked for coffee. I watched her leave.

"I think I'm in love," I said.

"Maybe you should call Janey."

I turned back to him. "No. That's over."

"If you say so. Look, about last Saturday . . ."

"What?"

"Taking you along on the Newberry ID. I'm sorry if I sounded like I was lecturing you or something."

"Hey. It could have been worse. I could've been taken for a ride by Nitti, not Ness."

He let go a rueful smile. "I suppose. Say, uh . . . were you out of town or something?"

"Yeah. For a couple of days."

"Where'd you go?"

"Out of town. Business."

"I don't mean to snoop."

"I know, Eliot, but you just can't help yourself."

"Say, did you pick up any work from Retail Credit?"

"Yeah, I did. Anderson's giving me some insurance claims to investigate. I appreciate the lead, and the recommendation, Eliot."

"Oh, that's okay, Nate."

"But I'm still not going to tell you where I was yesterday."

"If you don't want to . . ."

"Okay, I went to Atlanta and took on Capone as a client."

He smirked. "You don't have to be a smart-ass."

I shrugged. "Let's just say I'm working for an attorney and it makes the case more or less privileged information."

"That might be stretching a legal point, but I'll accept it. Besides, it isn't my business. I'm just curious, that's all."

"It's okay."

"What attorney?"

"Jesus, Eliot! Louis Piquett."

He didn't like that; he didn't say so, he just looked into his coffee with Norwegian gloom.

"I'm not thick with him, Eliot. Fact, I haven't even met him."

"Maybe you *did* go see Capone in Atlanta."

"Yeah," I said good-naturedly, pretending to kid him. "Maybe I did."

"Piquett's connected to Capone, they say."

"I've heard that."

"He was Jake Lingle's killer's lawyer, too."

So there it was: out on the table, between us. Jake Lingle.

"That assumes the guy they sent up really did kill Lingle," I said.

Eliot looked at me. "Oh, I'm sure he was the killer. There were reliable witnesses."

I said nothing; the sarcasm in Eliot's voice had been so faint I could've been imagining it.

"There's something I've wanted to tell you for a long time," Eliot said. "We never talked about the Lingle matter. That happened before we happened. But you seem to be in the thick of it again, in regard to the Capone gang . . . through no fault of your own." He pointed his thumb Cermak-ward again. "And, well . . . I can't help but be concerned."

"I appreciate your concern, Eliot. I really do. But . . ."

"But keep out of it. Fair enough. Only let me tell you this thing I've wanted to tell you. It isn't commonly known. Frank Wilson and I knew about Lingle . . . we knew he was close to Capone, and could be a major witness, as to the kind of dough Capone spent, to help us build a tax-evasion case. We called Colonel McCormick at the *Trib*. He knew of Lingle, but didn't know him personally. We didn't tell the Colonel why we wanted to see Lingle—if we had, the Colonel wouldn't have made such a sap out of himself, in the press, defending the fallen hero. But we asked the Colonel to set up an appointment with Lingle for us, at the Tribune Tower. He agreed. We were to meet with Lingle at eleven o'clock the morning of June tenth." He paused melodramatically, and this time it worked. "I don't have to tell you what happened June ninth."

Jake Lingle was murdered.

"No," I said, "you don't."

"It's always bothered me, circumstantial as hell though it is, that Piquett, with his Capone connections, a pal of Lingle himself, himself a witness at the trial for having seen Lingle shortly before the murder, that this very man Piquett should defend the guy who supposedly shot Lingle."

"I can see how that would bother you," I said.

"There've been a lot of theories about who was behind the Lingle killing. Who hired it. Some feel Capone was back of it, many feel otherwise. But I don't have any doubt that it was anyone but Capone."

"Neither do I, Eliot."

"Well," he said gravely, "we won't say anything more about the Lingle matter. But I thought you should know about the appointment at Tribune Tower that Lingle didn't get to keep."

"It's not a bad thing to know. Thanks, Eliot."

The waitress came back and we both had another coffee.

"Listen," Eliot said, "I wanted to see you this morning, not just to pry into your affairs. I wanted to give you some news."

"Oh?"

"I'm putting in for a transfer."

"Out of Chicago?"

"Yes."

"Why?"

"The show's over, here. I'm a lame duck. Chief prohibition agent in a city that'll be selling beer legal, 'fore you know it, and everything else, soon as FDR gets 'round to it. I want a real job again."

"Eliot, you always used Prohibition as a weapon against the gangs; an excuse to go after them. Why not keep using that excuse as long as you can get away with it?"

He shook his head. "No. It's over." He looked at me and his eyes were tired; he looked older than twenty-nine. "You know something, Nate. Sometimes I think getting Capone was just . . . public relations. They brought me in, they sicced me on him, and we did the job, and now he's gone, but hail, hail . . . the gang's still here. And with Prohibition gone, they'll be less vulnerable. More underground. But here. Still here. And I'm not sure anybody cares."

I didn't say anything for a while.

Then said, "Eliot—surely you knew how much the Capone conviction was a PR effort, from word go. Nobody was better at getting in the papers than you."

He smiled sadly, shook his head some more. "That's a nice way of saying I'm a glory-hound, Nate. I guess maybe I am. Maybe I like my picture in the papers, my name in headlines. But did it ever occur to you that the only clout I had, the only way I could build public support, the only way I could show the concerned citizens and the politicians who brought me in to do the job that I was doing that job was to get in the goddamn papers?"

Actually, it hadn't occurred to me; and I felt kind of ashamed of myself that as one of his best friends, I had been right in there giving Eliot an at least partially bad rap all along, where his supposed publicity hunger was concerned.

"Where will you go?"

"Where they send me. I'd imagine I'll be here through the summer. They may have some use for me during the fair."

"You'll be missed. I'll even miss you."

"I'm not gone yet. Anyway, I wanted to tell you about it. Kind of, you know. Get it off my chest."

"I'll be leaving town, myself. For just a week or two."

"Oh?"

"Yeah. I'll be down in Florida, early next month."

"Isn't that when Cermak'll be down there?"

Ever the detective.

"Is it?" I said, with what I hoped came off as genuine ignorance/ innocence.

"Think it is," Eliot said noncommittally, rising, picking up the check, putting down a dime for the tip. I added a nickel. He looked at me. "You *are* in love."

"I fall in love easy when I haven't been laid in two weeks," I said.

He smiled at that, and didn't have a tired look in his eyes anymore. We walked out on the street together, and I walked over to Dearborn with him and down to the Federal Building, where he left me, and I went on to Van Buren and 'round the corner to my office. It was windy, which was hardly a surprise in January in Chicago, but the wind had real teeth now, and I buried my hands in my topcoat pockets and walked with my head looking at the pavement, because the wind made my eyes burn when I walked into it.

My head was still down as I opened the door and came off the street and into the stairwell, and I raised my head only when I heard footsteps coming down above me.

In the stairwell, half a flight up, a woman was coming down. A woman in her early twenties with a face like Claudette Colbert's, only not as wide. She was rather tall, perhaps five eight or nine, and wore a long black coat with a black fur collar, nothing fancy, yet not quite austere. She had dark black hair, short, a cap of curls that lay close to her head, and another cap cocked over that: a beret. She carried a little black purse in one hand. As we passed on the stairs, I smiled at her and she returned it. She smelled good, but it wasn't a perfumy, flowery scent; it was a fragrance I couldn't place: incense? Whatever the case, I was in love for the second time in an hour.

Then when we'd passed, she called out to me, in a melodious, trained voice that seemed affected, somehow, in a way I couldn't quite define, like the fragrance.

She said, "Do you have an office in this building, or are you just calling on someone?"

I turned to her, leaned on the banister, which wasn't the safest thing in the world to do, but I was trying for a Ronald Colman air.

"I have an office," I said. With understated pride.

"Oh, splendid," she smiled. "Then perhaps you'd know what Mr. Heller's hours are."

"I'm Mr. Heller," I said, losing my air, but managing not to sputter. "Anyway, I'm Heller."

"Oh, splendid! Just who I've come to see."

And she came up the stairs and I allowed her to pass, her body brushing mine, the fragrance still a mystery, and once in the corridor, led her to my office. She went in, I took her coat and hung it on the tree, and she stood poised, purse in two hands like a fig leaf in front of her.

She was stunning, in an oddball way: she was deathly pale, partially from face powder, but her lips were dark red, a red with black in it; she wore black, completely black—a one-piece slinky dress that wanted to be satin but was cotton, with a slit up to her knee, black heels, sheer black hose with a mesh pattern. The effect, with the beret, was vaguely apache dancer, but also vaguely naïve. Play-acting was part of this, somehow.

I hung my own topcoat up, gestured to the chair in front of my desk, which I got behind; she sat with her back straight, her head back a bit. She reached a hand out to me across the desk, which I had to stand to take; I wasn't sure if I was supposed to kiss it or shake it, so I just kind of *took* it, taking the tips of four fingers in my hand and squeezing gently, acknowledging the hand's existence, then sitting down.

"My name is Mary Ann Beame," she said. "That's Beame with an *E*. A silent one. I don't have a stage name."

"You don't?"

"That's my real name. I don't believe in stage names. I'm an actress."

"Really?"

"I've done some little theater, here and there."

Very little theater, I thought.

"I see," I said.

She sat up even straighter, wide-eyed. "Oh! Don't worry. I'm not destitute. Just because I'm an actress."

"I didn't assume you were."

"I have an income. I work in radio."

"No kidding?"

"Yes. It makes a tidy living for me, till I can go on to something better. Do you listen to the radio?"

"When I get the chance. I been meaning to pick one up for the office."

She looked around, as if trying to see where to put this radio, once I bought it. She noticed the Murphy bed and pointed toward it; the gesture was theatrical, but somehow I didn't think this was coming from snobbishness. "Isn't that a Murphy bed?" she asked.

"It might be," I said.

She shrugged to herself, not bothering to understand either the Murphy bed or my remark, and looked across the desk at me, smiled and said, "Just Plain Bill."

"Pardon?"

"That's the sudser I'm on. 'Just Plain Bill.' I do several voices, one of them a lead. I do that regularly, and pick up a lot of other shows. Have you heard 'Mr. First-Nighter'? That's where I've done my best work, I think."

"I'm more an 'Amos 'n' Andy' man, myself."

"They do all their own voices," she said, rather sadly, as it wasn't a market for her wares.

"I'm glad a serious actress like yourself has no compunctions about working in radio. A lot of actresses might feel above it."

"A number of splendid actors and actresses are working in Chicago radio, Mr. Heller. Francis X. Bushman. Irene Rich. Frank Dane."

"Eddie Cantor," I offered.

"Not in Chicago," she corrected.

"Well, then. We've established you're gainfully employed. Now, why is it you wanted to employ me?"

Her face took on a serious cast; the pretension dropped, and concern came through. She dug in her little black purse and came up with a dog-eared snapshot.

"Here's a photo of Jimmy."

She handed it across the desk to me; it was a photo of her and a boy who looked a bit like her, though he was pudgy. It was several years old; possibly when they were still in their late teens.

"We were twins," she said. "Still are, I suppose."

"Not identical twins, I hope," I said, venturing a small smile.

"No," she said distantly, not getting it.

I started to hand the picture back, and she shook her head no.

"Keep that," she said. "I want you to find him."

"How long has he been missing?"

"Well, he isn't *missing* exactly . . . it's nothing you could go to the police about. I mean, it isn't a missing persons case or anything like that."

"What is it, then, Miss Beame?"

"Call me Mary Ann. Please."

"All right, Mary Ann. Why is your brother not exactly missing?"

"We come from Davenport, Iowa? On the Mississippi. One of the Tri-Cities. Heard of that? Rock Island? Moline?"

I'd heard of all three: Davenport was where Bix Beiderbecke came from—the jazz cornet player who, till bad bootleg gin killed him in '31, made Paul Whiteman worth listening to; Rock Island I knew from its railroad; and Barney had fought in Moline. But the term "Tri-Cities" was new to me. I didn't bother saying so, because she was off and away.

"My father was a chiropractor. That makes it sound like he's dead, and he isn't. He's alive and well. But Daddy was a chiropractor.

Davenport is the home of that, you know . . . the Palmers, they invented chiropractic. And my father was very thick with them. Very friendly, one of their first students. But he had an accident in an automobile, and his hands were badly burned. He had to stop practicing. He taught at the Palmer College for a while, and ended up as the manager of WOC Radio."

I stopped her. "How did he go from being a bonesetter to the manager of a radio station?"

"The Palmers own WOC. 'World of Chiropractic.' Like the *Tribune*'s station WGN stands for 'World's Greatest Newspaper.' Understand? That's where I had my first experience, in radio, was on Daddy's station. I read poems on the air when I was a little girl. When I was older, I had my own program for the kids, reading stories, like fairy tales. That's where I got my experience, and why I was able to come to Chicago and find work in radio, here."

Having a father in the business who could pull some strings (even if he couldn't crack bones) must not have hurt, either.

"Jimmy and I were always close. We had a lot of the same dreams. I wanted to be an actress, and he wanted to be a reporter. We both read a lot, as kids, and I think that's what fueled our fantasies, and our ambitions. But, anyway, that was Jimmy's dream, only Daddy wanted him to be a chiropractor, as you might guess. Jimmy had a couple of years at Augustana College, taking liberal arts, planning to take journalism, but Daddy wanted him to go on to Palmer, and when Jimmy wouldn't, Daddy cut off the money. And Jimmy left home."

"When was this?"

"A year and a half ago. About June 1931, I'd say. Right after his college got out."

"How long have you been in Chicago?"

"A year. I hoped to run into him here."

"Chicago's a big place to just run into people."

"I know that now. I didn't know that in Davenport."

"Understandable. But you had reason to believe he'd come here?"

"Yes. He wanted to work for the World's Greatest Newspaper."

"The *Trib*."

"Yes. Short of that, I think any Chicago paper would do."

"And you think, what? He came to Chicago and applied for jobs at the various papers?"

"I think so, yes. I called all the papers and asked if they had a James Beame working for them and they just laughed at me."

"They thought you were pulling their leg."

"Why?"

"James Beame. Jim Beam. You know."

"No."

"It's a whiskey."

"Oh. I didn't make that connection."

"Well, they probably did. He hasn't contacted your family? Your father, your mother, since he left in the summer of '31?"

"No. Mother's dead, by the way. When she gave birth to us."

I didn't know what to say to that; it was a little late in the game to express condolences. Finally I said, "I take it this is your personal effort to locate your brother . . . your father isn't involved."

"That's right."

"Is there anything else pertinent you can tell me?"

She thought. "He came by hopping a freight. At least that's what he told me he planned to do."

"I see. It's not a lot to go on."

"But you will *try*, won't you?"

"Sure. But I can't guarantee you anything. I can check with the papers, and maybe ask around some Hoovervilles."

"Why those?"

"A naïve kid, down on his luck, he might fall in with hobos or down-and-outers." If he lived through it. "Or he might have gone on by freight to someplace else. Do you want to know what my guess is?"

"Certainly."

"He came here and tried to land a job and got nowhere. He was too embarrassed to go back home, so he hit the road. My guess is, he's traveling the rails, seeing the country. And one of these days, God willing, he'll get back in touch with the family, and he'll be a grown-up."

"What are you saying, Mr. Heller?"

"Nate. I'm saying, save your money. I'll take the case if you insist but I think things would work out just as well if you let them work out on their own."

Without hesitation, she said, "Please take the case."

I shrugged. Smiled. "Consider it taken."

"Splendid!" she said. Her smile lit up the room.

"My rates are ten bucks a day. I'll put at least three days into this, so . . ."

She was already digging into her purse. "Here's a hundred dollars."

"That's too much."

"Please take it. It's a . . . what is it?"

"Retainer. I can't."

"Please."

"I'd rather not."

"Please."

"Well. Okay."

"Splendid!"

"Listen, do you have an address? A place where I can reach you?"

"I have a studio on East Chestnut. We have a phone." She gave me the number; I wrote it down.

"That's in Tower Town, isn't it?" I said.

"Yes. And you aren't surprised, are you?" That last was delivered impishly.

"No," I admitted. Tower Town was Chicago's version of Greenwich Village, home of the city's self-styled bohemians. "Say, how did you happen to pick me to come to?"

She looked at me with more innocence than I knew still existed in the world; or anyway, Chicago. "You were first in the phone book," she said. Then she stood. "I have to run. I've two parts on a sudser this afternoon."

"Where?"

"Merchandise Mart."

That was where the NBC studios were; CBS was at the Wrigley Building.

"Let me get your coat," I said, and got up from behind the desk.

I put it on her; the smell *was* incense. That was about as close as Tower Town got to perfume.

She gazed at me with the brownest eyes I ever saw and said, "I think you're going to find my brother for me."

"No promises," I said, and opened the door for her.

I'd give it the old college try, Palmer or otherwise.

I went to the window and looked at her out on the street, straining to see her through the fire escape between us, seeing little more than the top of her head, that beret, as she caught a streetcar.

"I think I'm in love," I said to nobody.

## 12

Sundays, I missed Janey.

I missed her other times, too; every night, for instance. Days hadn't been a problem: my new business was keeping me occupied, so far, and I didn't really have time to mope. I worked long days, so nights I was tired, and then there was always Barney's speak waiting for me when I dragged home; not that I got drunk every night, but I drank enough to go to sleep without much effort. Rum, mostly.

But Sunday, goddamn Sunday.

That was our day, Janey's and mine. Good weather, we'd go to a park or a beach or a ball game—summers we played tennis and pee wee golf; we'd go to a matinee in winter, maybe ice-skate at some lagoon, or just spend a day in her flat, and she'd cook for me, and we'd listen to Bing Crosby records, and play Mah-Jongg, and make love two or three times. Now and then Eliot and his wife, Betty, would have us over for Sunday dinner, like family, and we'd play some bridge. Eliot and Betty usually won, but it made for a nice afternoon. A preview of the sweet, quiet life Janey and I'd have after we got married and had a house of our own, maybe even in as respectable a neighborhood as Eliot and Betty's.

But I wasn't living in a dream cottage, I was living in an office, and that had its advantages, but spending Sunday alone in it wasn't one of them. I'd sit and look at the phone and think about calling Janey. I would manage, for minutes at a time, to convince myself there was a percentage in doing that. A full five minutes might go by before I admitted to myself that what was between us was dead.

And today was Sunday.

But I had another woman on my mind, this Sunday: a client. Purely business. I was able to convince myself of that for minutes at a time, too.

I hadn't had a chance, yet, to do much about tracking down Mary Ann Beame's brother. I had started on the case the afternoon of the day she came to my office. I followed the most obvious course of action, which was to check with all the papers in town, where he'd probably gone looking for work, just another naïve teenage kid from the sticks who expected the big town to spread its legs for him, never considering that the town might be on the rag. It had only taken me that one afternoon and part of the next morning. I showed his picture to the information desks and cashiers in their first-floor cages at the *Trib, News, Herald-Examiner;* I checked with the City News Bureau, too. Nobody remembered him, and why should they? A lot of people were looking for work these days; nobody had been hired in janitorial for a year and a half, let alone editorial. Nobody kept job application forms, because would-be applicants didn't get that far; any reporters that did get hired were pros who would go right to the city editor and ask if he had anything for 'em. Jimmy Beame's plan to be a big-city reporter was a pipe dream: I knew that going in. But I was a detective, and any competent detective knows that most of the legwork he does will account to nothing, so I checked anyway, knowing what I'd find: nothing.

Most of the next week I spent investigating insurance claims for Retail Credit in Jackson Park. Business was so good, I spent seventy-five dollars of Capone's money on a '29 Chevy that was the first car I ever owned: a dark blue coupe with a rumble seat. It made me feel like a rich man, but the people I called on reminded me I wasn't. Not that they were well-to-do—they lived in typical Chicago two-, three-, and six-flat buildings   but anybody with steady work and a nice place to live who could afford insurance seemed well-to-do these days. I called on a few merchants, and a lawyer; and a professor at the University of Chicago campus, whose claim was the only one that smelled phony to me: a family heirloom, his grandmother's diamond ring, which now was his wife's, was missing, having been "lost on an outing"; but the description of the ring was specific enough that I thought I might be able to turn it up at one of the North Clark Street pawnshops, and planned to advise Retail Credit as much.

The tree-lined boulevard that I followed out of the university campus was the site of the midway of the last world's fair, the Columbian Exposition. The only overt reminder of that fair—which had begun with much fanfare about the success of the modern age and had ended with the city in the throes of a depression—was the Fine Arts Palace, which had later become the Field Museum, and now was turning into something called the Museum of Science and Industry. Restoration was under way as I drove by, scaffolding still up, as workers worked at getting the joint ready to house exhibits for the next world's fair, opening in May.

I remembered my father talking about the '93 fair: he hadn't liked it; he found it offensive, union man that he was. Within the White City of the fair—its arcanely classical buildings out of sync with Chicago's reputation as the birthplace of modern architecture—fairgoers had lined up for rides on the first Ferris wheel, and men gawked at Little Egypt, while outside, in the Gray City, jobless men had wandered looking for parks to sleep in that weren't littered with Greek and Roman buildings.

Each day as I drove back to the Loop along Leif Eriksen Drive at twilight, angular-shaped structures would rise like a mirage along the lakefront; overtly modern buildings and towers not quite finished, some of them with their skeletons still showing, poked at the sky, testing it. The winter had been kind, thus far, and snow and cold had not got in the way of the continuing construction of this futuristic city upon land that had, in part, been dredged from the lake.

The new fair was coming: the Century of Progress General Dawes insisted on celebrating, even if it wasn't really a hundred years yet; who was counting?

On the site of the fair, less than a year ago, was a Hooverville. The jobless, the homeless had been made to give way for the Century of Progress. Well, what the hell, maybe the prosperity the fair would bring the city would give the jobless a job or two. And losing the lakefront sure didn't cost Chicago her Hoovervilles.

And the Hoovervilles were my next stop, where Jimmy Beame was concerned. As good a way as any to avoid spending Sunday in my office. And the Hoovervilles wouldn't be closed for the Sabbath, either.

I started with Grant Park, which didn't qualify as a Hooverville, but was an outdoor hotel for the down-and-out just the same; nobody dared put up any shacks there, of course, since the cops would put a quick end to that. But otherwise, as long as things didn't get out of hand, the cops looked the other way—they about had to, since they'd long since stopped picking up vagrants: there wasn't room in the jails to accommodate *that* big a crowd.

I walked up there, past the Adams and Congress hotels, and soon was showing Jimmy Beame's smiling well-fed face to gaunt, unshaven men in suits that had once cost more than mine but now were held together with safety pins and string. The men in Grant Park—Lincoln Park was the same—were those who had not succumbed to moving into a Hooverville; they had not accepted their rung on the depression ladder, and were usually not panhandling, yet, were still trying to eke out existences doing odd jobs, like shoveling snow, which is where one old codger I talked to told me he'd got the extra topcoat he had folded up to use as a pillow on the bench he had staked out for himself, this bitter cold Sunday morning.

And there was snow to shovel, now: it had finally hit Chicago; no blizzard, but the few inches we'd got mid week were clinging to the ground, thanks to the consistently cold weather. The old guy with two topcoats was in the minority; most of the men didn't have even one, and this tall, tough, skinny old bird might be man enough yet to wake up tomorrow morning and still own two.

"I ain't seen this boy," he said, looking at Jimmy Beame's smiling face. "The gal he's with's a pretty little thing. Like to've met her when I was in my prime."

"That's his sister."

"Looks it," the old guy said.

"Have you eaten today?"

"I ate yesterday."

I started to dig in my pocket; he put a hand on my arm.

"Listen," he said. "You plan on showing that picture around? Asking these has-beens and never-wases if they seen this kid?"

I said that I was.

"Then don't give anybody a red cent. Word gets around you're giving out dough, you'll get more information than you can use and none of it'll be worth a slug."

I knew that. But this poor old bastard was in his damn seventies, and out in the cold like this . . .

He must've known that was going through my mind, though, because he smiled and shook his head.

"Just 'cause I'm the oldest kid on the block, don't make me the neediest, or the worse off. If I had some information for you, I'd take your dough. But I don't, so I won't. These other boys won't take that attitude, though. See, I been in this game since before hard times. I been riding the rails twenty years, ever since a woman I lived with for fifteen years throwed me out for reasons that are none of your business. But these other boys . . . they don't know how to handle this life. It's new to 'em. So don't give any money away. You can't have enough to handle the business you'd do."

I shook his hand, and forced the buck in mine into his. He gave me an almost angry look, but I said, "You worked for that. Your advice was worth it."

He smiled and nodded, and stretched out on his bench for a snooze, the folded topcoat under his head.

Around the base of the statue of Alexander Hamilton, the founder of the Treasury of the United States, sat several more down-and-outers, and I could see they were the sort of man the old hobo had referred to: guys in their twenties, thirties, forties—men who'd had jobs, who'd played by the rules, who'd believed that for the man willing to work there was always work—sitting at the base of Hamilton's statue with faces that still had pride in them. But there was confusion, too, and anger, and as the months passed and these men moved into a shack in one of the Hoovervilles that dotted the outlying parts of town, those faces would turn blank, frozen, and by something more than just the cold.

One of the men, sitting on a step with a Sunday *Tribune* next to him, had his suitcoat off, and his vest, and was wrapping some newspaper around his trunk, and then buttoned his vest over himself and the papers, and then wrapped some more paper around himself and the vest, before climbing back into the suitcoat.

He noticed me watching him, and had a smile left in him and shared it with me. "Keeps ya from freezin', they tell me," he said.

I didn't have a snappy answer. I managed to say, "Bet it does," and he said, "Gotta make sure you keep one over your heart."

"Oh?"

He shrugged. "That's if you plan on waking up."

"Ever see this guy?"

I showed him the picture.

He studied it. Said, "Any dough in it if I have?"

"No," I said.

"I haven't seen him. I wouldn't even've seen him if there *was* dough in it."

"Thanks for your trouble," I said.

"Don't mention it," he said, and spread out the rest of the newspaper and lay down on it. He didn't put any on top of him, like blankets, though: there was just enough wind to make that inadvisable.

I showed the picture to the rest of the squatters on Hamilton's pedestal. None of them had ever seen Jimmy Beame; most of them liked the looks of Mary Ann; some of them seemed past caring about the looks of a Mary Ann, even in an abstract way. I questioned some more men, who sat on benches along the lakefront, looking out at the nearly completed city of tomorrow where a sea of shacks had been, not so long ago. One of the men, a gray-complexioned middle-aged guy in hat and topcoat, both of which had cost some dough, though the topcoat's buttons were mostly gone, hadn't seen Jimmy, either, but suggested I get a copy of the photo made and then he could help me show the picture around, and could turn an honest dollar. I turned him down, without a twinge—like that old guy said, I didn't have enough money to do the job without covering my heart over, and with something tougher than newspaper.

I drove to the Hooverville at Harrison and Canal. It was a vista straight out of Krazy Kat: a surrealistic town of shelters built from tar paper and flattened tin cans, scrap lumber and cardboard boxes, packing crates and old car bodies, chicken wire and flapping tarps, anything the city dumps could provide, with an occasional old stovepipe sticking out at an odd, raffish angle. The hovels were rather neatly arranged in a landscaped setting, with walks carved out of the earth and some trees and bushes planted—barren now, of course, except for a couple of evergreens, one of which had probably served as a Christmas tree; no weeds or rubbish in sight, just a strange little town in the snow, many of its occupants huddling around trash-cans, fires in which burned a vivid orange against the gray-white day. This, and a number of other Hoovervilles near the railroad yards and in vacant lots around town, had been around long enough to have become more than a temporary stop: these people lived here, men and women and children, people who seldom were able to wash themselves or their clothes, but who carried themselves with a quiet dignity that said they would if they could. And from the number of children and pregnant women, life here seemed to be going on.

It was the Hoovervilles like this that were the most promising to me in this search: some of these people had been here well over a year, whereas the hobos of the city and the down-and-outers of Grant and Lincoln Park were transient. If Jimmy Beame had come here by freight, in which case he would just about had to have fallen in temporarily with tramps, he could very likely have come back to a Hooverville to spend the nights during his fruitless search for a desk in Tribune Tower. So it was the permanent residents of the city's Hoovervilles who had the best chance of having seen him.

Nobody at Harrison and Canal had ever seen Jimmy Beame.

I hit three more Hoovervilles, the outlying ones, and called it a Sunday. The next morning I tried the loading platforms on lower Wacker Drive, and none of the men there could identify the picture; neither could the men under the Michigan Avenue bridge. The Hoovervilles near the railroad yards were perhaps the best bet, but I got nowhere. I ended up in Barney's speak about seven Monday night and drank rum till I stopped seeing unshaven faces wearing battered fedoras.

Then I spent two days on the near North Side, going up and down North Clark Street with that goddamn picture in my hand. North Clark Street was not the place to go for a man tired of looking at hobos; it was, in fact, hobohemia. Ramshackle old buildings with half-hearted store fronts catered to the drifters who had been the soul of the street since before hard times, and would be after; peddlers and street hawkers had every corner and many spots in between all sewed up. Just a few blocks from here were the fancy shops of North Michigan Avenue, where wealthy women in furs and jewelry bought more furs and jewelry. But this was North Clark Street: pawnshops, white-tile restaurants, chop-suey joints, chili parlors, poolrooms, sleazy theaters, cigar stores, newsstands, secondhand stores, mission soup kitchens, flophouses; a dingy, shabby street that at night turned into a "little white way" of bright lights and hot jazz, with cabarets and "open" dance halls where lonely men and women from the rooming houses could get acquainted and maybe set up some light housekeeping for a week or a year, as well as tens-cents-a-dance halls, where the hookers plied their trade.

But the hobos shuffling these streets, filling the men's hotels and rooming houses, hadn't seen Jimmy Beame; at least not the ones I talked to. Or on LaSalle, Dearborn, State, or Rush streets; or the cross streets below Chicago Avenue, where dozens of flophouses had a bed—or something like a bed— for a homeless gent . . . assuming he had a quarter a night or a dollar a week. And a lot of people in Chicago didn't.

Didn't have a quarter, and didn't know who the hell Jimmy Beame was, either. That would seem to sum up the hundreds of unshaven, shabbily dressed men I showed that picture to.

I spent a day trying the flops along South Clark, South State, and West Madison—stopped in at the Dawes Hotel for Men, the skid-row charity hotel the General had founded in memory of his dead son. And got nowhere.

Back to North Clark Street. Between Clark and Dearborn streets, in Washington Square, in front of the Newberry Library, was Bug-house Square. If my father were alive, and down-and-out, he'd be here: at night, crowds of men would stand along its curbstones, lis-tening to the oratory of whoever was atop the several soapboxes, pro-pounding upon the favorite topics: the evils of capitalism, and the nonexistence of God. The more intellectual of the drifters and down-and-outers would tend to find their way here, this focal point for reds and I.W.W. sympathizers, intellectuals and agitators. My father would have been at home here.

During the daytime, the soapboxes stood vacant, mostly, and the benches and curbs were taken up by the same sort of unshaven faces I'd been looking at all day for days now (not to mention in my sleep). The major difference was a number of these shabbily dressed citizens were reading newspapers, not wearing them.

A young man on the down-and-out, disillusioned by his rejection from the great newspapers he so idolized, might well end up in Bug-house Square.

I asked several men and got a negative response; then a pale, youn-ger one with wire-frames and longish brown hair seemed to know the face.

"Yes," he said. "I know who this is."

"Are you sure?"

"Yes. It's Mary Ann Beame. She lives in a studio in Tower Town. She's an actress."

Great

"Yeah. Well, thanks, kid."

"Isn't that worth something?"

"Not really."

"I'm not begging or anything, I just think since I identified the picture . . ."

"It's the boy I'm trying to find."

"Oh. Him I don't know. Why don't you look up Mary Ann? Maybe she knows him."

"I'll try that."

"I could use fifty cents. Or a quarter. I could use some lunch."

"Sorry."

"I'm not a hobo, you understand. I'm an inventor."

"Oh really." I started to move away.

He got up from the bench; he wasn't tall; his eyes were brighter than a puppy's—in terms of shine, anyway.

"I invented a lens," he said, and reached in a corduroy jacket pocket and withdrew a round thick polished piece of glass double the size of a silver dollar.

"That's nice."

"It enables a person to see things a billion times bigger than they really are." He held it up for the sun to bounce off it; the sun was under a cloud.

"No kidding."

"I ground it myself, with emery cloth." He was walking beside me, now; he leaned in and spoke in a hushed tone, touching my arm. "I've been offered a thousand dollars for it. I'm holding out for five thousand."

I removed his hand from my arm, carefully, with a polite smile; I even made some conversation: "How'd you find out that lens was so strong?"

He smiled. Smug. Proud. "I experimented on a bedbug. I put a live bedbug under this glass, and I could see every muscle in its body. I could see its joints and how it worked them. I could see its face; no expression in its eyes, though. Bugs don't have much native intelligence, you know."

"Yeah, I heard that. So long."

He was behind me now, but calling out to me. "You couldn't do that with an ordinary lens!"

No, you couldn't.

I drank too much rum that night, and decided I had to get rid of this fucking case before it turned me into a lush.

In a little over a week I'd be going to Florida; tomorrow, I had to see Mary Ann Beame and tell her I couldn't find her brother.

CHICAGO WATER TOWER

## 13

So the next afternoon I drove north on Michigan Avenue, past the Wrigley Building and the Tribune Tower and the Medinah Athletic Club and the Allerton Hotel, toward the landmark those skyscrapers now dwarfed: the old water tower, a Gothic churchlike building with its tower thrust in the air like a gray stone finger—perhaps a middle finger, considering the talk circulating of late that the North Side's sole surivivor of the Great Fire was to be torn down to speed the flow of Michigan Avenue traffic.

The water tower, at Michigan and Chicago avenues, gave its name to Tower Town, Chicago's Greenwich Village, and was at the district's center—though the exact boundaries of Tower Town were a bit hard to define. It vaguely encroached on the Gold Coast, north of Division Street, but came to an abrupt halt at Grand Avenue, on the south. It sneaked west of Clark Street, and crossed Michigan Avenue to move eastward into Streeterville, an area named after a squatter who lived in a shack (but which now ran to some of the fanciest apartment buildings in the city). State Street was its main north-south road, and Chicago Avenue bisected it east-west.

That's *where* Tower Town was; *what* it was was streets whose "quaintly" run-down buildings housed tearooms (Ye Black Cat Club), art shops (The Neo Arlimusc), restaurants (The Dill Pickle Club), and bookstalls (The Radical Book Shop). Above the shops were garrets and "studios," as demonstrated by the flower boxes hanging from sills above, and the *Studio for Rent* signs in some of the shop windows. Like most big-city "bohemias," there was an effort, conscious or not, to attract tourists, and slummers; but on a cold Thursday at dusk, the wind blowing the snow around like a minor dust storm, its streets were empty of anybody but the young artists and students who lived here, and they tended to have hands burrowed in the pockets of their corduroy coats, moving forward without looking, which was what they were good at, after all.

I'd been to the Dill Pickle Club before; it was a landmark like the water tower. But I never expected to be back a second time. I hadn't

been impressed by the garish nude paintings on the walls, or the
dark, smoky dance floor, or the little theater that seated fewer people
in the audience than onstage, or by the stale, paper-thin chicken
sandwiches that passed for food.

Now here I was back at the Dill Pickle, sitting at a table, just me
and a candle and no tablecloth, waiting for Mary Ann Beame, trying
not to listen as at a nearby table three long-haired boys in denim and
dark sweaters talked with two short-haired girls in long black skirts
and dark sweaters. They were all smoking, all drinking coffee or tea.
Each of them seemed to be carrying on his or her own conversation.
One of them was discussing the superiority of his poetry to that of a
friend's (not present) and went on at length to point out that if *he*
were an editor he would have none of that shit in *his* poetry
magazine; oh, Harriet Monroe might, but it wasn't good enough for
*his* (nonexistent) magazine. One of the girls was discussing a recent showing of "primitive art" at the Neo Arlimusc by a sixty-two-
year-old clothing peddler from Maxwell Street who painted Jewish
sweatshop scenes on cardboard: "The artist's expression will out! Poverty-stricken, he seizes upon the only medium within his grasp!" A
pale frail-looking male was denouncing Kipling and Shakespeare (to
name two) but later spoke admiringly of Kreymborg, while another,
better-fed male was telling of his landlady throwing him out because
she couldn't understand anyone not having beds and chairs in an
apartment, and also because he had long hair. The final girl, a *zoftig*
brunette with a nice full mouth, pretended to be upset that she was
prostituting herself by posing nude as an artist's model (outside
Tower Town) for a dollar an hour; actually, she was proud of herself. I
was about ready to check my wallet for a spare dollar when Mary Ann
Beame floated in.

She was wearing the black coat with the black fur collar again. I
rose and helped her out of it, and she slung it over an extra chair at
the table I'd been eavesdropping on; nobody seemed to mind, or for
that matter notice. She wore a beret, white this time, and a navy-
blue sweater with a diagonal white zigzag pattern throughout, like
lightning, with a navy skirt. She put her little purse on the table and
sat down, her wide, Claudette Colbert eyes looking at me expec-
tantly, a little smile hesitantly forming on the red Claudette Colbert
lips.

I hadn't spoken to her on the phone: I had got a male voice at the
number she gave me, and left a message for her to meet me here, or

to call me if she couldn't. So she probably thought I had news about her brother Jimmy. I didn't.

I told her so.

"I spent five days looking," I said, " and didn't find a trace of him. Nothing to indicate he's been in Chicago at all."

She nodded patiently, the eyes narrowing a bit, but still wide enough to get lost in; the lips pursed a bit, like a kiss.

"I tried the papers, most of the Hoovervilles, combed the near North Side . . ."

"You mean you thought he might've been that close to where I live?"

"Sure. Over on North Clark Street."

"That's full of derelicts."

"Right. And I asked around Bughouse Square. I did find one guy who seemed to know you, but that's as close to a lead as I got."

"What do we do now?"

"I'd suggest give up. My guess is he changed his mind at the last minute and took that freight to California or New York or someplace  someplace other than Chicago."

"No," she said firmly, shaking her head. "His ambition was to be a reporter for the *Trib;* that's what he would've tried first."

"And he well may have. Tried, got nowhere, and hopped a freight elsewhere."

"I want you to keep looking."

"I think it would be pointless. You'd be wasting your money."

"It's my money."

"It's my time. And I don't want to spend it looking for your brother."

For a minute I thought she was going to cry; but she didn't. She thought about it, but she didn't.

"Look," I said. "He'll turn up. The country's full of kids riding the rails, looking for excitement." And work, I thought.

A big bushy-haired guy in a black sweater and denims came up to the table and took our order. I asked him how the chicken sandwiches were; he said good as ever. I ordered ham. Mary Ann waved off my suggestion that she order a sandwich and asked only for a cup of tea. I asked for some of that, too.

"Did you just come from the Merchandise Mart?" I asked.

She nodded.

"What, another soap opera?"

She nodded.

"It sounds like interesting work."

She looked away from me, toward a painting of a fat redheaded nude woman.

"Take this," I said, holding my hand out toward her.

She looked at the hand, then at me. "What's that?"

"Fifty bucks change. I worked five days. You gave me a hundred."

"Keep it," she said.

"Quit pouting and take the money, goddamnit."

She glared at me and grabbed the money out of my hand; stuffed it in her little black purse. Apparently she was a free spirit who didn't like getting sweared at.

The ham sandwich came and it was thin and stale and as bad as I remembered the chicken. The tea was okay; it tasted vaguely of oranges. I liked it. She drank hers, too, but whether she liked it or not, I can't tell you.

When we finished, I helped her into her coat and I paid and we went out onto the chilly street; it wasn't snowing, but the wind was still blowing around the snow we already had.

"You want a lift?" I asked her.

"I can walk; it isn't far."

"It's cold. My car's just down the block there. See? Come on."

She shrugged, hugging her black fur collar up around her face, falling into step with me.

I helped her up onto the running board and inside, and got around on the driver's side and got in and started it up.

"I got a heater in this thing," I said, getting that going.

"That's nice," she said noncommittally.

"Where to?"

"East Chestnut." She gave me a street address.

I drove.

"Who was that guy who answered the phone when I called today?"

"That's Alonzo."

"Oh? Who's Alonzo?"

"He's a painter."

"What's he paint?"

As if to a child, she said, "Pictures."

"What kind?"

"Experiments in dynamic symmetry, if you must know."

"Oh. Where's he live?"

"With me."

"Oh."

It was dark now, though my headlights caught the swirling snow; over on the right, two men walked hand in hand. That didn't surprise me, not in Tower Town. Just like Mary Ann living with some guy called Alonzo didn't surprise me; it disappointed me, but it didn't surprise me: it wasn't uncommon to see two names on a mailbox in this neighborhood—one a man's, the other a woman's. Unmarried couples were part and parcel of Tower Town  like the talk of free love and individualism. Women in Tower Town liked to hold on to their individuality, and their independence—and their names.

After a while, I pulled over and she started to get out.

"I'll walk you," I said.

She looked at me; thought that over. Then shrugged.

I turned the car off and followed her down the boardwalk sidewalk to a dilapidated four-story frame building. The entrance was in the alley, up an outdoor staircase that was painted red, perhaps as a political symbol, perhaps symbolizing that one took one's life in hand as well as the flimsy banister when going up those creaky stairs.

We entered a small kitchen furnished with a table, a one-burner oil stove, and a chair; there was a sink with some dirty dishes in it, and a cupboard—no icebox. The walls were bare yellow plaster, cracking; pieces had fallen off. She lay her coat and beret on the table, and said, "Would you like some tea?"

"Sure," I said.

"Take off your coat and stay awhile," she said flatly, filling an oddly shaped copper teapot at the sink.

I lay my coat on top of hers.

"Go on in and meet Alonzo," she suggested.

What the hell, I thought; I went in and met Alonzo.

He was sitting in the middle of the floor. The room was dimly lit, and so was something he was smoking: from the smell of burning incense in the room, I figured it was a muggle, a marijuana cigarette. He was a little blond boy of about twenty in a vermilion sweater and corduroys; he didn't seem to notice me come in.

It was a big room, with a high ceiling and a skylight; but there wasn't much furniture in it—just a mattress covered by messed-up blankets, and a chest of drawers against one wall, looking lonely and out of place, like it had wandered in accidentally, off the street. The walls were hung with startling modernistic paintings: loud colors, dis-

torted shapes, sound and fury signifying guess what. They hurt the
eyes; they hurt mine, anyway.

"You paint this stuff," I asked him.

"I painted them."

"Does that one have a name?" I asked, pointing to a canvas where
red, green, and blue weren't getting along.

"Certainly. That's *Man's Inhumanity to Man*."

"How'd you arrive at that?"

He looked at me with a smirk and eyes the color of soot. "The way
I arrive at all my titles."

"Which is?"

He shrugged. "When I finish a work, I hold it one way, then another, and just keep tilting it till it suggests something. Then I title
it."

"Tilt and title, huh?"

"You could put it that way."

"I just did. I take it you're Alonzo."

He stood, smiling. "You've heard of me?"

"Mary Ann mentioned you."

"Oh," he said, a little disappointed. "I talked to you on the phone
today, didn't I?"

"I believe so."

He sucked on his muggle, held the smoke in; then he spoke, and it
was like somebody speaking while taking a crap. "I suppose I'm expected to get the hell out of here."

"I wouldn't know why," I said.

"I don't do *ménage*," he said, waving both hands, including the one
with the muggle, which had served its purpose by now. He dropped
it to the wooden floor and ground it out, walked to one corner of the
room, where an old corduroy jacket was tossed, and put it on and left
me alone with the paintings.

Pretty soon Mary Ann came in with two cups and saucers. She
handed them both to me and went across the room and through a
doorless doorway into darkness. I stood there like a cigar store Indian, balancing the two cups of tea, with no furniture to set them on,
and finally walked over and used the top of the dresser for hers, and
stood sipping mine.

She came out in a trailing black kimono with red and white flowers
on it; it was belted at the waist with a black sash, and the white of her

legs flashed as she walked toward me and then stood with hands on her hips.

"How'd you like Alonzo?" she asked, arching an eyebrow.

"About as much as his paintings," I said.

She tried not to smile, then said, "I think they're good."

"Really?"

The smile won out. "No. Not really. Come on."

I followed her through the doorless doorway, which as she pulled an overhead string lit up and turned out to be a small connecting hall, with a bathroom to the right, and another room straight ahead, which she led me to.

It was a smaller room, but big enough for the four-poster bed within; the walls were draped with blue batiks and so was the ceiling. It reminded me of a booth on a midway. Against the dark blue-batiked walls were a couple of pieces of furniture, for a change, including a small dresser and a makeup table with round mirror; on the makeup table was a small cylindrical art-deco lamp that provided the only light in the room. The only window was painted out, black.

"You and Alonzo don't share . . ." I searched for a polite way to put it.

"A bedroom?" she smiled. "No. Why should we?"

I shrugged. "You live together."

"We're roommates," she nodded. "But that's the extent of it."

I sat on the edge of the four-poster, then quickly got up; but she tugged my arm until I sat again and sat next to me, with a wry little smile.

"Poor baby," she said. "You're confused."

"I just don't understand Tower Town, I guess."

"Alonzo likes boys."

"You mean he's a fairy?"

"That's it."

"Oh. And you're sharing rent, then."

"That's right. It's a nice big studio apartment, but it took the two of us to throw in together to be able to afford it."

"Why Alonzo?"

"We're friends. He's an actor as well as a painter. We did a play together, with the Impertinent Players. You know . . . a little theater group."

"Oh."

"Would you like some more tea?"

"No. No, thanks.

She took the cup from me and went trailing out, flashing some more white skin.

I glanced around the room. Over the head of the four-poster was a pale electric quarter-moon, with a man-in-the-moon face, turned off.

She came back in the room, sat next to me.

"Do you smoke that stuff?" I said, gesturing to the other room.

"Muggles? No. I don't even drink. I was raised in a proper home; we never had that sort of thing around, and I never acquired an interest in it, let alone a taste."

"But you don't mind him doing it?"

"Alonzo doesn't drink."

"I meant smoke marijuana."

"No, I don't mind. Alonzo's no dopey, no viper, mind you; he just does that once in a while, to relax. When he paints, or before he goes out to . . . well, to look for a date."

"Does he . . . bring his dates here?"

"Sometimes. But he tells me first, if he's planning to. And I can stay in my room and study lines, if I'm in a play; or just read or sleep."

"It doesn't bother you, what's going on out there?"

"Why should it?"

I didn't have an answer for that.

"The motto around here," she explained, "is live your own life. *Live*, don't just exist."

"Most people these days find just existing tough enough."

She didn't have an answer for that.

"I'm glad to be in your bedroom," I said. "You're a lovely girl, and that's a lovely kimono, and you make a swell cup of tea. But I'm still not going to look for your brother anymore."

I thought that would make her mad; it didn't.

She said, "I know," a bit distantly.

"Then why did you bring me up here?"

Now she did get just a little bit mad; just a little. "Not to bribe you, if that's what you think. There's plenty of other detectives in town."

"That's right, and some of the larger agencies could track your brother nationwide, if you got the dough for it."

"I'm psychologically connected to my brother."

"What?"

"My psychiatrist says that most of my problems are connected to my being a twin. I feel incomplete because my brother is missing."

"You have a psychiatrist?"

"Yes."

"And he says you feel incomplete because your brother is missing?"

"No. I say that. He says most of my problems are connected to my being a twin."

"What problems?"

She shrugged. "He didn't say."

"Why do you go to him?"

"Alonzo suggested it."

"Why?"

"He thinks I'll improve as an actress if I get in touch with my primitive unconscious."

"This is Alonzo's theory, not the psychiatrist's?"

"That's right."

"How much does the psychiatrist cost?"

"Quite a bit."

"How much, if you don't mind my asking?"

"Five dollars an hour."

I sat there and burned. Five dollars an hour. I cut my twenty-buck-a-day rate to ten for her, because I feel sorry for the struggling young actress trying to make it in the big city, and end up shlepping around Hoovervilles and fucking North Clark Street flophouses for five days, and she's paying five dollars an hour to some Michigan Avenue witch doctor.

She said, "Why does that make you mad?"

"What?"

"That I go to a psychiatrist. Why does that make you mad?"

"I've just been looking into too many unshaven faces, lately, that's all."

"I don't understand."

"Men are selling apples on street corners and praying to pull in a buck a day, and you're pissing five bucks away for nonsense."

"That's cruel."

"I suppose. And it's your five bucks. You can do what you want with it."

She didn't say anything; she was looking at her hands, which were folded in her lap.

"You must make good money doing radio," I said.

"Not bad," she admitted. "And I can get money from home, if I need to."

We sat in silence for a while.

I said, "It really isn't my business what you do with your money. Guys selling apples on street corners isn't your fault . . . and your five bucks isn't going to solve the problem, so forget I said anything. Like I said, I seen too many unshaven faces while I was wandering around Hoovervilles, looking for your brother."

"You think my life's a bunch of hooey, don't you."

"I don't know. I don't go for Tower Town, that's all. All this free love you people talk about, it doesn't seem right somehow."

She smiled, teasingly. "You'd rather pay for it, is that it?"

I smiled back, against my will. "That's not what I meant."

She kissed me.

It was kind of a long kiss; and very sweet. Her lips were soft. Warm. Her lipstick was sticky.

"You taste better than a candy apple," I said.

"Have another bite," she said, and I kissed her, and my tongue slid in her mouth and it seemed to surprise her, but she liked it; she must've, because she slid hers in mine.

And that kimono slid off her shoulders and my hands were on her cool, pale flesh. Her body was soft as her lips, but muscular, too; almost a dancer's body. Her breasts weren't large—just nice handfuls; pretty handfuls with small, little-girl nipples, the areola not much bigger 'round than a piece of Lifesaver candy, with a nipple where the hole would be.

She began to undress me, kissing me while she did, and I helped, and soon we were under the covers in the four-poster. We lay kissing, petting, then as I was about to get on her, she said, "Wait."

"Do you want me to use something?" I asked. I had a Sheik in my billfold.

"No," she said, getting out of bed, going to her makeup table and switching off the lamp. She went out of the room and into the bathroom and came back with a towel, which she lay on the bed, positioning herself on it, then with a pixie smile reached a hand up and turned on the electric moon.

I tried to enter her gently, but it was difficult; she was small, tight.

"Am I hurting you?"

"No," she said. Kissing me. Smiling at me like a ghostly angel.

And I was in all the way.

It was only a few minutes, but it was a wonderful few minutes, and when she came, a moan came out of her that had pain and pleasure in it but transcended both; I came a moment later, withdrawing, spilling onto the towel she'd positioned herself on.

"No," she said, sadly, touching my face. "You should've stayed in me."

I eased off, looked at her; I was on my side. "I thought you wanted me to," I said, and motioned toward where the towel was.

She smiled enigmatically and said, "No. That's not what it was for."

She gathered the towel and got up from the bed; she didn't mean for me to see, but I did: the towel was bloodstained.

I leaned back, waiting for her to return. *Oh*, I thought, *she's in her period*.

Then I realized something.

She came back, got in bed, got into my arms.

I looked at her; she still had that cryptic little smile.

"You were a virgin," I said.

"Who says?"

"I say. You were a virgin!"

"Does that matter?"

I pushed her away, gently; sat up.

"Of course it does," I said.

She sat up, too. "Why are you disturbed?"

"I would never have . . ."

"That's why I didn't tell you."

"But you can't be a virgin."

"I'm not."

"Don't play games."

"I'm not."

"How old are you?"

"Twenty-three."

"And you're an actress living in Tower Town, sharing a studio with some fairy artist and seeing a psychiatrist and talking about free love and living not existing, and you were a *virgin*?"

"Maybe the right man finally came along."

"If you did this so I'd keep looking for your brother, all I've got to say is, it's maybe the one bribe nobody in Chicago ever thought of before."

"It wasn't a bribe."

"Do you—love me or something, Mary Ann?"

"I think that's maybe a little premature. What do you think?"

"I think I better find your brother."

She snuggled close to me. "Thanks, Nathan."

"I can't look into it again for a few weeks. I've got some other business to do—Retail Credit work—and then I'm going to Florida on a matter."

"That's fine, Nathan."

"Aren't you sore?"

"About what?"

"No, I mean aren't you *sore?* You know. Down there."

"Why don't you find out."

The electric moon smiled.

MIAMI, 1933

## 14

Cold hit Chicago like a fist. The wind conspired with the falling temperature and turned the city to ice; then eleven inches of snow joined in, turning it white. Those people in the Hoovervilles I'd talked to not so long ago probably made it through okay, because they at least had shacks to live in and sometimes a barrel with something burning in it to huddle 'round. But the down-and-outers in the parks froze. To death. Not all of them, but enough of them—though it didn't get much play in the papers. Not good publicity in the year of the fair. Of course the major role the papers played in the lives of the down-and-outers was insulation: wear it over your heart if you hope to wake up in the morning. I wondered if the guy who'd passed that piece of wisdom along to me had woken up this morning.

Me, I was in Florida, wearing a white suit, soaking up the sun, smelling the salt breeze. Men on the streets were in shirt sleeves and straw hats; women wore summery dresses and tanned legs. The buildings were as white as Chicago's blizzard—though the similarity ended there—and the palm trees along Biscayne Boulevard leaned, as if bored with sunshine. Mayor Cermak should get in town late this afternoon; the blond man Frank Nitti was sending to meet Cermak might already be here.

The first thing I did, when I got off the Dixie Express at a little after seven on this Wednesday morning, was pay a cabbie to take me to the nearest used car lot. A guy in his shirt sleeves with a gold incisor that reflected the Miami sun sold me a '28 Ford coupe for forty dollars. It didn't exactly run like a million bucks—it ran like forty bucks—but it ran, and soon I was having a look around the Magic City.

It was a synthetic paradise, like a movie's elaborate background painting that was supposed to fool you into thinking it was real, but didn't quite make it—and you didn't quite care, because there was a charm to it, to the ice-cream buildings, the transplanted tropical foliage, the bay so blue it made the sky seem not blue enough, the skyline that rose off the flat terrain like Chicago in the imagination of an eight-year-old child. Twenty years ago, this was mangrove swamp, sand dunes, coral rock. Jungle. Now it was a playground for the rich, and the only sign of anyone remembering it having been a jungle was the pith helmets worn by the cops directing traffic, their uniforms pale blue, belted white.

Despite hard times, Miami seemed to be doing good business. On showy Biscayne Boulevard, the palm-lined four lane that ran parallel to the sprawling, tropically landscaped Bayfront Park, cars with license plates from all forty-eight states (including, at times, Florida) could be spotted, by anyone so inclined. The shopping district, west of Bayfront Park, was a dozen blocks of predominantly narrow, one-way streets and was a Florida version of Maxwell Street and State Street, slapped together: open-front shops sold fruit boxes and juice, and neckties with colorful hand-painted designs, and ashtrays the shape of the state; department-store manikins lounged in display windows, wearing swimsuits and sunglasses, and contemplated tossing the beach ball around; photo galleries invited patrons to pose before cardboard seashores while holding up a huge stuffed fish and leaning against what purported to be a palm; Seminole families in full tribal regalia sat in curio shops to attract the curious (and their money); theater doormen in elaborate paramilitary attire hawked the latest screen thrill, while corner pitchmen offered suntan lotion and racing forms—the latter an especially hot commodity. As I waited for the light to change on Flagler Street, a newsboy about ten years my elder sold me a Miami *Herald*, but when I said I didn't want a racing form too, he gave me a look like I'd said I didn't like women.

I didn't see many down-and-outers as I strolled around downtown Miami, but there were some women in their thirties in pretty summer frocks, housewives I'd guess, who approached occasional pale-face tourist types like myself, requesting "a penny a day to keep hunger away from somebody out of a job"; they weren't begging for themselves, of course—the little boxes they carried said "Dade County Welfare Board." Another woman, this one in her forties, but also rather nicely dressed, approached me and handed me a leaflet; she was with the Citizens Taxation Committee—despite falling property values, taxes were being kept at "Boom" levels of earlier years, it seemed.

"Something must be done about the mayor," she said, with her mouth a firm line, her eyes hard behind wire-frames.

I nodded agreement, and went into a restaurant called the Dinner

Bell, where I had roast beef, peas, coffee, and apple pie for fifteen cents. A blond guy was sitting at a table nearby, drinking lemonade; he wore a white short-sleeve shirt and gray suspenders and buff trousers, and was about the right age. But he wasn't the blond guy I was looking for. Neither were half a dozen other blond men who passed me on the street that I gave as careful a once-over as I had him.

It wouldn't be that easy. I wanted it to be—I wanted to just bump into the blond killer on the street and put my gun in his back and duck him into an alley and slam his head into a wall and, if he was walking around unarmed (which he might be, till he closed in on his target), plant my gun in his pocket and drop him off anonymously on the doorstep of a hospital or a police station, like an unwanted babe. His packing a pistol would be enough to assure him a few days at the expense of Dade County, which should keep him out of circulation till Cermak headed home.

Or I could hang a close tail on him, let him lead me to his hotel. That would allow me to see if he was working with a backup man, in which case I'd plant the gun on the blond and sic a cop on him, and the backup man would probably fade away. As for any confrontation with the blond himself, the best thing would be to clobber him from behind, bad enough to put him in the hospital, but not kill him; another possibility was holding him captive in his room (and running up his room service bill while I did) till Cermak left town. But an approach like that would mean he'd see me, get a good look at me, and the backup man (if there was one) would probably have to be dealt with head on, too, all of which could have nasty repercussions concussion seemed the better approach.

The gun I'd plant on him, incidentally, would not be mine: it would be the .38 Colt Police Special that had been delivered to my office by messenger, along with my train tickets, five hundred dollars expense money, and a letter from the office of Florida's attorney general authorizing Nathan Heller to operate as a private investigator in Florida (including a temporary gun permit). Attorney Louis Piquett apparently had some friends in high places in Florida—or rather Al Capone did. Despite some public posturing by state and city officials when he showed up in Florida, around '28, Capone had been a welcome addition to the community—in fact, a fellow named Lummus, Miami's mayor at the time, was the real estate agent who sold Capone a mansion on Biscayne Bay.

There was no explanation as to why the gun had been sent; none was needed. Capone assumed there was at least the possibility of my killing the man I'd been sent to stop; toward that end, he'd provided something that couldn't be traced to me. I took my automatic along as well, having immediately had the thought of using the Piquett-furnished gun as a plant, should I happen upon the blond gunman prior to any attempt on Cermak's life.

Which was a fantasy I'd nurtured all the way down here on the Express, sitting by the window, watching the midwestern snow dissolve into the bluegrass of Kentucky; crossing rivers, cutting through valleys, skirting mountains, stopping at cities. An American panorama slid by me, and I saw it all . . . and none of it, because I was thinking about that blond assassin.

And now I was walking the crowded downtown streets of Miami, realizing how futile my fantasy was. There was only one way to do this job; I'd known it all the time, but had pretended not to. I had to shadow Cermak and wait till the blond showed up; in effect, wait until the attempt on Cermak's life was about to be made. And *then* stop it.

It was risky, to say the least: for Cermak, certainly, but for me, too. The smart thing to do would've been to turn this assignment down. Only it was never smart to turn Al Capone down. It was also never smart to turn down ten thousand dollars, which is what my client had promised me, after all—on the minor condition that I succeed.

So I did some groundwork. I got back in my forty-buck Ford and crossed the county causeway, passing by Palm Island (where the Capone masion was), white sunlight bouncing off pleasure-craft-cluttered Biscayne Bay. Then I was on the ten-mile-long, considerably narrower island that was Miami Beach, following Collins Avenue north through a collage of pseudo-Mediterranean hotels and apartment houses and mansions that (of course) faced the beach, with accompanying terraces and swimming pools (for those who found the Atlantic too crowded or salty or whatever). I rolled by white sand splashed with color by sun umbrellas and bathing-suited figures that scurried to and from cabanas bigger than my office back home; and glimpsed golf courses, private landing docks, the bougainvillea-spread walls of palatial estates, and palm-sheltered coves where yachts moored and speedboats raced. No Hoovervilles, though.

In a subdivision off Collins Avenue, away from the Atlantic and toward a placid lagoon called Indian Creek, were some comparatively modest homes, not mansions, just vacation bungalows with a meager three or four bedrooms. One of these homes, which were spaced rather far apart with well-tended but not overly tropical front yards, was the winter home of Mayor Cermak's son-in-law, a doctor who, not coincidentally, had recently been appointed Illinois Director of Public Health. A rather modern-looking single-level stucco house, set back from the street and partially obscured by shrubs and palms, this was where Cermak was likely to be staying. I parked my car on the street and walked up the lawn, where a gardener was working on the shrubs by the house.

"Hello," I said.

The gardener, a dark little bowlegged man in coveralls and a floppy hat, turned and glanced at me with a moronic smile and kept clipping the hedge as he did.

"I'm with the Miami *Herald*," I said. "I was wondering when Mayor Cermak is expected."

"He come pretty soon," the man said. Cuban?

"How soon?"

"Tonight sometime." He kept clipping.

"Is anybody home?"

"They not down here."

"Who?"

"The family. They in Chicago."

"Okay. Thanks."

He smiled some more, and then started looking at what he was doing.

I went back to the Ford. So much for Cermak's own security: that guy would've told John Wilkes Booth where Lincoln was sitting. On the other hand, Cermak would undoubtedly have a fleet of bodyguards with him, and security would be stepped up once he moved in.

Next stop was Coral Gables, which joined Miami on the west and, while not as overtly wealthy as Miami Beach, was a well-to-do little community. Some overly zealous city planner had put in a cream-color stucco archway you drove under as you "entered," limited the buildings to a mock-Spanish design, stuck matching awnings on everything, and tinted the sidewalks coral. The Miami Biltmore Hotel loomed above this contrived, palm-bordered landscape, a sprawling hacienda gone out of control, with a central tower adjoining an assortment of wings to face in a gently curving C the putting greens that were its lawn.

The attendant who took my car didn't seem to believe I could be staying at a place this grand; neither could I. I hauled my shabby suitcase across a lobby of potted palms and overstuffed furniture and potted, overstuffed politicos, who were scattered about the lobby in groups of three to six, smoking cigars, laughing, talking loud, having the grand sort of time the victors have when they've been dividing up the spoils.

FDR's right-hand man, Jim Farley—who was to be his postmaster general, and was currently his patronage chief—was not among the Demos loitering about the Biltmore lobby. But his presence was felt: between puffs of cigar and dirty stories were speculations about who would get what, and it was Farley these men were in Miami to see. It was Farley who was Cermak's target.

I had a reservation, and a bellboy took me up to a room with a double-bed and a view of the golf course. It was two in the afternoon; I called the desk and asked for a wake-up call in two hours. I went to sleep immediately, and when the phone rang, I jumped awake. But I felt rested.

I shaved and threw water on my face and got back into the white suit; I had a Panama and sunglasses, too. I looked like a few thousand other people in Miami. I left my suitcase in my suite, but took the two guns with me, my automatic in my shoulder holster (it didn't bulge much under the coat) and the .38 in my belt, where its short barrel nudged my lower belly.

The train station was in downtown Miami, on First off Flagler, near the majestic Dade County Courthouse, a big Gothic wedding cake of a building whose layers rose twenty-eight stories. The Florida East Coast Railway Station, on the other hand, was a long, low-slung mustard-color wood-and-brick affair with an arched overhanging roof from which a large sign said MIAMI, in case you forgot what town you were in: a dinosaur of a building left over from pre-boom Miami, a frontier-style station where you might expect to catch a stagecoach instead of a train. I left the Ford in the parking lot in back and wandered inside, where I bought a Miami *Daily News* at the newsstand, and found a place on the end of one of the slatted high-backed benches where I could get a view of all doors, and could sit and pretend to read while I watched and waited.

It was five, and Cermak was due in at six. The place was pretty empty when I first got there, but began to fill up quickly with others who, like me, were meeting folks arriving on the Royal Poinciana, which was what the Dixie Flyer out of Chicago turned into at Jacksonville.

I saw several pretty young women—white teeth flashing in tanned faces, tanned legs flashing under colorful print dresses—and exchanged flirty smiles with those who weren't arm in arm with a sweetheart, and a few who were, when the sweetheart wasn't looking. It occurred to me that this wouldn't be a bad town to get laid in. Unfortunately, every time I saw a blonde, it reminded me of my quarry; and every time I saw a dark-haired girl—particularly one with short dark hair—I thought of Mary Ann Beame.

That blond killer hadn't been the only thing my mind had turned over and over, obsessively, on the train ride to Miami. Mary Ann Beame was dancing around my brain like Isadora Duncan; she'd really done a job on me. I hadn't been with that many women. I was no virgin, of course—but I thought the same of her. And it disturbed me. I thought maybe I was in love with her. I also thought she was using me, like an actor in a play she was directing in the little theater of her mind. I never wanted to see her again; I wished I was with her now.

Why *not* pick up a Florida filly for the night? I didn't owe Mary Ann Beame anything; she was just a client. So she'd given me her virginity; so what? It was just another retainer, wasn't it?

Well, I wasn't in Miami for the sunshine. I was here on a thousand-dollar retainer, which wasn't exactly anybody's cherry, but it was nothing you'd want to lose easily, either. And my night was already planned for me: I'd have to stick by His Honor, when he showed up, possibly through the night. That's why I'd grabbed the two hours sleep at the Biltmore; that's why I had a Thermos of hot coffee waiting in the Ford.

Pretending to read the front page of the *News* for an hour led to my actually reading most of it, in bits and pieces. There was news of Chicago; it had been two days since I had left, after all, the snow just starting. The storm had paralyzed the city, but fifteen thousand of the unemployed had been hired to dig out Cook County, and efforts to provide relief housing for the down-and-outers in the parks and Hooverville residents had been stepped up. So there were no more deaths by freezing, though some emergency snow-shovelers got hit by streetcars or had heart attacks. That was as far as the *News* article went. No doubt some of the Chicago papers were cheeky enough to point out that Mayor Cermak left for Florida just after the storm hit: even in the year of the fair, that couldn't go unreported.

General Dawes was on the front page, too. He was in Washington, D.C., subpoenaed by the Senate Stock Exchange Committee to testify about his role in connection with Samuel Insull. Insull was the utilities tycoon who during the twenties headed companies worth some $4 billion and had a personal fortune around $150 million. There was a new board game I had played with Janey a few times: Monopoly. Insull had turned the business of electricity and gas, and railroads, into a game of that; and when he was finished, his paper empire was worth about as much as the little colored "money" you used to buy Boardwalk.

Just two years ago, the Chicago banks were turning the city's requests for loans down and honoring Insull's; one of those loans came from the Dawes bank, to the tune of $11 million. Now the General was in front of a Senate committee, and Insull was in Europe somewhere.

Not that anything would come of it: the General would weasel his platitudinous way out of it. But the fact that this had made the front page of the Miami *Daily News* meant that the embarrassment was nationwide—hardly the sort of publicity the General might hope for, in the year of the fair. It made me smile.

More pertinent to my present interests was the small inset article announcing a testimonial dinner for James A. Farley, chairman of the Democratic National Executive Committee, to be held by the Roosevelt for President Club at the Biltmore Saturday. Also as honored guests would be "a group of leading Democrats who are guests of metropolitan Miami this week." That would include Cermak, undoubtedly. Tickets were two dollars each and reservations could be made at the Biltmore. Looked like I better rent a tux. I wondered if I could rent one my automatic wouldn't unduly bulge under.

It was ten till six, and I'd seen a lot of pretty girls, but no blond killer. Normally, that would be okay with me; but any hope of my getting this over with quickly was slipping away. I'd have to be Cermak's shadow for the next few days or week or however long His Honor decided to stay in a sunnier clime; and tailing somebody who knows you isn't the easiest thing in the world to pull off, particularly over a relatively long stretch of time.

You met the trains outside, in front of the station, right out in the middle of the street, with the courthouse looming at left. The sun was on its way down, but it wasn't quite twilight yet, and I felt conspicuous, though I probably wasn't. It was just light enough out to justify leaving the sunglasses on, and I leaned against the building and watched the people waiting, watched the Royal Poinciana come up the middle of a Miami street. Then it was a scramble of redcaps with carts and porters and people getting off the train and others greeting them. Several of the pretty girls I'd been daydreaming about met their husbands or boyfriends and walked out of my life. I watched for the blond. He could be meeting the train; he could even have been on it. I didn't see him.

I saw Cermak. He came down off the train, looking overweight and tired, a hand on his stomach, a conductor helping him down the couple steps. Two watchful bodyguards preceded him—one of them was the son of Chicago's chief of detectives, a pale fellow about thirty; the other was Mulaney, the skinny cop I'd seen in Cermak's suite at the Congress, that time with Miller.

Speaking of whom, Miller and Lang followed Cermak off the train, and I said a silent *Shit*. I'd hoped they wouldn't be along; I'd hoped their notoriety in the Nitti matter would've precluded Cermak's bringing them. But here they were.

Now my work was really cut out for me. The chances of Lang and Miller making me were far greater than Cermak, who might not recognize me if I walked right up to him; to him, I was just another nobody. But with Miller and Lang around, I'd have to keep my distance.

On the other hand, the four bodyguards, and their watchfulness, indicated Cermak was somewhat aware of the danger he was in. It meant this Florida trip might be at least partially an attempt to get away from Chicago till it cooled off, figuratively speaking.

Well, there was no blond killer here to greet the mayor. Instead, two wealthy-looking businessman-types in their late fifties approached him with smiles and outstretched hands. Cermak's tiredness fell away like a discarded garment and he beamed at them, his cheeks turning red, immediately pumping their hands like the politician he was. All the while, the four bodyguards kept around him, almost circling him, looking the crowd over. No one from the press seemed to be present; no fanfare at all, just these two businessman friends, who stood and talked with Cermak while a redcap rounded up his luggage.

I kept well back as I followed them around the station to the parking lot behind. Cermak and his wealthy-looking friends (who seemed to be apologizing for Miami's shabby train station) and Miller got into one of two waiting chauffeured Lincolns. So did Lang and the other two bodyguards; the luggage went with them.

I followed them over the county causeway to Miami Beach; as I expected, they went to Cermak's son-in-law's house. I didn't turn down the street after them, but pulled over and waited till they'd had a chance to unload the Lincoln and go inside. It was twilight by the time I parked across the road and down three quarters of a block, in the shadow of some palms, to keep watch.

The night was cool; I rolled the windows most of the way up, locked the doors, and sat in the back seat. That may sound stupid to you, but it's standard procedure: a person in the back seat is less noticeable, and people at a glance see only the empty front seat and assume the car has been parked and left.

Between eight and eleven, Cermak had several visitors: several more prominent-looking types—I thought I recognized Chicago millionaire John Hertz—called on him. So did a carload of what I took to be politicos, come over from the Biltmore. Once in a while one of the bodyguards could be seen strolling across the front yard. That was a good sign, actually: if Cermak's bodyguards were keeping on their toes, I wouldn't have to keep an all-night surveillance.

I stayed till two, and noticed that a shift of bodyguards was keeping watch; once an hour, one of them—so far it had been the young son of the chief of detectives, followed by thin, pale Mulaney—would prowl around the lawn with a flashlight and a gun.

I drove back to the Biltmore and put in for a wake-up call at six. By seven I was sitting down the street from Cermak again, down the other way, three quarters of a block. It was raining; it was cold. Florida was doing its best to make us Chicagoans feel at home.

At eight, a chauffeured limo drove up to the house, and in a few minutes, Cermak and his four bodyguards were getting in, Mulaney holding an umbrella for the mayor.

I followed them back to the Biltmore. That was no surprise: I expected Cermak to meet with Farley as soon as possible. I waited till they were inside before turning the Ford over to the attendant; when I got into the lobby, Cermak was glad-handing it with six or seven politicians who were gathered around him, protecting him at least as well as the bodyguards, who seemed nervous about the crowd. I threaded my way through the lobby, but didn't see the blond—just the cigar-puffing, bullshitting Demos.

A buck bought me Farley's floor from a bellboy, and I went up and looked around: no bodyguards. Apparently Cermak was the only politician here on the run from gangsters. I waited around the corner from the elevators and listened as Cermak and his bodyguards and a couple of other men loudly got off. They went directly to Farley's room; I ducked down the stairs before Lang and Miller and company had a chance to look the floor over.

I had breakfast in the restaurant downstairs, and sat in the lobby and pretended to read the paper again. At eleven-thirty all heads turned as Farley, a big, bald-headed, pleasant-looking man, and a beaming Cermak, bodyguards bringing up his considerable rear, paraded across the Biltmore lobby. This public display meant the Roosevelt forces were at least pretending to be making up with Cermak for his failure to back their boy at the Chicago convention.

They went out and got in a Cadillac limo that was apparently Farley's, with only Miller accompanying Cermak. The other bodyguards followed in the Lincoln. I followed in the Ford.

Soon I was driving along an avenue of royal palms towering eighty or one hundred feet, and up ahead was Hialeah Park Racetrack. Amid more palms was the massive, vine-covered grandstand with its bougainvillea-overgrown trelliswork. It was early, but there were plenty of people, despite the damp weather (the rain had let up but the sky remained overcast), and I had plenty of faces to look at.

Farley, Cermak, and crew disappeared into the clubhouse, a little Spanish villa whose back was turned to the grandstand. They went in the side entrance, next to the grandstand, up wide steps that passed a terraced porch where millionaires sat behind a wrought-iron fence, like prisoners, and lunched. I followed Farley's party, or tried to: they went in through an archway, where a guy a bit too big to be a jockey was dressed like one. He stopped me.

"Are you a member, sir?" he asked.

"Pardon?"

"A member of the Jockey Club. It's a private club, sir."

"I'm sorry. I thought it was just a restaurant."

"It's a fine restaurant, sir. But you have to be a member."

I reached in my pocket. "No temporary memberships?"

Deadpan, he said, "No, sir. Excuse me."

That meant I was supposed to leave.

I hung around in front of the grandstand, studying the crowd.

At one-thirty, Farley and Cermak and an ever-increasing entourage went in to watch the races. So did I. They shared a special, centrally located box. I got as close as I felt prudent, and used the binoculars I rented from a vendor to study the crowd around the box.

I didn't place any bets; the damp, grass track would've made handicapping unreliable, anyway. But the crowd—the dampness had kept no one away, apparently, except maybe my blond quarry—was having a loud, roaring time; many familiar faces from the Biltmore lobby were among the spectators, and they particularly were having a ball.

Even on this dreary day, Hialeah was impressive. It was a new track, built just a year or so ago, or actually rebuilt, as a track had been operating here since 1925, even though legal pari-mutuel betting didn't come to Florida till '31. But Joe Widener, the man who had reportedly spent fifty grand getting that bill pushed through at Tallahassee, had transformed Hialeah into something special. Along the backstretch was a green wall of feathery pines, against which the jockeys' colors were a bright, bold moving design. The wide oval track surrounded a huge, landscaped area where lawns and flower beds circled a lake that seemed to be a bed of pink water lilies. The water lilies were actually a couple hundred pink flamingos.

"How do they keep those birds quiet?" I asked the guy next to me, between races. "Why don't they flap around more, with all the horses galloping and gunshots and everything?"

He shrugged. "They catch 'em down in Cuba and bring 'em up here and then clip their wings."

I thought about that. The pool of pink flamingos had seemed beautiful; now it didn't.

I had a hot dog and a Coke. The voice on the loudspeaker was getting the crowd worked up over today's big race, the Bahama Cup, which may have explained why so big a crowd was here on so dismal a day. I took a look at Cermak and Farley through the binoculars. They were all smiles, but the smiles seemed forced; they seemed to be talking, more than watching the race. Anyway, Cermak did. Maybe things hadn't gone as well at their meeting this morning as the mayor's smile in the Biltmore lobby might've led one to believe.

The Coke went right through me, and during the Bahama Cup, I figured it would be a good time to hit their normally crowded public facility. I walked out of the stands down to the john and went in. I had it to myself; I stood and emptied my bladder, and thought about what a dull business it was I was in.

A hand settled on my shoulder.

I looked back.

It was Miller. Lang was just behind him. Their smiles were as dull as their eyes.

"Zip up, Heller," Miller said. "You're coming with us."

LANG AND MILLER

## 15

I zipped up.

Unbuttoned my coat.

Turned around slowly and smiled. "Nice room you got," I said, reaching back, flushing the urinal. "You guys're lucky to find something so suited to you, at the peak of the tourist season. Close to the track and all."

"I said, you're coming with us, wise guy," Miller said, and grabbed my right arm.

With my left I jerked the Police Special out of my waistband and buried it in Miller's gut so hard it backed him up; but I followed him, and the gun stayed where it was, as I reached in under his suitcoat and got his .45 revolver.

I backed him right into a toilet stall, and said, "Sit."

He sat.

Lang had his mouth open and his gun out, a .45 revolver; his .38 was back in Chicago being held as evidence in the forthcoming Nitti trial.

I pointed the Police Special at the seated Miller and Miller's .45 at Lang. Pretty soon Lang put his gun away, holding his hands out, palms up, empty, and put on a small but ridiculous conciliatory smile.

I didn't put my guns away.

I said, "You boobs are finished telling me where to go."

"Go to hell," Miller said, still sitting.

I leaned in the stall and rapped him on the side of the head with the Police Special; his hat fell off, hitting a damp spot near the stool. He wasn't bleeding, but he wasn't cracking wise anymore, either.

Lang had taken this as an opportunity to move on me, and he was as fast as a fat old lady; I slapped him with Miller's .45 and he went down on his side. He bled, a little. I put the Police Special away, dropped the .45 in the refuse bin, went over and got Lang a couple of paper towels, got one of them wet at the sink, tossed 'em to him.

"Did you guys want to talk to me or something?" I asked.

Lang, on the floor, and Miller, from his stall, exchanged glances; they were big men, and the two of them together could certainly take me. But the Police Special was stuck in my waistband where I could get at it quickly, and they knew my mood was such that going any further with this was going to be expensive.

About this time a man came in and took a leak. With Lang on the floor, and Miller sitting on the stool with his pants up, and me with a thumb and a gun in my waistband, it was obvious something was going on; so the guy didn't bother washing his hands. He probably only did half of what he came to.

"There's better places to talk," Lang said, getting up, brushing himself off. Miller was coming slowly out of the stall, examining the damp spot on his hat, keeping his owllike face blank, but the eyes behind the Coke-bottle lenses were seething.

I buttoned my coat. "Let's go talk outside," I said.

I held the door for them.

The results of the Bahama Cup were being announced over the loudspeaker, and enough people must've placed the right bet, because a cheer went up. We walked down out of the stands and down the stairs onto the lavishly landscaped grounds of Hialeah Park. We found a palm tree to stand under, which was no trick.

"What's going on, Heller?" Lang said. It wasn't a demand: my presence here, understandably, had him confused, and he seemed to be doing his best not to come on tough.

"I'm down here on business," I said. "For a client. An attorney."

Miller, who was standing behind Lang like another palm, said, "What are you doing carrying a heater?"

"I'm here as a private cop," I said. "I'm licensed to work in Florida, and I got a special permit to carry a gun. I'm legal and aboveboard. You boys are nothing but glorified bodyguards, in Miami. Not that you're anything else in Chicago. But you got no jurisdiction here. You got no call to put the strong-arm on me, or anybody."

Miller was openly scowling, now, but Lang was thinking that over.

"Okay," he said. "That sounds reasonable, I guess. What were you doing watching the mayor?"

"What do you mean?"

"We caught the sun glinting off your binoculars, Heller. You been watching Cermak, and he ain't running today."

"Maybe he should be," I said.

Miller said, "What's that supposed to mean?"

"I'll tell Tony," I said. "That's who I'll talk to. Not his stooges."

Lang thought some more. "The mayor can't be bothered right now. He's with some VIPs at the moment."

"He's begging Jim Farley for scraps, you mean."

Lang and Miller looked at each other; it bothered them that I even knew who Farley was.

I surprised them some more: "Is Tony going to move to the Biltmore, now, or stay at his son-in-law's place again?"

That really threw them.

"What do you mean?" Lang said.

"Just answer."

Lang shrugged. "His son-in-law's."

"Is he going to see Farley again tonight?"

Lang didn't answer.

"If he isn't," I said, "I could drop by around seven."

"I'll have to ask the mayor," Lang said.

"Why don't you?"

Lang looked at Miller, motioned with his head to come along, and the two went back up into the grandstand.

The rain had let up; the sun peeked through the palms. Some people started to drift out of the stands, now that the Cup was over. Panama hats and pretty women.

Lang came back alone.

He said, "The mayor says he'd like to meet with you in a public place."

"Why?"

"Maybe he thinks there's less likely to be trouble. He's got some people coming to the house this evening, and doesn't want you there, okay?"

"Okay. Where?"

The Miami Aquarium was a beached ship, the *Prinz Valdemar*, an old Danish barkentine that sank in a storm in the early twenties, blocking the harbor, paralyzing shipping traffic for months. A hurricane in '26 raised the ship and left it on the beach, like driftwood; but it was mostly intact, and in '27 it was turned into an aquarium. At the entrance of the white four-masted ship-turned-building, pretty girls in pirate outfits drew sketches of patrons, for a modest fee. I stood and let a dazzling brunette do mine and gave her a buck and she gave me a smile and if she hadn't made me start thinking of Mary

Ann Beame, I might have done something about it. Behind her, two monkeys chained to a revolving ladder went round and round—like my thoughts.

I strolled through the ship and looked at the glassed-in exhibits: sea turtles, alligators, crocodiles, a couple sea cows, stingrays, sharks, morays, and a slew of mounted specimens. On the upper deck of the sand-locked ship was a restaurant, where Cermak was waiting.

Cermak had a table at portside, perhaps so he could have Miller and Lang toss me overboard—they sat at a separate table opposite him, behind the chair where I'd be sitting; the other two bodyguards were at a table at His Honor's back. At any rate, we had a ringside view of Biscayne Bay, which at twilight was like a mirage, its many houseboats and yachts looking small, unreal, like toys floating in a big blue-gray bath.

The mayor was in a dark gray suit with a blue bow tie, and he rose from the table—there was no one else there—and extended his hand and gave me a smile that must have looked friendly to anybody looking at us. The eyes behind the dark-rimmed glasses were as cold as I remembered.

I shook the hand; as before, it seemed a trifle damp. Whether from nerves or a recent trip to the lavatory, I didn't know. He gestured for me to sit and I did.

"I'm surprised to see you in Miami, Mr. Heller," Cermak said, still standing, looking down at me.

"Make it 'Nate.'"

"Fine," he said, sitting, putting his napkin in his lap. "Fine. I hope you like lobster. I took the liberty of picking one out for you."

"Sure. Thanks."

A busboy in white sailor garb came and poured us both some water, asked if we'd like some coffee, and we said yes. A waiter in a blue sailor suit walked by with a tray that bore a quartet of bright red lobsters, with claws like catcher's mitts.

"First goddamn aquarium I ever saw," Cermak said, "where you can eat the exhibits."

I smiled politely. "Right."

He sipped his water. "Why are you in Miami, Heller?"

"Nate. I'm here for a client."

"Who?"

"An attorney."

"What attorney?"

"I consider that privileged information, Your Honor."

"Really."

The waiter put some clam chowder in front of us. I started in on the soup; we'd been served some crackers on the side, Saltines, and Cermak began breaking them up over his chowder. He dipped his spoon into the mixture and said, "You were watching me today, Nate. Why?"

"I was watching you at the train station, too. And at your son-in-law's place. And at the Biltmore."

Cermak dropped his spoon; he dropped the smile, too.

"You want to tell me what this is about, Heller?"

"Nate."

"Fuck you, Heller." He was smiling again, and his voice was very soft: no one in the world could hear him but me. "Fuck your cute tough-guy shit. You can be dead in an alley in an hour, if I want it that way, you little bastard. Now what the hell are you doing here? And what does it have to do with me?"

"That's no way to talk to somebody who's trying to keep you alive."

"What the hell are you talking about?"

"The attorney I'm working for has a client. The client has an interest in your well-being."

"*Who* are you talking about?"

"I'm telling you more than I really should, Your Honor. There's a line I can't cross."

The waiter brought us each a plate of coleslaw; I began to eat mine. Cermak ignored his.

"You're saying my life's in danger."

"What do you think? Are you down here strictly to court Jim Farley's favor? Or are you here partly at least to duck Frank Nitti's *dis*favor?"

"Keep your voice down."

"I wasn't speaking loud. Those words just seem loud, Your Honor."

"You were sent here to *protect* me? I have bodyguards."

"I know. I said 'boo' to two of 'em in the toilet at Hialeah and they peed their pants."

"They're good men. What makes you especially qualified to be my protector?"

"I can recognize the man Nitti is sending."

"I see."

"I know what he looks like. I've seen him before."

"When? Where?"

"After he shot a man. That's all I care to say about it."

Cermak looked at me for a long time.

Then he said, "What attorney are you working for?"

I thought about whether to answer him or not. Maybe he thought this was a shakedown, or a scam of some kind, growing out of hard feelings I harbored over the lies I'd agreed to tell for him; maybe I needed to make one more point, before he could buy it, before he could believe the truth.

"Louis Piquett," I said.

His face turned whiter than the chowder.

The waiter in blue served the lobsters. He put one in front of the mayor and another in front of me; they were enormous: like the flamingos at the racetrack, they were beautiful, ugly things. I began to crack mine open with the pliers we'd each been provided. The cracks were like gunshots, but Cermak didn't seem to hear them, or see the dead scarlet crustacean on the plate in front of him; he was staring, and not at me, and not out at the darkening bay. He was looking off, somewhere. Nowhere.

Then, suddenly, he dug into the lobster, cracking it apart like the enemy. He sat, determinedly, eating, dunking the lobster's flesh into the pot of melted butter, using his fingers as often as his fork, till they were dripping with butter and juice from the lobster. His table manners were lousy. He ate fast; he ate as if ravenous—but I don't think he tasted anything. He was obviously a man who enjoyed eating, who regarded eating a carnal pleasure—but he wasn't enjoying this meal. He barely noticed it.

He finished way ahead of me. It was the first lobster I'd ever eaten, and I was learning as I went. I liked the way it tasted, though it was nerve-racking, eating the last third of the thing with Cermak staring at me with large eyes behind the round frames of his glasses, looking out at me like the fish behind glass in the aquarium I'd walked through a few minutes ago.

"It surprises me," he said, "that Mr. Piquett's client would still have my best interests at heart, after all these years."

"Quite frankly," I said, through a mouthful of lobster and butter, "I don't think Mr. Piquett's client gives a goddamn whether you live or die. I just think he's somebody who learned the kind of damage bad publicity can do. After all, Saint Valentine's Day is just a few days away, if you get my drift."

He said, "It's a power play, then. To remind 'em who's boss. An attempt to one-up Nitti from inside."

I shrugged. "You know how it is. Politics."

He nodded. Then he looked out at the pleasure craft on the bay. Twilight had turned into night and the lights on the boats winked at the mayor. The skyline of Miami shimmered on the water.

A waiter came and took our desert order: we both requested vanilla ice cream, but before it came, Cermak grimaced, apparently hit by a sharp pain. He stood, excused himself, and Miller trailed after his boss, who walked with one hand on his ample belly.

My ice cream came and I ate it. By the time Cermak returned, his ice cream had begun to melt; he ate it slowly, nibbling at it, with uncharacteristic lack of interest.

When he'd finished, he said, "You mean to shadow me, then? And wait for the assassin. And stop him."

I nodded. "I hoped to stop it before it got that far, but, realistically, yes."

"But Miller and Lang saw you at the track and you decided not to try to bluff your way out."

I shrugged. "I could've bluffed my way out if I was prepared to drop the matter. But I've got to stay on it, as long as you don't take steps to stop me."

He let out a short laugh. "Why the hell should I? You're here to keep me alive."

"It means a pretty penny to me to do so, Your Honor."

We had coffee.

"I'd like you to describe this man to me, and to my people," Cermak said.

"Sure."

"And you can maintain your surveillance on me with nothing but cooperation from Lang and Miller and the rest. You can report to me from time to time, if you like. Check with me daily regarding any of my plans."

"Good. What plans *do* you have?"

"I've done everything where Jim Farley's concerned that I can. He's made a few promises, but precious few. And I have a bigger fence to mend."

"What do you mean?"

"Farley told me Roosevelt plans to come to Miami next Wednesday. It hasn't been announced to the press yet. But there's a lot of big shots in Miami who put the pressure on to have him end up his yacht trip here. Good publicity for the city, and good for the president-elect, too. He's going to give a public speech. All the newsreel boys will be down here, brass bands, radio, the works."

"So?"

"You know about Roosevelt and me, Heller?"

"I know you backed Smith at Chicago."

"Did you know I turned down Farley's repeated personal pleas to switch sides? We were all set to give the favorite-son nomination to that dumb bastard J. Ham . . ."

J. Ham was J. Hamilton Lewis, the aging, dandyish senator from Illinois who, although a Democrat, was aligned with the reform-minded former mayor, Republican Carter Harrison II, son of Chicago's first world's fair mayor, who before the White City closed down had died from an assassin's bullet.

". . . and then J. Ham double-crossed us, pulled out, and I stuck that banker Traylor in as favorite son in his place."

"But that got J. Ham in solid with Farley, and he stole your patronage thunder."

Cermak frowned at that, but could hardly deny it. He said, "I delivered Chicago to the sons of bitches. Largest presidential vote in Illinois history. They owe me."

"Anyway, that's what you've been telling Farley today."

Cermak looked through me. Sipped his coffee. "I need to make a gesture. I need to be seen in public with FDR. I need to get his ear, privately if I can." He leaned forward. "Farley's going home. Sunday, after his banquet. Then the rest of the boys are planning a side trip to Cuba. By Wednesday, everybody'll be back home in New York or wherever, else layin' on their fat ass on a beach somewhere. But I'll still be here. It'll make an impression on him."

"On Farley? You said he'd be leaving Sunday."

"No! I mean Roosevelt. He'll take it like a personal tribute. Like a public apology for my doing him wrong at the convention."

"You really think so?"

Cermak laughed; it was sort of a snort. "Roosevelt is not only weak in the legs, he's also weak in the head."

"I don't think you should do it."

"What do you mean? Don't be stupid."

"Don't *you*. You figured you were safe down here. You figured because the Syndicate boys vacation down here themselves, because

Capone and Fischetti and the rest have homes here, and stay on their good behavior to stay welcome here, you figured nobody'd try to hit you down here."

Cermak shrugged. "Yeah. Right. You don't shit where you eat, Heller."

"Not unless you can make it look like you're doing something else."

"How do you mean?"

"Political assassination. You're down here in the midst of politicians from all over the map, including Roosevelt's entire Kitchen Cabinet. Some nut starts shooting up the Biltmore lobby while you and a hundred other politicians are standing around, and you happen to catch one of the bullets, nobody's going to think Syndicate. They're going to think of the poor unemployed bastards out on the breadline who're looking for somebody to blame for their troubles. And nobody better to blame than a politician. And now you want to shoulder up to Roosevelt in public? Did you bring that bulletproof vest you were telling me about along?"

Cermak leaned his elbows on the table, folded his big thick hands, and looked over them at me. "I have to do this. There's no way 'round it. I hate that crippled bastard, but we got troubles in Chicago, bigger troubles than fucking Frank Nitti. We got teachers that ain't been paid in months. We need loans from the federal government, and we need 'em fast. Can you grasp that, Heller? Can you grasp something bigger than your own goddamn dick?"

Well, I could've made a smart comment or two. I could've mentioned that I knew one of the patronage posts he was after Farley for was one he intended for yet another son-in-law, that position being internal revenue collector for Chicago, which would come in handy, because word was Cermak was being investigated for income tax evasion. Oh, there were maybe a hundred cynical things I could've said, but, you know, somehow I thought the bohunk bastard meant it. I thought he really did want to get Chicago on its feet again; I thought, for just a moment mind you, that he really did care about the teachers and the cops and the other city workers who were getting paid in scrip . . .

Cermak said, "Besides, the Secret Service'll be all over that place. There hasn't been a successful presidential assassination since McKinley, you know, and there never will be. 'Cause those boys are good. And my boys'll be there. And you'll be there, Heller. Won't you?"

I nodded. "But till then, stay low. No more public places."

"Just the dinner honoring Farley on Saturday."

"That could be tricky. It's open to the public."

"Only six hundred seats."

"All right. We can cover that. We'll just run tight security."

"Otherwise, I'll stay at my son-in-law's. With my bodyguards. I have some people to see, but they can come see me."

"Good," I said. "Nitti won't expect that. He won't expect you to lie low. And I don't think he'll hit you at home. I think it *has* to be a public appearance, to make it look like something the Syndicate wasn't part of."

"Then we've just got two events to deal with. The Biltmore dinner for Farley, Saturday; and Bayfront Park, Wednesday."

"What?"

Cermak pointed off to his left. "Bayfront Park. That's where Roosevelt is speaking."

"You really ought to take a rain check on that one, Mayor."

For the first time, the cold eyes softened a bit, and the smile seemed genuine. "I underestimated you, didn't I, Heller?"

"Maybe not. Maybe I'm just coming into my own."

"Maybe."

"Where are you headed next?"

"To the toilet," he said, standing, grimacing, holding his gut.

This time I followed him, and he motioned Miller to stay put.

His Honor was washing his hands when I said, "You got to tighten your security up on the home front, too."

"What do you mean?"

"I told your gardener I was with the *Herald* and he told me everything but your date of birth."

Cermak dried his hands on a paper towel; he shrugged with his face. "We don't have a gardener."

"What?"

"Not really. Some neighbor kid does it; when my son-in-law's down, he does it himself. Relaxes him."

"Your neighbor's kid isn't Cuban, is he?"

"Not hardly. Why?"

"Some Cuban was trimming your shrubs the other day."

Cermak shrugged again, this time with his shoulders. "My son-in-law probably hired somebody else to do the yard, to get it ready for when I got here."

"Yeah. You're probably right."

Anyway, it wasn't a Cuban I was looking for. Not unless it was a blond Cuban. But my blond could have a Cuban backup man, couldn't he?

"We'll call long distance and check on it," Cermak said, "if it'll make you feel better."

"Please," I said.

"Now," Cermak said, "let's go break the news to Miller and Lang that you're pals."

## 16

A Goodyear blimp glided overhead. Out on a strip of land opposite the park, pelicans and gulls came in for flapping landings, then took off again. It was late Wednesday afternoon and sultry, and couples of varying ages strolled around Bayfront Park, sometimes stopping for a game of shuffleboard or to sit on a bench and watch the blue bay and the white boats.

I about tripped over one of the nearly invisible guy wires anchoring a big palm against the wind; those wires were a danger you could overlook, in this peaceful, lushly landscaped park. The main promenade, from the foot of East Flagler to the bay, was lined with flower beds, clipped pine hedges, royal palms, and couples on benches. It made me wonder what Mary Ann Beame was doing; it made me wonder if she was thinking about me at all, while I was down here trying to keep Chicago's mayor alive.

Other than the guy wires, the park seemed free from hidden danger. I strolled all forty acres of it, forty acres that had been pumped from the bay less than a decade ago and turned into a tropical paradise. I didn't see the blond anywhere; the automatic was under my shoulder, and the Police Special was nudging my middle, and if he came early, to look over what might be the scene of his crime, I might still get to plant the .38 on him and get this over with, before it started.

With the sun still sharing the sky with the blimp and a few lazily soaring planes, I took a seat in the front row of the amphitheater. Green benches that would seat eight thousand sloped down in a wide semicircle to face the band shell. The central dome of the stage was painted a garish red, orange, yellow, and green design, vaguely oriental, and on either side of it were two towers with acorn domes decorated in bands of silver, green, yellow, orange, and red. It looked like a Shriner's idea of Egypt, right down to the yellow stucco stage with its blue platform, red-fringed brown curtain, and paintings of Cairo street scenes on either side of the proscenium. On the stage, a makeshift wooden reviewing stand had been assembled, six rows high, with room for maybe twenty-five or thirty dignitaries, of which Cermak would be one. He was, in fact, to be in the front row.

Fortunately, the public wouldn't be able to get close enough to the stage for anybody to take a shot at His Honor, not unless it was with a rifle, and short of climbing one of the royal and coconut palms separating the amphitheater from the Miami skyline, Cermak should, even in the first row, be safe. Because the area in front of the bandstand, a semicircular paved area, was where the president-elect would be speaking, from his car.

I sat there studying the situation, and began hearing muffled conversation behind me; I turned and looked and, though it was barely five o'clock, the green benches were starting to fill up. I got up and had a walk around, but didn't see the face I was looking for. By five-thirty, I realized I needed to stay put, if I wanted to hold onto my ringside seat.

A little after six some Secret Service guys began having a look around. I identified myself to one of them as one of Mayor Cermak's bodyguards, showed some identification, and another of them checked a list on a clipboard, found my name there, nodded, and let me be. As twilight settled in, there wasn't a seat to be had in the joint—and FDR wasn't set to talk till nine-thirty.

Of course, if this mixture of Miamians and tourists had read the paper, like I had, they'd known downtown traffic was going to be stopped at eight-thirty, and had decided to get down here while some parking—for their cars and their backsides—was still available. A parade would be leaving the pier where Astor's yacht, *Nourmahal*, would dock, around nine, and hundreds of local cops, by foot, motorcycle, and motorcar, would accompany Roosevelt and his people and some local dignitaries along Biscayne Boulevard to the band shell. They'd be preceded by various drum-and-bugle corps, and the press would bring up the rear.

I was nervous about Cermak making this public an appearance. But the blond killer was a pro, and he'd have to know this was a suicidal situation—with FDR here, the place would be swarming with security: cops and Secret Service and bodyguards. And here it was barely seven, and the areas to either side of the sloping benches were already filling with people. The crowd might give him a certain anonymity, but it would be impossible to move through quickly. Of course, if he used a silencer, his slug could take Cermak down before anyone knew what happened; and he might be able to disappear into the throng. The street was close by; Miami was close by. It could be done. But it was hardly ideal.

I was beginning to think either Capone's information was wrong, and the blond had never come at all; or my efforts to have Cermak lie low had paid off. His only public excursion had been the Farley banquet, which I attended in black tie and shoulder holster, and I'd stood by the doorway within the Biltmore Country Club and watched every dignitary and his lady enter, and there was no ringer; nor was any of the Biltmore help a blond hired killer posing as a busboy or waiter. I sat in the front, facing the head table, and Cermak's four bodyguards were variously placed—one on either side of the banquet room, standing, and the other two outside, one in front of the building, one in back. I'd given Lang, Miller, and crew a description of the blond and figured them competent enough to spot him, should he try to party-crash.

But he didn't, and I suffered through a night in a monkey suit, swallowing cigar smoke and dull speeches and tough beef, for nothing.

The rest of the time Cermak stayed at home; I kept a watch from outside, sitting in my forty-buck Ford, stopping in a couple times a day to report to the mayor, and keep track of his itinerary. He entertained various Demos, and an alderman from Chicago, James B. Bowler, showed up, and various millionaire Chicagoans who kept winter homes in Greater Miami called on him; but he made no public appearances. It turned out his son-in-law *had* hired a gardener to get the place beautiful for the mayor, so the bushy-haired bowlegged guy, while not the neighbor's kid, was apparently legit.

I had hoped for a cool night: the wind was swaying the palms gently, but it was muggy, and I wished I could take my coat off; the guns prevented that. Around eight—the crowd having swelled to at least twice the arena's capacity, many of them sitting on the sides of the grassy bowl   Miller and the thin bodyguard, Mulaney, showed up.

"Too many people," Miller said.

"Could be a blessing," I said.

"Only a goddamn crazy man would try something here."

"Yeah, I agree with you. But keep your eyes open anyway."

"I know how to do my job, Heller."

"I know you do."

Miller looked at me, searching for sarcasm; there wasn't any to find, and he figured that out, and took a position over toward the left of the stage. The other bodyguard moved over right. A few uniformed cops were on hand, by now; they were keeping people off the paved area, except for occasional children playing, who the cops tolerated good-naturedly. Vendors were moving through the crowd, as best they could, selling peanuts and lemonade. I had some.

Floodlights—red, white, and blue—swept the palms that fringed the amphitheater. A silver-helmeted drum-and-bugle corps from the Miami American Legion, preparing to march down the pier to greet FDR, assembled in the paved area in front of me and blared out half a dozen "tunes." They apparently didn't know I was armed.

The aisles were filled now; the areas to either side of the band shell and, I imagined, behind were clogged with people: men in shirt sleeves, women in thin summery frocks, a man's white shirt alternating with a woman's colorful dress, a flower bed of a crowd, a smiling crowd, despite the balmy night. The air hummed with conversation, as the crowd anticipated the presence of the man who, in just two weeks, would be inaugurated our thirty-second president, the crippled aristocrat who promised to lead us out of hard times. What the hell I voted for him myself, and nobody paid me to, which in Chicago speaks well for both voter and candidate.

Once the band had gone, limos bearing dignitaries swung around through the paved area, and the crowd, getting waved at, waved back and applauded, occasionally cheered; the limos went back behind the band shell, the dignitaries were unloaded, and they walked around front and up the steps at the center of the stage, and climbed the makeshift reviewing stand. Cermak, escorted by Lang and the other bodyguard, the chief of detectives' son, was one of the last to take his place, in the front row of the stands.

Lang came over to me. "Anything?" he asked.

"Nothing so far," I said.

"Nothing's going to happen."

"It might. Stay on top of it."

He smirked and wandered off, toward Miller.

The chief of detective's son, whose name was Bill, said, "You think something's going to happen?"

"I don't know. I don't like the mayor sitting in the front row of those stands. I don't think anybody in this crowd could hit him, with a revolver, where he is. But he'd be better off on one of the back rows."

"Impossible. He's got to be able to get down quickly to Roosevelt before that car pulls out of here."

"What do you mean?"

"We got word Roosevelt isn't staying the night. He's catching the ten-fifteen train out of here."

"That means Cermak's got to make his move, where FDR's concerned, here and now."

"That's right."

I heard myself sighing. "He'll make a nice target," I said.

Bill shrugged; but he seemed a little uneasy, even frightened. I was glad somebody else was taking this seriously: Miller and Lang were talking, over at the left, smiling, smoking. The dopes.

Me, I was still watching the crowd, looking for that blond head, seeking that face that had been seared into my memory the afternoon Jake Lingle died in a subway tunnel. I didn't find the face I was looking for; but there were twenty or twenty-five thousand faces here by now, I figured. It was just possible I'd missed one or two.

The crowd was getting excited now, and a little loud, but off in the distance the sound of a John Philip Sousa march could be heard. That really got 'em whipped up; that meant the parade was making its way here, and as the march got louder, the crowd did too, and they were cheering by the time the drum-and-bugle corps marched through the paved area in front of the band shell, blaring the president-elect's imminent arrival.

The band filed back around the band shell and a motorcycle escort rumbled across the paved area, and, just behind them, a light green touring car, its top lowered, rolled in to a stop in front of the steps leading to the stage. In the front seat was a uniformed police chauffeur and a plainclothes bodyguard. Half a dozen Secret Service men ran alongside the car or rode the running boards. In the back seat was the mayor of Miami—a heavyset balding man—and, in a dark suit with bow tie, hatless, Franklin D. Roosevelt.

The crowd was on its feet, now, cheering; Roosevelt's smile was infectious, and when he waved, the sound of cheering swelled even louder, and Miami waved back at him. On the stage, the dignitaries were on their feet, too, applauding, and I could see Cermak anxiously trying to catch Roosevelt's eye. When Roosevelt turned to acknowledge those on the reviewing stand, he immediately recognized Cermak and registered surprise—as Cermak had known, the other bigshot Demos had all headed home or to Havana by now, and this made him the ranking national figure on the stage—and FDR waved at Cermak, called out to him. I couldn't hear over the crowd's roar, but he seemed to be inviting Cermak to come join him; surprisingly Cermak shook his head no, smiling as he did, and shouted something down to the president-elect, which I also couldn't make out, but assumed was something on the order of, "After you've finished speaking, sir."

Behind the light green touring car was a blue convertible of Secret Service men; several carloads of press had emptied out behind the band shell, and reporters with flashbulbs popping were moving around the edges of the paved area. A newsreel crew was hastily setting up at right. There had been a press conference on Astor's yacht, which this same batch of newshounds had just covered, so there'd been no opportunity to set up in advance.

From the touring car, the mayor was speaking into a hand mike. He was saying, ". . . We welcome him to Miami, we wish him success, and we are promising him cooperation and support, and bid him Godspeed."

The crowd began applauding again, and the applause really built as Roosevelt raised himself up, using his arms to push up into a sitting position on the lowered top at the rear of the car. The microphone was passed to him; he looked tanned, relaxed, after his twelve days of fishing. Loudspeakers sent his voice out to the eager crowd, most of whom were on their feet.

"Mr. Mayor, friends," Roosevelt began, with a smile like a half-circle, adding, "and enemies . . ."

He paused, so the crowd could laugh, and they did.

"I certainly appreciate the welcome of my many friends in Miami," Roosevelt said. "But I am not a stranger here . . ."

Looking at him perched there, a perfect target, I was glad it was Cermak I was here to protect and not Roosevelt; the crowd was milling a bit, reporters moving about, the newsreel cameras grinding, people pushing through the throng to try to get a closer look. Meanwhile, the president-elect continued his chatty, regular-folks monologue.

"I have had a wonderful rest and caught a great many fish," he was saying. "However, I will not attempt to tell you a fish story."

That's when I saw him.

He wasn't a blond anymore; that's part of why I'd missed him. He was to my left and stage right, off to the side, just where the green benches stopped and the standing-room-only started; he must've been back behind a layer of people, but had squeezed out in front, now. He wore a white suit; hatless, his hair was now dyed brown or had it been dyed blond? He was pale; that was the tip-off: among the tans of the Miamians and even most of the tourists, his pale countenance glowed like neon.

"I put on ten pounds during the trip," Roosevelt was saying, "and one of my first official duties will be taking the ten pounds off."

I moved away from the bench and the wall of flesh behind me closed tight as I edged along the front of the first row; no one bothered me, or noticed me, because reporters and Secret Service men were stirring around, anyway. Miller and Lang were closer to the ex-blond than me, but their eyes were on Roosevelt, caught up in his charisma instead of watching the people like they were being paid to.

"I hope that I am able to come down next winter," Roosevelt said, finishing up, "see you all and have another ten days or two weeks in Florida waters."

Roosevelt smiled wide and nodded and waved and the roar of applause would have led you to believe the Gettysburg Address had just been spoken for the first time. Everybody was on their feet, some of them jumping up and down, whooping, hollering, and the people began moving forward, to get near him, right onto the paved area—the cops and Secret Service men didn't bother to try to stop the mass of humanity, perhaps realizing it wouldn't do any good. I could still see the ex-blond, moving in himself, unbuttoning his coat, but his eyes weren't on Roosevelt: his eyes were on the stage.

The newsreel boys were climbing up on the back of the green car, hollering at Roosevelt to go through the speech again, because one of their cameras had got fouled up; he said, "Sorry, boys," and slid down onto the back seat, motioning to Cermak up on the stage.

As I did my best to plow through, moving against the tide, I could see Cermak, beaming, come down the steps off the platform toward Roosevelt. I even heard Roosevelt raising his voice above the din: "Hello there, Tony!"

Then Cermak was shaking hands with Roosevelt, talking to him, on the side of the car next to the stage, away from the crush of people.

And the ex-blond was reaching under his coat—but I was there. I grabbed the arm and pulled it away from the coat, and the hand came out with no gun in it, he hadn't got that far, but I saw the gun under his arm as his coat flapped, and he looked at me amazed and I buried a fist in his belly, and he doubled over. The people around us didn't seem to notice, as they continued to press forward.

I yanked the automatic out from under my shoulder and grabbed him by one arm and put the barrel in his face. He didn't look at it, though: he looked at me.

And the damnedest thing happened: he recognized me.

"You," he said. Eyes wide.

It had never occurred to me that the blond would recognize me; he'd only seen me that once, in the street, but the same was true for me, and I remembered *him*, didn't I? And he had no doubt followed the Lingle case, having a vested interest in its outcome, and my picture turned up in the papers in regard to that, so I was a part of his life, just as he was part of mine. My image was as seared into his brain as his was in mine, and I said, "I got you this time, fucker."

Firecrackers went off.

That's what it sounded like, but I knew better. I whirled, without releasing my grip on him, and saw Cermak, well away from Roosevelt (who was being presented with a gigantic mock-telegram from the city of Miami), double over.

Shot.

And the firecrackers continued to go off.

I looked to where they were coming from, over to the right, stage left, and a bushy-haired head on a stumpy body was floating oddly above the mass of people around him, about five rows back, and then I realized the man had stood on one of the benches to do his shooting. The muzzle flashes from his long-barreled revolver made fireworks above the crowd.

And more people were going down.

The blond pulled away, and I swung at him, hard as I could, putting every fucking thing I had into it, right in the side of his face, and he crumpled, unconscious, and I moved toward Cermak, pushing, shoving, almost throwing people out of the way to get there.

Miller and Lang were crouching near him, and lanky, white-haired Alderman Bowler was kneeling, too, as if praying.

Cermak looked up at Miller and Lang; his glasses had been lost in the shuffle. He said, "Where were the goddamn bodyguards?"

I pushed my way past Bowler. "I had the blond, Your Honor. He didn't fire the shots."

Cermak smiled wanly. Sort of shrugged. "What the hell. They got me, Heller."

Roosevelt's touring car was still in place; the air was filled with screams, men and women both, and over toward where the shots had been fired, the crowd had turned into a mob.

"Kill him!"

"Lynch him!"

Roosevelt, momentarily shielded by his bodyguard, a sea of Secret Service men around him waving their arms, urging him to get out but getting a repeated curt "No!" from him, climbed out from under and pushed himself up in the back of the car and waved and smiled at the crowd, and yelled, "I am all right!"

A Secret Service man shouted, "Get out of here!" to Roosevelt's cop chauffeur. "Get the president out of here!" The cop moved forward and a couple motorcycle cops hit their sirens and began clearing a path.

I yelled to the moving car. "For Christ's sake, Cermak's shot! Take him out of here!"

Roosevelt must've heard me, because he turned and looked and leaned forward and spoke to the chauffeur and stopped the car. Cermak had caught it in the front, under his right armpit, along his rib cage, and he was bleeding, but able to get to his feet. Bowler and a couple Miami politicos helped me walk Cermak to the waiting car. We helped him in back with Roosevelt, who looked at me and smiled and nodded. Cermak looked at Roosevelt and smiled—he finally had his private audience with the president-elect; then he passed out, and the car shot away.

A white-haired man holding his head, blood seeping between his fingers, staggered by; over on the steps to the band shell, a woman in her thirties in an evening gown crouched in pain, a hand on her stomach cupping red. The blue convertible that had followed Roosevelt into the paved area was still there, and a confused-looking young uniformed cop was still behind the wheel; I went over to him and said, "Get another man and load these wounded people up and get 'em the hell to a hospital."

"I'm supposed to stay with the car," he said.

I grabbed him by the shirtfront and some shiny buttons popped off. "Fuck the car!"

He swallowed, said, "Yes, sir," and got out of the car and started rounding up the wounded.

Off toward the left, people were piled on top of each other like a couple football teams all in on the tackle. Some uniformed cops and Secret Service men were trying to pull the people off.

Over the loudspeaker came: "Please leave the park! Please leave immediately!"

I went over and started pulling people off the pile and one of the cops used his nightstick judiciously, and we got the assassin out from under the onslaught, and it was a small man, little more than five feet tall, naked but for a few shreds of his khaki clothes, which had been ripped from his body by the mob.

The cop I'd got tough with was helping the white-haired bleeding man into the blue convertible; the woman in the evening gown was already in the back seat. So was another man bleeding at the head. I pointed at the car, and two uniformed officers who had the small, barely conscious figure by either arm, and another who held the assassin's nickel-plated revolver, nodded at me and we made our way toward it, and tossed him on the trunk rack of the car. The cops climbed on top of the little man, sat right on him, and the car moved away. As it did, the groggy little assassin looked at me and managed a little smile and blurted something; the cops sat on him harder. It wasn't the gentlest way to treat him, but it probably saved his life: the crowd wanted blood.

If they wanted it, all they had to do was look on the paved area where Roosevelt's car had been: pools of blood were scattered here and there, like color in one of the paintings in Mary Ann Beame's Tower Town flat. The people were still milling around, but the crowd *was* thinning.

I sat on the steps to the band shell. Next to me was some of the wounded woman's blood.

Miller and Lang wandered up to me. They stood and looked at me and shrugged.

Lang said, "What now?"

"If you want to stay employed," I said, "I'd find out what hospital Cermak was rushed to, and be on hand."

Miller and Lang exchanged glances, shrugged again, and wandered off.

One of the other two bodyguards, Bill, had overheard this; he came slowly up. He looked haggard.

"We should have stopped it," he said.

"Right," I said.

"Do you think it was an accident?"

"What?"

"Maybe the guy was after Roosevelt."

"Go away."

He went away.

The blond, who was now brown-haired, was long gone. I'd had him, and he was gone. Cermak was shot, possibly dying; and a little bushy-haired man had pulled the trigger.

The gardener I'd seen at the son-in-law's.

Well, I knew where they'd taken him: the county courthouse. That was where the jail was. I wanted to get in and talk to that Cuban or whatever the hell he was. Maybe the fools *would* believe Roosevelt was the target.

But they hadn't heard what the bushy-haired assassin had muttered to me, as the three cops sat on him and drove him away.

"Well," he'd said, looking right at me, with brown shiny eyes, "I got Cermak!"

## 17

The towering Gothic Dade County Courthouse was starkly white against the night, lit up so you could see it for miles. Or anyway for blocks: it was only a matter of eight or so from Bayfront Park to the courthouse, which I walked, since traffic was still blocked off. Cops and sheriff's deputies swarmed the two flights of steps that rose to the entryway, where a row of two-story fluted columns loomed, like a reminder of more civilized times.

A cop, his hand on the butt of the revolver at his side, was pacing nervously at the curb.

I approached him. "I was at Bayfront Park," I said, showing him my identification. "A Cermak bodyguard."

"You did a swell job," he said.

"You're telling me. I take it they aren't here with the gunman yet."

"No. I don't know what the hell's keeping 'em; it ain't that far from the park."

"The car they threw the guy on the back of had some of the wounded in it. They probably went to the hospital first."

The cop nodded. "That must be it."

When the blue limo rolled up a few minutes later, the assassin was off the luggage rack and in the back seat with two cops sitting next to him, not on him; the chauffeur cop and the other cop were in front. They ushered the dark, bushy-haired little man out of the limo and up the steps—he was completely naked, even the khaki shreds I'd seen hanging on him at the park were gone now, and no one seemed concerned about providing him with something to cover up with, not that he seemed particularly concerned about it: he seemed calm, and had the faintest of smiles on his face. The swarm of cops parted like the red sea and moved in waves up the steps. I dove in.

That was when I noticed a guy at my side, in plainclothes; he definitely wasn't a deputy. He was wearing a gray snap-brim fedora, a black suit, a dark blue shirt, and a yellow tie. He was in his mid-thirties, but his brown hair was grayed, and he had a nervous, ferretlike manner.

We were in the midst of the crush of cops and inside the high courthouse lobby, when I turned to him and said, "Can I have your autograph, Mr. Winchell?"

He had a smile about two inches wide—tight, no teeth—and beady blue eyes that were cold as the marble around us. He pressed something in my hand. I looked at it: a five-dollar bill.

"Keep your trap shut, kid," he said, "and let me tag along with you."

"Be my guest," I said.

"Atta boy," he said. "There's another fin in it for you, you play your cards right."

I managed to pocket the five as, across the lobby from us, the elevator was opening and the assassin and a few of the cops squeezed in, apparently. Anyway, as soon as the elevator went up, the crowd of cops and deputies began to thin a bit, and they began milling about, and going their separate ways.

"Shit," Winchell said.

"How'd you get here so fast? You're the only reporter around."

"The rest of those jerks are probably at the hospitals and tagging after Roosevelt."

"I didn't see you with the press at the park."

"I was at the Western Union office, sending my column off to the *Mirror*, when I heard two guys arguing about how many shots the nut got off at Roosevelt. That's all I had to hear; I got over here so fast my ass won't catch up till Tuesday."

"The rest of the newboys'll catch up with you before it does."

"I know. Can you get me upstairs? The jail's on the twenty-eighth floor, I hear."

"I can try."

We moved over to the elevator, where two cops were stationed to keep the likes of Winchell away, I supposed. We wouldn't have got any farther than that, but one of the cops had been at the park and had seen me helping load the assassin on the back of the limo. So when I said I was Mayor Cermak's personal bodyguard and wanted to question the assassin and flashed my ID, he let me on the elevator.

"What about him?" the cop said, pointing at Winchell. He didn't seem to recognize the columnist; normally that would've hurt Winchell's feelings, I supposed. But he didn't seem to mind, under the circumstances.

"He's with me," I said.

The cop shrugged and said, "Okay. It's the nineteenth floor. That's where the isolation cells are."

We got on the elevator.

Winchell rocked on his heels, looking up at the floor indicator.

"I didn't think this sort of thing was your line," I said.

"My by-line's my line," he said, "and anytime I can pin it on a story that's more than just entertaining the poor slobs on Hard Times Square with how some chorus girl got a diamond bracelet for laying some millionaire, I will."

The door opened on the nineteenth floor, and the sheriff, a big, lumpy man in dark suitcoat, white pants, colorful tie, and misshapen hat, was standing talking to a uniformed cop, who had a nickel-plated .32 long-barreled revolver in the palm of his hand, like something he was offering the sheriff. The sheriff turned a glowering gaze upon us, his dark eyebrows knitting, but before he could say anything, Winchell stepped forward with a smile as confident as it was insincere.

"I'm Walter Winchell," he said, extending his hand, which the sheriff, whose mouth had dropped open, took. "Let me in there for five minutes with that lunatic and I'll put your name in every paper in the world."

The sheriff's expression had shifted from foul to awestruck and, now that fame was pumping his hand, to a fawning, simpering grin.

"Glad to have you in my jail, Mr. Winchell."

"As a temporary visitor, I hope," Winchell said, spitting words like seeds. "What can you tell me about the guest you just checked in?"

"He says his name's Zangara. Giuseppe Zangara. That's about all we got so far. His English is pretty bad. But I'm something of a linguist myself . . . speak a little Italian. I can translate for you, if you can't make out what he's trying to say in American."

"You're a gentleman, Sheriff. Lead the way."

"Wait a minute," the sheriff said, and turned to me. I was standing just behind Winchell, trying to be inconspicuous. "Who are you?"

I told him; the cop standing nearby, who had been one of the three I'd helped in wrestling the assassin onto the limo luggage rack, confirmed what I said.

"No Chicago people," the sheriff said, waving his hands. "We don't want any of you Chicago cops in here. We'll handle this our own way."

Winchell said, "Sheriff, he's with me."

The sheriff thought about that, said, "Well, okay, then. Come along."

We followed the sheriff, and I said to Winchell, "Thanks."

"Now we're even," he said. "Or we will be when you cough up that fin I gave you."

I gave him his five back.

The sheriff and the cop, the gun the assassin had used stuck in his belt, led us down a cellblock lit only by the lights coming from the corridor behind us. The individual cells stood empty, for the most part; we walked past one where a Negro squatted on his cot, watching us, mumbling. He was the only other prisoner on the floor.

At the end of the cellblock corridor, standing naked in the middle of his cell, was the man named, apparently, Giuseppe Zangara. He stood erect, unashamed. But not exactly defiant. As we joined two cops standing staring at their prisoner, I got a good look at him: about five feet six inches tall, weighing perhaps 115, with a wide scar across his stomach; his face long, narrow, square-jawed; his hair jet-black; his eyes bulging, dark, intense. That faint smile was still on his face; when he saw me—recognized me—that smile, momentarily, disappeared.

The sheriff looked through the bars at the calm, detached prisoner. He said, "I'm going to put you in the electric chair, friend."

Zangara shrugged. "That's okay. Put me in chair. I no afraid."

The sheriff turned to Winchell and said, "That's what you're up against, Mr. Winchell."

Winchell moved in, stood as close to the bars as he could get. "You know who I am?"

"No," Zangara said.

"My name's Walter Winchell. Ever hear of me?"

Zangara thought about that. "Maybe."

"'Good evening, Mr. and Mrs. America, and all the ships at sea . . .'"

Zangara grinned. "Radio. Sure. I know you. Famous man."

"You want to be famous, Giuseppe?"

"Joe. Call me Joe. I'm American citizen."

"You want to be famous, Joe?"

"I want to kill president."

"To be famous?"

He thought about it.

"You talk to me," Winchell went on, "and you'll be famous. Talk, Joe."

Zangara looked at me. Waiting for me to spill the beans, I guess. I wasn't talking.

He was: "I try kill president. I try kill him because I no like government. Capitalists all crooks. Everything just for money. Take all president—kings, capitalists—kill. Take all money ·burn. That's my idea. That's why I want to kill president."

"But you didn't kill the president, Joe."

Zangara didn't seem too broken up about that. "I failure," he shrugged.

"You shot a lot of other people. They may die."

Another shrug. "Too bad."

"Then you're sorry?"

"Yeah, sure, sorry like when bird, horse, cow die. Not my fault. Bench was shaky."

"What do you mean?"

"Bench I stand on to kill president, it shaky."

"It wobbled, you mean? That's why you missed?"

"Sure." He looked at me again, puzzled this time. He wondered why I wasn't asking him about seeing him at Cermak's son-in-law's place; he wondered why he was getting away with his "Kill-the-president" routine. I let him wonder.

Winchell got out a notebook, finally, said, "Let's start from the beginning, Joe."

"Fine."

"How old are you?"

"Thirty-three."

"Where were you born?"

"Italy."

"How long have you been in America?"

"Been here, 1923, September."

"Ever been married, Joe?"

"No."

"Your parents living?"

"My father living. My mother die when I was two years old. I no remember my mother. I have stepmother. Six sisters."

"Where is your family now?"

"Calabria."

"In Italy?"

"Yeah."

"What have you been doing since you got to America, Joe?"

"Oh, work. Bricklayer." He glanced at me, smiled briefly, nervously, rubbed his small hand over his stubbly chin and cheek with tapering fingers, added, "Sometimes gardener."

Winchell kept shooting questions, taking the answers down with the fastest pencil I ever saw. "Where have you lived in America?"

"Lot of time in New Jersey. Sometime Miami, sometime New York. I suffer with stomach"—he pointed to the six-inch scar across his belly—"when cold, so I come Miami."

"What have you been doing since you've been down here?"

"Nothing. I have little money."

The sheriff touched Winchell's arm. He said, "He had forty dollars on him, in what was left of his trousers."

Winchell nodded, filing that away, went on. "Ever been in trouble before, Joe?"

"No, no trouble, no, no. I not been in any jail. This is first time."

"Did you ever try to hurt anybody before?"

"No, no, no."

"How long did you plan this shooting? When did it first come into your mind?"

"All the time my stomach is in my mind." He held two hands like claws in front of his scarred stomach and frowned; this much he seemed to be telling the truth about.

"Tell me about your stomach, Joe."

"When I work in brick factory, I burn my stomach. Then I become bricklayer."

"Your stomach still bothers you?"

"Sometimes I get big pain in my stomach. I suffer too much. Fire in my stomach. Make fire in my head and I turn 'round like I am drunk man and I feel like I want shoot myself, and I figure, why I shoot myself? I am going to shoot president. If I was well, I no bother nobody."

"Don't you want to live, Joe? Don't you enjoy living?"

"No, because I sick all time."

"Don't you want to live?"

"I don't care whether I live or die. I don't care for that."

"Joe, there's something I gotta ask."

"You famous man. Ask what you like."

"Is there any insanity in your family, Joe?"

"No."

"Nobody crazy?"

"Nobody in crazy house."

"Are you a drinking man, Joe?"

"I can't drink. I can't drink. If I drink, I die, because my stomach is fire. I can't drink nothing."

"Can you eat?"

"I can't eat. Eat just a little bit, hurt me. Burn me. I come Miami for specialists but nobody can help the trouble."

"You said you're a citizen, Joe?"

"Yeah. Bricklayer union make me."

"Anybody in this country ever harm you?"

"No, nobody, no."

"You made a living here, didn't you? What kind of trouble did you have here?"

Zangara grimaced, impatient with Winchell for the first time; he pointed a finger at the scar. "Trouble is *here*. What is use of living? I better dead, suffer all the time, suffer all the time."

That stopped Winchell; amazing that anything could stop him, but it did, momentarily, and I stepped in and said, "Are you dying, Joe? Did you come here to Miami to die?"

His teeth flashed in the whitest grin I ever saw. "My job done," he said.

Winchell glanced at me, irritably, probably wishing he hadn't allowed me along, and started back in. "Why did you wait till Mr. Roosevelt had finished speaking? He was a better target when he was sitting up on the car."

That threw Zangara, just a bit, and he almost stuttered as he said, "No have chance because of people in front. Standing up."

"They were standing up when you shot at him. You had to stand on a bench to do it, right?"

"I do best I can. Not my fault. Bench shaky."

"That's where I came in," Winchell said to himself, glancing at his notes so far.

I said, "Did you know Mayor Cermak?"

The hand nervously stroked the rough chin and cheek again; the dark eyes avoided mine. "No, I didn't know him. I just want to kill the president."

"You don't know who Mayor Cermak is?"

"No, no, no. I want just the president. Just know president because I see picture in paper."

"Cermak had his picture in the paper lately. A couple of times."

Winchell butted back in, but picked up my thread. "Are you worried that Cermak might die?"

"Never hear of him."

"Joe, what's the Mafia?"

"Never hear of him, either."

Winchell looked at me; I smiled at him blandly.

He said, "You didn't shoot at Mayor Cermak? The Mafia didn't hire you to shoot at Mayor Cermak?"

Cocky now, almost laughing, Zangara said, "That's a baloney story."

"Why didn't you try to get away in the park, Joe?"

"Couldn't get away there. Too many peoples."

"Wasn't that suicidal, Joe?"

Zangara blinked.

"Risky, Joe," Winchell said. "Wasn't that risky?"

The naked little man shrugged again. "You can't see presidents alone. Always peoples."

"Are you an anarchist, Joe? A Communist?"

"Republican," he said.

That stopped Winchell, too.

Then he said, "So you wouldn't try to kill President Hoover, I suppose."

"Sure. If I see him first, I kill him first. All same, it makes no difference."

The sheriff interrupted. "Zangara, if Mr. Roosevelt came in this jail and you had your pistol back in your hand, would you kill him now?"

"Sure."

"Do you want to kill me? Or the policemen who caught you?"

"I no care to kill police. They work for living. I am for workingman, against rich and powerful. As a man, I like Mr. Roosevelt. As a president, I want to kill him."

Winchell jumped back in. "Do you believe in God, Joe? Do you belong to a church?"

"No! No. I belong to nothing. I belong only to myself, and I suffer."

"You don't believe there is any God, heaven or hell or anything like that?"

"No. Everything on this earth like weed. All on this earth. There no God. It's all below."

Winchell had run out of questions.

Zangara turned and walked toward the window in his cell. He could see Biscayne Bay out of it. A gentle breeze was coming through: I could feel it from where I stood.

The sheriff said, "We'll get you a lawyer tomorrow, Zangara."

His bare back still to us, he said, "No lawyer. I don't want nobody to help me."

The sheriff asked Winchell if he was done, and Winchell nodded, and we walked back out through the cellblock, our footsteps echoing, the black man still sitting on his haunches on his cot; he was laughing, now, to himself. Rocking back and forth.

At the elevator the sheriff shook Winchell's hand and spelled his name for Winchell three times; and we went down.

Winchell was silent in the elevator, but outside, in the Miami night air, he put a hand on my arm and said, "What's your name, kid?"

"Heller."

He smiled; showed some teeth for a change. "Aren't you going to spell it?"

"I don't want to be in your story."

"Good, 'cause you're not. You're Chicago, right?"

"Born and bred."

"What do you make of that back there?"

"You're New York. What do *you* make of it?"

"Hogwash."

"Is that what they call it in New York?"

"It's one of the things you can call it in print. Bullshit by any name would smell as sweet."

"That scar on his stomach isn't bullshit."

"No. It's real enough. Ever hear of Owney Madden?"

Raft's gangster friend.

"Sure," I said.

"He's a pal of mine," Winchell said. "He saved my life when Dutch Schultz got mad at me. I got a little fresh in my column, where Schultz and Vince Coll were concerned. Predicted Coll's murder the day before it happened."

"And Schultz didn't like that."

"No, and I was on the spot. I lived under the threat of a gangland execution for months; I had a goddamn nervous breakdown from it, kid, I ain't ashamed to say."

"Your point being?"

"I'm a public figure. They shouldn't have been able to bump me off without a major stink. I pointed this out to Owney. You know what he said?"

"What?"

"They could find a way, he said. They could find a way and nobody would even know it was them who bumped me off."

We stood halfway down the steps of the courthouse, the balmy breeze fanning us like a lazy eunuch.

"I think that little bastard hit Cermak," Winchell said. "I think he thinks he's dying from that stomach of his anyway, and they probably promised to support that family of his back in Italy in return for him taking Tony out, and for his silence. What do you think?"

"I think you're right on the money," I said. "But if you print it, nobody'll ever believe it."

"What's a guy to do?" Winchell asked. "The bullshit they'll believe."

And he walked off, looking for a taxi, now that traffic was moving again.

## 18

The next morning around seven, I read the *Herald* over breakfast in the Biltmore coffee shop: peeking out between the eyewitness accounts of last night's shooting at the park was an item about General Dawes. He was finally testifying to that Senate committee about the Insull case. Yes, it was true that he had loaned Insull eleven million dollars of the twenty-four-million-dollar capital and surplus of the Dawes bank; and he copped to "putting too many eggs in one basket." Puffing his pipe and nodding ruefully, he admitted, "The bankers of this country in retrospect look pretty sad." When asked for suggestions for new banking laws, he said, "I don't want to give any half-baked views on new laws—though that is a habit not unknown in Washington." The latter apparently got the General a laugh from the gallery. But not from me.

Then I went up to my room and packed my white suit and my two guns, and checked out and drove the forty-buck Ford to the northwest section of Miami. Up a winding lane lined with hibiscus, oleanders, jasmine, and crocus bushes was Jackson Memorial Hospital, a two-story building with any number of long rambling white stucco wings with red tile roofs and awnings on the windows, set amid lush palms.

I parked in the adjacent lot and walked to the entrance, where twenty or so beautiful young nurses were standing around chattering, all smiles and excitement, apparently awaiting the arrival of someone special; that someone did not seem to be me.

Within the reception area in the main wing were most of the reporters from the park last night, and then some. No Winchell, however. He'd filed his big story and was leaving the pickings for lesser lights. Over against one wall Western Union had set up wires and typewriters for the press.

Two Secret Service men stopped me as I entered and asked who I was; I told them, showed them ID, and asked if there was any possibility of seeing Cermak. Without answering, one of them took me by the arm and walked me through the wall-to-wall reporters to a corridor just past the reception desk.

Still holding onto my arm, the Secret Service man said, to two more of his ilk guarding this corridor, "This is the guy Cermak's been asking to see."

Everybody except me nodded gravely, and I was escorted by the same guy down the corridor—which was bordered on either side by more pretty nurses. It was like a hospital scene in the latest production of Earl Carroll's *Vanities:* the cuties were all smiles and giggles as if about to break out into a song and tap dance.

The Secret Service man saw me falling over my feet, trying to look at both sides of the nurse-lined corridor at once, and said, "There's a nurses' training school here. The reporters have been taking a lot of pictures this morning."

"I bet."

Between clusters of nurses, doorways to hospital rooms stood open, and patients in bed were sitting up, leaning over in some cases, to get a look at me. Or who they hoped I'd be.

"When are you expecting Roosevelt, anyway?" I said.

The Secret Service man frowned at me, like I'd just let something big out of the bag. "He's due any time now."

Like any good parade, this one had pretty girls *and* flowers: floral displays lined the walls, stretching to the end of the corridor, where some people were grouped, among them Alderman Bowler, some more Secret Service men, a couple Miami detectives, and several white-coated doctors. Standing on either side of the door to the nearby hospital room were Lang and Miller.

"Doctor," the Secret Service man said. "This is Mr. Heller. The gentleman Mayor Cermak has been requesting."

Lang and Miller exchanged smirks at the word "gentleman."

White-haired Alderman Bowler gave me a weary smile and extended his hand. I took it, and Bowler said, "You kept your wits about you last night, young man. Thank you for that."

"That's more thanks than I deserve," I said. "How is the mayor doing?"

One of the doctors, a middle-aged man who, prematurely, was as gray as Bowler, said, "We're hopeful."

The other doctor, a younger man with glasses and a parchment tan, said, "There's no use deluding ourselves. The mayor's life's in danger. The bullet—which is still in him, just over his right kidney pierced his right lung, and he's been coughing up some blood. There's a strain on his heart. And there's always danger of pneumonia developing, and/or infection."

The other doctor shot a withering glance at the younger one, who didn't seem to notice, or anyway care.

"I suppose," the older doctor said, "my colleague's reason for telling you all this is to give you a sense of the caution you need to take."

"What are you talking about?"

"Just that the mayor insists on seeing you; he's a stubborn man, and arguing with him on the subject will cause the very sort of excitement that we would like to avoid. So we're acquiescing to his wishes, where you're concerned."

"I'll take it easy with him, Doc. How are the other victims?"

"Only Mrs. Gill was seriously wounded," the younger one said. "She's in critical condition. The other four sustained only minor wounds."

The older doctor said, "Why don't you go on in."

I put my hand on the door to push it open and, just before I went in, said to Miller, as if noticing him for the first time, "Oh? Do you still work here?"

Cermak, propped up in bed—an older, nontrainee nurse hovering at his side—looked at me and managed a lopsided smile. His skin was gray, his eyes half-closed, his lips pallid. His hands were folded over his belly. All around the room, and in an adjoining sunroom where the other two bodyguards sat, were flowers.

"I haven't seen so many flowers since Dion O'Bannion got killed," I said.

He laughed at that, just a little, and the nurse frowned at me, then at him.

I was at his bedside now. "How you feeling, Mayor?"

He shrugged with his face. "I wouldn't buy me if I was for sale," he said. His voice was breathy. "We need to talk."

"Fine."

He turned his head toward the nurse; it was an effort, but he did it. "Get out," he said.

She didn't think that was at all friendly, but she didn't bother arguing the point. She'd already spent some time with His Honor, apparently, and knew the futility of fighting him.

When she had gone, he said, "Shut the sunroom door for me, Heller."

I did that.

"And the window," he said.

I did that, too; two uniformed cops were standing outside the first-floor room, and they turned and glanced at me as I brought the window down.

Then I went to his bedside; on the stand next to the bed was a stack of telegrams, thick as a book. The one on top was from the mayor of Prague.

"You know, Heller," he said, "I didn't know I'd been shot. I felt something stun me, like a jolt of electricity. But I didn't hear the shots, what with the noise of the crowd. Then my chest felt like the center of it was on fire."

"He got away, Your Honor."

"I was told they got him."

"I mean the blond."

"Oh."

"Assassins work in teams, usually. One of them shoots, the other is simply backup. The blond was the backup. Only if the assassin had missed you would the backup have started shooting, and probably would've got away with it, too, since the crowd's attention was on the little man emptying his gun at the president's car. The blond probably had a silenced gun, or was planning to pass himself off as a cop or Secret Service man in the confusion. He's worked a crowd before. Anyway, I made the mistake, because I knew he'd pulled a trigger in the past, of assuming he'd pull the trigger this time. I was wrong."

"You did what you could. If the other people working for me had done as good as you . . . well. They didn't, did they?"

"You'll get no argument from me on that score."

"I guess ultimately I got myself to blame."

I wouldn't have argued with him on that score, either, but didn't say so. Instead I said, "Have you seen the papers?"

"They haven't shown them to me," Cermak said. "I've been told the basics. Zangara? Is that the name?"

"That's the name."

"Italian, they say."

"That's right."

"What do the papers say exactly?"

"That this guy Zangara was trying to shoot Roosevelt."

He smiled a little. "Good."

"I thought maybe you'd feel that way. That's one of the reasons why I've been keeping my trap shut."

"About what?"

"Remember that gardener I was suspicious about? I had you check with your son-in-law to see if he'd hired any yardwork done?"

Cermak nodded.

"Well, I didn't check that out thoroughly enough. Another mistake I made. Your son-in-law undoubtedly did hire a gardener; but the guy I saw trimming the hedges around that house wasn't who he hired. It was Zangara. Checking out the lay of the land."

Cermak said nothing.

"I got into the jail last night. I heard Zangara's story. It isn't much of a story, but it's probably going to hold up. He'll stick by it, anyway. I can see it in his eyes."

"You think Nitti sent him."

"Yeah. And so do you."

Cermak said nothing. His breathing was slow, heavy.

"I was hired to stop this," I said, "and I didn't. But one of the reasons I was hired to stop it was to avoid bad publicity. My client's business interests would not be served by having it widely known that you were shot by a Syndicate torpedo."

Cermak said, "Nor would mine."

I shrugged. "Fine. Then I'll keep your gardener's identity a deep dark secret, and you'll be a hero to all concerned—despite the fact that half the eyewitnesses say Zangara was shooting directly at you. By the way, did you really say that to the president?"

He looked puzzled. "Did I really say what?"

"The papers have you saying, 'I'm glad it was me instead of you.'"

Cermak laughed. "That's a crock of shit."

"Good for your public image, though."

He thought about it. Then he said, "I was elected to clean up Chicago's reputation, Heller. I was elected to be the goddamn world's fair mayor. And that's what I'm gonna be."

"Take it easy, Your Honor."

"It'll take more than one fucking bullet to pull this tough old hunky down. You go back and tell Chicago I'm gonna pull through."

"But don't tell 'em anything else," I said.

"Right," he said.

The door opened and Bowler stuck his gray head in. "FDR's coming up the drive. Mr. Heller, would you mind . . . ?"

I started to go, but Cermak said, "Why don't you stay."

"Okay," I said.

Bowler found that curious, but said nothing and went out.

Cermak said, "I could use a steak right now."

"What, with that stomach trouble of yours?"

"Yeah, and I can feel it acting up. But I could still use a steak."

"Or some liver and dumplings?"

"Yeah, that's an idea. That'd plug up this goddamn hole."

There was scattered applause out in the corridor: the nurses were finally getting to greet who they'd been waiting for. No singing or tap-dancing, though.

Bowler stepped in and held the door open and President-elect Roosevelt, in a wheelchair, rolled in with a big smile and a number of people following him, among them the two doctors and the Secret Service man who'd earlier taken my arm. Roosevelt, in a cream-color suit, looked tan and fit, but, despite that patented smile, the eyes behind his glasses were red, worried.

"You look fine, Tony!" Roosevelt said, wheeling over to the bedside and extending his hand, which Cermak managed to take. "The first thing you know you'll be back on your feet."

"I hope so," Cermak said, his voice sounding suspiciously fainter than it had when we had spoken moments before. "I hope that'll be in time for your inauguration."

"Well, if you can't make it by then, you'll come and see me at the White House a little later."

"It's a date, Mr. President."

Roosevelt glanced at me. "I know you," he said.

"Not really, sir," I said.

"You called out to me last night, and asked me to wait for Tony, here."

"I guess I did."

"I'd like to shake your hand."

I went over and shook his hand; it was a firm handshake.

"It's your quick thinking that has saved Tony's life," he said. "What's your name, son?"

I told him.

"Are you with the Chicago police?"

"Formerly. I'm a private operative. A bodyguard, last night, I'm reluctant to admit."

"I had good people all around me, Mr. Heller. There's not much you can do about a madman with a gun. Bob Clark, with the Secret Service and one of my best people, was right there, and he couldn't do anything about it—except get wounded himself. Just a graze, I'm pleased to say. You know, he's the man who accompanied one of your fellow Chicagoans to Atlanta Penitentiary a while back. A Mr. Al Capone. Of course I don't imagine either of you would run in the same circles as *that* fellow."

Roosevelt smiled at each of us, one at a time; Cermak and I returned his smile, but I was wondering if Roosevelt was just making a little joke or, if he knew of Cermak's reported Capone connections, a veiled reference indicating he suspected last night's gunplay was Chicago-bred.

In any event, Cermak changed the subject immediately. "Before you got to town," he said to Roosevelt, "I had a nice visit with Jim Farley."

Roosevelt looked at Cermak with surprise. "Yes, Jim has mentioned that to me. I spoke with him long distance today—he sends his best."

"We talked about the schoolteacher's salaries in Chicago, that have gone unpaid so long."

Roosevelt nodded.

"We've had difficulty collecting taxes in Chicago for two years. Big Bill left us a real mess; you know that, Mr. President. I am hoping you will be able to help us obtain a loan from the Reconstruction Finance Corporation sufficient to pay the teachers' back salaries."

Roosevelt was smiling, just a little; I thought I could see amazement in his expression. Amazement at Cermak's shamelessness in making political hay out of his situation. Cermak had him over a barrel: once the press got wind of the selfless requests from the hospital bed of the man who'd taken a bullet for him, Roosevelt would have little choice but to do his best to honor those requests.

"I'll see what I can do, Tony," Roosevelt nodded.

"Frank . . ."

"Yes, Tony?"

"I'm glad it was me instead of you."

And Cermak winked at the president-elect.

In the background, Bowler's eyes went wide.

Roosevelt smiled slyly; he'd seen the papers, too. For a moment I thought he might agree with Cermak: *I'm glad it was you, too, Tony*.

But instead he said, "I'll see you at the world's fair, Tony."

And wheeled out of the room, the entourage following—all but one doctor, the older one, who said to me, "Mr. Heller? Please?"

"Okay," I said, and moved toward the door.

As I did, Cermak began to cough; the doctor rushed past me. There was blood on Cermak's chin.

"Get the nurse," the doctor said to me.

I went out in the corridor and got her.

The doctor was wiping the blood off Cermak's face when I got back, but Cermak was grasping his stomach, his fingers like claws.

"How much pain are you in?" he asked.

"Terrible pain," Cermak said. "It's the . . . old trouble of mine. The stomach. Causing me terrible pain. Stomach hurts. It hurts."

I slipped out of the room; I didn't say good-bye to Lang and Miller.

I drove my forty-buck Ford back to the guy I bought it from and he informed me it was now a twenty-five-buck Ford, and I sold it to him for that and caught my 2:30 P.M. train back to Chicago.

JOE ZANGARA

## 19

Mayor Cermak's funeral was held in Chicago Stadium, where, the summer before, Franklin Roosevelt had been nominated for president. The floor of the stadium was elaborately landscaped into a huge cross of lawn and flowers. About twenty-five thousand people filled the stadium—approximately the same number who'd filled the bowl at Bayfront Park. Eulogies were presented by a priest, minister, and rabbi—a "balanced ticket," as one cynic said, reflecting Cermak's only true religion: politics.

And many politicians were on hand, of course; but President Roosevelt wasn't one of them. Just a few days before had been his inauguration. And today he was still in the midst of the banking crisis that had him declaring bank holidays and pushing an emergency banking act through a special session of Congress, among the many other bold moves that marked the opening days of his administration. He did send a representative to the funeral, though: Jim Farley, whose attention Cermak now, finally, commanded.

Governor Horner gave the political eulogy. He said, among other things, "The mayor met his public foes in battle array and attacked with such force and rapidity that the well-organized army of the underworld was soon confused and scattered."

The greatest public funeral in Chicago's history, they called it; and no matter where you were in Chicago on the bitterly cold morning of March 10, 1933, you couldn't miss it. I was in my office, trying out the radio that I'd finally bought—and found the two-and-a-half-hour ceremony being broadcast on most of the stations. I also found myself drawn to listening to it, dull as it was. I was fascinated by Chicago's efforts to turn Cermak into the "martyr mayor," and a little surprised at how little trouble Chicago was having swallow ing it.

A few newspaper articles suggesting the mob connection appeared in the days following the shooting; but the chief of detectives—whose son was one of Cermak's bodyguards, remember—had publicly dismissed the theory, and it hadn't reared its head since.

And then the papers had been full of the up-and-down battle Cermak was waging for his life; that, more than anything, had turned him into a hero. The doctors issued statement after statement citing Cermak's "indomitable courage and will to live"; from the start he was given at least a fifty-fifty chance to pull through.

As for Zangara, he was tried for attempted murder, four counts: Roosevelt, Cermak, and two of the other victims. His story remained for the most part the same as the one he related to Winchell. Occasionally details would shift, but usually it was the same—often word for word the same, delivered with the quiet smile of somebody who knows something you don't know. The psychiatrists examined him and termed him sane; and the judge gave him eighty years. Zangara laughed and said, "Oh, Judge, don't be stingy. Give me a hundred years." And was taken back to his skyscraper jail cell.

A few things came out at the trial that nobody—including the defense—seemed very interested in. One was the testimony of several Miami Beach hotel clerks who said that Zangara was constantly receiving mail and packages postmarked Chicago, and always seemed to have plenty of money. The manager of the pawnshop Zangara bought his .32 revolver from said that he'd done business with Zangara for nearly two years and that ". . . he was supposed to be a bricklayer, but he didn't work at that trade—he always seemed to have money."

Zangara had money, all right: he admitted losing two hundred dollars at the dog track a day or so before the shooting, and in addition to the money he'd had on him—forty bucks—he had two hundred and fifty dollars in a postal savings account. His bankbook showed that the account had, not long ago, contained twenty-five hundred dollars. No one asked Zangara what became of the money, whether he'd sent it home to his father and stepmother and six sisters in Italy, with whom even now he was corresponding. The prosecution did ask Zangara where the money came from, and he had no explanation other than insisting that he'd earned it as a bricklayer—even though he'd been out of work three years.

Other stories circulated that had no apparent basis in fact: some of the papers reported that Zangara had a drawerful of clippings about Roosevelt's visit to Miami, as well as others about the assassinations of Lincoln and McKinley. Testimony on the witness stand by investigators made no mention of any such clippings.

But Zangara's litany—"kill the president, kill any president, kill a president"—drowned everything else out. Nobody seemed to notice that Zangara's raving usually was accompanied by a nervous smile like a child actor who knows the lines but doesn't really have the maturity to give a convincing performance.

I didn't see any of this in person, of course; but it made the newsreels. That sheriff whose shorts Winchell had dropped the fame bug down appeared with Zangara in most of the reels; and Zangara seemed to have been bitten by the bug, too, as he was pictured more than once sitting in his cell surrounded by newspapers with his name in headlines. The judge at Zangara's trial also made the newsreels, giving interviews about the special summation he'd made before pronouncing sentence, in which he'd made an urgent plea for control of handguns; several civic groups took the judge's lead but went another step with it, urging handguns be outright banned.

On hearing of Zangara's eighty-year sentence, Cermak, in the midst of a rally (a political rally, by the time Cermak got through with it), said, "They certainly mete out justice pretty fast in this state." He went on to wistfully wonder why other states didn't learn from Florida's example, and stamp out crime via speedier trials.

And when, after the daily reports of improvement alternating with crisis came to an end, Cermak died in a coma on the morning of March 6, the state of Florida didn't disappoint him. Zangara was retried within three days, and sentenced to die at Raiford Penitentiary on March 20. The papers said the electric chair sat in the midst of a little cubicle at the end of a long corridor; when Zangara sat in it, he must've looked like a kid in a grotesque high chair.

He'd taken that seat of his own accord, shaking free from the grasp of two guards who meant to lead him to it; he sat and said, smiling, "See? I no scared of electric chair." But then he looked about and saw no cameramen among the handful of reporters present in the visitors' gallery. And he said, "No camera? No movie to take a picture of Zangara?"

The warden said, "No. That isn't allowed."

"Lousy capitalists!"

Guards placed a black hood over his head and he said, "Goodbye—*adios* to all the world, lousy world." And then: "Push the button."

And Zangara got his way.

Of course it came out, within days of the execution, that the real cause of Cermak's death was colitis, despite an autopsy report attributing the primary cause of death to the gunshot wound, enabling Florida to rush Zangara to judgment. The nine physicians who signed the report, with colitis listed only as a contributing factor, later admitted that the wound was at best "indirectly" responsible; that, as earlier reports indicated, the wound had in fact healed; that Cermak had indeed died of ulcerative colitis, that "old problem" of his.

Of course the way I saw it, fair was fair: Zangara's bellyache had killed Cermak, in a way; why shouldn't Cermak's bellyache return Zangara the favor?

The morning the state of Florida was frying Joe Zangara, the state of Illinois was attempting to try Frank Nitti for shooting police Sgt. Harry Lang in the hand while resisting arrest. I hadn't been called to the grand jury indictment hearing in January, due no doubt to Cermak's string-pulling and the general assumption that the case was cut-and-dried; but for the trial I was present, sitting next to Lang with Miller on the other side of him, as we all waited to see if we'd get to speak our pieces today. Lang and Miller had been very friendly to me, so far; just three pals getting their day in court.

Nitti and his counsel approached the bench. Nitti, looking tan and healthy but a trifle thin, was wearing a blue serge suit with a blue tie; he looked like a business executive, except perhaps for the barber-slick hair.

I heard Lang whisper to Miller, "Jesus, look at Nitti. He's brown as a berry. Where'd the wop get the tan?"

I said, in less of a whisper than Lang, "Haven't you guys heard? Nitti's been in Miami vacationing, and looking after his business interests."

They turned and looked at me blankly.

Then Lang whispered, "No kidding?"

"No kidding. He went down the day after Cermak got shot. Probably a show of support for the people who work for him, down Miami way. Sort of a busman's holiday, while he healed up from your police-work."

Lang thought about that and swallowed; behind the Coke-bottle lenses, Miller seemed to be putting two plus two together, too.

Then, forgetting to be nice, Lang sneered and said, "What makes you so well-informed?"

"Ever hear of a guy named Ness?" I said.

They thought about that awhile, too, as up at the bench Nitti's lawyer—a well-dressed Italian shorter than his client—was filing a motion for a continuance.

"I want to question the three officers in the case," the attorney said. "I just got into this case last Friday, and need time to prepare thoroughly."

The judge asked Nitti to step forward and approach the bench, and asked him to plead.

"Not guilty," Nitti said. "And I want a jury trial."

Lang was shifting nervously in his seat.

Nitti's attorney asked for a ruling on the continuance, and, despite the prosecutor's demand for an immediate trial, the case was held over till April 6.

I had the end seat, and got up and started to leave.

Lang stopped me in the aisle, smiled. "I guess I'll be seeing you in April."

Miller was standing behind him like a fat shadow.

"I guess so," I said.

Then, in a stage whisper, Lang said, "A deal's a deal, Heller."

I smiled at him. "That deal's with a dead man. You're on your own, jackass."

Lang sputtered. "Listen, Heller, Cermak——"

"Is dead. See you in court."

And I left. Behind me, Lang and Miller huddled like a football team that wondered where the hell their quarterback went to.

I wasn't sure yet whether I was just giving them a bad time, or if I really meant something by all that; but the prosecutor, a feisty little guy who didn't dress as good as Nitti's lawyer, was waiting for me out in the hall.

"Got a minute, Heller?" he asked.

"I got to get back to my office."

"I just want to say one thing: You didn't give testimony at the inquest. And you weren't called at the grand jury hearing."

"That's two things."

"No it isn't," he said. "It's one thing: you haven't perjured yourself yet." Like any good trial lawyer, he knew when to pause dramatically; he paused dramatically, and said, "Now. Got a minute?"

We went to his office.

## 20

It was Thursday, April 6, and I was sitting in a speakeasy with Eliot Ness.

"I don't usually have a beer for breakfast," Eliot was saying, raising the mug to his wry smile.

It was Barney's speak, of course, and it was closed. We were the only ones in the joint, except for Barney himself, who was sitting in the booth next to me and across from Eliot, saying, "Might be your last chance to break the law this way, Mr. Ness."

Despite the fact they were both my friends, Barney and Eliot barely knew each other; and on the few occasions I did get them together, they insisted on calling each other "mister." I tried to stop 'em, but it didn't do any good: they respected each other, and I just couldn't seem to talk 'em out of it.

"So it's all over, tonight at midnight," I said.

Eliot shrugged. "It's been over for months. But, technically, just because beer's legal again doesn't mean the dry agents'll dry up, not right away anyway." He gestured over toward Barney's bar, behind which bottles lined the mirror. "That stuff's still a crime, you know."

Barney said, "I just haven't crated that up, yet. We're only serving setups, till Repeal comes in a hundred percent."

"It's only in three point two percent, at the moment," Eliot said. "Can I have another one of these?"

"Sure. I'll get it . . ."

"I can get it. It'll be a change of pace, drawing a beer without using an ax."

Eliot went over behind the bar and got himself a beer.

"No kidding, Barney," I said, "you're really packing the hard stuff up and sticking with beer and setups?"

He nodded. "Winch and Pian have been on my case about a nice respectable Jewish contender like me running a speakeasy, so now that I can open up legal, I'm gonna. You'll be able to buy your rum here aboveboard and over-the-counter, 'fore too long. Roosevelt'll come through for us, wait and see."

Eliot was back; sat down. Sipped his beer and said to Barney, "When are they going to give you your shot at Canzoneri? After you put Billy Petrole away at the stadium last month, I don't see how they can deny you."

"You spoiled my surprise, Mr. Ness," Barney grinned. "I haven't told Nate yet, 'cause we won't get the contracts back signed and sealed till this afternoon. But I put my John Henry down a couple days ago. I'm getting my title shot."

I said, "Barney, that's great. When's it set for?"

"June. Gonna take advantage of those world's fair crowds."

"That's just great, Barney."

"I'll have tickets for you guys if you want 'em. I hope you both'll be there."

Eliot said, "Try and stop us," and raised his mug of beer in a toast.

Barney turned to me. "Can I get you a beer or something? Help me celebrate a little?"

"No thanks, champ. I got to testify in half an hour."

Eliot looked at his watch. "That's right." He drained the beer. "Let's go."

Near the Bismarck there was a parking lot, where Eliot left his government Ford, and we walked over to City Hall, half of which was the County Building, where the courtroom was. The day was cloudy and in the lower forties, windy enough to be chilly; a light rain fell. We walked with our heads lowered and our hands dug in our raincoat pockets.

"Eliot," I said.

"Yeah?"

"This prosecutor."

"Charley, you mean?"

"You just answered my question."

"What question?"

"I've just been wondering if the prosecutor was a friend of yours, that's all."

He pretended not to get my drift.

But before we went in the building, I stopped him, put a hand on his arm and we stood in the rain, close enough that I could smell the beer on his breath.

"I know you got my best interests at heart," I said.

"Yeah, 'but' . . ."

I grinned. "No 'buts' about it. I know you got my best interests at heart. Thanks, Eliot."

He grinned back. "I don't know what the hell you're talking about."

Eliot sat next to me in the courtroom, and that made Lang, a couple rows up, nervous. He kept craning his neck around to look at us, a vaguely desperate look on his face. He'd brought some of the nervousness along with him, apparently, as he'd also brought his lawyer, who sat next to him—the same dapper little fat attorney who'd come to that ditch in the Indiana dunes to identify the body of Ted Newberry, back in January—and who noticed Lang turning to look at me and stopped him doing it.

But Miller, sitting on the other side of Lang, wondering what his partner was looking at, turned and looked at us, too, and seemed similarly disturbed.

I hadn't had any contact with either of them since Nitti got his continuance, in this same courtroom, a few weeks before. No threatening phone calls or bribes or confrontations. Not that I had expected them to try anything. They probably wouldn't have risked doing anything to me themselves, at this point; and as far as I knew the only gang affiliation they had was with the Newberry/Moran group, who weren't much of a threat to anybody these days, many of their various members having defected to sign up with other factions, primarily the major one: Nitti's. But I'd been sleeping with my gun under my pillow just the same.

Besides, for all they knew I might get on the stand and tell the story they wanted me to.

The judge came in, and we all rose, and, despite his lawyer's admonitions, Lang turned and looked at me again, and I winked at him, like Cermak did at Roosevelt.

And Lang was the first witness called.

He walked to the stand and as he passed Nitti, Nitti muttered something, presumably nasty. It wasn't loud enough for the judge to rap his gavel and reprimand Nitti—but it was plenty to unnerve Lang another notch. He took the stand and, after the prosecutor had asked a few perfunctory questions to establish the legality of entering the office at the Wacker-LaSalle without a warrant, Nitti's lawyer rose from the defense table and approached the bald cop.

"Who shot you?"

Lang looked at me.

"Who shot you, Sergeant Lang?"

The answer to that question, of course, was supposed to be, "Frank Nitti."

But Lang said, "I don't know who shot me."

Over at the prosecution table, the prosecutor jumped to his feet, as did several associates of his, and a wave of surprise—noisy surprise rolled over the courtroom. Several people stood; one of them was Miller. His fists were clenched, and he said, "Dirty son of a bitch."

The judge rapped his gavel, and everybody shut up, or anyway kept it down; the jury sat looking at each other, wondering if all trials were like this.

Nitti's lawyer leaned against the rail in front of the witness stand and, calmly, asked, "Can you say under oath that the defendant, Frank Nitti, shot you?"

"No."

A group of surprised prosecutors and police officials were on their feet and moving forward, and the chief prosecutor pushed his way to the forefront.

His face was red as he thrust a finger at Lang.

"Do you see the man who shot you?" he shouted. "Is he in the courtroom, sergeant?"

"No," Lang said. A calm had settled over him; with his bald head, and his folded hands, he looked damn near cherubic.

Nitti's lawyer stood next to the prosecutor but turned to the judge, who seemed to be having as much trouble believing his eyes and ears as the jury, and said, "I object, Your Honor! The prosecution is impeaching its own witness!"

The prosecutor turned to Nitti's lawyer and said, with contempt, "Yeah, he's my witness. But he turned out to be yours."

That left Nitti's lawyer momentarily at a loss for words.

The prosecutor jumped back in. "I want to ask him if he committed perjury just now. Or did he commit perjury when he testified before the grand jury, when this indictment was voted? Because before the grand jury, he said Nitti shot him."

I could see Nitti, sitting in his chair sideways; he was amused by all this. He was leaning back, a smile turning the downward V of his thin mustache into an upward one.

I leaned toward Eliot and said, "Your friend the prosecutor is getting pretty worked up about this."

We both knew that the prosecutor wasn't finding anything out about Lang he didn't know already.

"I don't know what he's so steamed about," Eliot said. "*You're* the one Lang's upstaging."

I was supposed to climb the stand and contradict Lang's Nitti-shot-me story; who could've guessed the pressure of the *possibility* of my doing that would be enough to make Lang contradict the story on his own?

Well, one person might have predicted it: Lang's lawyer, who was rising from the gallery to go toward the bench, saying as he went, "Your Honor! Your Honor! I am appearing here as this policeman's lawyer. As his counsel I advise him not to answer any more questions."

"Your Honor," the prosecutor said. "This man has no part in this proceeding. A witness has no right to a lawyer."

The judge agreed, but Lang's lawyer did not retire to the gallery; he stood beside the defense table, where Nitti and his lawyer were sitting, just two more spectators fascinated by a trial straight out of Lewis Carroll.

"Either you lied before the grand jury," the prosecutor said to Lang, "or you're lying now. I am giving you the chance to straighten yourself out here."

Lang's lawyer called out, "I advise my client not to answer "

The judge's gavel interrupted him.

Lang said, "Right after I was shot, my memory wasn't as good as it is now. Because of shock."

"You weren't suffering from shock in January, when you testified before the grand jury," the prosecutor said. "You were out of the hospital and cured by that time!"

Lang said, "I was suffering from shock. I can bring doctors to prove it."

The prosecutor let out a short laugh and turned his back on the witness, walking away saying, "You'll probably have that chance—in a trial of your own."

And sat down.

The judge sat behind his big wooden box wondering why the room got so silent all of a sudden; and then, remembering he was in charge, called a recess, instructing the prosecutor to meet with him in chambers.

People stood in little groups out in the corridor; reporters mingled with the various groups, not getting anywhere particularly. Lang and his lawyer stood talking solemnly; Miller and some plainclothes dicks stood well away from Lang, but Miller was bad-mouthing his partner loud enough that the echoey corridor carried it to anyone who cared to listen.

"I think Miller feels double-crossed," Eliot said.

I shrugged. "The minute Lang recanted, it made Miller look dirty. He's been supporting Lang's story all along, remember."

"He looks dirty because he is dirty," Eliot said.

"Good point," I said. "But this is Chicago. I wouldn't go looking under any cop's nails, if I were you."

Frank Nitti and his lawyer were standing down the corridor from us, talking; Nitti was all smiles. I saw him look my way a couple of times, but perhaps because I was standing with Eliot, he didn't come over right away. But eventually he did, and he looked at Eliot and nodded and said, "Mr. Ness."

"Mr. Nitti," Eliot said, nodding.

It occurred to me that Eliot and Nitti, like Eliot and Barney, shared a certain respect; and if my suspicions were correct about Eliot working on his pal the prosecutor to help see I didn't perjure myself, then Eliot had, in a roundabout way, been working to help Nitti here. The irony wasn't lost on Nitti, either.

"You're not here to root for *me*, are you, Mr. Ness?" Nitti asked.

Eliot shrugged. "If somebody tried to assassinate you, I am."

Nitti shrugged. "There's a lot of that going around."

Eliot's expression turned cold. "Yeah. So I hear."

Nitti had overstepped his bounds, and knew it. He turned to me and said, "I get the feeling you're behind this."

"Oh?"

"Yeah. I don't figure Lang's conscience is why he suddenly don't remember who shot him."

"You don't, huh."

"If I'm indebted to you, and it looks like maybe I am . . . well. I pay my debts, that's all."

He shrugged again, smiled almost nervously, and turned to rejoin his lawyer, only his lawyer was right behind him; it made Nitti look a little awkward, and Nitti snapped at the man in Sicilian. The lawyer took it stoically, and they walked back down the corridor a ways, and Nitti was smiling again by the time they came to a stop.

"If you don't believe him," Eliot said, "just ask Cermak."

"What?"

"Whether Nitti pays his debts or not."

When court resumed, the prosecutor had a perjury warrant ready for Lang, and Lang was placed under arrest.

"I'd like a ten-thousand-dollar bond, Your Honor," the prosecutor said.

The judge said, "Bail will be two thousand dollars. That seems large enough. He is a policeman, after all, with a policeman's pay — which as a city employee has been infrequent of late."

"You mean he *was* a policeman," the prosecutor said.

Eliot leaned my way and whispered, "His policeman's pay seems up to hiring a high-priced attorney."

The prosecutor said, "The State calls Nathan Heller."

And I took the stand.

Lang and his attorney were sitting in the front row of the gallery; one deputy sat next to Lang, several others hovered. Lang was looking off to one side, not terribly interested in what I had to say.

Why should he be? It was nothing he didn't already know: I told what had really happened in the office at the Wacker-LaSalle.

Despite Lang's upstaging me, all eyes (except his) were on me; the reporters were scribbling fast and furious. Miller was glaring, fat and furious.

At one point I was asked to step down and show how I had held Nitti by both wrists just before Lang came in and shot him.

"How was Lang shot?" the prosecutor asked.

"Nitti was unconscious," I said. "Lang must've shot himself."

A murmur passed across the courtroom, and Lang's eyes finally turned my way; he looked sad.

I stepped down; I had expected at least a few questions about or references to the guy I'd shot, in the window. But neither the defense nor the prosecution brought it up. I think Lang's lawyer would've got into it if he could, but Lang wasn't on trial. Technically.

Miller was called.

"Lang came in and said, 'He shot me,'" Miller told the prosecutor. "I went into the room where the shooting happened and picked up a revolver with one shot fired."

Nitti's lawyer had some questions for Miller.

"Why was Nitti put in that room before he was shot?" he wanted to know. "Was it to murder him, away from witnesses?"

"You'd have to ask Lang."

"Where did you go between four o'clock and five-thirty?"

"The mayor's office."

"With whom did you talk there?"

The prosecutor rose and objected. "Irrelevant and immaterial, Your Honor."

The objection was sustained.

Eliot shifted uncomfortably in his seat.

I said, "Cermak still has a few friends, I see."

Eliot said nothing.

Nitti's attorney tried again. "Did Lang have a conversation with anyone just before the shooting?"

"Yes," Miller said. "Ted Newberry."

And yet another wave of surprise rushed across the courtroom.

The judge rapped his gavel, and Nitti's attorney said, "You refer to the reputed gangland leader, Ted Newberry?"

"Yeah," Miller said. "The dead one. He offered Lang fifteen thousand to kill Nitti."

The judge had to bang his gavel again to quiet the courtroom, but the excitement was winding down: Miller was getting into an area that Nitti's lawyer obviously felt was best left unplumbed, and he said he had no further questions. The prosecutor seemed content to leave Miller and his Ted Newberry story to the grand jury. The Nitti case, however you figured it, was coming to a close.

The prosecutor asked for, and got, a directed verdict of not guilty for Nitti.

The next day, at the grand jury indictment for Lang, I was questioned again, this time by State's Attorney Courtney. The same ground was gone over. Nitti testified, corroborating my story, of course. He told reporters he would prefer to forget the whole thing, however; he didn't want to prosecute anybody for anything—he just wanted to get back to Florida and "regain his health."

Whether Nitti wanted to participate in the prosecution of an assault charge against Lang or not, Lang's perjury charge would go through.

And Lang's pal Miller tried, in the grand jury hearing, to desert a sinking ship. He was, the papers said, as helpful as could be, and repeated the Newberry story in detail. Cermak was one detail, however, that got left out.

Lang took the Fifth.

A John Doe warrant was used on Nitti, to keep him in town.

Outside the grand jury room, as I was coming out, Nitti and his lawyer were standing waiting to be called.

He stopped me and said, "Heller—something I want to ask you, now that your pal Ness ain't around."

"All right, Frank. Shoot. If you'll pardon the expression."

"What were you doing in Miami? What were you doing in the park, when that crazy anarchist bastard tried to kill the president?"

So I was right: the blond *had* recognized me, and reported back to his chief.

I said, "I was playing bodyguard for Cermak. Some job I did, huh?"

"About changed the course of history, didn't you, pal?"

"'About' doesn't count for much, Frank."

"Why'd Cermak hire you on, an ex-cop, when he had Lang and all the other cops in town at his fingertips, and for free?"

"Cermak didn't hire me."

"Oh, yeah? Who did?"

"One of his longtime backers."

Nitti considered that, or pretended to: there wasn't a flicker of a reaction to indicate he suspected Capone's role in this; but that didn't mean he didn't.

"Well," he said. Smiling. "No harm done." His lawyer was wanting him to move along; it was their turn at bat. Nitti put a hand on my arm. "About what you did for me, in this Lang thing . . ."

"I didn't do it for you, Frank. I just told the truth."

"Sure. I know. But I appreciate it. I owe you one, kid."

And he winked at me, and went in to testify.

I had a talk with some reporters, who I'd managed to duck the day before; they wanted to know about my quitting the force, and what my future plans were and so on.

And suddenly I knew what a part of my future plans would be; Nitti had reminded me of a debt somebody else owed me.

"I'm going to be working at the world's fair, boys," I told the newsmen. "I used to be with the pickpocket detail, you know, and General Dawes himself has contracted me to work with the fair's special security force in that regard."

They put that in their stories, and the next morning the phone rang.

"Hello, Uncle Louis," I said into it, without waiting to hear the voice on the other end. "When does the General want to see me?"

## 21

My appointment with General Dawes was at ten, and I figured I'd be out of there by noon, easy, for my luncheon date with Mary Ann Beame at the Seven Arts, a joint in Tower Town on the second floor of an old stable that made the Dill Pickle seem like Henrici's. I'd been seeing her a couple times a week since I got back from Miami, and by seeing her, I mean sleeping with her, and she was still driving me crazy with her small-town-girl-goes-bohemian ways, and one minute I wanted her out of my life and the next I was thinking about asking her to marry me, though with all her talk of a career I wasn't sure *where* I fit in.

Today I was going to tell her I'd pursued every avenue I could think of to find her brother—in Chicago at least—and the only idea I could think of, to pursue it further, was to start at the source: to go back to their hometown and try to track him from that end. Whether she'd go for that, since it would involve telling her father, who she'd kept out of this so far, I didn't know. But it was about all I had left. I'd checked with every newspaper in the suburbs and small towns around Chicago, and nobody recognized Jimmy's picture, and I hit the employment bureaus and the relief agencies and a hundred other places—and I'd run through that retainer of hers (which I'd initially thought was overly generous) weeks ago, with no intention of asking for anything else from her—except the right to keep seeing her. I was definitely going soft in the head department: that radio I bought I'd been using to listen to her on that silly soap opera—though I never admitted that to her.

At nine-thirty, after "Just Plain Bill," just as I was getting ready to walk over to the bank, a messenger delivered an envelope to me with a thousand-dollar bill in it.

There was also a note—"For services rendered"—typed on a sheet of Louis Piquett's law firm's stationery.

I called Piquett up; his secretary, after checking with him, put me through.

"I trust you've received my message, Mr. Heller. I hope it was satisfactory."

"Best message I've had in some time. But why? I didn't deliver on what your client hired me for. The man I was sent to protect isn't with us anymore, you know."

"Correct. And you haven't received the full ten thousand dollars promised, either. But my client does recognize you performed your services as best as circumstances would allow, and felt services rendered should be compensated."

"Thank your client for me."

"I will. And we're sorry for the delay in getting this message to you. My client's business transactions don't move as swiftly as they did before his confinement."

"I understand. Thanks, Mr. Piquett."

"My pleasure."

I got up from the desk and folded the thousand and put it in my pocket; too bad I didn't bank with Dawes—it would've saved me a trip. Of course the only banking I did with anybody these days was keep a safe-deposit box. Maybe happy days *were* here again; but bankings days weren't, as far as I was concerned.

The Dawes bank was on the corner of LaSalle and Adams, in the shadow of the Board of Trade Building and across from the Rookery, and was as pompous as the General himself: a massive graystone edifice with stone lion heads lording it over eight three-story pillars cut out of its face, little stone lions lurking above like regal gargoyles. A corridor ran the length of the building clear over to Wells Street, through a promenade of shops; the bank was on the second floor. Dawes had his office on the third. Just off the street entrance were rows of elevators on either side, and my uncle Louis—wearing a gray suit the price of which would feed a family of four for as many months—was pacing between them, getting in people's way.

"You're late," he said, barely opening his mouth, which was like a gash under his salt-and-pepper mustache.

"My limo stalled," I said.

He glared at me and we got on an elevator empty but for the operator; we had it all to ourselves. There's nothing like a family reunion.

"I hope you realize the position you've put me in," Uncle Louis said.

"What position is that?"

He glared at me again, and for the rest of the ride stood fuming silently, possibly searching for the words to put me in my place, but not finding them before the elevator operator opened the door for us at the third floor.

My uncle led me to a door without any lettering on it; inside was a male secretary at a desk in a large wood-paneled anteroom. The secretary nodded at us and buzzed us through, into a big bleak office that was more dark paneling with one of the walls covered by photos of the General and notables.

Dawes was sitting behind a big mahogany desk on which the stacks of papers were so neat it looked posed; so did the General, in a blue pinstripe, his hand touching his pipe. He didn't rise; his stern expression apprently meant he wasn't pleased with me, either.

"Sit down, gentlemen," he said.

There were chairs waiting for us; we filled them.

"Mr. Heller," the General said, then clarified: "*Young* Mr. Heller. What was the idea behind giving that story to the press?"

I pretended to be surprised. "Was I meant to keep our business arrangement a secret?"

Dawes sucked on the pipe; his brow was knit. "What business arrangement is that?"

"We spoke in December, at Saint Hubert's. You suggested that I let the chips fall where they may and tell the true story at the Nitti trial. In return, as a token of gratitude for performing this possibly dangerous civic duty, I was to be paid three thousand dollars for working with your security people at the fair, to help control the anticipated pickpocket problem there."

Dawes relit his pipe. It was an elaborate operation. He said, "I believe you're quite aware that the situation has changed since we spoke."

"The truth is still the truth. And a bargain is still a bargain."

"And Mayor Cermak is deceased."

"Yes. But what does that have to do with our contract?"

"I don't remember signing a contract with you, Mr. Heller."

"We had a verbal contract. My uncle here was witness to that."

Uncle Louis went pale as death.

I said, "I'm sure my uncle will attest to that."

My uncle said, "Nathan, please, you're being most rude "

Dawes interrupted with a wave of the hand. "Louis, I quite understand your position." He turned his gaze on me and it was like one of those stone lions was looking at me. "You should not have spoken to the papers about this. It was quite a breach of confidence."

I shrugged. "You said nothing about our agreement being a confidential one. Besides which, I didn't tell the reporters *why* you offered me the job at the fair—that *might* have been a breach of confidence. My testimony at the trial made news, you know; my views are of interest to the press at the moment. And they asked me my future plans."

Dawes leaned his head back and quite literally looked down his nose at me and, as if lecturing, said, "Once a reporter asked me if I were going to take my knickers with me to London—black silk knee breeches are usual court dress, over there—and I asked him if he wanted a diplomatic answer, or the kind the question deserved? And then I told him to go plumb to hell. You might in future take that example to heart."

"But if you void our deal, General, I'm going to be placed in an embarrassing light; I'll have to let the press know the circumstances. You've already had some unfortunate publicity of late, General—if you'll pardon my adding Insull to injury."

He looked at me solemnly. "This reeks of blackmail, young man."

"This reeks of business. And business is about money, and three thousand dollars to a private detective just starting out is good business indeed."

Uncle Louis was breathing hard.

The General said, "In my very young days, I had a burning ardor for money, Mr. Heller. But since then I have been interested in it only intermittently. One of the Rothschilds once said he made his fortune because he discovered there are times when one should *not* try to make money. It strikes me that money is something you are unduly interested in."

"The Rothschilds can afford that attitude. The Hellers—this Heller, anyway—can't. Now, I apologize for my bad etiquette with the press. But our agreement is binding, as far as I'm concerned, and if you feel differently, I'm going to be noisy about it. I'm not a big wheel, like you, General. But us little wheels can get awful goddamn squeaky when we don't get our grease."

Uncle Louis sat shaking his head, staring blankly at the wall of photos of the famous: Coolidge and Dawes; Hoover and Dawes; Pershing and Dawes; Mellon and Dawes.

The General lowered his gaze and began shuffling papers. He said,

"My secretary will have contracts ready for you to sign this afternoon at four. Please return then, and sign them, Mr. Heller. Good afternoon, gentlemen."

I rose and went out; Uncle Louis stayed behind, speaking to the General, but the General didn't seem to be having any. Uncle Louis caught up with me at the elevators.

"Let's you and me talk, Nate," he said, pointing down the hall. "I have an office, too."

That he did—and his own secretary, an attractive if bookish woman in her early thirties—but the interior office was perhaps a quarter the size of the General's, albeit bigger than my own. And Uncle Louis didn't seem to have a Murphy bed.

He did have a desk, and he sat behind it and tried to look as authoritarian and stern as the General. He damn near pulled it off; but I didn't help matters by refusing to take a chair.

He fairly spit the words at me. "You know damn good and well that the General's offer was made at a point in time when besmirching Mayor Cermak's name was a desirable thing. Now that Cermak is dead, and a martyr, your testimony at the Nitti trial has only caused the very sort of bad Chicago publicity the General wishes to avoid. You *know* all that, don't you? You knew that all along."

"Sure."

"And yet you take advantage of the General, and of me, and hold us to a bargain that was made under vastly different circumstances. Where do you get your damn nerve?"

"I think it's called *chutzpa*, Uncle Louis."

"You're an embarrassment to me. You *must* know all I have to do is tell the General that I'm willing to deny being a witness where that verbal contract is concerned, and your windfall at his—and my expense will be forfeit."

"Maybe. Maybe not. The General has old-world notions about keeping his word; part of the way he sees himself includes keeping promises, pretentious old fart that he is."

He stood and, his face redder than a Communist, thrust an arm out and pointed a finger as close to my face as he could get without hurtling the desk. "Consider yourself disinherited, disowned, you smartass, you *gonif* . . . you just traded three thousand dollars for more money than you could ever dream of. You're disinherited!"

"I don't want your money."

He suddenly seemed embarrassed for his outburst. Whether it was a pose or not, I can't say; but he sat down and folded his hands and, nervously, said, "I have no sons, Nathan. I have two daughters I love very much. But I always thought of you as . . . the son I never had."

"Horseshit."

Maybe it *had* been a pose: the hands flattened on the desk, fingers spread out but arched, like spiders, and his face turned hard. "You stood to inherit a lot of money, you ridiculous, ridiculous fool. And you threw that money away. Just threw it away. And nothing you can ever say will change it."

"Fine. So long."

I started to go.

"Get out! You're no nephew of mine. As far as I'm concerned, you're dead. As dead as Cermak."

"As dead as my father?"

Uncle Louis blanched. "What does your father have to do with it?"

"Maybe plenty. Maybe he's why I put you on the spot with Dawes. You don't dare *not* back me up, do you, or Dawes will lose respect for you. He doesn't like outright liars, and he has an overriding sense of family. He idolizes that dead son of his, building fancy flophouses in his memory, and he wouldn't take kindly to the sort of man who would turn on his family, for mere monetary or business concerns."

"Nate. Nathan. Why—why this bitterness? What have I done to you?"

"You haven't done anything. You've done me favors."

"Yes I have. I got you on the force. Could your father have done that?"

"No, and he wouldn't if he could. He hated the cops, and it was the saddest day of his life when I joined up. And you knew that; that's why you helped me get on. You didn't do it for me. You didn't give a damn about me, one way or the other. It was to get back at Pa. Because him you hated."

Silence hung between us like a curtain.

Finally he said, "I didn't hate him, Nathan."

"Then why did you kill him, Uncle Louis?"

"Kill him? What obscenity are you speaking . . ."

"You kept your eye on me, didn't you, Uncle Louis? Kept track of your nephew on the force. You were thick with Cermak, way back when, and you've always been thick with the politicians and all the boys behind the scenes."

He shrugged, not following me, exactly. "I—I suppose that's right."

"Well, somebody in the know told my father where the money came from that I gave him for his shop. Somebody told him it was blood money. Somebody told him his son Nathan was a crooked cop."

Uncle Louis, looking more than ever like a thin version of my father, a shadow of the man my father had been, said nothing; his eyes were wet and his bottom lip trembled.

"You told him, Uncle Louis. You told him. And he killed himself."

Uncle Louis said nothing.

My eyes were wet, too. I pointed my finger at him. "I disinherit *you,* fucker. I disown you."

And I left the guilt there with him.

THE CHICAGO WORLD'S FAIR

# 3
# TOWER TOWN
## APRIL 9–JUNE 25, 1933

"LITTLE BIT O' HEAVEN"

## 22

Winter was over, but it was still cold. Mary Ann Beame and I set out for a Sunday drive under overcast skies that didn't let the sun peek through once in six hours—which is how long a Sunday drive we took, starting out around noon and heading across the state toward the Mississippi River and the Tri-Cities, where Mary Ann and her lost brother Jimmy had been born and raised.

This was my first cross-country trip, and even with paved roads, I was a little uneasy about it. The '29 Chevy had been getting me around the city well enough, but clear across the state? That suddenly seemed overly ambitious, particularly under a sky this nasty.

But soon I was going a confident 40 mph down U.S. 30, farm country whizzing by us on either side—though I did slow down for the dozen or so little towns along the way. Eviction notices in the farmyards, and out-of-business signs in store windows, said that hard times wasn't something Chicago had cornered the market on. All that farmland, stretching out flat to the horizon, looking wasteland-barren this time of year, broken only by the occasional farmhouse/silo/barn, came as a shock to a city kid. I knew this rural world surrounded Chicago, but I'd never really seen it before, and when we pulled up to a gas station outside of DeKalb, a farmer in coveralls and floppy straw hat, his face as barren as the land, leaned against his pickup truck, which was getting filled at the next pump, and regarded us like visitors from another planet. So did a couple more farmers sitting leaned back in chairs in front of the station, chewing tobacco, apparently not minding the somewhat chilly day.

Mary Ann didn't seem to notice these folks as anything special; she'd come from a rather rural community herself, and in fact she sat with her nose in the air, ignoring the riffraff, going high-hat like so many expatriates do when they finally condescend to come home.

She sat in the Chevy in her white hat and black-and-white-checked dress and waited for me to get her a grape Nehi from inside, where I found more farmers playing rummy at a table, drinking bottles of Zollers beer. I got two bottles of pop from the cooler and paid the attendant, a kid about twenty with red cheeks and bright eyes who asked me where I was from. I told him Chicago.

"Are those Cubs gonna take it this year?" he asked me.

He meant the pennant; first nonexhibition game of the season was this coming week.

"Wouldn't be surprised," I said. They'd won it last year and were favored to again.

"I been to a game in Chicago," he said, grinning. "More'n once."

I grinned back at him. "Me, too."

I went out and stood by the car and handed Mary Ann in her bottle of grape pop; mine was orange. Over to one side of the station, some farm kids were pitching horseshoes.

"It's a whole different world," I said.

"What is?" Mary Ann asked flatly, doing her best to drink from the pop bottle with dignity.

"This is," I said, pointing to two barefoot farm kids about eleven who were going in the station. A minute or so later, they came out, a kid clutching a half-pint of Hey Brothers Ice Cream and another with two small wooden spoons in one fist, fishing a jackknife out of a pocket with his other hand. They sat over by the slightly older kids playing horseshoes, and the kid with the knife cut the carton of ice cream in half and handed one half to the other kid, and they both dug in with the wooden spoons.

"Doesn't that look good?" I said.

"What?" Mary Ann said.

I pointed the kids out to her again.

She made a face, said, "Too cold for ice cream," and handed me back the empty Nehi bottle.

I finished my Nehi off, put the bottles in a wooden carton up by the door near the tobacco-chewing farmers, and gave the red-cheeked kid a buck for the gas and told him to keep the change. His face lit up like nobody had ever done that to him before, and maybe they hadn't.

We rumbled down the road, sitting silently for maybe a hundred miles. I was irritated with Mary Ann. All day so far she had chattered about herself and her ambitions (Hollywood was figuring in her fantasies now), but when I had tried to point out the simple rustic charms of the countryside along the way, like that gas station back there, she had nothing to say—except, perhaps, "They're just a bunch of hicks, Nathan," or something similar.

We ate supper at a roadside café called Twin Oaks, just the other side of Sterling-Rock Falls, where we would catch Illinois highway 3. The place was busy, and we had to sit at the counter, and Mary Ann didn't like that; she also didn't like the looks of the greasy Greek who served us, and she didn't like the way I looked at the young woman doing the cooking, who came out to ask me how I'd liked her pie.

"Little tramp," Mary Ann said as we drove away.

I shrugged. "She was cute. And the cherry pie was good, too."

"She was common."

"What's wrong with common?"

"Nothing, in your eyes."

Now she was irritated with *me*, and didn't speak till we hit the Tri-Cities, cutting through Moline to Rock Island, where a government bridge crossed over to Davenport, connecting also to the nearby Rock Island Arsenal. The riverfront, on the Illinois side anyway, was given over to railroad tracks and factories; what residential sections we saw seemed to be nothing special – these were workingman's towns, or had been before times got bad. As we crossed the black steel bridge, the lock and dam on either side, the Mississippi below looked dark and choppy. A lot like the sky.

We turned left into Davenport, through a warehouse district and into the downtown. It seemed puny to me, like a scale-model of Chicago that might be displayed at the fair next month. The tallest building, which was maybe twenty stories, of which a good portion was a clock tower, had a beacon light, sort of a pocketwatch version of the Lindbergh Beacon atop the Palmolive Building. But to somebody not Chicago-bred, the Tri-Cities might have seemed like a metropolis Davenport's population alone was sixty thousand, Mary Ann said, third largest city in Iowa—and the five or six blocks of shops and restaurants probably seemed like the big city to the farmers and small-town folks of the surrounding area.

Mary Ann directed me up a hill, which was Harrison Street, and had me turn to the left, up into an area where Gothic mansions perched on the bluff to look down upon the Tri-Cities; some of the mansions were starting to look a bit down at the mouth and long in the tooth—some seemed to have been turned into apartment houses. The house Mary Ann guided me toward was not one of the Gothic ones, however, but something more modern, a Frank Lloyd Wright-style two-story brown-brick affair that might best be described as a modernistic castle, right down to the art-deco turrets. Sitting at the end of the block, mansions of an earlier day all around, it perched on the edge of the steep hill that fell sharply to a side street below. I pulled into a paved driveway that curved around to the left to a double garage and left the car there. I got my overnight bag and Mary Ann's suitcase out of the rumble seat and a light went on over a side door, near the garage.

He was thin and distinguished-looking, gray-haired with a dark mustache, wearing a pale gray suit and darker gray tie and, most significantly, gray gloves. He stood in the doorway and waited for us to come to him, but his manner, as he swung open the screen door, was friendly ·he had a reserved but unfeigned smile going.

We stepped into a white, modern kitchen, with a nook off to the left, and I put the bags down as Mary Ann hugged her father and gestured toward me, almost offhandedly, saying, "This is Nathan Heller, Daddy," and left us there in the kitchen alone.

His reserved smile turned into a more open, if embarrassed one, and he said, "You'll have to excuse my daughter, Mr. Heller. If you've traveled all the way here from Chicago with her, I suppose you know by now that she has a mind of her own. Unfortunately, that mind at times seems in no way connected to the real world."

This was said with obvious affection for his daughter, but I did appreciate this immediate honesty from a man whose bearing suggested reticence.

"Good to meet you, sir," I said, and extended my hand without thinking, even though Mary Ann had told me about her father.

He extended a gray-gloved hand, which had only two fingers in it, the thumb and forefinger, and we shook hands. Despite his having only a fraction of a hand to do it with, the grip was as firm as you'd expect a chiropractor's grip to be. I noticed his other, similarly gloved hand appeared to have all its fingers.

My face must've revealed my indecision as to whether or not I should apologize for my faux pas, because he smiled compassionately and said, "Think nothing of it, Mr. Heller. Shaking hands with people is something I have never given up, despite a shortage of digits."

I smiled back at him. "Is that coffee I smell?"

It was perking over on the stove.

"It certainly is," he said, going over to a cupboard. "Have you eaten?"

"Yes, we stopped at Sterling-Rock Falls."

"Good. My cook has Sunday off, and while I've been a bachelor for

twenty-some years now, coffee is as yet my only culinary achieve-
ment. I'm afraid you'd have been in for cold cuts, had you needed a
meal. The coffee, however, I can guarantee. Care to try a cup?"

"Love to," I said.

He gestured toward the nook, and I went over and sat down. He
brought two steaming cups over and we sat and drank in silence. He
was, I believe, trying to figure out where to begin with me; I was just
enjoying the coffee and not being in the Chevy, though the nook was
a little reminiscent of a cramped car, at that. A bath and bed sounded
good to me.

But Mary Ann's father wanted to talk, and, since I was here to
gather information about Jimmy Beame, I wasn't about to discourage
him.

"My daughter called me a few days ago, Mr. Heller," he said, "and
told me who you are, and why you've made this journey."

"Make it Nate, please."

"Fine. And my name is John."

"All right, John. Do you disapprove of my trying to locate your
son?"

"I would've, six months ago. Now . . . well, I'm inclined to support
your efforts. In fact, if my daughter hasn't paid you sufficiently, I
would be glad to underwrite your efforts myself."

"That isn't necessary," I said.

Somebody cleared her throat.

We turned and looked over where, in the doorless doorway of the
kitchen, Mary Ann, in a baby-blue bathrobe that covered her from
neck to slippers, stood, arms folded, rather cross. Pouty.

"I just wanted to say good night," she said.

"Good night, darling," her father said.

She came over and hugged him again, remembering, I guess, that
it was me she was irritated with, not him; and she kissed him on the
cheek and smiled at him, then glanced over at me and put the smile
away and went over and got her suitcase and turned her back and
padded out with it.

I called out to her: "Good night, Mary Ann."

"Good night," she said, like a child, her back to me, already
through the doorway and halfway down the hall.

John Beame studied me, like he might a difficult patient.

"That's something she *didn't* inform me of," he said.

"What's that, sir?"

"That she's in love with you."

"Well, uh . . ."

"Are you in love with her?"

"Sir, I . . ."

"She's a wonderful girl. Difficult. Childish. Self-centered. But quite unique, and loving, in her way."

"Yeah. Wonderful."

"You *do* love her, don't you?"

"I guess I do. Damned if I know why, if you'll excuse me for saying so, sir."

"John," he said, smiling wryly. "I love her because she's my daughter, Nate. What's your excuse?"

I laughed. "I just never met anybody like her before."

"Yes. And she's attractive, isn't she?"

"No argument there, sir . . . John."

"Spitting image of her mother, rest her soul. More coffee?"

"Please."

He brought the pot over and filled my cup; his gloved hands seemed able to cope pretty well. I tried not to look at them.

"Oh, these hands of mine function well enough, Nate," he said. "I can even give chiropractic adjustments with them, though I haven't practiced for years, in terms of hanging a shingle out. I was afraid, with some justification I might say, that my patients would be repulsed by my hands being disfigured. Of course I could've worn gloves, but even then—with only two fingers on my right hand and considerable pain in those early years—it didn't seem worth the trouble. My friend and mentor, B. J. Palmer, offered me a position teaching at his college, which evolved into my managing his radio station. WOC was the second licensed radio station in the United States, you know. At any rate, it's been, and continues to be, an interesting life. And certain of my friends still come to me privately, gratis, for chiropractic care. I have a room with an adjusting table upstairs."

"Mary Ann said you injured your hands in an automobile accident."

He looked into his cup of coffee; stared in. "Yes. Years ago, when she and Jimmy were very small."

"They were in the accident, too?"

He nodded. "I often took them on house calls. I had one out in the country, one evening, a farmer who'd twisted his back in a hayloft fall. A lot of my patients were rural   I come from rural stock myself.

It was my father's greatest disappointment that I didn't follow in his footsteps as a farmer, but I had a brother who made him happier, by staying in that field, if you will pardon a pun. But you asked about the accident. It was dark, and the road was narrow, unlit . . . a dirt road with deep ditches. Some drunken fool, driving without lights, ran into us, and . . . I was not entirely blameless. Like him, I was driving rather more fast than would seem in retrospect prudent . . . anxious to get my children home, wondering why I'd used such bad judgment in bringing them along on an evening call . . . but then, widower that I was and am, I had no one to stay with them, so I often took them along . . ."

He stopped. Sipped the coffee. The cup in the thumb and fore-finger of the gloved hand looked like an affectation, and added to the peculiarly formal tone of our conversation.

"Mr. Beame. John, I was just curious—it's my nature as a detec-tive, I guess. If this is something you'd rather not discuss . . ."

"Nate, there's not much left to tell. The collision was head on; both cars ended in the ditch, and there was a fire. I burned my hands pulling my children from the wreckage; burned them worse pulling the drunken fool from his wreckage—but he died anyway. His head had hit the windscreen with such force the glass cracked."

"Mary Ann and Jimmy, were they injured?"

"Minorly. Cuts. Scrapes. They needed considerable chiropractic care. They'd always been close, being twins, but with a boy and a girl, you might expect them to be less close than if they'd been of the same gender. But this experience—this brush with death, if you'll allow an old man his melodrama—brought them even closer together than before."

"I see."

"They were, if I recall correctly, seven years old at the time. I believe the experience may have also encouraged their flights of fancy. The world of make-believe was always a better place than the world of reality, for them."

"That's true for all children."

He nodded, sadly. "But most children grow out of it. Jimmy—and, as you can see, Mary Ann—never abandoned their romantic fancies. A boy reads *Treasure Island* and wants to be a pirate when he grows up; but then he grows up and he is an accountant or a lawyer or a teacher. A girl reads *Alice in Wonderland* and wants to dress up and chase mythical white rabbits down holes; but then she grows up and is wife and a mother to her own little girls and boys."

"Sounds like you don't believe in Peter Pan."

He smiled sadly again. "Unfortunately, it would seem, my children do."

"Aren't you being a little unfair, sir? Your daughter *is* an actress, and that's a recognized profession, in which she seems to be doing rather well."

He shrugged. "With some help from me."

"Let me tell you some facts of life about the big city. You can get strings pulled for you, to get into a job; you can have a relative with money or position buy or clout your way in for you. But once you're in, if you don't cut the mustard, you get cut, but fast. If Mary Ann wasn't doing a good job for those radio people, she'd've had her pretty rear end fired by now, if you'll excuse the crudity."

He folded his gloved hands, the fingers of his left hand resting over the knuckles of his right, where fingers had been. His smile was gentle. "I'll excuse it gladly, Nate. Because you're right. I suppose I have been unfair, where my children are concerned. Mary Ann *is* doing quite well. I only hope Jimmy is."

"Tell me about him."

"You have to understand something. During the years Jimmy was growing up, the Tri-Cities was a wild place . . . in the Chicago, gangster sense, that is. And it still is, to a degree. At any rate, the papers then were full of gunplay and sensationalism, as events admittedly warranted. A gangster named Looney trained his own son as a gunman, and when the son was shot down by rival gangsters, Looney ran on the front of the scandal sheet he published—which he used for purposes of extortion—a photograph of his dead son in his coffin. He accused the other, legitimate newspapers in town of *hiring* the murder."

"Your son was a little boy when this was going on?"

"Yes. And I would sit at this very table and, I must say, rant and rave about this deplorable situation; and my wide-eyed son would sit and take it all in, impressionable lad that he was. I would tell my son that this Looney gangster, by publishing his scandal sheet, was disgracing one of America's most honorable institutions: the press. That he was making a laughingstock of one of our greatest freedoms: freedom of the press."

"And that's when Jimmy caught the newspaper bug?"

"I suspect so. That, and the lurid stories that even our respectable papers were printing, because those things were indeed going on— bootlegging, wide-open gambling houses, houses of ill repute, riots in which innocent bystanders were slain, gangland slayings, all of it. It captured his imagination."

"That seems normal enough."

"Then, when he was older, I introduced him to Paul Traynor, a police reporter with the *Democrat*."

"When was this?"

"His high school days. Paul liked Jimmy; endured the boy's questions, let him accompany him to trials, took him home and he and Jimmy would talk for hours. I admit to feeling jealous of Paul, a bit. But I saw nothing unhealthy about it, though Jimmy's fascination with gangsters—he often brought home Chicago papers, and kept a scrapbook of bloody clippings—disturbed me greatly. And Looney's gang had by this time been replaced by another, equally vicious bunch, some of whom are still around."

"What about Paul Traynor? Is he still around?"

"Oh yes. I can arrange for you to talk with him, if you like."

"That might be helpful. Did your son live here with you while he was going to college?"

"Yes. He attended Augustana, which is just over in Rock Island. I thought I had him convinced to switch to Palmer, when he left."

"Rather unceremoniously, I take it."

"I'm afraid so. My initial bitterness over his going came from Jimmy's manipulation of me. You see, for several years—since his last years in high school, in fact—we had quarreled on the subject of his future. But that last week he had changed his mind, he said. I know now he was only pretending to agree with me, to avoid conflict, to be able to slip away quietly. And, in fact, I had given him several hundred dollars, for his Palmer tuition. He was very convincing. Mary Ann is not the only person in this family with acting ability, it would seem."

"I see. What were his personal habits, those last few years he lived here?"

"He was out nights, often. We quarreled about that, as well, for what good it did. All the Sen Sen in the world could not disguise the fact that he had often been drinking, which he knew was anathema to me."

"So for a while after he left, then, you felt, 'good riddance.'"

"That's harsh, Nate. But I suppose it does sum up the way I felt, yes. But that was well over a year ago. I had thought surely he'd get in touch with us by now—perhaps not me, but his sister, as close as they were . . ."

"She hasn't heard from him."

"Nor have I, and I *am* concerned. Now I am concerned."

"Well, I'm going to do my best to track him down. But it's a big country, and a young guy like him could be most anywhere and up to most anything."

"I understand that. But I do appreciate your efforts, Nate, and I appreciate Mary Ann's concern for her brother's welfare."

"I need to talk to some people. Besides Traynor, was anyone else close to Jimmy?"

"There was a fellow named Hoffmann at the radio station, a boy in his early twenties who was an announcer and did a bit of sportscasting. But he's not with WOC any longer—he moved on with no forwarding address. He broke in our new boy before he left, however, and perhaps it would be worth talking to him—the new boy, I mean."

"Would he have known Jimmy?"

"No. Dutch has only been with us a few months. But he and Hoffmann were socially active, and Jimmy may have come up in conversation. He's worth talking to."

"Anyone else?"

"I can't think of anyone. Jimmy's high school and college chums have graduated and scattered to the four corners of the earth, for all I know. And outside of journalism, he wasn't very active and had few friends. Mary Ann was probably his best friend in that period, and I'm sure you've questioned her thoroughly about those days."

"Yeah. Well, the two names you've given me are a start. This sportscaster, when could I meet him?"

"Tomorrow morning. I'll put it in motion. And I'll arrange an appointment with Traynor in the late morning or early afternoon."

"Good."

"Let me show you where you'll be sleeping, then. It's Jimmy's room, upstairs."

The house was as modern inside as out: pale plaster walls and wood floors, wood beam ceilings, a minimum of wall decoration. Only Beame's study, a large book-lined room with several comfortable-looking leather chairs and a matching couch, looked lived in. This I glimpsed as we walked down a hallway and around to the stairs. I took my overnight bag up with me.

It was a corner room, not terribly large, with a double bed and little else; there were some shelves on two of the walls, but they were empty. Any traces of Jimmy's presence were missing from the room; this must have registered on my face, because John Beame picked up on it.

"I'm not one for maintaining shrines, Nate," he said, with his sad smile. "I'm sure Mary Ann will be unhappy with me, for removing the model planes and pirate ships and the antique crossbow and the rest of Jimmy's paraphernalia."

"Well, the way he took a powder, who can blame you for tossing the junk out."

I'd used the word "junk" to test the old boy, and he passed: he flinched as I said it.

"I didn't throw his things out, Nate," he said. "They're crated away in the basement. Except those damn scrapbooks of his. Those I burned."

He touched his face, for a moment, with a gray-gloved hand; he wasn't as strong as he liked to think. Then he excused himself, saying he'd let me get settled and come back later, and I stripped down to my drawers and got into bed. I looked over toward the window, where the moonlight was coming in, though I couldn't see the moon itself.

I thought about Mary Ann, in a room nearby; next door maybe. Part of me wanted to go looking for her; part of me wanted her to come looking for me.

And part of me didn't want anything to do with her, not tonight, anyway. Not here. Not in her brother's room. His bed. That would've bothered me, though for the life of me I didn't know why.

Thunder woke me.

I sat up in bed; rain was at the windows, rattling them, pelting them. I checked my wristwatch on the small table by the bed: just after three. I tried to go back to sleep, but the insistent tattoo of rain, and the ground-shaking thundercracks, worked against me. I got up and went to a window and looked out. That nasty sky we'd driven here under had finally kept its promise, and I was glad I was inside and not driving across Illinois in a Chevy. Then, while I was still there at the window, the sky burst open, showering hailstones; it was like a dozen Dizzy Deans were up there hurling baseballs at the house. It made an incredible racket.

"Nathan?"

I looked back and Mary Ann, still in the baby-blue robe, arms folded to herself protectively, was rushing across the room to me. She hugged me. She was trembling.

"Just a hailstorm, baby," I said.

"Please. Get away from the window."

Down on the lawn, the hailstones were gathering. Christ if they *weren't* the size of baseballs. One of them careened off the window, and I took Mary Ann's advice.

We stood by the bed and I held her.

"Let me get in under the covers with you," she said.

She sounded like a kid; there was no ulterior motive here: she was really scared.

"Sure," I said, and went over and shut the door.

She curled up against me in bed, clinging to me, and, gradually, her shaking stopped, though the hailstones kept up for a good twenty minutes.

"I'm sorry about today," she said; I could barely hear her over the hailstones.

"We were both a little childish," I said.

"I suppose maybe I am sort of a snob," she said.

"Who isn't?"

"I do love you, Nathan."

"You do, huh?"

"I do."

"Why?"

"I'm not sure. Do you know why you love me?"

"Besides the physical? I'm not sure, either."

"I feel safe with you, Nathan."

"That's nice," I said, meaning it.

"You're stronger than me. You see the world as it is."

"In my trade, you see it any other way, you don't last long."

"I guess I've always seen it through rose-colored glasses."

"Well, at least you know that. That means you're more of a realist than you think."

"Everybody who sees the world through rose-colored glasses is a realist. That's why they put the rose-colored glasses on."

"Come on now, Mary Ann. You've had a nice life so far, haven't you? I mean, you don't exactly seem to've had it tough. Your father appears to be a terrific guy."

"He is. He's wonderful."

"And you obviously got along well with your brother, or you wouldn't be going to all the trouble of hiring me to track him down."

"Yes. Jimmy and I were very close—I—would crawl in bed with him sometimes, like this. Don't get me wrong. It wasn't like—like that. I suppose we played doctor and kissed and did the silly things kids will do growing up. But I wasn't in love with my brother, Nathan. We didn't do anything wrong."

"I know."

"I *know* you know, because you're the only man I've ever been with. And you know that's true."

"I know."

"But Jimmy and I . . . we banded together. Daddy is wonderful, but he can be—distant. He's sort of formal. It's the doctor side of him, I guess; or the professor side, maybe. I'm not sure, exactly. I grew up aware of not having a mother. I grew up aware of her having died giving birth to me. And Jimmy. I used to cry about it, at night, sometimes. Not often—don't get me wrong—I'm not neurotic or anything. The psychiatrist I go to is simply for understanding myself better—that's only healthy for an actress, don't you agree?"

"Sure."

"Did my father tell you about the accident? When he burned his hands?"

"Yes."

"It was my fault. Did he tell you that?"

"No . . ."

"I saw the other car. I saw the other car coming at us, and I got kind of—hysterical, I guess, and I grabbed Daddy's arm, and I think—I've never said this out loud to anybody but Jimmy—I think that's why Daddy couldn't avoid the other car."

"Mary Ann, have you ever talked to your father about this?"

"No. Not really."

"Look. The other car was driven by a drunk driver. Without any lights on, is what your father told me. Isn't that true?"

"Yes," she admitted.

"So if it was anybody's fault it was that guy's. And even if it *had* been in some way your fault, you were a little *kid*. You got scared, and so what? You should let go of this."

"That's what my psychiatrist says."

The hailstones were trailing off; the rain kept at it.

"Well, he's right," I said.

"I just wanted to tell you about it. I don't know why I wanted to. It's just something I wanted to share with you . . . if 'share' is the right word."

"I'm glad you did. I don't like secrets."

"I don't either. Nathan?"

"Yes?"

"I know another reason why I love you."

"Really?"

"You're honest."

I laughed out loud at that. "Nobody ever accused me of *that* before."

"I read about you in the papers. I said I came to your office because you were first in the phone book. Well, that was partially true. I also—I recognized your name, too. I remembered reading about you quitting the police, after that shooting. I asked some of my friends in Tower Town about it, and they said they heard you quit because you didn't want to be a party to the corruption."

"That sounds like the kind of high-flown horseflop that might pass for thinking in Tower Town."

"It's true, isn't it? And you told the truth at that trial, last week. Because you're honest."

I took her by the small of the arm; not hurting her, but firm enough to engage her attention. "Look, Mary Ann. Don't build me into something I'm not. Don't put your rose-colored glasses on when you look at me. I'm more honest than some people I know, but the soul of honesty, I'm not. Are you listening?"

She just smiled at me, like the child she was—or chose to be.

"Is that why you love me?" I asked. "Because I'm a detective? A private eye? Don't build me into a romantic figure, Mary Ann. I'm just a man."

She picked my hand off her arm like a flower and gave me that impish grin of hers, which she really had down pat by now. Then she hugged me and said, "I know you're a man. I've been paying attention."

"Have you, Mary Ann?"

"Maybe I am naïve, Nathan. But I know you're a man, and an honest one—for Chicago, anyway."

"Mary Ann . . ."

"Just be honest with me. Don't lie to me, Nathan. No secrets. No deceptions."

"That's good, coming from an actress."

She sat up in bed; the blue robe hung open and I could see the start of the gentle curves of the cups of either breast. "Promise me," she said. "No lies. And I'll promise you the same."

"Okay," I said. "That's fair."

She grinned, and not impishly—not in any way contrived or calculated—a good, honest grin, and a beautiful one.

"Now," she said, suddenly serious, slipping the robe off, "make love to me."

I didn't argue with her, even if this was her brother's bed. But I did reach for my billfold, to get a Sheik, and she stopped me.

"Don't use anything," she said.

"That can lead to little Mary Anns and Nathans, you know."

"I know. You can pull out if you want, but I want to feel you in me. And I want to feel me . . ."

The intensity of the rain kept pace with us, and the reflection of the rain on her ghostly pale flesh as I arched over her, driving steadily but sweetly into her, was ever-shifting, creating streaky, elu-

sive patterns on her, and her mouth was open in a smile, in her
passion, and her eyes gazed at me with an adoration that I'd never
seen in any woman's eyes before; and when I withdrew from her, she
had a momentary look of pain and then she grabbed that part of me in
her hands so that I would spill into them, and she cupped my seed in
her hands, then clasped her hands together and held the warm seed
there and looked up at me with a closemouthed smile that I will take
to my grave.

Finally, back to reality, she took some tissues from the pocket of
the robe and, with droll reluctance, wiped her hands, putting the
robe on, kissing me, touching my face, leaving me there, as the storm
dissipated.

In the morning her father had grapefruit and coffee ready for us.
He wore gray again—a different suit, a different gray tone in the tie,
but gray again—perhaps that was because gray seemed the least conspicuous color for the ever-present gloves.

Mary Ann and I sat on one side of the nook, her father on the
other; I stayed out of the breakfast conversation, for the most part,
while father and daughter filled each other in on what they'd been up
to lately. John Beame dutifully reported that he had indeed been
listening to his daughter's radio programs—he even took a morning
break for "Just Plain Bill," in his little office at the college; and he
particularly liked an adaptation of "East Lynne" that he'd heard her
in on "Mr. First-Nighter."

That seemed to please Mary Ann, who was wearing this morning a
feminine yellow-and-white print dress that I could not picture her
wearing in Tower Town.

I took a quick look at the morning *Democrat:* hailstorm damage
locally amounted to one hundred thousand dollars; one of the
Scotsboro boys had been found guilty in that rape case; Roosevelt was
asking Congress to approve of something he called the Tennessee
Valley Authority.

"Can I give you a ride over to the college, sir?" I asked him, as the
conversation between father and daughter seemed to have wound
down.

"I usually walk," he smiled, "but I'm willing to be a loafer this
once."

"Hope you don't mind the rumble seat," I said.

"I've put up with worse indignities," he allowed.

"That must mean I'm invited along," Mary Ann said.

"Sure," I said. "For right now."

She went mock-snooty. "Well, I like *that*," she said, getting out of the nook, going after her purse. Her father and I let her lead us out to the car, where the drive and lawn were strewn with melting hailstones; it was cloudy and a little cold. Somebody somewhere in town was burning garbage: the smell hung in the dank air like rotten fruit. Soon we were going down Harrison, cutting left on Seventh Street, and heading up the steep hill of Brady.

At the crest of Brady, across from a mortuary, was Palmer College, a collection of long rambling brown-brick buildings crowded together, taking up two square blocks. In front of what seemed to be the central building was a round deco clock on a skinny pole and a neon sign that said:

### RADIO STATION

### W

### O

### C

### VISITORS
### WELCOME

and, beneath that, CAFETERIA, inside a neon pointing arrow. From atop adjacent buildings, twin black antenna towers rose like derricks.

I found a place on the street to park and followed Beame and his daughter into the building the neon hung from. There were students in their twenties all about, mostly male, but a few female. Inside, the place looked like pretty much any college, with one strange exception: epigrams were painted in black on the cream-color plaster walls, just about everywhere you looked: over doors, on the ceiling, on the wall going up the stairs, everywhere. Their wisdom seemed a bit obscure to me, at best: "Use Your Friends/By Being of Use to Them"; "Early to Bed, Early to Rise/Work Like Hell and Advertise"; "The More You Tell/The Quicker You Sell." Was this a medical school for bonesetters, or a training school for Burma Shave salesmen? Mary Ann must've caught me making a face, and shook her head no, letting me know this was not a subject to get into with her father.

We went up an elevator to the top floor of the school, the doors opening onto the reception room of the radio station, which was even stranger than the motto-strewn floors below: it resembled, more than anything, a den in a hunting lodge. A heavy chunk of wood with wavy letters spelling RECEPTION ROOM carved out of it hung by chains from a ceiling that was crossed by several varnished tree trunks; the rustic wood-and-brick room was wall to wall with photos of celebrities, both local and national, in misshapen roughhewn frames. Visitors were apparently expected to sit on benches made of varnished tree limbs and branches; amid this rustic nonsense was an electric sign with lit-up red letters that demanded SILENCE and reminded you, vaguely, that this was the twentieth century.

This time Beame noticed me smirking, I guess, because he seemed a little embarrassed, as he gestured to the area and said, "B.J. does have his eccentricities." He meant B. J. Palmer, of course, head of the school and the station, and judging from the sotto voce Beame used, which wasn't just because of the SILENCE sign, B.J.'s being eccentric wasn't a thought you expressed openly, at least not loudly.

There was no receptionist, but we hadn't been there long when, through a rectangular window that seemed at first to be just another (if oversize) photo on the wall, a face peered, belonging to a handsome collegiate-type with crew cut and glasses, wearing a brown suit and green tie.

He came into the reception room, moving with an athlete's assurance, and Mary Ann smiled at him and he smiled shyly back at her and then the smile turned almost brash as he held his hand out to me, saying, "I understand you're from Chicago."

"That's right," I said.

"I tried to get work there," he said. "They said I should try a station in the sticks." He grinned and nodded up at the wood overhead. "So I took 'em at their word."

Beame put a hand on the kid's shoulder and said, "Nate Heller, this young man is Dutch Reagan. He's our top sportscaster. In fact we're losing him to our sister station WHO in Des Moines, in a few weeks."

"Glad to meet you, Dutch," I said, and we shook hands: Yes, he was an athlete all right. "Hope we're not interrupting you."

"I don't go on the air for another fifteen minutes yet," he said.

Beame introduced Reagan to Mary Ann, who was obviously impressed by the handsome kid.

"Mr. Beame said you're here to talk to me about his son," Reagan said, adjusting his glasses, "but I never knew Jimmy. I've only been at WOC four months."

"But you were a close friend of another announcer here who *did* know Jimmy."

"Jack Hoffmann. Sure."

"Mr. Beame thought Jimmy might have come up in conversation with Hoffmann."

Beame said, "It's a long shot, Dutch. But Jimmy had so few friends . . ."

Reagan thought about it; his face was so earnest it hurt. "Can't think of anything, sir. I'm really sorry."

I shrugged. "Like the man said, it was a long shot. Thanks, anyway."

"Sure. Oh, Mr. Heller. Could I have a word with you? Could you step in the studio for a second?"

"Fine," I said.

Beame looked curious, and Reagan said, "I want to ask Mr. Heller to look up a friend of mine in Chicago. No big deal."

Beame nodded, and Reagan and I went into the studio, a room hung with dark blue velvet drapes, for soundproofing purposes, though the ceiling was crossed by more trees, bark and all, attached to which were various stuffed birds, poised as if in flight, though they weren't going anywhere.

"I didn't want to talk in front of Mr. Beame," Reagan said. "I *do* know some things about his son, but they aren't very flattering."

"Oh?"

Beame was watching us through the window; stuffed birds watched us from tree beams above.

"Yeah. He was in with a rough crowd. Hanging around in speakeasies. Drinking. Fooling around with the ladies, using that term loosely, if you get my drift."

"I get it. You know what joints he might've been frequenting?"

Reagan smiled on one side of his face. "I'm no teetotaler. I'm Irish."

"That means you might know where some of those places are."

"Yeah. Jack Hoffmann and I used to hit some of 'em, occasionally. And those I haven't been in, I know about. Why?"

"You working tonight?"

"No."

"Busy?"

"Are you buyin'?"

"That's right."

"I live at the Perry Apartments, corner of East Fourth and Perry. I'll be waiting out front at eight tonight. Swing by."

"I'll do that," I said, and we shook hands, and he smiled at me, and it was an infectious smile.

"Irish, huh?" I said.

"That's what they tell me," he said, and went back in his announcer's booth, which was visible through a window in the left draped wall, where a bulky WOC microphone could also be glimpsed.

In the rustic reception room, Mary Ann's father said, "What was that all about?"

"Old girl friend of his he wants me to check up on."

"Oh."

"Nice guy."

"Yes. Yes, he is. Now, then. I've made an appointment with Paul Traynor, for ten o'clock, at the newspaper. In the meantime, I've got to stay up here and get to work. I'll leave you at my daughter's mercy."

"Come along," Mary Ann said, taking my arm as we got on the elevator. "That appointment's at ten and it's only half past eight now. I'm going to take you on a tour of my favorite place in the world. Or anyway, the Tri-Cities."

"Really? And what's that?"

"'A Little Bit O' Heaven.' Ever hear of it?"

"Can't say I have. Where is it?"

"Next door."

Soon I was walking with Mary Ann across an oriental courtyard, past a thirty-foot-long writhing rock-and-tile and chipped-stone snake, by two idols with human heads and monkey bodies, under shell-and-stone umbrellas, through a four-ton revolving door inlaid with thousands of pearl chips and semiprecious stones, into a big pagoda of a building in which ancient hindu idols coexisted with Italian marble pieces that luxuriated in lushly lit waterfalls; where rock gardens and pools and ponds and fish and fauna and petrified wood and growing plants and shells and agates came together to form a place I   and no one—had ever seen the like of before. Trouble was, I wasn't sure I wanted to.

I said little as she led me around; she was enthralled—I wasn't.
The money that had been sunk into this combination rock garden and
museum seemed excessive, considering the times. This was not a
curator's notion of a museum, it was a collector's conceit, a con-
glomeration whose sum was considerably less than its parts.

"This is B. J. Palmer's personal collection, you know," Mary Ann
said, as we stood in front of an immense black idol, a sign telling us
this "Wishing Buddha" was over a thousand years old. "I think it's
wonderful of him to open it up to the public like this."

"We paid a dime."

"What's a dime?"

"Two cups of coffee. A sandwich."

"Don't get serious on me, Nathan. Can't you see the benefit of a
place like this?"

"You mean a world that isn't the real world? Sure. It's nice to go
someplace unreal once in a while."

"You're damn right," she said, and tugged at me, and said, "This is
my favorite part," and soon we were in a tiny wedding chapel,
formed of pebbles and stones and mortar, with a rock altar eight feet
wide, eight feet deep, ten feet high.

"The smallest Christian church in the world," she said in a hushed
tone.

"No kiddin'."

We were holding hands; she squeezed mine.

"Hundreds of couples are married here every year," she said.

That she could be warmed by a cool, stone closet like this was a
testament to her imagination and sense of the romantic.

"Isn't it splendid?" she said.

"Well . . ."

She put her arms around me, looked up at me with that innocent
look that I had come to know was only partly artifice.

"When we get married," she said, "let's get married here."

"Are you asking for my hand, madam?"

"Among other things."

"Okay. If we get married, we'll do it here."

"If?"

"If and when."

"When."

"All right," I said. "When."

She pulled me out of there, almost running, like a schoolgirl.

When we were out in the oriental court, with a little brook babbling nearby, she babbled, too: "This was our favorite place."

"What?"

"Jimmy's and mine. When we were kids. We came here every week. We'd make up stories, run around till the guides'd get cross and stop us. Even when we were teenagers, we'd come here now and then."

I said nothing.

She sat on a stone bench. "The day before Jimmy left, we came here. Walked around and took it all in. There's a greenhouse we've yet to see, Nate." She stood. "Come on."

"Just a second."

"Yes?"

"Your brother. I don't mind looking for him. It's my job. You're paying me to do that. Or you were. I'm not inclined to take any of your money, from here on out. But, anyway, your brother . . ."

"Yes?"

"I don't want to hear about him anymore."

Her face crinkled into an amused mask. "You're jealous!"

"You're goddamn right," I said. "Come on. Let's get the hell out of heaven."

She kissed me.

"Okay," she said.

## 24

"Jimmy's a good kid," Paul Traynor said, "just a little on the wild side."

Traynor was only a few years older than me, but his hair was already mostly gray, his lanky frame giving over to a potbelly, his nose starting to go vein-shot, the sad gray eyes looking just a shade rheumy. He was sitting at his typewriter at a desk on the first floor of the newspaper building, in a room full of desks, about half of which were occupied, primarily by cigar-puffing men who sat typing through a self-created haze.

"He grew up during the Looney years," Traynor said, "and developed this fascination for gangsters. And, you know, we always have run a lot of Chicago news in the *Democrat*. We cover the gangland stuff pretty good, 'cause it has reader appeal, and 'cause the Tri-Cities liquor ring is tied to the Capone mob. So a kid around here could easily grow up equatin' that stuff with the wild west or whatever."

"His father said you and Jimmy were pretty friendly. You let him tag along to trials now and then."

"Yeah. Since he was maybe thirteen. He read the true detective magazines, and *Black Mask*, and that sort of thing. Kept scrapbooks about Capone and that crowd and so on. It seemed harmless to me. Till he got out of high school, anyway, and started feelin' his oats."

"Drinking, carousing, you mean? Lots of kids do that, when they hit eighteen or so."

"Sure. A kid out of high school wants to get laid, wants to go out with his pals and get blotto. Flamin' youth. And so what? No, I *wish* that was the way Jimmy'd gone: hip flasks and raccoon coats. Oh yass."

"You mean instead of hanging around speakeasies."

He had a smile like a fold in cloth. "Yeah. But it's more than even that. He got thick with the local bootleggers themselves. It's possible—just possible—he did some work for 'em. But don't tell his old man; it'd kill his old man."

"Don't worry. Did the kid actually want to *be* a gangster?"

"Did Jimmy want to be Al Capone when he grew up? Naw. That wasn't it. It was a combination of a couple of things. First, he was just *taken* with that crowd, road-show Capones that they were. It was the Nick Coin bunch, and Talarico's crowd, that he was hanging around with."

"Those names don't mean anything to me."

"Well, Coin and Mike Talarico were sometimes rivals, sometimes partners. You know how that business goes. Coin was shot down in front of his house last summer. Shotgun. Never found the killers, though they held a guy from Muscatine for it, then released him. Somebody brought in from Chicago did it, was the rumor, of course. Probably hired by Talarico, 'cause Coin had reportedly squealed to the feds. Anyway, Jimmy knew Coin and his crowd. And . . . well."

"Go on."

"Look. John Beame's a good man; if he's trying to find his son, I'd like to help. But there's something that I can only tell you if you swear to secrecy. Absolute goddamn secrecy."

"All right."

"You gotta understand Jimmy's second reason for hanging around with those lowlifes: he wanted to be a writer, a reporter. He wanted to go to Chicago and write about gangsters for the *Trib*. He didn't want to get *in* the game, see; he wanted to sit on the fifty-yard line and do the play-by-play, if you get me."

"I get you."

"And this is the part you got to keep to yourself, Jesus, keep it to yourself." He lowered his voice, leaned toward me. "Jimmy was feeding me stuff. He was hanging around with the Coin crowd, and even doing some minor things for 'em—driving a truck, here and there, no guns or anything, just bootlegging. But he'd keep his ears open, and he'd tell me things. Pass along the scuttlebutt, get it? If something big was up—and we've had our share of Chicago-style shootings and bombings and kidnappings and what-have-you—Jimmy'd pass along what he heard. To me."

"Did you encourage this?"

He looked at me hard, the gray eyes looking like smoky glass; his cigar was out, but he didn't seem to have noticed.

"I paid him," he said.

"I see."

"No you don't. You gotta understand the kid was doin' this on his own. And I told him he'd get his damn head blown off if he kept it up, but dammit if he didn't start feeding me some good tips. I couldn't help myself; I'm a reporter. And he was eighteen, nineteen, twenty years old when this was goin' on. He was old enough to be held responsible for his own actions."

"You wouldn't happen to know some of the places he hung out, would you? And who his 'friends' were?"

"Are you nuts? I never went with him: he couldn't be seen around with me, if he was gonna do this half-assed undercover work. But I can tell you where some of the speaks in town are, if you like."

He started rattling 'em off, and I stopped him till I could get my notepad out. When he'd finished, he said, "I can't really give you any names of the wharf rats he was hanging around with, 'cause he never really said. He wasn't close to the big boys, so talking to Talarico or Lucchesi wouldn't do any good. They probably wouldn't know Jimmy from Adam. Coin knew Jimmy, but Coin's dead."

"Anything else you can tell me?"

"Well. I do know he made some trips to Chicago. This was while he was in college, but during the summers. As early as the summer of '30. That always bothered me. See, his friend Coin was tight with the Chicago boys. Ever hear of a guy named Ted Newberry?"

*The body was in a ditch near a telephone pole.*

"Yeah," I said. "I heard of him."

"He was the Chicago big shot the Tri-Cities liquor ring was tight with. I covered a trial in the fall of '31, where Newberry and Coin, Talarico and Lucchesi were codefendants. Anyway, Jimmy went to Chicago a couple times, and I always wondered if he was running an errand or something for Coin. I grilled him about it, but he always claimed it was just pleasure trips. Still, I always had the queasy feeling that Jimmy was getting in over his head. All I could think of were those scrapbooks he put together in junior high and high school, full of Chicago and Capone, and couldn't help but wonder about those 'pleasure trips.'"

"Did you talk to him about his plans to go to Chicago and try to get a job there?"

"Yeah. I told him his expectations were unrealistic. That they'd toss him out on his butt. But he had to try, he said. And I guess every kid does have to try. So I didn't try to stop him. I even wrote him a letter of recommendation, in case he did get in for a real interview by some miracle. And I told him if he flopped, he could come back and I'd try to get him on the *Democrat* here, as a copyboy if nothing else. And he said—what was it he said? He seemed confident they'd give him a shot. Almost cocky, the little snotnose. 'Oh, they'll print my stuff,' he said. Something like that. Ever heard anything so ridiculous?"

I hadn't, and I said as much to Mary Ann, in the Palmer cafeteria over lunch. The cafeteria was in a narrow one-story building with a half-roof slanting up against the side of one of the main school buildings; above the archway going in was a motto: "Is Life Worth Living? That Depends On the Liver!"

Well, I wasn't having liver, though it had been one of the selections; I was having a go at the meat loaf, and it wasn't a Little Bite O' Heaven.

"I knew Jimmy had some rough friends," Mary Ann said, "and knew he went out drinking and all. But I didn't know about any . . . gangsters or bootleggers or anything."

"Maybe you weren't as close to him as you thought."

Her eyes stung me. "We were *very* close." Then, offhandedly, she said, "I knew he had an interest in criminology."

"He had an interest in criminals."

"It's the same thing."

"No it isn't. Ever hear of a guy named Reinhardt Schwimmer?"

She was having liver. She swallowed a bite of it and then said, "Why of course. Rudolph Schwimmer's name is on the tip of every tongue," and stuck hers out at me, just a bit. Some college boys who were watching her from a nearby table about fell over when she did that; they'd fallen deeply in love with her back in the cafeteria line.

"*Reinhardt* Schwimmer," I said. "He was an optometrist. He had a fascination for gangsters. And since his practice was in Chicago, he had access to some. He took to hanging around with them, at the speakeasies they frequented, even at some of their places of business, including a garage where trucks of hooch got loaded and unloaded. One day Doc Schwimmer dropped by the garage to talk to the boys, who were waiting for their boss Bugs Moran and his second-in-command, a fella named Newberry, to show, when some cops came barging in and told everybody to put their hands in the air."

"And the innocent doctor got arrested right along with the bad guys," she said.

"Not exactly. This was Saint Valentine's, 1929."

Mary Ann didn't play naïve; she knew what I meant.

"They killed him, Mary Ann," I said. "He probably told the men with machine guns he wasn't one of the gangsters; that he was just an optometrist. But they killed him anyway. He was there, and he got killed."

Her eyes were damp. "Why are you saying these things, Nathan?"

We were on the verge of a scene.

"Hey," I said, trying to shift gears, "I shouldn't have got into this here. I'm sorry. I didn't intend to upset you, it just came out . . . but a picture's starting to form, Mary Ann. A picture of your brother. And he isn't looking too very smart."

"For your information, my brother was an A student."

"Mary Ann. There's school, and there's *school*. Like the hard-knocks kind. Your brother is a kid from Davenport, Iowa. He may have hung around with some bootleggers"—I'd been a little vague with her on this point not wanting to betray Traynor's confidence—"but he was still a kid from the sticks."

"What's your point?"

"I don't know. I'm starting to have a sick feeling, that's all. Maybe it's the meat loaf."

"You've said all along you think Jimmy's off somewhere . . . riding the rails, seeing the country."

"I think he probably is. But he's not seeing Chicago, or I'd probably turned him up by now. Some things bother me, Mary Ann. Like his hanging around with hoods, here in Davenport. And did you know your father gave him two hundred dollars for tuition to Palmer, which he pocketed and took with him to Chicago?"

She turned pale. "No. Jimmy didn't tell me that."

"He told you he was going to hop a freight, though, didn't he?"

"Yes."

"If he did, and if he had two hundred dollars on him, well . . . that worries me."

"What are you saying?"

"Nothing. But if he made it to Chicago with his two hundred, I'll eat another serving of this meat loaf."

Her lower lip was trembling; I reached across and touched her hand.

"I'm sorry if I seem a bastard," I said. "It's just . . . I want you to be prepared, in case."

"In case what?"

"In case you have to look at something without the rose-colored glasses on."

She thought about that; she pushed the plate of liver away.

"Find him, Nathan," she said. "Please."

"I'm going to try."

"Don't try. Do it. Find him for me."

"I can't promise that."

"You *have* to."

"Okay. I promise. All right? Are you all right?"

She managed a smile. "Yes."

"How about helping me find this brother of yours?"

"Sure," she said.

She had arranged for me to talk to her brother's journalism instructor at Augustana, across the river in Rock Island; it was a beautiful campus on a rolling green bluff and the building we entered didn't have a single motto on its walls. But the matronly English literature instructor who also taught journalism had nothing illuminating to say about Jimmy, except that he was a fine writer and showed a lot of promise; that his marks in everything from literature to math were top-drawer. Nothing about Jimmy's personal life; nothing in the subject matter of his stories for the school paper that reflected the interest in crime that Traynor had told me about.

Back in Davenport, we stopped at a market, then went back to her father's modernistic castle, where I helped her in the kitchen, and she surprised her father with a roast beef dinner with all the trimmings, and she and I surprised each other by both being good cooks. I'd done a lot of cooking at home, growing up; and she'd been the only woman in this house for many a year. So we agreed to alternate days in the kitchen when we got married, though I silently promised myself to let her handle it, except for special occasions.

After dinner Mary Ann and her father, his arm around her, a gray-gloved hand gentle on her shoulder, went into his study. They asked me to join them, but I declined: this was a family moment, and I wasn't family yet. Besides, I had an appointment.

Dutch Reagan was waiting for me in front of the Perry Apartments, wearing a sweater over a shirt and tie, and brown slacks. His hands were in his pockets and he was leaning back against the building; with his glasses and crew cut, he didn't look like somebody who could get in a speakeasy, let alone give me a city-wide tour of 'em. I pulled up and he got in.

"Right on time," he said, with a ready smile.

"Take a look at this," I said, and handed him my notepad, folded back to the page where I'd jotted down Traynor's list of speaks. I pulled away from the curb.

"This is most of 'em," Reagan said. "Where'd you get this?"

"A reporter. Anything significant left out?"

"These are all mostly right downtown here. I'd suggest hitting the roadhouses, too."

"How many of them are there?"

"Just a couple. But we better stick to drinking beer tonight, and one per place, or we're not going to make it through the list. At least I won't."

Anyway he was honest about it.

"We'll take it easy," I assured him. "Are you a regular at any of these places?"

"I've been in most of 'em, once or twice."

"Just once or twice, huh?"

"I didn't say I was a drinking man, just Irish."

"Is there a difference?"

"You got red hair, you tell me."

I grinned at him. "I'm only half-Gaelic—you look like the full ticket."

"Well, my dad puts it away pretty good—too good, actually. Most of my drinking's been done on the fraternity back porch or in a parked car. Look, you may want to avoid the food in these joints. Most of 'em have to advertise they serve food, to stay open, you know."

"That's par for the course."

"Well, I just thought I should warn you. You seem to be heading toward Mary Hooch's, and I know a guy who ordered a sandwich there and when he took a bite, it bit him back."

We hit the speaks downtown first, starting with the one on West Second Street run by the heavyset old lady known as Mary Hooch, a friendly old gal who looked like she could go a couple rounds with Barney. Her place, like most we went to, was a narrow hole in the wall with no sign out front, but otherwise running wide open. Legal sale of beer hadn't hurt her business any—the dozen or so workingmen at the bar were putting away the specialty of the house: near beer spiked with alcohol, exceeding the legal 3.2 limit and then some.

"I know Jimmy," Mary Hooch said. She had a puffy face with two

beady eyes hiding in it and hair as frizzy as Joe Zangara's. "Good kid.
But I hear he took off for Chicago, long time ago."

"Do you know any of his friends? Did anybody he hung out with
hang out here?"

"Not to speak of."

"If you know Jimmy, you ought to know his friends."

"Everybody was his friend. All the fellas and gals."

"Anybody here tonight, for instance?"

She looked around the room. "Not really. These guys are working
stiffs, or out-of-work stiffs. Jimmy hung around with a different type."

"If I offered you a fin would you get more specific?"

"I don't think so. You're a friendly fella, but you're from out of
town, right? I think I told you all I'm going to."

It went like that everyplace: a joint on East Fourth, where the
shrimp and oysters looked edible, and Reagan forgot his advice to me
and had a basket of the former; another over a garage at West River
Drive and Ripley, where sandwiches apparently more legitimate than
Mary Hooch's were being served; a place up on Washington Street
that actually had a small sign out front (Yellow Dog) and sold German
food. Bartenders remembered Jimmy, knew he hung around with
some "locals," but wouldn't get specific about who. With one exception: Jack Wall, the manager of that place over the garage, a smooth,
well-dressed guy with a Nitti-style pencil mustache and a shovel-jaw.
The impression I got was that he was up high enough in the Tri-
Cities liquor ring to talk more freely than the others, if he felt like it,
which he did, when I explained I was a private op from Chicago
working a missing persons case.

"Jimmy hung around with some of Nick Coin's boys," Wall said,
"in particular Vince Loga."

"Know where I could find Loga?"

"A speak. Not this one."

"Oh?"

"He ain't here. Trust me."

It seemed prudent to do so. I had left Reagan at the bar, where he
sat nursing a beer, studying some of the sad faces around him. In the
car, he said, "Lot of those guys are out of work. Mighty sad situation."

"They found dough for a drink, though, didn't they?"

"You're awful cynical, Mr. Heller. Doesn't it make you feel a little
sick inside, when you see out-of-work men on street corners?"

"On street corners, yes. In bars, no."

"Well, somebody's got to do something about it."

"Oh yeah? Like what? Like who?"

"I can tell you what *I* do. Every day when I walk up the hill to the station, I give ten cents to the first guy who asks for it."

"If it's the same guy every day, you're getting taken."

"Very funny. I got *plenty* of guys to choose from, believe me. Well, the president'll straighten this out."

"Voted for him, did you, Dutch?"

"I'll say I did. And so did my father. He's even working for the government."

"Your father? Doing what?"

"Giving out scrip to the unemployed to exchange for food."

We hit a couple of roadhouses on the outskirts of Davenport, both of them on the rough side: chicken-wire ceilings and sawdust on the floor and factory and foundry workers who liked to fight when they got drunk; I was glad I was with a husky former football player, even if he was wearing glasses and a sweater. Then we headed for a place Reagan had heard of but never been in, on highway 6, a route that took us along the Mississippi and through several little towns. The night was clear, the full moon reflecting off the smooth surface of the river, turning it an eerie gray.

Reagan asked me about Jimmy, and I filled him in. He said he could sympathize with the frustration Jimmy must've felt, going from newspaper to newspaper looking for work.

"I had swollen feet from pounding the Chicago sidewalks," he said. "And I got all the reception-room fast shuffles you'd expect. It was a woman at NBC in Chicago who told me to head for the sticks. Even then, I was damn lucky, landing that WOC spot."

"How'd you manage it?"

"The station had been advertising for an announcer, but I showed up the day after they filled the slot. It was Mr. Beame who gave me this news, after I'd driven seventy-five miles in my father's car. Instead of staying cool, I kind of lost my temper, and asked him how the hell a guy can get to be a sportscaster if he can't get inside a station? And mentioning sports did it—they needed somebody to help announce some Iowa games, and that's how I started. Five bucks per. And that's where I met Jack Hoffmann, who was Jimmy Beame's drinking buddy."

"And you ended up taking Hoffmann's place at the station."

"More or less. Oh, he was a capable man, and he could ad-lib and all that, but he didn't know football. Still, I learned a lot from him, and he went off to find something in radio that wasn't sports."

"You like your work?"

"Sure. I wouldn't mind being the next Quin Ryan or Pat Flangan. Of course, my dream's to get into acting, not that this job *isn't* acting 'A chill wind is blowing through the stadium and the long blue shadows are settling over the field.'"

"Not bad," I admitted.

The roadhouse was up ahead, a white two-story building on the right, with a gravel lot full of cars and a small blue neon out front that said FIVE O'CLOCK CLUB. I pulled in.

This was not a workingman's joint, at least not the men who worked in the area's factories and foundries. The men at the bar were in suits and ties and hats, as were the ones at tables with women in low-cut and/or tight-fitting dresses who might have been working girls, but didn't, I thought, work here; this seemed to be a place you *brought* a moll. It was modern-looking: black and white and chrome with subdued lighting, a nightclub atmosphere. A five-piece band was doing some Dixieland jazz on a small platform over in the far left corner; they sounded like the reason Bix left the area.

The bartender was heavyset and pockmarked, but his apron was clean, which was a first for the evening. I asked him if he knew Jimmy Beame, and he said no. I asked him if he knew Vince Loga and he said no. I gave him a fin and asked again. He still didn't know Jimmy Beame, but Vince was in back playing cards.

He pointed to a door at the rear and I headed there, Reagan next to me, the eyes behind the dark-rimmed glasses blinking as he tried not to look down the pretty necklines at the tables we passed, and considering the size of some of the guys sitting at the same tables as those necklines, that was a wise decision. As I reached to open the door, a bouncer the size of a Buick drove over and advised me the game was closed. I gave him a buck, opened my coat to show him I wasn't armed, and he opened the door for me, and I went in.

He stopped Reagan. Said to me, "You gave me one buck. If he goes in, I want another."

I didn't feel like giving him another, so I told Reagan to stay out there.

The room was smoky and the low-hanging shaded lamp cast its pyramid of light across the green-felt, money-strewn table. Six people were playing; the game was poker. Five of the men had their coats off, ties loosened, hats on, except a hatless, dark-haired dude who had his back to me, and had kept his fancy pinstripe on. I waited till the end of the current hand and said, "Who's Vince Loga?"

A guy about twenty-two with the sort of bland, baby-faced looks that could, in company like this, mean somebody with something to prove, was right across from me.

"I'm Loga," he said, not looking at me, looking instead at the cards being shuffled to his left. "I'm also busy. I also don't know you. Beat it."

The dude with his back to me turned and it was George Raft.

He stood and smiled at me, extended a hand, which I took. "Heller," he said. "What the hell are you doing here?"

"You're asking me?" I said. "I'm on business. What are you doing? Making a movie? Sequel to *State Fair*, maybe?"

"I been in the Tri-Cities for three days," he said. "Makin' stage appearances at the Capitol with *Pick Up*. That's the new movie. You know, I came here from Chicago Saturday; stopped in with Max Baer and saw Barney while I was in town—didn't he mention it?"

"No, but I was kind of busy last week."

"Yeah, I know. I saw the papers."

"Can I have a word with you, George? In the other room?"

"Sure."

We stepped out into the other room, where Reagan was waiting at the bar. I introduced Raft to him and the kid was grinning ear to ear; he'd apprently never met a big Hollywood star before.

"Look, George. I could use a favor."

"Name it."

"Tell that guy Loga I'm okay. Tell him he can level with me."

"Okay. You mind telling me what it's about, first? I don't want the whole story, mind you. Just an idea of what kind of limb I'm out on."

"It's just a missing persons case. It doesn't connect with anything big that I know of."

"Fair enough." He turned to Reagan. "You like that announcing racket?"

"Sure," Reagan said. "But I'd like to be an actor, like you, Mr. Raft."

Raft's smile, as usual, was barely there. "Well, be an actor if you like; but don't be one like me. Listen, if you do go out to Holly-wood . . ."

"Yes?"

"Lose the glasses."

Reagan nodded, thinking about it, and Raft took me back in and said to Loga, "This guy's a friend of Al Brown's."

Loga swallowed hard; he was in the middle of a hand, but he put his cards down and went out with me. Raft nodded at me and smiled and sat back down and played cards.

"You're a friend of the Big Fellow?" Loga said, like I was a movie star.

"Never mind that. The question is, are you a friend of Jimmy Beame's?"

Loga shrugged, but not insolently, which was an effort for him. "Yeah. So what?"

"Heard from him lately?"

"Not since he left here, year and a half ago or so. Why?"

"You know where he is?"

"Chicago, I guess. That's where he said he was going."

"To do what?"

"Just look for work."

"What kind?"

Loga smirked. "Whatever pays the right money, what else?"

"Did he have a contact or anything in Chicago? Anyplace lined up to stay?"

"Not that he said."

"I hear he hopped a freight to get there."

"Where'd you hear that? That's the bunk. He had a ride."

"Oh?"

"Yeah, Dipper Cooney. He's a ___"

"Pickpocket. Yeah, I know him."

Loga shrugged again. "He worked the Tri-Cities for a few weeks; he's been all over Wisconsin and Illinois and around. The pickpocket dicks in Chicago put the collar on him once too often, he said, so he started floating city to city."

"But he was heading back?"

"Yeah, he was going back. And Jimmy hitched a ride with him."

I chewed on that awhile.

"That's all I know, pal," Loga said. His being impressed with my knowing Capone was wearing off, possibly because I was making noises that sounded like a cop. "It was a while ago, and you're damn lucky I got a good memory. Y'mind I go back and play some cards?"

"Sure. Tell Georgie I said thanks."

"Will do."

He went back in the smoky room, and, just as the Dixieland combo was starting up again, Reagan said, "Did you get something?"

"Maybe," I said. "We better cash it in for the night. You look like you're about one beer over your limit. And I got to get some sleep—I got a long drive back to Chicago tomorrow."

## 25

Saturday, May 27, a beautiful sunny day. A Goodyear blimp glides overhead. The oblong bowl of Soldier Field, where Mary Ann and I sit well back in the bleachers, is packed with people—now and then sections of the crowd begin singing "Happy Days Are Here Again," apparently believing it. Outside, crowds swarm either side of Michigan Avenue to watch the parade, as if expecting the president of the United States to be grand marshal.

But the president hasn't been able to get away from Washington to open Chicago's big fair; he's sent instead his postmaster general, Jim Farley. The only president on hand is Rufus C. Dawes, the General's brother, the president of the Century of Progress Exposition.

The crowd is noisy, festive, as the parade pours into the amphitheater, the motorcycle police, sirens blaring, leading the way for band after band, horse troop upon horse troop, the stadium awash in waving flags, flashing sabers, gleaming helmets. Then touring cars bearing dignitaries: big, bald, genial Jim Farley; Rufus Dawes, whose pince-nez seems designed as a means for the rest of us to tell him apart from his brother; the recently appointed mayor, Edward J. Kelly, a big man with a full head of hair and glasses that lend a needed dignity; Governor Horner, smaller, slightly rotund, bespectacled, bald; moving past the reviewing stand where high-hatted officials sit, beaming, movie cameras grinding nearby, as the procession moves around the arena. And the cheering crowd gobbles it all up; or most of the crowd, anyway. A few, like Mary Ann, don't like being part of a crowd: starring roles only, no mob scenes, please—though the show business aspect of the event clearly excites her. Others, like me, have seen parades before.

At the platform in front of the reviewing stand, the speeches begin; Dawes, Kelly, and Horner make the expected grandiose claims for the fair and Chicago. Farley is the keynote speaker, and not a bad one.

His bald head reflecting the noon sunlight, Farley first solemnly explains the president's absence. Loudspeakers fill the stadium with

Farley's tale of the president's regret at not being able to attend: "It was here in your Chicago stadium that his party nominated him for the presidency . . . moreover, there is the tie of friendship . . ."

And the uninvited guest, the last man Rufus and General Dawes want to see here, sneaks in: the man Mayor Kelly has replaced through party machinations devious even for Chicago, with legislation rushed through Springfield to authorize the city council to select the new mayor (to "save the public the expense of an election"), turning scandal-ridden Park Board Chairman Edward Kelly into a world's fair mayor ("A man of vision!"), a mayor who represents the Irish faction of the Demos ("Fuck the Irish!" having been the previous mayor's war cry), backed by Jewish Governor Horner, who owes his election to that uncouth, patronage-minded hunky whose departure from this vale of tears has been a blessing disguised by a period of several weeks of public mourning, weeks ago, months ago, history now, dimly remembered if at all; but Farley, possibly not fully understanding the twisted nature of Illinois politics, has brought the uninvited guest up onto the reviewing stand.

". . . the tie of friendship with your martyred mayor, a friendship the warmth of which rose above political affiliation and typified the mutual admiration of two outstanding public men, each of whom recognized the sincerity of the other."

Mayor Kelly, Rufus Dawes, and Governor Horner shift in their seats, in perfect unison, like dancers in *The Gold Diggers of 1933*.

Farley continues: "The most intense moment in our president's career was when he held in his arms the friend who had stopped the deadly bullet aimed at his own heart."

There are few dry eyes in the bleachers; I wonder how Cermak's family is taking all this. A small article in yesterday's *Trib* told of the family's disappointment at not being invited to be on the reviewing stand; the city council responded by assuring the Cermaks reserved seats in the bleachers nearby.

General Dawes is among the dignitaries on the reviewing stand, but he does not speak. He is content to allow the public to think his brother Rufus the sole guiding force of the exposition—Rufus and the visionary Mayor Kelly—though Dawes must certainly be somewhat disappointed having another *Democrat* take Tony's place, and a scandal-tinged one at that. The extent of General Dawes' public activities at the Century of Progress, this sunny day, will be to take the first two-wheeled carriage ride of the fair, sitting in his stovepipe hat, puffing his pipe, his back-seat chauffeur a college kid. The papers will take pictures of this earth-shattering event, saying "Who says Dawes can't be pushed around?"

We have aisle seats, and Mary Ann doesn't argue when I suggest we leave early, while speakers are still having at it, and get over to the fair, which has been open for business since nine this morning.

Even leaving that stadiumful of people behind, it's crowded getting in, partially because there are so few turnstiles for everybody to push through. In the background the dignified, imposing Field Museum and Shedd Aquarium look on, as if jealous of the crowds their new neighbor is attracting. I pay Mary Ann's fifty cents, and offer my pass in its little leather billfold to the attendant, who checks my picture and punches the card.

And, then, spread out before us is General Dawes' and Cermak's—dream city, a city of futuristic towers, geometrically shaped buildings, flat angular planes of white, blue, orange, black, yellow, red, gray, green, windowless bold splashes of color. Before us is an avenue overseen by flapping red flags angling in from overhead at either side, an avenue filled with people and an occasional tour bus, the buses getting out of the way of people, for a change, and at its far end, the Hall of Science, Camelot out of Buck Rogers, fluted white pylons alternating with sheets of cobalt blue. To our left is the Administration Building, an ultramarine box with a silver facade; at the left a lagoon shimmers—across it the long, low, green-and-black Agricultural Building, and the three white towers of the Federal Building, which loom over its triangular Hall of States like the prongs of a big upturned electrical plug.

And it goes on like that: the Sears Roebuck Building, an off-white, blue-trimmed tower rising from a sprawl of modernistic wings; the Swedish, Czechoslovakian, and Italian pavilions, looking just as futuristic as the next guy, with little old-world flavor in evidence; then up a ramp to the Hall of Science, the "capitol" of the fair, with its U-shaped front facing the lagoon. Inside, a ten-foot transparent robot human says to us (and others gathered around him), "Now, ladies and gentlemen, I shall swallow. You can see this mouthful of food passing down my esophagus. Now you see the swallow entering the top door of my stomach. Watch my stomach contract to churn up food."

I *had* been hungry, before that, and when the memory had faded a bit we did partake of a couple of red hots from a futuristic white stand by the Sky Ride; Mary Ann was anxious to take this ride—with it

six-hundred-some-foot towers standing a couple thousand feet apart.
At about two hundred feet up, so-called "rocket" cars traveled back
and forth on steel cables, above the lagoon. It was not something I
wanted to do after having a hot dog.

Once you got past the assault upon your senses by geometry and
color gone berserk, the fair turned out to be a fair: we wandered
among plaster dinosaurs; saw Admiral Byrd's *City of New York*, the
ship he used to explore Antarctic seas; hit the two-block stretch of
midway, and rode the roller coaster, the Bozo, and the Cyclone, but,
hoping to keep the red hot down, I begged off the Lindy Loop, passing up, too, the Pantheon de la Guerre, where the world's largest war
paintings were on display, and doing without the flea circus and the
Florida alligator show. We crossed the lagoon and had a look at the
Enchanted Island, where parents could dump kids (after a doctor in-
spected each tyke) and gigantic cutouts of Oz characters and a two-
story boy riding in his red wagon ruled the five-acre roost.

The whole fair was big on giantism, despite a midget village on the
midway   the Time and Life Building had, on its either side, towering huge mock covers: a *Fortune* cover depicting planets in space; a
*Time* cover featuring the man of the year—FDR—whose face loomed
over the fair, even if he hadn't been able to make it there. The Havi-
land thermometer was just this big goddamn thermometer, several
stories high, with a red neon stem; no wonder that kid at Enchanted
Island was trying to get away on his wagon.

We walked hand in hand. Mary Ann wasn't saying much, but was
trying to maintain a cynically bohemian attitude—she wore a black
beret with a black slit dress, and heels that must've killed her, while
everybody else in sight wore colorful, holidaylike apparel; but while
her look was Tower Town, her eyes were full of Iowa. This place
made Little Bit O'Heaven look sick. This was the most unreal unreal
place on earth, and Mary Ann, whether she would admit it or not,
loved it here.

So did the rest of the people, and it was a swell place to hide from
the depression, even if a lot of families did have to pass up the many
food concessions and find a bench to eat the lunch in brown bags
they'd brought with 'em. Most of the tourists were staying in private
homes, usually at fifty cents per person, meals included; and many a
frugal head of the family—whether in trousers or skirts—insisted on
getting the full fifty cents worth by bringing their lunch.

Of course a lot of people *were* buying their lunch here, in which case it was likely their money—at least some of it—would go into Syndicate coffers. Capone might have been in Atlanta, and Cermak in the ground, and Chicago superficially a cleaner city, but Nitti's boys were cleaning up at the fair. Quite literally, since they controlled the fair's street-sweepers union, and the union the college-boy rickshaw pullers/carriage pushers formed, and half a dozen others. The San Carlo Italian Village restaurant was run by Nitti people; they had the popcorn concession, hatcheck, parking, towel/soap/disinfectant concessions; every hot dog and hamburger sold at the fair was theirs, and Ralph "Bottles" Capone, Al's brother, had seen to it that, with the exception of Coca-Cola, no soft drinks sold on the grounds came from any other bottling works than his own. Most of the beer here was Nitti's, too, of course. And why shouldn't Nitti make money off the fair? He built it.

Word from the street, confirmed by Eliot, seconded by the private police I'd been working with on pickpocket prevention, was that Nitti-dominated unions and employers' associations had controlled the trucking and much of the construction work in the clearing of Northerly Island and the turning of the lakeshore into a futuristic landscape of geometry and giantism. And all contractors accepting construction jobs on Northerly Island had added an extra 10 percent on top of their bids—because Nitti had decried 10 percent off the top for the mob.

Nobody was talking about this, really: not the papers; not the Dawes boys, certainly. You had to look the other way in certain matters, after all. For example, with all these tourists coming in, prostitution was bound to go through the roof, so the city fathers had required prostitutes to register as "masseuses," and to submit to weekly examinations by a city-appointed doctor who would look for, well, "skin diseases." And now all around town neon signs had sprung up saying MASSAGE PARLOR, and so what? Hadn't the General admitted to me once that he only wanted to clean the town up "within reason"? The world wasn't going to end because some bird from Duluth got laid—and if we wanted him to bring his business back to Chicago again sometime, better to send him home without the clap.

This fair that Mary Ann was wandering through so gaga-eyed was not the City of Tomorrow, it was just another never-never land; harmless, but transitory. In a few months the brightly colored plywood and glass would come crashing down. These tourists from Iowa and every other hick state were all aglow, thinking their future was all around them; some poor souls even imagined they were in Chicago.

They weren't, of course; they were in Chicago only in the sense that the fair was what Chicago—which is to say, Dawes and Cermak and Nitti—had planned it to be. In that sense, they were in Chicago, all right.

In every other sense, they were in Tower Town, with Mary Ann.

BARNEY ROSS

## 26

"I haven't mentioned you looking for my brother," Mary Ann said, "for ages."

We were seated at a small round table in the open-air gardens at the Pabst Blue Ribbon Casino, overlooking the fair's south lagoon, just to the rear of the Hollywood pavilion. There was a lake breeze.

"Actually," I said, pouring a legal Pabst from its bottle into a glass, "it's been two weeks. But you *have* been good about it, I must say."

Ben Bernie and his Lads were taking a break; they'd been playing on a circular revolving platform right out in the open, next to a canopy-covered dance floor that extended into the garden. We'd had to wait half an hour for our table, even though it was only around three-thirty in the afternoon, well away from either lunch or supper crowds. But this was opening day at the Century of Progress, and the Pabst Casino (casino in the cabaret sense only—no gambling was going on) was the largest, swankiest joint on the exposition grounds; it was, quite legitimately, touting itself as the place "to dine and dance with the famous," and the three round white-red-and-blue interlocking buildings, one of them twice the size of the other two, were jammed to capacity.

She poked at her Hawaiian salad. "It's been over a month since you told me you 'finally had something.' Remember?"

"You're right. And what else did I say?"

"'Just don't hound me about it.'"

"Right."

She poked at her salad some more. Then she looked up and her eyes got wide. She leaned forward. "Glance back over your shoulder."

I did.

"Now what?" I said.

"Don't you see who that is, walking toward us?"

"Oh, yeah. It's Walter Winchell. He and Damon Runyon and all the big-shot New York newshounds are in town. So what?"

"Didn't you say you met him in Florida?"

"That's true."

"Here he comes! Introduce me, Nathan! If I had a mention in his column, well, it could mean—" She shut up. Winchell was nearing us.

As he went by, I said, "Hello."

He glanced at me, smiled without smiling. "Hiya," he said, not recognizing me, and was gone.

The smirk settled on the left side of Mary Ann's face. "I thought you said you *knew* Walter Winchell."

"I said I met him," I said. "I didn't say I knew him."

"Well, you *know* who this pickpocket is that Jimmy hitched a ride with, don't you?"

"Yeah."

"Well, why don't you *find* him, already?"

"Jimmy or the pickpocket?"

"Nathan!"

The people at the next table looked at us and Mary Ann, uneasy about center stage all of a sudden, said, "You know who I meant."

"Mary Ann, this pickpocket is a guy we used to bust all the time. He was good, one of the best, but he had a bad habit of hitting the same few places over and over again. The train stations. The Aragon. The College Inn. And he ended up getting busted so often, he left the area."

"But he came back here with Jimmy."

"Apparently, but that doesn't mean he stayed. In fact, according to my old working buddies on the pickpocket detail, he was run in by 'em shortly after the time he would've brought Jimmy into town."

"Why didn't you tell me this before?"

"I didn't want to get your hopes up. They also told me they haven't seen hide nor hair of Dipper Cooney since. Word is he's stayed in the Midwest, but is floating city to city."

"Oh. Then why did you tell me you thought he would turn up, eventually?"

I gestured toward the fair, spread out across the lagoon before us like Frank Lloyd Wright's scattered toys.

"That," I said. "The fair. It's pickpocket heaven. He won't be able to resist it."

"You think you'll find him here, at the exposition?"

"Of course. I got two hundred helpers, don't I?"

The two hundred helpers were the fair's private police, the men I'd

been training the better part of the month and a half since the Tri-
Cities trip. The General was paying me good money, so I was giving
him value for the dollar. I had taken the two hundred men—many of
them ex-cops and out-of-work security people, but none of whom
were pickpocket detail veterans, like yours truly—and handled them
in classes of twelve in the fancy trustee's room in the blue box that
was the Administration Building, using three of them who I'd known
before, when they worked for the department, to act out some standard pickpocket techniques.

"There's one hard-and-fast rule on the pickpocket detail," I'd start
out. "'Look for people who seem inconsistent with their surroundings.'"

That meant, in a department store, you looked for people walking
around looking not at the items displayed for sale, but other shoppers. At a prizefight, you looked for people studying not the action in
the ring, but the crowd. At the El stations, you looked for people not
looking in the direction of their train, but at the guy standing next to
'em.

And at the world's fair, you looked for people not looking at the
futuristic towering pavilions or the exhibits therein; you looked for
people on the midway whose attention was not drawn to the Fort
Dearborn Massacre show, or Carter's Temple of Mystery; you looked
for people in the Streets of Paris show whose eyes weren't on Sally
Rand: you looked for people looking at people. And a lot of 'em would
turn out to be pickpockets.

I trained the three ex-cops—pickpockets usually work in teams of
three—to demonstrate some of the typical routines. For instance, a
whiz mob—pickpocket team—will spot a wealthy-looking dame walking along with an expensive shoulder-strap bag hanging like it's fruit
and she's the tree, and guess who's harvesting? The whiz mob, who
decide to "beat her on the stride," as it's called. Two fairer-sexed
members of the mob—moll buzzers, in the dip's own vernacular
will walk in front of the mark, then suddenly stop or maybe back up a
step, as if avoiding stepping in something. The mark will unavoidably
bump into them, and as the mark is being jostled, and being pro-
fusely apologized to, the third member of the mob—the hook—will
have come up from behind to open the mark's bag and have at it.

There are a lot of variations on this, and I taught as many of 'em as
I could to my pupils. Common ones at the fair would include action
at the refreshment-stand counter, with the buzzer reaching across for

some mustard and jostling the mark as the hook works the mark from behind.

Of course there would be the occasional solo artist, and redheaded, freckle-faced Dipper Cooney, a man of thirty-five or forty who unless you looked close looked twenty, was one of the best. A real live cannon, a dip deft enough to take a wallet from the back pocket of a prosperous, alert mark—without benefit of buzzers to jostle said mark's attention.

A live cannon like Cooney would never be able to pass up the fair; he would see it as duck soup, and he'd be right . . . normally.

Of course he wouldn't know that each and every one of the two hundred boys in white pith helmets, red jackets, blue trousers, and holstered sidearms would have seen his police file photo; that each was instructed, if catching the Dipper in the act, to hold him for me personally.

This was about as far as I'd gone in putting word out I was looking for Cooney. The boys on the pickpocket detail were among the few on the Chicago department who had not come to view me as persona non grata for having talked against Lang and Miller in court; but I still didn't trust the boys so far as to let them know how urgently I was looking for Cooney. One of the reasons Cooney had left Chicago was that my superior on the detail had demanded a percentage of the cannon's take to allow him to have free reign at the train stations; Cooney had unwisely turned the offer down, and had been collared so many times by the detail thereafter that Chicago became a place he didn't want to be anymore. I let the guys on the detail know only that Cooney was a guy I needed to talk to, regarding an insurance matter I was tracking, and that if they caught him and called me, it was worth a fin. If I'd made more out of it than that, well, Cooney might get told I was after him: the pickpocket detail knew very well that a live cannon like Cooney was worth more than a private cop like me, and he or Billy Skidmore would pay well for the information.

And of course I avoided talking to Skidmore himself, the portly, bowler-wearing junk dealer/ward heeler/bail bondsman with whom most serious pickpockets, gamblers, and shoplifters did their bonding business.

I had to keep it low key if I wanted to reel my fish in; the boldest move I made was to ask one of the pickpocket detail boys to lift Cooney's file photo for me, so I could borrow it and get some copies made. But I just made a couple; I wasn't going to go handing them out. If word got out on the streets I was after him, Cooney'd spook, sure as hell.

I considered calling Nitti and using up that favor he said he owed me. It was pretty well known that Cooney, through Skidmore, had done occasional work for the Capone/Nitti crowd; he was that good a dip, the kind you could send on a specific assignment, to pick a key out of somebody's vest pocket, or slip something incriminating into somebody's wallet.

But I couldn't risk it: Nitti seemed a dangerous last resort, as his loyalty to Cooney might outweigh any sense of obligation he felt to me; and besides, he was in Florida, on his estate, resting up, still recuperating.

I did go to two of Cooney's favorite hunting grounds: the Aragon Ballroom on the North Side, where Wayne King the Waltz King foisted watered-down Chicago jazz on his public between rounds of Viennese schmaltz in a mock Moorish setting; and the College Inn, where the Old Maestro Ben Bernie and his Lads performed in front of a dance floor that resembled a big backgammon board, while couples danced in the dimmed lights of a room where radium-painted fish glowed off pastel walls, turning the room into a sort of aquarium. But my fish hadn't shown, the bouncers told me, when I showed them his picture, promising anybody a fin who called me if Cooney swam in.

And now it was weeks later, and Ben Bernie was playing at the Pabst Casino—which was run by the College Inn management—and none of my efforts to turn Cooney up had done a bit of good. Still, the fair had opened today; he'd show. He'd show.

Or so I thought. May turned into June, and I found myself several days a week, supposedly as a function of my role as pickpocket adviser, haunting the fair. My pith-helmeted pupils would nod to me as I'd pass, and whenever I'd remind them about that specific pickpocket I was looking for, I'd get a shrug, and a "Can I see that picture again?"

At the same time, my relationship with Mary Ann was getting a little strained; I was on the verge of telling her to hire another detective—but the part of me that wanted to stay with her, to sleep with her, to maybe God-help-me marry her, was afraid to say so.

She didn't go to Barney's big fight, June 23. I wanted her to, but she pretended she didn't want to see my friend Barney get hurt, which was horseshit, because she didn't give a damn about Barney.

I'd introduced them months ago, and Barney had loved her on first sight ("What a terrific girl you lucked on to, Nate!" he'd told me, later); but Mary Ann, I'm afraid, was jealous of Barney, not so much because he and I were close—but because he was somebody I knew who was more famous than she was.

So Eliot and I went, and sat in the third-row seats Barney had provided us, in the same Chicago Stadium where FDR got nominated and Cermak got eulogized. We were watching the second prelim, in which one light heavyweight was knocking the stuffing out of another. I was watching, but I wasn't really seeing. This was Barney's big night, his big fight, and I was nervous for him. Somebody had to be—the cocky little bastard was cool as a cuke at his speak this afternoon, or pretending to be, and the butterflies in my stomach were in full flight.

Barney couldn't have had a better, more beautiful starry summer night for it, and the turnout should have been terrific—Barney was, as the sports page put it, "the most popular fistic figure to develop in these parts in years"—but the stadium was only half-full. The massive floor of the arena was spectator-covered, but only the first few rows of stands were filled, and I wondered if the fair had hurt tonight's attendance, or maybe it was just the price of a ticket in times like these, for a fight you could hear on the radio free.

Whatever the reason, it wasn't because Barney was a shoo-in. In fact, it was almost the opposite: the odds favored the champ, Canzoneri, to hold on to his title. But by no means was Canzoneri a shoo-in, either (the odds were 6 to 5 in his favor), and the mostly male crowd here tonight, the stadium air turned into a hazy fog of cigarette and cigar smoke caught in bright white lights, seemed confident the fighters would fan the smoke to flames. Christ, I was nervous. Eliot picked up on it.

"How much dough you got on this fight?" he grinned.

"A C-note," I said.

"On Barney?"

"On Seabiscuit, you jerk. What do you think?"

"I think you're going to take some money home. Relax."

"Does it show?"

"You're damn near shaking, son. Ease up."

"I just want this for him, that's all. He deserves this one."

Eliot shook his head, smiled. "That isn't the way it works. He's

going to have to earn that title, in that ring, in just a few minutes . . .
but I think he can do it."

"Is that who I think it is?" I said, pointing discreetly.

"Your old buddy Nitti? Sure. Who else? Canzoneri's got a big following in the Italian community."

"Nitti's Sicilian."

"Don't get technical. The mob guys are big Canzoneri boosters."

"Do they own him?"

Eliot shrugged. "Not that I know of. Just ethnic pride."

"I thought Nitti was in Florida."

"He's pretty much living down there right now, yeah. But he had
another matter in court to attend to, so he's back for a few weeks."

"That's Dr. Ronga, his father-in-law, next to him, you know."

"He's staying with Ronga, I hear. It's nice to have a doctor around
the house, when you're recovering from bullet wounds. Did you see
who's over on the other side?"

"Who?"

"Mayor Kelly and his boss Nash and bunch of other big political
muckety-mucks."

"I'm so impressed I could shit."

"Well, they're here rooting for Barney, no doubt. Kelly called him
'Chicago's pride and joy' the other day."

"Yeah, well, I guess it's all right for 'em to stick around, then."

The bell sounded and the last of the prelims was over; there had
been no knockout, but one of the fighters was battered and bloodied.
From the way my stomach was jumping, you'd think I was the one
climbing in that ring next.

And a few minutes later the ring announcer was yelling into his
microphone: "In this corner, ladies and gentlemen, Tony Canzoneri,
world's lightweight champion."

Canzoneri, dark, moonfaced, neck and shoulder muscles bull-like,
grinned at the audience, clasping his hands over his head in a predic-
tion of victory; he got a good hand. Nitti, Ronga, and a brace of
bodyguards did their share.

"In that corner, Barney Ross, his worthy opponent — "

And the thousands of friends Barney had in the arena—myself included—went berserk. Maybe the house was only half-full, but it
sounded packed when Barney's cheer went up; he waved at the
crowd, grinning shyly, looking almost embarrassed. He caught my

eye and grinned a little more naturally and nodded at me. I smiled, nodded back.

"Barney's faster than Canzoneri," Eliot said. "That's going to make the difference."

"Could," I said. "But pound for pound, Canzoneri's the hardest-hitting puncher in boxing. I hope Barney can take it."

Eliot nodded; we both knew that Barney, despite a hard-fought, impressive record, which had earned him this shot, had never had an opponent in the champ's league.

When the bell sounded, Canzoneri, wanting to get it over with quick, rushed out to meet the cool, cautious Barney midring, and swung a wild right, then another one, both of which Barney ducked so easily it was as if Canzoneri had done it on purpose, to prove Barney was, as reputed, one of the hardest fighters to land a glove on in the business.

Then Barney tore into him, not playing it at all safe, as if to prove *he* didn't believe Canzoneri's reputation as a killer-puncher; suddenly it was like *Barney* was champ, and wanted to put this pretender away as fast as possible.

And by the end of the third round, Barney had a nice early lead. Canzoneri landed some, including a series of lefts and rights to the head that made Barney's cheering section groan and wince en masse; but Barney was landing more often, and usually staying out of harm's way.

Maybe a little bit too much.

"Barney's too careful tonight," I told Eliot, having to push it to be heard over the crowd noise. "He's missed a couple perfect opportunities to really put that guy away."

Eliot nodded, leaned toward me, and said, "Yeah, but he's taken the hardest stuff Canzoneri's got to give, and it isn't slowing him up any."

But Canzoneri was a champ, no doubt about it; and in the next round, he took command, and started working on Barney around the eyes. By the fifth round, Barney was bleeding. And slowing down.

So was Canzoneri. The two of them boxed, trying to outpoint each other, clinching often; they'd been trading blows like flyweights, but hitting like heavyweights, and they were getting tired—and saving up for the final rounds.

Then in the ninth round, and I don't know if he'd been playing possum or not, Barney came alive, turned into a left-hook machine.

Canzoneri didn't know what the hell to think; he did his best to dodge the onslaught, barely retaliating at all. Barney backed him into the New Yorker's own corner and whaled away at him and the bell rang.

Round ten; final round. The crowd on its feet, yelling, cheering.

Barney landed a light left to the face and a hard right, rocking Canzoneri's jaw, and followed quick to the face, jab, jab, jab. But Canzoneri found a hard right hand somewhere and sent it to Barney's cocky face and the two fell into a lover's clinch. When they came out of the clinch, they went into a brutal slugfest; the killer side of Canzoneri was clear, now, but Barney's left, bless it, kept the champ off-balance, and the damage to a minimum. When the flurry ended, it was Barney who'd landed the more, the better, blows. Canzoneri looked tired, but angry, and he swung a stiff right to Barney's midsection; Barney started in slugging with both hands, and suddenly Canzoneri found himself on the other side of the ring. In the midst of backing away, though, Canzoneri lashed out with a hard right to the head, which looked like it had knockout written all over it, from where I stood.

Then again, Barney wasn't standing where I was; but he *was* standing, and he was coming back with, Jesus! A great fucking right to the head and the bell rang.

They kept fighting and the ref had to pry 'em apart.

Barney trudged over to his corner—the southwest corner, his lucky corner, the one he worked out of to beat Bat Battalino and Billy Petrolle, in his climb to this night.

We, the crowd, were still on our feet, but we weren't cheering; there was a hush over the stadium like somebody died.

"Who the hell won?" Eliot said, almost in a whisper.

"Damned if I know," I said.

"I think Barney."

"I don't know. Maybe a draw."

"In which case the championship stays with Canzoneri."

"Yep."

"He's got it in points, Nate."

"Who?"

"Barney. Just wait. He's got it on points."

We waited; the fighters waited. Forever.

After a while the ring announcer went to the mike, but instead of announcing the winner, begged the crowd's indulgence for the time this was taking; this was, after all, a championship fight . . .

I didn't hear the rest because we booed the son of a bitch out of there.

Finally he came back and did what he was paid for.

He said: "The new lightweight champion of the     "

And that's all anybody heard, because that meant Barney had won, and the stadium went stark staring nuts, cheering. From ringside, the photogs started flashing, and Barney grinned down at them, tears and sweat streaking his face. I'd never seen him look so happy. Or so tired. He'd given it every ounce he had, and I was proud of him.

Besides, I'd won twenty bucks on the deal.

While the windup fight was under way, a six-rounder between a couple middleweights, Eliot took his leave, as he had to work tomorrow and it was getting late; so I made my way down to Barney's dressing room alone.

Barney was sitting on the training table, fielding questions from reporters, and not terribly well: yes, he would give Canzoneri a return bout; no, he didn't know who he'd take on next. His trainer was working on the cuts over his eyes as the reporters fired their questions, and Barney, bushed, dazed, could barely answer, doing little more than flash his shy grin, which was enough to win the press guys over.

The two managers, Winch and Pian, a couple deadpan, stocky guys, cleared the room of the reporters, Winch going out with them. Balding Art Winch was an Italian guy who looked Jewish, and dark-haired "Pi" Pian was a Jewish guy everybody took for Italian. Both of them were so businesslike you wanted to hit 'em with pies—Pi particularly.

Pi was enthusiastic tonight, however; with a mug that made Buster Keaton look like Santa Claus, he allotted Barney a pat on the back and said, "Well done, fella, well done."

Half a dozen or so of Barney's old West Side pals were let in the dressing room, and they were bubbling; they had a big party planned for him at the Morrison, which I knew about and had been looking forward to. Barney promised to drop by.

"Drop by?" blurted a guy of twenty-eight, with the acne of a thirteen-year-old. "Don't you even wanna celebrate your champeenship?"

And then Barney's face lit up; the door had opened and Winch was there, escorting a plump, beatifically smiling late-middle-aged woman in a blue dress; behind wire-frame glasses her eyes were Barney's.

"Ma!" Barney shouted.

He ran to her, hugged her, tears running down both their faces. Then he held her at arm's length and looked at her. "It's *Shabbes*, Ma! How'd you get here?"

Solemnly, she said, "It's *Shabbes*, Beryl," which was Barney's real name, making with an elaborate, Jewish-mother shrug. "I walked. What else?"

"It's five miles!"

"I had to come. You see, I knew if I come to see you fight, you win."

"But you hate fighting, Ma."

"Sitting home waiting, I hate. Besides, I figure if you can take the punishment, I can take it."

"Anything you say, Ma. Nate, come over here!"

I went over. "Hello, Mrs. Ross. Why don't you let me drive you home? You can make an exception on riding on the *Shabbes*. Sick people do it."

"Aren't you the smart *Shabbes goy?* Do I look sick?"

Barney said, "Nate's right, Ma. You'll collapse or something, and then you *will* be sick. Let me drive you."

"No."

"All right," Barney said, "I'll walk home with you."

Barney's West Side pals, listening to all this, protested: what about the party?

"I'll be there later," Barney promised them. "First I got to walk my girl home."

And he did; all five miles, with his Ma on his arm.

Or so he said; I didn't walk along with 'em. I wasn't crazy, and I wasn't near as Jewish.

I went upstairs and the windup fight was over and folks were wandering up the ramps out into the lobby. They were all wound up, still caught up in the Ross-Canzoneri bout, some of them arguing the decision, most of them saying it was a fight they'd tell their grandkids about, and as I was going down the ramp into the gray cement lobby, I saw him.

Dipper Cooney.

He was dressed like a college kid: sweater, slacks—that was his game. That was how he turned looking twenty when he was nearly twice that into a living; red-haired, freckle-faced, friendly, he did not look like a pickpocket.

But brother, was he.

I moved through the crowd as quickly as I could without attracting attention or getting swung at; Dipper was following a guy and studying him to make the hook, and I had time.

Then about ten feet from him I got overanxious, and pushed past a guy, who pushed back and said, "Hey! Watch it, bub!"

And Dipper turned, and saw me.

And recognized me.

To him, I supposed, I was still just a pickpocket detail cop. And he could see I was moving toward him, fast enough, furious enough, to have caused a commotion (goddamnit!), and he started pushing through the crowd himself, and was out the door and into the starry night.

I followed him, and he left an angry trail of people, as the fans in front of the stadium, lingering, chatting about the great fight, were in both our ways, and got pushed out of it, and we had to be well away from the stadium and into the residential district surrounding it before either of us could really run.

And one thing a pickpocket can do is run.

Cooney, who'd kept his weight down to help with the college kid pose, was light, small, wiry, and he had half a block on me.

But I wanted him bad.

I ran full throttle after him, feeling like a track star, and I shouted, "Cooney! I'm not the cops anymore!"

He kept running.

So did I.

"Cooney!" I yelled. "I just want to *talk*, goddamnit," and that last was just to myself; my side was starting to ache. I never ran this fast, this far, before.

The neighborhood was mostly two-flats and row houses, and it was almost midnight, so we were alone on our sidewalk track, nothing, nobody in our way, and I began to cut the distance, and then he was just out in front of me and I threw myself at him, tackled the son of a bitch, and we skidded, skinned ourselves on the sidewalk and landed in a pile.

I didn't have a gun on me, but that was okay: pickpockets rarely carry guns, as it takes up stash space and weights 'em down. And I was bigger than this forty-year-old college kid, and I crawled on top of him like a rapist and grabbed the front of his shirt and the two green eyes in the midst of that freckle-face looked up at me round as the colored kid's in *Our Gang.*

"What the fuck you want, Heller?" he managed. He was panting. So was I. I hoped my breath was better than his. "You ain't no goddamn cop no more."

"You know about that?"

"I can read. I seen the papers."

"Then why'd you run?"

He thought about it. "Force of habit. Let me up."

"No."

"I won't run. I'm winded, Heller. Let me up."

Cautiously, I did. But I kept the front of his shirt wadded in one fist.

"I just want some answers," I said.

"You still sound like a cop."

"I'm private."

That stirred a memory. "Oh. Okay. Yeah, maybe I remember reading that. You're a private dick now."

"Right. And this isn't police business."

We were on a side street; a car angled down it, somebody leaving the stadium, probably. I let go of his shirt, so it wouldn't attract the driver's attention. Cooney thought about running. Just thought.

"In fact," I said, "there's a double sawbuck in it for you."

His attitude changed; running was now out of the question. "You're kiddin'? What do I know that's worth a double sawbuck to you, Heller?"

"It's just a case I'm working, a missing persons case."

"Yeah?"

"Kid named Jimmy Beame. His sister and father are looking for him."

He rubbed his chin. "I think I know a Jimmy Beame."

"Give."

"*You* give. You were talkin' double sawbuck a minute ago."

I dug in my pocket and got out a ten; gave it to him.

"You can have another," I said, "if I like what you have to say."

"Fair enough," he shrugged. "I was in the Tri-Cities, must've been a year and a half or two ago. This kid Beame was thick with the local mugs. Small-timers . . . but they were connected to some Chicago folks."

"Go on."

"This kid wanted in."

"In where?"

"The mob. He wanted some fast money, he said. He'd been boot-legging and such—some of it in Chicago, he said, for these Tri-Cities mugs. But he wanted something bigger."

"What, exactly?"

"He wanted to work with the Capone gang."

"What? He was just a hick kid!"

"Yeah, but he'd been around a bit. Had a gun on him, when he traveled with me. And I helped him out; he paid me to."

"So what did you do for him?"

"How 'bout the other sawbuck?"

I grabbed his shirt again. Another car came rolling down the side street and I let go.

"Easy," he said, brushing his college sweater off.

"What did you do for him?"

"I called Nitti. I done work for him, you know, time to time. Said the kid was all right, and Nitti said send him, and I gave the kid the address and that's that."

"That's that?"

"That's that," Cooney shrugged, and the car going by slowed as the driver extended an arm with a gun in its fist and I dove for the bushes as three silenced bullets danced across Cooney's chest.

Then the car was gone, and so was Cooney.

SALLY RAND

## 27

Night at the fair.

White lights bouncing off colored surfaces, colored lights careening off white surfaces, the modernistic lines of buildings brought out by tricks of incandescent bulbs, arc lights, neon tubes, a night aglow with pastels, like some freak occurrence, like a diamond necklace caught fire and flung along the lakeshore.

That was the view from atop the east tower of the Sky Ride, on Northerly Island, anyway, where Mary Ann had dragged me. But even down on the grounds of the fair, the effect was otherworldly. This was not the first time Mary Ann had asked me to bring her to the fair at night: the half dozen times we'd been here together, with the exception of that first afternoon, had been after the sun fell and the lights came up, and the futuristic city looming along the lake became even more unreal.

Of course I hadn't really brought her here tonight; I had met her at the Hollywood pavilion, which was her favorite place at the exposition—and where, tonight, she'd been working. A special broadcast of "Mr. First-Nighter" had emanated from one of the two radio studios within Hollywood, which sprawled over five acres on the tip of Northerly Island, just south of the Enchanted Island playground. Much of Hollywood was a bulky structure in shades of red that despite the massive round Sound Stage entryway was strangely lacking the futuristic grace of the rest of a fair which was itself more a reflection of Hollywood's notion of the future than science's. Outdoor sets surrounded the building, and movies were shot here daily by a crew making two-reelers for Monogram, often featuring name stars, admittedly not of Dietrich or Gable stature, but stars (Grant Withers was here for the duration), and amateur movie photographers and the just plain star-struck could watch talkies being made, and afterward have a beer and sandwich in the outdoor replica of the Brown Derby restaurant. And there were several sound stages indoors, one of them an auditorium that seated six hundred, which was also used for radio broadcasts, and was where Mary Ann and the rest of the "Mr. First-Nighter" troupe had broadcast this evening.

I'd seen Mary Ann doing radio before: several times I'd picked her up at the massive nineteenth-floor NBC studios at the Merchandise Mart, in Studio A, the largest radio studio in the world, where I stood in the glassed-in soundproofed balcony and listened to whatever soap opera she was working on that day come in via small speakers. She would stand before the unwieldy microphone and read her script, and she was good, all right, but I can't say her talent bowled me over.

Tonight, though, I'd sat in the audience at Hollywood, and Mary Ann had impressed me. It was odd to sit in a theater and—where stage or screen should be—see a big glassed-in sound stage, inside of which were padded walls like an asylum, where not inmates but actors with scripts were caged, standing before mikes, sound effects man at his table with his blank gun and frame door to slam and quarter-flight of steps to climb in the background. Above the forty-foot glass enclosure were two smaller glass-enclosed rooms for the sound engineers; the control rooms were dimly lit, but lights on their console panels winked at the crowd. An impressive theater, unlike anything I'd ever seen before.

But it was Mary Ann that impressed me most.

Even with the glass curtain separating her from the audience, they loved her. And she loved them back. The awkwardness of standing reading a script did not keep her from making eye contact with them, from playing out to the hilt her role of damsel-in-distress in the ludicrous private eye melodrama she was cast in tonight. She had dressed simply, in a milk-chocolate linen dress, with tiny pearl buttons down the front, some puff in the shoulders, the skirt clinging, then flaring a bit at the knees, and of course a matching beret; somehow it made her look innocent and worldly at the same time. When the show signed off the air, and the actors-under-glass took their bows, it was Mary Ann, not guest star Adolphe Menjou, who got the big hand.

"You were terrific," I said.

She grinned, crinkling her chin. "You never said that about my acting before."

"I never saw you wrap an audience around your pinkie before. Say, what kept you?"

She'd been nearly half an hour after the performance before meeting up with me outside.

"You won't believe this," she said, "but a scout for Monogram was in the audience."

"Somebody connected with the movies they're making here, you mean?"

"Yes, but he works for Monogram in Hollywood. *Real* Hollywood."

I wasn't sure there was any such thing, but I said, "And you've been offered a part?"

She was beaming. "Yes! Isn't it exciting? In August, if I can get a week off from 'Just Plain Bill.' They can write me out; give me the flu or send me on a trip or something. Isn't that just *splendid?*"

I was happy for her; I didn't mention that in the weeks previous she had dismissed Monogram as "poverty row," and had poohpoohed the making of two-reelers here at the fair as a "small-time publicity scheme, catering to these hick crowds." But I also knew she'd filed her name with the Monogram people's casting office, as had most of the actors in Chicago.

We were walking past the Enchanted Island, and its giant boy on his Radio Flyer wagon. It was a little windy tonight; almost chilly, for summer, but pleasant enough.

"Mr. Sullivan—he's the director I'll be working with—says it will be a sort of paid screen test. If Mr. Ostrow in Hollywood likes my work in the two-reeler, I could be flown out to Hollywood and put under contract!"

"It sounds like money in the bank to me," I said, meaning it. She'd been good tonight; she'd connected with that audience like Barney's left and Canzoneri's chin.

"Nathan," she said quietly, as we moved among the crowd, wandering past the circular court of the Electrical Building, where a fountain fanned water and light in a silver arc before the pastel orange-and-blue building. "You'll come out there with me, if they send for me—won't you?"

"Sure," I said.

"Do you mean it?"

"Sure. I can pack my business in a suitcase in a minute flat. California's perfect for my kind of work."

"You're not just saying this?"

I stopped her; put my hands on her arms. I looked into the

Claudette Colbert eyes and said, "I'd follow you anywhere. To hell, or Hollywood. Got that?"

She smiled and hugged me; some people going by smiled at us.

"Then take me to the fair," she said impishly.

"Where the hell do you think you are?"

"There's some things we haven't done."

"Like what?"

"The Streets of Paris. I want to see Sally Rand take off her clothes."

"Sally Rand doesn't take off her clothes; she already has her clothes off when she comes out. The trick is to catch a look at her when she's waving these damn ostrich plumes around."

"You speak as if from experience."

"This is what the boys tell me. I wouldn't know, myself. Why would I want to go see a gorgeous blonde parade around in her skin? For that matter, why would you?"

"Just checking out the competition. They say you haven't seen the fair if you haven't seen Sally Rand."

Actually, I did know why she wanted to check Sally Rand out. It'd been in the papers, just recently: several of the Hollywood studios were after the sensation of the fair to sign with 'em. So Sally Rand *was* competition.

But I had been hoping to go right home, either to my place or hers, and I told her so. What I didn't tell her was why.

Yesterday somebody had tried to kill me; I was convinced of that. I didn't know whether or not Dipper Cooney had been silenced on purpose, or had just happened to be there when an attempt on me was made. But my instinct was that I had been the prime target last night. And the only thing I'd been up to lately, outside of working at the fair, was snooping around looking for Mary Ann's brother.

I couldn't tell her about last night. I couldn't tell anybody, not Eliot, maybe not even Barney. That dark residential side street had been deserted enough for me to risk leaving poor Cooney dead, there on the sidewalk, and I'd walked quickly back the number of blocks to my car in the stadium parking lot and went home, to my Murphy bed. Because me being involved with another shooting right now what with the hostile cops and yellow journalists that would attract was something I could do without.

Apparently nobody had seen what happened: there'd been no screams, no shouts, when Cooney took those silenced slugs—no lights going on suddenly in windows. Just me tumbling into the

bushes, and when the car had gone by and showed no sign of return-
ing, and it seemed safe to come out, I took my powder, and unless
somebody had recognized one of us when I'd gone pushing through
the crowd after Cooney, I didn't see how I could be pulled in on this.

And today had borne this out. I'd had a call from one of the boys
from the pickpocket detail, telling me Cooney had been killed, wondering if that news was worth the fin I'd been offering 'round; and I'd
said no, Cooney wasn't worth squat to me dead, but if my pal came
around to Barney's sometime, I'd buy him a beer for his trouble. And
we'd left it at that.

Also, Cooney had got a small mention on the inside pages of the
afternoon papers: a longtime pickpocket with a record had been
gunned down, and police figured it was a mob-related slaying, but
had no leads. It would be added to the list of hundreds of gangland
slayings in Chicago these last ten or fifteen years; if a gangland slaying
had ever been solved in Chicago, I hadn't heard about it. Except for
Jake Lingle's, of course.

But what did Cooney's death mean? I was afraid I knew. I was
afraid that Mary Ann's brother, with his connections to Ted Newberry via the Tri-Cities liquor ring, had got in hot water with the
Nitti crowd, and now that my snooping was leading me to Nitti's
doorstep, the bullets were starting to fly.

Nitti was supposed to owe me one, but I hadn't thought this was
what he had in mind.

So I called him. Or tried to—I couldn't get through to him at his
office over the Capri restaurant on North Clark Street (which was
across from the City Hall, incidentally), but whoever I talked to relayed the message, and around seven that night, just before I was
going to head out to the fair, Nitti returned my call.

"Heller, how are you doin'?"

"Better than Dipper Cooney," I said. "He died last night."

"So I hear."

"I was with him."

"That I didn't hear."

"Are you on the level with me, Frank? I did you a favor once, you
know."

"I didn't have anything to do with what happened to Cooney. You
want me to find out who did?"

"That, I'd appreciate."

"Let's talk. Meet me at my office tomorrow afternoon. Two o'clock. I want to know about this punk you're trying to find."

"Jimmy Beame?" So he'd heard about that.

"Right. Who knows, I might even be able to help you out on that score."

"I'd appreciate that, Frank."

"See ya tomorrow, Heller."

And the phone had clicked dead.

I sat staring at it, wondering if I was being set up; I had the clammy sort of feeling you get waiting in a doctor's office for the results of your tests.

So I took my gun with me to the fair, and now I was trying to get Mary Ann to leave with me, since being at the fairgrounds with all these people was making me nervous.

"Nervous? What about? Nathan, don't be a grouch. Look. I'll let you take me to see Sally Rand some other night. But it's about time you took me up on the Sky Ride."

"We went on the Sky Ride last week."

"Not the observation deck."

"I'm not crazy about heights, okay?"

"Tough guy! Come on." And she tugged on my arm.

We were almost there, anyway; I glanced behind me, half-expecting to be followed. But I couldn't see anybody suspicious. Nobody that seemed inconsistent with his surroundings. And there were pith-helmeted guards with sidearms all around who knew me, and I could call on, if trouble turned up. So what the hell.

The Sky Ride towers were like twin Eiffels, and why not? That tower had been the hit of the Paris Exposition of '89, and these towers loomed over the Century of Progress in much the same way. The steel-web frameworks rose over six hundred feet, higher than any of Chicago's skyscrapers, the tallest towers this side of the Atlantic coast. A third of the way up, the silver, red-striped "rocket" cars, carrying thirty or forty passengers, crossed the lagoon on overhanging cable tracks. Last week, when we'd taken that trip, I felt we were up plenty high enough; now, as we entered the pennant-flapping SKY RIDE entryway, getting into one of the two elevators that went to the top (two others went to the rocket-car platform), we'd be going up another four hundred feet, to the observation deck.

It took a whole minute to get there, and we looked first from the windows of the enclosed observation room, the fair spread out before us like a colorful electric map. One of the fair's pith-helmeted security guards was on-duty in the observation room; not too many people up here tonight—maybe a dozen, mostly couples. I said hello to the guard, a florid-faced guy of about forty who used to be a traffic cop; he said hello back, and whispered he'd got a pickpocket earlier that day, seeming proud of himself. I patted him on the arm and told him atta boy.

Mary Ann was still looking out the window, breathless; she loved looking down on the lights of the fair and, beyond that, of the city. But I was ready to go, and said so.

"Oh, Nathan! We haven't even been up on the observation deck."

"This is as far as I go."

She hugged one of my arms with both of hers. "Don't be a wet blanket. It's a beautiful night; there'll be a nice breeze."

"Freeze our butts off, is more like it," I said, but then we were walking the final flight up, and Mary Ann dragged me to the highest exhibit at the fair—the Otis Elevator exhibit, which showed the machinery that operated the Sky Ride's high-speed elevators—also the dullest exhibit, I might add—which was in a building that covered all but the outer walkway area of the unenclosed observation deck.

Outside, on the deck, there weren't many people; the wind was blowing a bit too much for standing on top of a tower six-hundred-some feet off the ground. We found a place around one side of the building, where the deck jutted out like a porch so you could get a better look at the fair, and stood by the rail, having a gander, enjoying some privacy.

And seeing the fair stretched out before you, not through a window, but right before you, leaning against a rail and looking out at it, well, dammit if it didn't take *my* breath away. Searchlights cut across the sky, from the very tower we stood upon, intersecting with the arc lights of the fair below; the fair's geometric buildings turned into abstract shapes and colors as if on the canvas of some Tower Town modern artist.

I turned to Mary Ann to comment on this, to leave cynicism behind for a moment and be frankly impressed with all this, and Mary Ann's eyes were wide and she was intaking breath, and not because of the view.

Somebody was coming up behind me.

Fast.

The outstretched hands hit me just as I was turning, my right hand reaching toward the automatic under my coat, but not quite getting there, and it was a guy in a straw hat and pale yellow suit and just as I was going over the rail, backward, I saw Mary Ann slapping at him with both hands and his hat flew off, got caught by the breeze and went flapping by me as I fell, and I recognized him, and the sole thought in my panic-stricken brain was, *the son of a bitch is blond again*.

I hit a steel support beam, hard, on my back, and it knocked the wind out of me, but somehow my mind or instinct or some goddamn thing overrode, and I grabbed at the beam, catching it in the crook of one arm, and I clung to it, hugged it, wrapped both arms, both legs around it. The support connected the platform to the tower structure at a 45-degree angle, and thank God I hadn't got to my gun, because I needed both hands. The support was about as big around as a man's leg, and had rough sharp edges all 'round, digging into my flesh as I hung there in the breeze, my tie, my suit, flapping.

I was on the underside of the beam, like some animal clinging to a tree limb. I didn't look down; I knew what was down there—my fucking stomach, for one thing.

So I looked up, back up, toward where I'd fallen from, and Mary Ann was leaning over the side, reaching her hand out to me, but she was far away, ten feet, ten miles, ten years, and the guy was behind her, and I had to swallow before I could yell, "Look out!"

And she was struggling with him, he had her halfway over the side, and I let go with one arm, clutching with the other, legs hooked 'round the slanted support, and got my automatic out from under my arm, Christ knows how, and the guy just about had her over the side when he saw the eye of my automatic looking at him, and, before I could fire it at him, he disappeared from view.

Mary Ann, thankfully, did not; the blond gone, she leaned over and reached out again and I said, "No! Too far!" and she began to cry. I think she was trying to scream, but couldn't find the sound. Or maybe she *was* screaming and the wind in my ears was keeping me from hearing as I clumsily tucked the automatic back under my arm.

I yelled at her: "Go down to the observation booth!"

She nodded, and disappeared.

The support I called home angled under the platform, connecting underneath it; I'd fallen past the windows of the observation booth, but apparently nobody had seen me, and I was at a position that prevented them from noticing me, hanging here like Harold Lloyd.

The support below me paralleled this one but connected right to the corner under the observation booth and its windows. If I could drop down to the next support, I might crawl up it and get in view of the people in the booth, besides which Mary Ann would by now have alerted them to my situation anyway, and I might with somebody's help make it in through a window.

It was only about five feet down; I wouldn't have to be an acrobat to make it. But it would have helped.

I tried not to look at the fair below me. I tried not to think about the six-hundred-foot drop below me. Just that support beam five feet down. *Why was it so cold up here? So windy? Why was my mouth so dry, and my eyes so damp?* I let my legs loose and hung by my arms only; my feet touched the support beam below. I looped one arm around the support, let the other one loose, hanging by the crook of my arm, trying to stand on the beam below, trying to get my balance so I could risk letting go of the upper support altogether. A calm came over me; a passive, quiet feeling I couldn't hope to explain. I let go of the beam above, and then I was standing, I had my balance, but it was like standing on the tilted floor of a fun house, only much narrower, and, Christ! I began to slide, my feet began to slide, and my balance went and the fair whirled below me, and I hit the beam in a belly flop and clung, grabbed, hugged, slid. Then stopped sliding. Home again.

I looked up. Mary Ann's wide-eyed face was in a window, the corner window, and her mouth was open in a silent scream; I grinned up at her, like I was showing off, while resisting the urge to pee my goddamn pants. Then she was pointing, and the florid-faced guard was busting the glass out with his gun butt.

I edged up the beam toward them, on top of the beam this time, like a baby crawling, then I was up to where the beam joined with the underpart of the platform and the windows were right above me and the guard, some college-kid fairgoer bracing him from behind, was reaching out a hand down to me and I took it, hanging over the fair for one long moment before he pulled me up and in.

Mary Ann hugged me; she was crying, but she wasn't hysterical. Happy. Real happy.

Actually, I didn't have time for that. "Go back to your flat," I said curtly, moving past her. "Wait for me!"

"What —"

"Just do it, baby. Just do it."

I thanked the college kid who'd helped the guard reel me in, then turned to the guard. "Keep this one under your hat, pal."

He glanced at the eight or ten people standing around open-mouthed, talking among themselves, as if they wondered if this were part of the show. "I don't know if I can do that "

"There's a half a C-note in it for you if you do. And I'm covering the damages."

He grinned, shrugged. "Do my best, Mr. Heller."

Then I went to the two elevators and grabbed one—I caught a glimpse of Mary Ann, her face tight with irritation, hands on hips, staying behind, but reluctantly. The elevators took only one minute to go down, and I didn't figure I'd been hanging out there more than two or three minutes, so my old friend, my blond friend, the man who killed Jake Lingle, the man who helped kill Cermak, had a lead on me; but not much of one.

The ticket-taker in the lobby of the Sky Ride entryway said yes, he had seen the blond guy in the pale yellow suit, moving quickly, and pointed toward the lagoon. There wasn't a huge crowd at the fair tonight, but enough of one, and the lights were designed to make the world an out-of-focus pastel wonderland, not to heighten visibility or clarity.

So I stood there looking for a figure moving quickly, but didn't see one; then I moved quickly, toward the Sixteenth Street bridge, and stopped the first pith-helmeted security guard I came across, and he recognized me and smiled and I asked him if he'd seen this guy.

He had, and he pointed across the bridge, toward the Hall of Science, its square buildings and towers burning orange and green and blue against the night. In the foreground, gondolas, canoes, sailboats glided; a peaceful scene, and my brain was on fire.

*The Eighteenth Street entrance. That was the closest way out; the closest way to the parking lot.*

I ran.

Like a bat out of fucking hell, and knocked a few people down and to hell with excuse me, and almost got stopped by more than one security guard, but when they saw who I was, figured I was after some pickpocket, and one guard, in fact, fell in stride with me and yelled, "Need any help, Heller?"

I shook my head no, and the guy fell away.

Then the fair was behind me and all the cars in Chicago were parked in front of me, row after row, car after car.

But it was private parking, and there were only a few ways in and out. Maybe, just maybe, I had him.

I showed my fair ID to the two attendants at the entry to the parking area; they were in street clothes but had coin changers on their belt, and they told me, yeah, they saw a blond guy run through here, and pointed down to the left. I saw no one. I jogged down the first row of cars, glancing to either side; when I'd put some distance between me and those attendants back there, I got the automatic out. A car was pulling out, so I ducked to one side, waited and watched as it passed. An elderly couple.

I kept looking: the parking area wasn't lit, but the aurora borealis of the fair, at left, provided light enough. I was nearing the end of the first row when I saw a car pull out over on the next row, a little black Buick coupe with a white canvas top. It was the car that had glided by and gunned down Cooney last night. I ran between parked cars into the next lane and as the lights bore down on me, I saw him. Behind the wheel.

The blond.

I stepped to one side and pointed the gun at him but he swerved toward me, and as I backed up out of the way, squeezing between two parked cars, he got a shot off at me, a silenced one, and it grazed my arm, and, dammit, goddamnit, reflex sent my automatic flying.

And he saw that, and hit the brakes, and then he was hopping out of his car, moving toward me, gun in hand, the silencer making it look bulkily modern, as if a souvenir of the fair.

At the same time, I fell back, on my back, grabbed my chest as if he'd hit me there and kind of curled up and moaned and as he was standing over me, smiling, pointing the gun down at me, I kicked his balls up inside him.

This time *he* dropped the gun.

He dropped it, his hands popping open when he doubled over, and a wheeze came out of him, not a scream, just a dry pain-racked wheeze, and as he was still bent over I slammed a fist into his jaw that about took it off its hinges and he fell on his side, but the moment of white pain had passed, apparently, because then he was scrambling for his gun and suddenly he had the damn thing, was bringing it up toward me when I dove at him, and with both hands grabbed the wrist and turned it in on him and together we pulled the trigger. The sound was no more than a *snick* but the ghostly pale face went slack and I barely had time to say it: "This time I *did* get you, fucker."

I stood, his gun in my hand, and looked around. The only sound was the muffled roar of the fair; otherwise, the night was as silent and empty as the dead man's mind. Even the breeze had died. Nobody had seen this. Nobody had heard it—not with the blond's silenced gun as the instrument of death.

His car, the engine running, was only a few steps away; I dragged him to it, and hauled him up over the running board into the seat on the rider's side. I made him sit up straight, though his chin was on his chest; his belly was bright blood-red, and spreading. I shut the door and got in on the driver's side.

I flashed my ID to the attendants as we drove past and they smiled and nodded. I laughed to myself, remembering whose concession parking was.

I stopped at an all-night drugstore on Michigan Avenue and bought a bandage for my arm and used a phone book. Ronga was listed. I didn't have to jot the address down; I could remember it. It was only ten or fifteen minutes away, too. Good.

I went back to the car and the blond was still sitting there. Where was he going to go?

Me, I was going to call on the man who sent him: his boss.

I told him so, not starting the car back up yet, getting out of my coat and bandaging the nick on my arm.

"I'm taking you to Nitti, pal," I said.

But he made no comment; in fact he slumped over to the right and rested his head against the window as if bored the glaze on his barely open eyes seemed to confirm that. I was sitting up nice and straight, in fact leaning forward; I was a little crazy, as a matter of fact.

"What good's your opinion, anyway?" I said to the blond, pulling out onto Michigan Avenue. "You're dead."

As dead as Lingle.

As dead as Cermak.

"As dead as Nitti," I said to my rider, stopping at a light.

Then it turned green and I went.

## 28

Dr. Ronga lived on West Lexington, on the near West Side. I caught
Harrison, took it over to Racine, and when I reached the corner of
Lexington and Racine, I knew I was a stone's throw from the address
I was looking for. On the corner was a sandy-colored brick pharmacy,
MacAlister's, with an apartment jutting out above—a perfect spot for
a lookout post. But I didn't see anybody in the window.

We were in the midst of Little Italy, my silent blond passenger and
I, but this was a remarkably nice neighborhood for the area—and a
sleeping one: it was approaching midnight, with no one on the street,
no other cars at the moment, nobody but the blond and me. Down at
the end of the long block was Our Lady of Pompeii Church, with an
open bell tower that could also be used as a lookout, if Nitti was
feeling especially threatened.

In fact, the location seemed designed to be easily defensible. The
Ronga apartment was in the middle of the block, a massive three-
story graystone that came right up to the sidewalk; this was unusual,
as other buildings in the neighborhood were set back from the walk,
with a little yard and stairs going up a story to an entrance. Across the
street were more apartment buildings, also three stories, where men
could be posted on rooftops, if necessary.

I drove past; the next block over, on the left, there was a little cul-
de-sac park. Lexington otherwise seemed to be fancy two-flats, row
houses, small mansions, all set back with modest fenced front yards.
A ritzy neighborhood, for Little Italy. Cabrini Hospital and Notre
Dame Church were nearby; maybe that explained it.

I turned right at the church and cut down an alley behind it, taking
a jog over to another alley that would take us directly behind Ronga's
graystone. It was more a glorified gangway than an alley, and it was
tricky, weaving around garbage cans; my passenger leaned from one
side to the other as we went. Another alley intersected and I glanced
down to my left, past my inattentive companion, and saw an old-
fashioned lamp over the side door. Ronga's side door.

I continued down the gangway-style alley, stopping behind the building, but not killing the motor. A series of three open porches, one stacked atop the other, joined by one open staircase, ran up the back wall. Underneath the porches was a row of garbage cans, tucked away there. I sat and let the motor run and waited for something to happen.

Two figures appeared on the middle porch; two men in shirts with rolled-up sleeves and ties loose around their necks and no coats or hats. Two men with guns in their hands. One revolver each. They leaned over the porch and assessed the situation.

The motor still running but cutting the lights, I opened the door, stood out on my running board; if I'd opened my door wide, it would've smacked into the wall of the adjacent building—the alley was that narrow.

"Any of you guys know me? I'm Heller."

The two guys looked at each other. One of them was starting to look familiar, a small, dark man with a cigarette in his slack lips, its amber eye looking down at me.

Louis "Little New York" Campagna said, "What the hell ya doin' here, Heller?"

"This isn't my idea," I said. "This guy said I should bring him here."

Campagna exchanged glances with the other man, who was fat, dark, with eyebrows that joined in one thick line over beady black eyes. Campagna and his cigarette and his gun looked down at me. "What guy?"

"I don't know his name. He's wounded. He says he works for Nitti and made me bring him here."

"Get the hell outa here," Campagna said.

"He's got a gun," I said.

Campagna and the fat guy backed away, but they were still up there looking down.

"I think he's passed out," I said. "Give me a break! Handle this."

Campagna came clomping down the wooden steps; he didn't move fast. He looked at me with more distrust than one person should be able to muster and, revolver at the ready, squeezed past the car on the opposite side of me, by the window the blond sat next to. I stayed on my own side of the car; I had a gun in my hand, too, but with the car between me and Campagna, that wasn't readily apparent. Above me the fat gunman was watching.

"Jesus," Campagna said, looking in. "He looks dead."

"Could be," I said. "He was gut-shot."

"Whaddya doin' bringin' him here for, ya stupid bastard?"

"He had a gun. Stumbled in my office, bleeding, and said he was shot and wanted me to drive him. I did what I was told. You do *know* him, don't you?"

"Yeah, I know him. I don't know what I'm supposed to do about it, though. Get him outa here."

"Fuck you, jack. He's your dead meat."

Campagna glared at me.

I tried to look apologetic. "Come on, take him off my hands. Look, it's *his* car—you can dump it someplace. I'll catch a cab."

"All right. Shit. Fatso!"

Fatso came trundling down the steps. As he reached the bottom, I stayed where I was while Campagna stepped away from the car, and he and Fatso faced each other within the tight dark alleyway.

Campagna tucked his gun in his belt. "Go someplace and fuck yourself, Heller," he said, dismissing me, barely glancing back at me.

Fatso put his gun away, too, and asked Campagna what it was all about, and I shut the engine off and stepped out from around the side of the car and laid the silenced gun across the back of Campagna's head, and he went down like so much kindling. Fatso's mouth dropped and his hand moved toward his waistband, but then he saw the look on my face—it was a sort of smile—and thought better of it.

Campagna was down there with red on the back of his head and on one ear; he looked out. He was out.

Holding the silenced gun on Fatso, I bent down and yanked Campagna's revolver out of his belt and emptied the cylinder of its bullets onto the brick alleyway, tossed the gun down the alley, where it fell a good distance with a dull clunk. Fatso had his hands in the air and I got his revolver out of his waistband and repeated the procedure.

Then, in a stage whisper, I said to Fatso, "Use his tie to tie his hands behind him."

He did what I told him. Huffed and puffed a bit, but he did it.

"Who's up there?" I said, still whispering.

"What do you mean?" he said, glancing back at me as he bent over working, picking up on the sotto voce. The single eyebrow across his forehead was raised almost to his hairline.

I put the silenced gun's snout near his. "Guess what I mean."

"Just Nitti."

"No other bodyguards?"

"A guy in the apartment over the pharmacy. He just stays there, sort of on call."

"Nobody else?"

"Two men in the apartment above; they're the day shift. Asleep, now."

"And?"

"Most of the people in the building are family or friends. Dr. Ronga owns the building. But no more bodyguards."

"Where's Ronga now?"

"At Jefferson Park. The hospital."

"When'll he get back?"

"Not till morning. He's on duty all night."

"Nitti's wife? Ronga's?"

"Mrs. Nitti and her mother are in Florida."

"Is that the truth?"

"Yeah. Yeah, it's the truth!"

"If it isn't, I'll blow your guts all over this alley."

"If you live that long."

"Take that chance if you like."

"I'm tellin' the truth, Heller. There? Is that good enough?"

Campagna's hands were bound tight with the tie; he was breathing heavy, but was still dead to the world.

"Haul him over under the steps and put him behind the garbage cans. Get him out of sight."

He dragged Campagna like a sack of something and put him down the same way, as he moved the cans out a bit to make room. Then he heaved Campagna back there.

"Now what?" he asked.

"Now turn around," I said.

He sighed and shook his head and did. I laid the barrel of the gun across the back of his head.

He landed in the garbage cans and made a clatter. I just stood there looking up, the gun in my hand, waiting for someone to stick his head over the porch and look down. Just fucking waiting.

Nobody did.

I used Fatso's tie to tie his hands behind him. I rummaged around in one of the garbage cans looking for some paper or cloth; I found a nice dirty dish towel that had got burned, along the bottom, and discarded. I ripped it in half, wadded each piece, and shoved it in either unconscious man's mouth. Then I tied each man's shoelaces together, before laying the fat man on top of Campagna. That stood more likely to kill "Little New York" than my slugging him.

*Kid games,* I said to myself silently, thinking about the shoelaces. *I'm playing kid games.* I looked over at the car; the blond was visible behind the windscreen, tilted to one side, his eyes still open a bit. *Not really,* he seemed to be saying.

Somewhere, way down the alley, a tomcat let go a yowl; then the night went silent again. It was cool for late June, but I felt hot; well, I'd been working.

I went up the stairs. Onto the first landing; the lights were off in the flat on this level. I went on up to the next. Ronga's apartment. I could see a light on in there, past a second, enclosed porch.

There was a heavy door with a lock, standing open, from when Campagna and Fatso had come out to check up on the car that had stopped in the alley, and a screen door that was shut, but not locked. I peeked in. A figure was moving in the white room beyond; the room was a kitchen. The man seemed to be Nitti.

I didn't like the way the silenced gun felt in my hand; the automatic was still under my shoulder, but I supposed I should use this bulky goddamn gun, since it belonged to the blond, and the portion of my brain that was still rational said it was a good idea to use the other man's gun for what I was about to do.

So I went in through the screen door, with a killer's silenced gun in my hand; I went in to shoot and kill Frank Nitti.

Who was in his pajama bottoms, at the oak ice chest across the kitchen from me, with his back to me, as he bent down, rummaging around in the icebox. His back was slimly muscular and tan, the latter from his naturally swarthy complexion and Florida; there was a nasty fresh red scar on his lower back, where Lang had shot him. In his right hand was a bottle of milk. His left hand was in there picking at stuff in the icebox.

He heard me come in but didn't turn.

"What's the commotion, Louie? A couple of kids in a car losin' their cherries, or what?"

"Well there's going to be blood spilled," I said. "You're that far right."

Nitti didn't move; the muscles in his back tensed, but he kept his pose. Then, slowly, he glanced back at me. I couldn't see much of his face, but I could see the confusion.

"Heller?" he said.

"Surprised?"

"Where's Louie and Fatso?"

"In the garbage."

"Are you feelin' okay, kid?"

"Take your hand out of the icebox, Frank. Nice and slow."

"What, you think I got a gun in the icebox? You fall off your rocker or something Heller?"

"I fell off something higher. Just take the hand out and turn around slow."

He did. There was another small but nasty red scar on his chest; and one more on his neck, where he'd also been shot by Lang. It looked like an ugly birthmark. He still had the milk bottle in one hand, nothing in the other.

"I was just raidin' the icebox, kid," he said, keeping it casual, but his narrowed eyes were anything but. "There's some leftover roast lamb in there. You wouldn't want to help me finish it, would you?"

The kitchen was white and modern; cozy, with a table in the midst. There were some cards on the table, from where Campagna and Fatso had been sitting, I supposed.

"Anybody else in the apartment, Frank?"

"No."

"Show me around."

He shrugged. Walking slowly, he led me through the place, going down a hallway that had several rooms off either side, bedrooms, a sitting room, a study. At the end of the hall was a big living room. The rooms were large, well-furnished; the walls were decorated here and there with Catholic icons. Nobody but Nitti was home.

In the kitchen again, I let him sit at the table, with his back to the door I'd come in. I sat with my back to the sink, so I could see the back door at my right and the hallway at my left. Nitti was studying me. He'd grown out his inverted-V mustache, I noticed; it was thicker, now. He looked older; skinny; small. While he hardly looked like a man on death's door, he was clearly not the man he'd been before Lang shot him.

"Kid. Mind if I take a swig of this milk?"

"Go ahead."

He took two gulps, right from the bottle, and for a moment a milk mustache mingled with his own, till he wiped it off with the back of one hand.

"Ulcers," he said. "All I do these days is drink milk."

"My heart bleeds."

"Yeah, well so do my ulcers, you little punk bastard. What the goddamn hell's this about? You're committin' goddamn suicide, you know."

"There's a dead man downstairs."

He sat up. "Louie? If you killed Louie, so help me I'll—"

"Campagna's all right. He won't know his name for a couple hours, but he's all right. So's Fatso."

"Then, who . . . ?"

"A blond guy. I don't know his name. But I've seen him around."

Nitti raised his chin and looked at me from slitted eyes.

"Last time I saw him," I said, "was at Bayfront Park, when you sent him to help kill Cermak. The time before that I saw him running down Randolph Street; that was when Capone sent him to kill Jake Lingle. And tonight, tonight you sent him to kill Nathan Heller. And he didn't get the job done, did he?"

Nitti was shaking his head. "You're wrong. Wrong."

"Tell me about it. Tell me you sent that son of a bitch to Florida just to catch some sun."

He pointed a finger at me, like my gun pointed at him. "I didn't say I didn't send him to Florida. What I do say is I didn't send him to kill you."

The gun in my hand was starting to shake. I heard myself say, "He pushed me off the Sky Ride tower, Frank. Six hundred feet in the sky, and by all rights I should be a twisted sack of bones and meat on a morgue tray right now, but I'm not. I'm here, and he's dead, and so are you, Nitti. I wish to Christ Lang had killed you that day. I wish to Christ I hadn't made 'em call an ambulance for you, cocksucker."

Nitti sat there quietly; when I ran out of speech, he patted the air softly, as if quieting, settling down, a child.

"Heller," he said. "I didn't send him. I didn't even know the bastard was in town. He doesn't work for me."

"Fuck you. You're dead."

"Wait. Just *wait*. Lower that goddamn thing, will you? Hear me out. I didn't say he never done work for me. He's from the East. He's a guy Johnny Torrio recommended to Al, back on the Lingle deal; and I use him now and then—on ticklish matters."

"So that's what I am. A ticklish matter."

"I know how you feel. I know the kind of emotions that are running wild in you, kid. I know all about revenge. If Ten Percent Tony wasn't in hell already, you could ask *him* if Nitti doesn't know all about revenge. But I didn't hire a contract on you. I swear by all that's holy."

As if on cue, a church bell began ringing. Midnight. I wondered idly if it was Notre Dame or Our Lady of Pompeii.

I said, "Who sent him then?"

"I don't know the answer to that. Not for sure. But I can figure it out. So can you, if you try."

I was starting to feel confused; I was starting to wonder what the hell I was doing. The momentum, the moment, was slipping away from me . . .

"The Lang trial is comin' up in September," Nitti said. "Or have you forgotten? Is that all past history to you now? Well, it isn't past history to some people."

"Are you saying Lang sent that guy? He doesn't have the money or the connections to —"

"He doesn't have the brains, or the guts, either. No. Not Lang. Nobody. Nobody sent him. You sang on the stand, Heller. You made news in Chicago: you told the truth. How do you think your blond buddy felt when he heard you were doin' that? You can identify him as the real killer of Jake Lingle; you can identify him as a second gunman at the Cermak kill. What sort of thoughts do you suppose went through his head when he found out Nate Heller's got a sudden case of telling the truth on witness stands? Who can say *what* might come out at this Lang trial. Lang was at Bayfront Park, too, you know."

I was resting the elbow of the arm with the gun-in-hand, on the table; now I leaned on the other elbow, too, and was rubbing the side of my face. I swallowed. My mouth was dry. And I felt sick to my stomach.

So did Nitti, apparently, because he took another swig of milk.

He wiped off his mouth, smiled, and said, "Put the gun down. Just set it on the table."

It sounded like a pretty good idea, but I wasn't ready to believe him just yet.

I said, "What about Jimmy Beame, then?"

"Forget Jimmy Beame. And I'm doing you a favor, giving you that advice. So put the gun down, take the advice, and go. Just go away."

I felt a surge of something; my face felt flushed. "I almost believed you for a minute, Frank. But now the truth comes out, whether you meant it to or not. Jimmy Beame was tied to Ted Newberry, I don't know how exactly, except that it was through the Tri-Cities liquor ring. And then he infiltrated your organization, and you found out, and you what? Had him killed? You're smiling. I'm right, aren't I? I'm right. And I started snooping around, and when I connected with Dipper Cooney—you were at the goddamn fight *yourself*, Frank—you tried to kill us both, but managed only to shut *Cooney* up, and        "

"Cooney died because he was with you. That's my guess, anyway. And that dead blond son of a bitch out there was who did it."

That's right: the car he was sitting out there in right now was the car that had glided by shooting last night.

Nitti's voice was a calm drone. "I've known you were looking for Jimmy Beame for a long time," he shrugged. "Since you first started hitting the flophouses on North Clark Street. Nothing much 'scapes my notice, kid."

"He is dead, though, isn't he?"

"Yeah. And he did do some work for Ted Newberry—ran some errands for Ted and his pals in the Tri-Cities. But you're forgetting something: between Saint Valentine's Day, '29, when him and Bugs Moran just missed the party, and that ditch in the dunes this January, Ted was one of ours. Back when the Beame kid was working for him, Ted was working for me and Al. So that fairy tale you built won't wash."

"Tell me a tale that will wash."

"No. You go home. I owe you one. And here's how I'm gonna repay you: the blond's going for a midnight swim in his car, in the Chicago River; and I'm gonna tell Louie and Fatso it was all a misunderstanding and they shouldn't kill you. That's how I'm gonna repay you. Now leave the gun—it's the blond's, ain't it? Dicks don't pack silencers, at least that I ever heard of."

I shifted the silenced gun to my left hand and with my right got out my own automatic; then, awkwardly, I managed to take the clip out of the silenced gun, and put the clip in my pocket, leaving the emptied gun on the table. Then I shifted my automatic to my right hand and said, "I haven't finished with this."

"Yes you have."

"No. You don't get it, do you, Frank? Jimmy Beame isn't just another job I'm doing, just another missing persons case. He's my fiancée's brother. That's right: my fiancée. I met her months ago, when she hired me to find the kid. When she finds out he's dead, she's going to insist on me looking into it. I'm going to have to find the guy who did it, Frank. And while you probably didn't pull the trigger, I got a feeling in a very real sense you're the guy."

Nitti laughed; it was a laugh that had no humor in it—something like sadness was more like it.

"Actually," Nitti said, "I owe you one for something else. Something you don't know about. You did me a favor once, and you don't even know it."

Capone said almost the same thing to me, at Atlanta.

"I didn't know this Beame kid by that name," he said. "I didn't know about the Newberry connection, either, at first. All I knew was Dipper Cooney—who knew better than to stiff me—okayed this kid, and when I talked to the kid, I found him different. He was a little wiseguy, for one thing, but more than that, he was smart. I said, you been to college, ain't ya, kid? And he said, don't let it get around. I liked that. He was real good with figures, and we made him kind of an accountant, in a wire room. Joe Palumbo's wire room. Ring a bell yet, Heller?"

No church bells rang on cue this time; but a bell was ringing.

"Got Jimmy Beame's picture handy, Heller?"

I dug at my billfold; got the picture out.

"Lemme see," Nitti said, reaching across. "I never seen him this young, or this fat, either. Baby fat. His hair was longer, too, curlier. And he had a mustache. Must've grew that to look older."

The kid in the window.

*"You* killed him, Heller," Nitti said.

*Then he wasn't in the window anymore.*

"You killed him," Nitti continued. "That's the favor you did us. See, one of my guys recognized the kid was somebody who'd done some running for Newberry and the Tri-Cities boys. Only he knew the kid's name wasn't Hurt—that's what he was calling himself, Frankie Hurt—but the guy couldn't remember what the other name was. Well, hell, a lot of guys use more than one name in a lifetime—I was born Nitto, ya know—but better safe than sorry. I had Louie check out the kid's flop.

"And Louie found something bad. He found notebooks. Lined paper, like a school kid. Only these notebooks were full of writing, and it wasn't no school kid's work. This Hurt was writing down everything he saw and heard, and because Palumbo's wire room was a place I was at a lot, the kid heard a lot. Just bits and pieces, of course, but good bits and pieces, or bad ones, depending on how you look at it. He also found the kid's real ID, a driver's license, and saw his name was James something Beame. James Palmer Beame, I think it was. And found an address book with the kid's father's name in it, and the father was a doctor in Idaho or something, and something else. The damn kid had his damn college diploma in the drawer, and guess what it said he studied in?"

"Journalism," I said.

"Right! The kid was going to peddle his story  *our* story—to the papers! Something had to be done. Do I got to spell out what? But here's the catch—Louie found this out the morning of the day you and Lang and Miller raided the wire room at the Wacker-LaSalle. The kid was there, and Louie hadn't had a chance to tell me any of this—obviously, it was better for me to know about the kid before the kid knew he was found out. So I was in there mouthing off about this and that, as I was placing some bets, and Louie grabbed the notepaper I was jotting bets down on—I had Anna's grocery list on it, too, can you top it?—and wrote me a quick message about the kid, and then you guys showed."

I felt strange—almost dizzy. "That note," I said. "Was it . . . ?"

"Yeah. That was the note I chewed up, the note I got shot over. Not that Lang wouldn't've found some other excuse. Then I got shot, and in the other room, the kid was getting nervous—this I found out later, of course, from Louie. The kid knows if he gets pulled in by the cops, he stands to get found out. He must've wanted to fill a couple more notebooks before goin' public. Anyway, so Louie tells the kid to make a break for it. The kid doesn't know. Louie says, do it. Go on. Go. And you come in the room, and Louie tosses the kid a gun, and you did us all a favor."

I just sat there. The gun was in my hand, but wasn't pointing at anything. The gun I'd used. The gun my father used.

Then Campagna was in the back doorway, unarmed, but angry, teeth bared, blood caked on the side of his face. He was moving toward me, not giving a damn that I had a gun, but Nitti put an arm out and stopped him. Campagna, confused, leaned over and Nitti whispered to him; and Campagna, rolling his eyes, sighing, said, "Well, then. I'll go help Fatso. He's still out."

"Good idea," Nitti said.

I put the gun back under my arm.

"You want a drink, Heller? I got some nice vino. Can't drink it

myself, this damn stomach of mine. Been killin' me. Hey—cheer up.
You'll think of something to tell your girl."

"I killed her brother," I said.

"I know that. You know that. Nobody else does. He's buried in
potter's field; just another dead nobody. Leave him there."

I got up; my legs wobbled, but I got up.

Nitti, bare-chested, came around and put an arm around my shoulder. "You been through a lot, my friend. You go get some sleep. And
let go of this."

"I was going to kill you."

"But you didn't. You did me some favors, I did you some. Now
we're even."

"The blond . . ."

"What blond? Forget it. This nonsense with guns, it's gettin' old.
When people think of Chicago, let 'em think of the fair, not guns and
gangsters. How do you like my fair?"

"Your fair?"

He smiled, nodded. "If a wheel turns on the fairgrounds, I got a
cut of the grease on the axle. Got the joint sewed up. It's like . . . a
trial run."

"Trial run for what?"

He shrugged elaborately. "For everything. For the country. We
got the world by the tail with a downhill start. We got the bartender's
union, which means we'll have every bartender in the country pushing our brands of beer and liquor. They'll have to handle our soft
drinks. They'll get their pretzels and potato chips from us. That goes
for every hotel, restaurant, cocktail lounge, and private club in the
forty-eight states. Like Al used to tell us, we'll see the day we make a
profit off of every olive in every martini served in America. This is big
business, kid; that's why this playing guns crap has got to stop. Let
these asshole bank robbers play guns all they want; like this guy Dillinger, let *him* have the headlines—I don't want 'em. Bunch of hicks
shooting up small-town banks, it gives the cops something to do,
keeps the heat off us. Here. You sit back down. I'm going to call you
a cab. There's glasses in the cabinet over the counter, if you want
some of this milk. And help yourself to the lamb in the icebox."

He left me alone.

The gun under my arm felt heavy.

The photo of Jimmy and Mary Ann Beame, together, younger, was
on the table; I put it back in my billfold.

I folded my arms on the table and rested my head.

After a while Nitti woke me up and, still in his pajama bottoms, walked me down his last mile of a hallway, an arm around my shoulder, guided me into his living room and to a doorway and down the front steps where a cab waited.

"Where to?" the cabbie said.

"Tower Town," I said.

## 29

I went up the red stairway and knocked on the door. I heard a chair move inside and then the door opened and she was there and her eyes were red from crying and her lips were trembling and she said, "Oh, Nathan," and fell into my arms. I held her there, on the porch over the open stairs, for a long time; stood there holding her in the cold and we were both trembling, but I don't think the cold had much to do with it.

Then we went into the yellow crumbling-plaster kitchen, with its oil stove and sink of dirty dishes and no icebox. A real comedown from Nitti's kitchen. She'd been sitting at the table, chain-smoking an ebony ashtray held the evidence of that. I'd only seen her smoke a few times, and then it was at the Dill Pickle or some other Tower Town tearoom, when she was striking a theatrical pose. Tonight the smoking, it would seem, had been no pose; she'd really been worrying about me, and that made me feel good, somehow, and guilty.

She was still in the chocolate linen dress; no beret, or shoes, or any other affectation, though. Her makeup had long since been cried off. She sat at the table and so did I and she held one of my hands with both of hers.

"Thank God you're here," she said. "Thank God you're all right."

"I'm fine."

"I thought that maniac would kill you."

"He didn't. I'm fine."

"I've been beside myself. I've been so . . ." And she came over and sat on my lap, tumbled into my arms, hugged me 'round the neck and cried. And cried.

"I   I thought I'd lost you," she said.

I stroked her hair.

"What was it about? Nathan, why did he try to kill you?"

"Baby. Baby. Not now. I'm not up to it now."

Her arms still 'round my neck, she leaned back enough to look at me; study me. "You look—"

"Awful. Yeah. I can imagine."

She got off my lap; took command. Miss Efficiency of 1933. "We can talk later. Come on. Let's get you to bed."

She took me by the hand and led me through the big open studio room. Alonzo had moved out long ago—he was living with a man, now—but had left a couple of his "experiments in dynamic symmetry" behind. He'd told Mary Ann she could choose any two, and, to her credit, she picked the two smallest. But for some unexplainable reason, I'd taken a perverse liking to both of the paintings, meaningless abstract splotches of color though they were.

In the bedroom, with its blue-batiked ceiling and walls, its single, painted-out window, its four-poster bed, I felt safe. Secure. Hidden away from reality. The man in the moon over the bed seemed to be winking at me. We had a secret.

"You look so tired," she said, looking at me with furrowed brow, taking my coat off me.

"Yes. I am."

She undressed me—except for the gun, which she didn't like handling, and left for me to deal with—and then she slipped out of her clothes and put me to bed.

I said, "Could you hold me? Just hold me."

She held me. She was the mother; I was the child. I fell asleep with her cradling me in her arms.

When I woke, she was cradled in my arms. The room was dark, though she'd left the electric moon glowing. I got up and looked at my watch, on the dresser. Four in the morning.

She stirred. "What woke you?"

"I remembered something."

She sat up; the covers were around her waist. Her breasts looked at me curiously.

I said, "I remembered I haven't made love to you tonight."

She gave me that impish grin. "It's too late. It's morning already."

I felt my face turn serious; I couldn't make it do anything else. "It's not too late," I said, and went to her.

I came inside her. It was the only time I ever did that, came without using something, without pulling out. I came inside her and it was wonderful. We were both crying when we came.

We lay in each other's arms.

"That can lead to little Nathans and Mary Anns, you know," she said, looking over at me, with a faint smile.

"I know," I said.

The next morning I told her. Not the truth, exactly, but something close to it. I woke, and she was making tea, and I went into the kitchen and she smiled, standing there in that black kimono with red and white flowers she'd worn the first night, and poured me tea and I told her.

"Jimmy's dead."

She put a hand on her chest. Then she sat slowly down.

"Your brother was working for gangsters. With gangsters. He may have been doing it to get material for a story, to try and make his dream about being on the *Trib* come true. But that doesn't matter now. The point is he was working for gangsters and he got killed."

She raised the back of a fist to her face and bit her knuckles; her eyes were very, very wide. She looked about eleven years old.

"That's why I got pushed off that tower last night. I've been snooping around and it almost got me killed. I didn't tell you, but I was shot at night before last; a man I was with, a man who knew your brother, was killed. Standing right next to me. Killed."

She was shaking. I pulled my chair around and put an arm around her. She was staring straight ahead; it was like I wasn't there.

After a while I said, "There's nothing we can do."

"But—how—when—where's his—I      "

She got up, pushing me and the chair away, rushed out of the room.

I went after her.

She was in the bathroom, kneeling over the stool.

When she was through, I helped her out into the studio. Sun streaked down through the skylight. Alonzo's mattress had been moved out and a secondhand sofa put in its place; we sat there. Dust motes floated.

"Do the authorities know?" she asked. It was a strain for her to keep her voice from cracking.

"No," I said. "I can't even prove it happened."

She looked at me sharply, confused. "You can't—what?"

"I don't even know where he's buried."

"Then how do you know he's really dead?"

"Frank Nitti told me."

"Frank Nitti . . . ?"

"That's where I went last night. From the fair. I thought that man had been sent by Nitti to kill me. I was wrong, but never mind. I'll try to explain. A gangster named Ted Newberry tried to have Frank Nitti killed; your brother died as a result."

Her eyes narrowed as she tried to think, tried to make sense of it. "Newberry," she said. "He's dead, isn't he? Wasn't it in the papers? *He* was the man responsible for Jimmy's death?"

That was only vaguely true, but I nodded.

"Shouldn't we do something? What can we *do*, Nathan?"

"There's nothing we can do. Newberry's dead. Nitti disposed of your brother's body. Nothing can be proved. I'm sorry. It's ugly, but you're going to have to learn to live with it."

"We should tell somebody. The police. The newspapers. *Somebody . . .*"

I held one of her hands in both of mine. "No. Your brother would be made out to be a dead gangster. Is that something you want to carry with you? You've got a career, Mary Ann . . ."

"Do you think I'm that *crass?*"

"I'm sorry."

"I have to—have to at least—tell Daddy."

"I wouldn't."

She looked at me, confused again.

I said, "I think it'd just about kill him. Let him think Jimmy's riding the rails someplace. Let him think his son will turn up one of these days. It's kinder."

"I—I don't know."

"Mary Ann, believe me, there are some things people are just better off not knowing."

She thought about that, said, "I suppose so," and got up.

With her back to me, she said, "Nathan, could you leave me alone for a while? I think I need to be alone for a while."

I got up. "Sure."

I went out of the room.

I was going out the door when she caught me; she wasn't crying, but she was close to it. She hugged me again.

"Call me tonight," she said into my chest. "I love you, Nathan. I still love you. This doesn't change anything. Not anything."

"I love you too, Mary Ann."

She looked up at me. "I told you never to hold anything back from me. No secrets. No deceptions. You could have hidden this from me, but you didn't. That was brave of you, Nathan. That was very brave. I want you to know I respect you for it."

I kissed her on the forehead and went out; I could feel her eyes on me as I went down the steps.

Well, I had her respect; I didn't deserve it, but I had it. As for her love, that was already fading. Try as she might to turn me into a brave knight who had the courage to tell his fair lady the bitter truth, I knew I would never again be the same in her eyes. She didn't know I killed her brother; but she might as well have.

I killed her romantic notions about me, and that was just as bad. I killed the dream that I was the true detective who would find the heroine's brother and make the world right again.

I killed the happy ending.

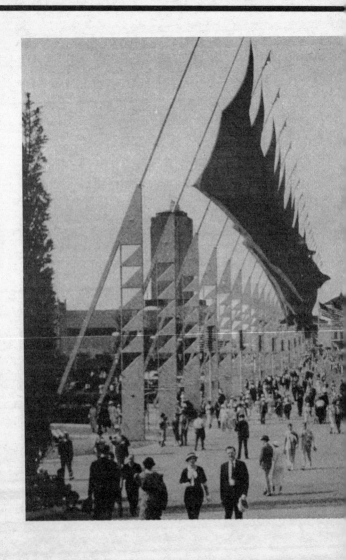
THE CHICAGO WORLD'S FAIR ■ THE AVENUE OF FLAGS

# 4
# THE BIG FALL
## SEPTEMBER 1, 1933

"I'M GLAD IT WAS ME INSTEAD OF YOU"

ANTON J. CERMAK

MAYOR OF CHICAGO

BAYFRONT PARK, 1983

## 30

I was sitting working up some insurance reports, rain pelting the office windows behind me, when Eliot came in, dripping wet, not wearing a raincoat.

"Damn rain came out of nowhere," he said, coming over and taking the chair across my desk from me.

"Glad to see you know enough to come in out of it," I said.

"Looks like you're keeping busy."

"I'm having a good first year."

"Job at the fair alone made it a good year."

I nodded. Put my pen down. "So. You're leaving tomorrow."

"Morning. Me and Betty and a Ford full of belongings."

"What exactly did you do to the Treasury Department to deserve Cincinnati?"

"Well," he shrugged, "where else are they going to send a prohibition agent when Prohibition's winding down? I'm supposed to clean up the 'Moonshine Mountains.' Think I'm up to it?"

"A hillbilly's squirrel gun can kill you just as dead as a machine gun."

"I suppose. Still, I never pictured myself as a 'revenooer.'"

"'Still' is right."

That made him laugh a little. But he seemed kind of sad. I knew how he felt.

He said, "See if you can't get out Cincinnati way, one of these days."

"Will do. Your folks are here. I imagine you'll be getting back now and then."

"I imagine."

"Was it worth it, Eliot?"

"What?"

"Fighting the good fight. Putting Capone away. All that."

"Putting Capone away was satisfying. Trouble is, nobody's doing a damn thing about Nitti. The FBI's busy running after outlaws like Dillinger, because the public *sees* what the likes of that breed does."

"Then you figure Melvin Purvis'll take care of Chicago while you're gone."

"That jerk! That pip-squeak doesn't know his dick from a doughnut."

Then Eliot realized I was baiting him and we both sat grinning at each other.

He said, "I stopped in downstairs and Barney wasn't around."

"He's at his training camp in the Catskills. Canzoneri rematch is coming up in a few weeks."

"Speaking of rematches, I wish I could be around to see the Lang trial."

That was coming up in a few weeks, too.

"Won't be much to it," I said. "I don't imagine much'll come of it other than Lang and Miller getting good and kicked out of the department." Both were on suspension at the moment.

"Well, just the same, I'd like to be there. Have you heard from Mary Ann lately?"

"She dropped me a card last week. She's up for a part in a picture."

"Hollywood must agree with her."

"It's the place for her."

"I kind of . . . thought you were serious about her."

"I was."

"You doin' okay, Nate?"

"I'm getting there."

"You want to take a break? Those reports can wait, can't they?"

"Got something in mind?"

Eliot stood. "Yeah. Let's go downstairs. I want to buy you a drink."

I saw Eliot only occasionally after that; but I kept track of him, and most of the others.

Eliot spent two years chasing moonshiners in Kentucky, Tennessee, and Ohio; later he became public safety director of Cleveland, Ohio—at thirty-two, the youngest in the city's history. During World War Two, he was the director of social protection for the Federal Security Agency—a fancy title meaning he was charged with combating venereal disease on U.S. military bases.

He did that from '41 till '45, and while he was waging a battle against VD, so was an old friend of his: Al Capone. Al did get out of Atlanta Penitentiary, but not as he hoped: he was transferred to Alcatraz, the "rock," which had been especially designed to be "a place of confinement for the more dangerous, intractable criminals." Syphilis began eating his brain away, and by '39 he was out of Alcatraz, but he was already partially paralyzed, both in mind and body. By his death in '47, at age forty-eight, VD had made him pretty much a vegetable.

As for Eliot, he went into private business, became president of a Pennsylvania paper company. Some of his friends—myself among them—urged him to put the story of his war against the Capone mob in writing. I guess he had enough of the old publicity-hound left in him to go along with it, because he wrote his autobiographical book, *The Untouchables*, which sparked the TV series that made his name a household word, and did the same for Capone, to a generation who hadn't even heard of the Big Fellow.

But Eliot didn't live to see any of that; he had just finished correcting the final galley proofs of his book when he died of a heart attack, in 1957. He was fifty-four.

On September 12, 1933, Barney took Canzoneri in the rematch, in New York, Canzoneri's home turf. The speakeasy became the Barney Ross Cocktail Lounge, and when Henry Armstrong defeated Barney for the title in '38, Barney devoted himself to the club and to gambling, and wasn't terribly successful at either. When World War Two came along, Barney joined the marines and fought at Guadalcanal, and got the Silver Star, a presidential citation, and malaria. The medics treated him for the latter with morphine, and, like more than a few GIs, Barney ended up an inadvertent addict. It's still hard for me to think of Barney as a junkie, but that's what he became—till he kicked it and went public with the story, winning the championship all over again. It finally took cancer ("the Big C," he called it) to beat him, in '67.

Frank Nitti had ten golden years—killing Cermak and getting away with it had given him power and credibility in the eyes of everybody from the high-hats to the hoods, the politicians to the harness bulls. Clearly this was not a gangster of the crudity of Capone, no hothead who would machine-gun a garageful of competitors and fill the headlines with blood and bad publicity. Nitti was an executive, a businessman; he, more than Capone, invented the modern corporate gangster.

And, like a lot of executives, he had stomach trouble: ulcers had developed in the wake of the attempt on his life by Sergeant Lang, and those wounds, though long since healed, had continued to give him pain, particularly the back wound. In 1943, faced with racketeering charges and certain imprisonment for his efforts with Campagna and others to extort big bucks from the movie industry, Nitti left his house in suburban Riverside and took a walk in the rain along some railroad tracks, about a block from Cermak Road (Twenty-second Street, renamed for the martyred mayor). His beloved wife, Anna, had died eighteen months before; he was fifty-eight. His stomach hurt him, and they say he just couldn't face another long prison term. Two witnesses saw him shoot himself in the head. The date was March 19, just one day short of ten years since the day Joe Zangara said, "Push the button." Nitti's gravestone reads: "There is no life except by death."

General Dawes died reading in his study, in 1951. He had given an interview shortly before, in which he told the reporters he had no interest in imparting any wisdom to the people through the mass media. He concluded with what might as well be his epitaph: "God give us common sense!"

Janey married a Republican county official from the suburbs. He rose to state senator, then finally to United States Representative he was defeated for reelection after serving for many years, but was offered a post with the Nixon administration. He was a minor figure in the Watergate scandal and served eighteen months at a prison farm, during which time Janey divorced him and is now living alone in Evanston—their three children are grown. I understand she is seeing a local businessman, an ex-mayor of Evanston who owns condos.

My uncle Louis died in 1948 after a stroke. We never reconciled.

Walter Winchell's sagging career was given one last boost when he was hired to do the voiceover narration for "The Untouchables" TV show.

George Raft made a movie in '34 called *Bolero*, in which he finally got to do more dancing than acting. One of his co-stars was Sally Rand, who did a laundered version of her famous world's fair fan dance. She flopped in the picture, and never had much of a movie career. She did her fan and bubble dances till her death a few years ago. Raft's career faded by the 1950s, partially because of his insistence on playing only "good guy" roles—Humphrey Bogart built a career on Raft's rejected "unsympathetic" parts, like Sam Spade in *The Maltese Falcon*. Raft's personal associations with the likes of Bugsy Siegel and Al Capone's brother John brought him public criticism, and toward the end of his show biz career, he acted as a shill for various mob casinos, from Havana to London. His most successful role in the last few years of his life was as a convict in an Alka Seltzer

TV commercial, spoofing his image. He also gave a good performance weeping at his tax-evasion trial.

Dutch Reagan went into acting, too.

Campagna was fishing in Florida in 1955, reeling in a thirty-pound catch, when he had a heart attack and died. He was fifty-seven.

I lost track of Miller; he was kicked off the department and left the city, as best I know. Lang was found guilty at his trial but was immediately granted a petition for a new trial. He had loudly told reporters he would "blow the lid off the Democratic party" if he went to jail. A year and some eighteen continuances later, the case was thrown out of court. Lang waited a few years for the heat to die down, then sued the city for reinstatement as a detective sergeant and got that and restoration of full pay for the time he'd missed. I had run-ins with him from time to time thereafter, as you well might guess; but I don't know what became of him after he finally did retire from the department.

Mary Ann, of course, went to Hollywood and changed her name to something you would recognize more readily than Mary Ann Beame. She did several pictures for Monogram before Twentieth Century-Fox bought up her contract. I was supposed to go out to Hollywood and we would get married. Mary Ann got married, all right; several times—never to me. She died last year of lung cancer; she was a heavy smoker, the *National Enquirer* said.

When I read of Mary Ann's death, it brought memories rushing back. I was (and am) living in Florida, having retired some years ago. I am married to a wonderful woman who is not a character in this book. We live in Boca Raton, but we get to Miami from time to time. We were walking through Bayfront Park one sunny February afternoon when I came to the memorial with the inscription "I'm glad it was me instead of you," and started to laugh. My wife wanted to know what was so funny, and I told her. And she suggested I write this book.

So I have.

As for the Century of Progress, it was held over for another year. And when they finally closed the fair down, crowds swarmed the lakefront to watch the demolition crews dismantle the City of Tomorrow. Last to go was the east tower of the Sky Ride. On Saturday, August 31, 1935, two hundred thousand people were on hand to watch the biggest crash since Wall Street. Engineers had placed seven hundred and fifty pounds of Thermit explosive in boxes wired to the north legs of the structure, and at the appointed time Rufus Dawes pushed the button and "the great tower" fell.

It made quite a racket.

# *I Owe Them One*

Because of the inconsistencies in "nonfiction" books about the gangster era in Chicago, and the tendency of history books to dismiss Zangara as "a demented bricklayer who failed to assassinate FDR," I went back to the newspaper files of the *Tribune, The Daily News* and other Chicago papers of the day, as well as the Miami *Herald* and *News*, where eyewitness accounts of such events as the shooting at Bayfront Park, and lengthy accountings of testimony at the Zangara and Nitti trials, were at variance with "history's" version of the events in question.

Nevertheless, this is a work of fiction, and a few liberties have been taken with the facts, though as few as possible—and any blame for historical inaccuracies is my own, reflecting, I hope, the limitations of my conflicting source material and the need to telescope certain minor events to make for a more smoothly flowing narrative.

Several hardworking people helped me research this book, primarily George Hagenauer, whose contributions include helping develop the family history of the Hellers; discovering the Nydick killing in the newspaper files, a related case not touched upon in any of the nonfiction books covering the Nitti shooting/Cermak assassination; and uncovering a massive scrapbook on the Century of Progress, which allowed me to "go" to the fair. George is a lifelong resident of Chicago, and he—and Mike Gold, another Chicagoan who is a Chicago history buff with an eye for detail—provided invaluable help and support. Jay Maeder, of the Miami *Herald*, was similarly helpful. If I have re-created any sense of Chicago in the 1930s—or, in Jay's case, Miami in the 1930s—much credit must go to them. Jim Arpy, of the Quad City *Times*, shared his expertise (and files) with me. Also helpful was retired police reporter (of the Davenport *Democrat* and Quad City *Times*) Paul Conway, as were Rick McQuire and Dave Lund of WOC-TV. My friend and frequent collaborator, cartoonist Terry Beatty, also lent his support and help to this project (and the loan of another Century of Progress scrapbook/diary, kept by his grandmother when she attended the fair). And I'd like to thank Dominick Abel, my agent; Tom Dunne, my editor, and his associate, Ellen Loonam; Rick Marschall, who when he was editor at Field Enterprises encouraged me to do a story about a private eye in the '30s period; Bob Randisi, who encouraged me to do a story about a private eye, period; and Sarah Lifton, another former editor of mine, who seems to make a habit out of being in my corner.

Thanks are also due to Donald E. Westlake and Mickey Spillane, for more reasons than just the moral support they lent during the writing of this novel.

Photos selected by the author for use in this edition are courtesy the Chicago Historical Society (Maxwell Street, General Dawes, Water Tower, Al Capone, Hooverville, and Barney Ross); other photos are courtesy the Miami *Herald*, the Chicago *Tribune*, and UPI; the Bayfront Park, 1983, photo was taken by Marice Cohn, staff photographer with the Miami *Herald*. Remaining photos have been selected from the personal collections of George Hagenauer, Barry Luebbert, and the author. Efforts to track the sources of certain photos have been unsuccessful; upon notification these sources will be listed in subsequent editions.

Literally hundreds of books and magazine and newspaper articles have been consulted in researching *True Detective*. I am particularly indebted to the anonymous authors of the Federal Writers Project volumes on the states of Florida, Georgia, Illinois and Iowa, all of which appeared in the late '30s; also helpful were several University of Chicago sociological studies, including *From the Gold Coast to the Slum* (1929) and *Chicago Police Problems* (1932). A few other books deserve singling out: *A Corner of Chicago* (1963), Robert Hardy Andrews; *Al Capone* (1930), Fred D. Pasley; *The Bootleggers* (1961), Kenneth Allsop; *Boss Cermak of Chicago* (1962), Alex Gottfried; *Captive City* (1969), Ovid Demaris; *Chicago Confidential* (1950), Jack Lait and Lee Mortimer; *Dining in Chicago* (1931), John Drury; *The Dry and Lawless Years* (1960), Judge John H. Lyle; *Four Against the Mob* (1961), Oscar Fraley; *George Raft* (1974), Lewis Yablonsky; *The George Raft File* (1973), James Robert Paris with Steven Whitney; *Headquarters* (1955), Quentin Reynolds; *Maxwell Street* (1977), Ira Berkow; *Mayors, Madams, and Madmen* (1979), Norman Mark; *No Man Stands Alone* (1957), Barney Ross and Martin Abramson; *That Man Dawes* (1930), Paul R. Leach; *The Twenty Incredible Years* (1935), William H. Stuart; *The Underworld of American Politics* (1932), Fletcher Dobbins; *The Untouchables* (1957), Eliot Ness and

Oscar Fraley; *Where's the Rest of Me?* (1965), Ronald Reagan and Richard G. Hubler; and *Winchell* (1971), Bob Thomas.

When all the debts have been paid, or at least acknowledged, one remains: this book could not have been written without the constant help and support of my wife, partner, and toughest (and best) critic, Barbara Collins.